Nothing Left To Lose

A J WILLS

Cherry Tree Publishing

Nothing Left To Lose
AJ Wills

Copyright © A J Wills 2022

"The most dangerous creation of any society is the man who has nothing left to lose."

- James Baldwin

Chapter 1

Where the hell is she?

It's gone half nine and a niggle of worry rumbles in my gut. A vision of Abi on a hospital trolley flashes through my mind. I shove it away. I'm being silly. Worrying unnecessarily. I'm sure she's fine.

I snatch up my phone and hit the redial button, willing her to answer, hoping for a slurred apology and the sound of music thumping in the background. At least I would know she was safe.

I listen to a long hiss-filled silence, the blood gushing through my ears.

A click.

Her voice.

And for a split second, I dare to believe I'm through.

'Abi?'

'You've reached Abigail Pilkington-Hutton. I can't take your call right now but leave a message.'

I slump in my chair and pinch the bridge of my nose as I ring off, my heart beating a little faster and a little harder. A kaleidoscope of images of my wife's body dumped by the side of the road, bleeding, lifeless, her eyes staring blankly, spiral through my head.

Stop it.

I refuse to be that husband. She's perfectly capable of looking after herself. She's not a child. And yet, I can't help but worry.

Of course, the lasagne's ruined. A fiery blast stings my face as I flip open the oven door. I step back to let the curls of steam rush towards the ceiling and peer inside despondently at the charred remains. Shavings of Parmesan cheese are blackened beyond salvation and crusty tracks of meat sauce have bubbled up and hardened over the sides of the ceramic dish. It's as good as cremated, even though I turned the heat down hours ago.

I slam the door shut. Wasting good food irks me, especially when I've put effort into cooking. It's not as if it's one of those vile cardboard-tasting ready meals, straight out of a packet. It's an authentic Italian recipe from a dusty old cookbook I picked up in a secondhand bookstore in town. I used a pinch of rosemary and cubes of pan-fried pancetta for the ragu and a sprinkling of nutmeg in the bechamel sauce. A surprise treat to celebrate the end of Abi's trial.

I've lost count of the number of evenings and weekends she's given up working on the case. The missed bedtime stories with the girls. The hours going through witness statements "one more time". After everything she's sacrificed over the last couple of months, I thought tonight we could spend some time together.

But she's not come home and her phone's off.

It's not like her. Even when she has to work late, she always calls or messages. But I've heard nothing from her all day and her phone is going straight to voicemail. I've left at least half a dozen messages, but either she either forgot to switch her phone back on when she left court or she's let the battery run flat. What else can I do but wait and hope she's back soon?

Apart from the slow, monotonous tick of the clock and the occasional rumble of a passing car, the house is eerily quiet. I made sure Norah and Katie were in bed early because I wanted Abi to myself this evening. Just the two of us. I'd prepped the lasagne as soon as I'd got in from picking up the girls, then once they were asleep, I'd laid the table in the kitchen diner and lit a dozen candles which had slowly melted and flopped until I'd had to blow them all out again.

I'm sure she's okay. It's just odd not to hear from her, especially as I thought she'd want to share her news. Instead, I found out from an alert that popped up on my phone.

Guilty verdicts on two men in torture-murder trial

I had to read the story twice, not quite able to believe it. Abi had put her heart and soul into the case while under intense scrutiny from the press who'd been drawn to court like flies to a rotting carcass. It was one of those one-in-a-thousand trials that had lit up the public's ghoulish imagination and been covered extensively by all the papers and almost nightly on the evening news.

Abi probably had her hands full in the aftermath of the verdicts, caught up in the whirlwind of media interviews, and knowing my wife, spending time with the victim's family, ensuring they comprehended what was going to happen next. Making them feel included and understood.

But where is she now? Probably out celebrating. I only wish she'd pick up her phone and let me know she's safe. It's not too much to ask, is it?

With nothing else to do, I sit at the table and peel open the family laptop. I should use the unexpected free time to write up that new pecan and maple pudding recipe I've been working on for my blog. But I can't concentrate. I stare at a blank screen with my mind wandering.

While other people like to drink, watch TV or read a book to unwind, I like to cook. I love the creativity and the theatre of it all, losing myself in the rituals of chopping, stirring and tasting, concocting dishes that look, smell and taste divine. And like an actor on stage revelling in the adulation of an audience hooked on his words and actions, I live for those moments when someone takes their first mouthful of my food, their eyes roll to the heavens, their bodies seem to melt, and they announce (like I don't already know it) the food is amazing. Heavenly. To die for. The fizz of pleasure that makes my skin tingle is a powerful drug.

I even have my own blog, Abi's idea. It started as a local restaurant review guide but recently I've been uploading my own recipes onto it too. If nothing else, it's a good excuse to get into the kitchen to try out new dishes.

I click away from the blank page and open a web browser. Since I last looked, a news story about Abi's case has been updated with a brief video clip. Abi standing on the steps outside court with her black robes flapping around her legs and a flash of her tightly pinned russet hair peeking out from under a grey wig. Her courtroom armour. She's surrounded by people, staring dead-eyed over her shoulder at the camera. The victim's family and friends, I guess, although there's no hint of jubilation on their faces.

Abi starts to speak, her chin raised, shoulders back. My Abi. The mother of my children. The smartest woman I know.

'Today, two men are beginning life sentences for the brutal murder of a much-loved father, brother, uncle and friend,' she says, delivering her words slowly and deliberately. 'Billy Bowden was loved and admired by everyone who knew him, but on the evening of October the nineteenth last year, his life was cruelly cut short by two men who tricked their way into his home with the intention of torturing him into revealing the combination to his safe - a safe containing a little under two thousand pounds. A paltry price to pay for any life.'

My pride stirs as she speaks, standing there magnificently in her gown and wig. A champion of the people. A defender of justice. I push the other feeling away and bury it deep.

'This has been a long and arduous case, fraught with difficulties even as the trial was under way,' she continues, an oblique reference to the key witnesses who'd unexpectedly pulled out at the last minute and the cock-up in the lab which resulted in the DNA evidence being discounted.

'And although the family are pleased that justice has finally been done, they take no pleasure in today's outcome. Justice will not bring Billy back, nor undo the unthinkable pain he must have endured at the hands of the cruel and sadistic men who made his final hours on this earth a living hell.

'They would like to thank the media for their support during these difficult last few weeks but would ask now that they are left alone to rebuild their lives.'

The video ends and the screen goes black.

Maybe she's hooked up with Felicity or Colette and met with them in town. They've all been close since school and if they've heard about Abi's success on the news, it's possible they've taken her out to celebrate. I already feel better Abi might be with friends who'll make sure she gets home in one piece.

I find Colette's number in my phone. She's the sensible one. The headteacher at Norah and Katie's school.

My finger hovers over the dial button.

Is that the sound of footsteps on the drive? A key scraping in the lock?

I rush into the hall as the front door crashes open and Abi stumbles in, tripping over the doorstep.

'You're back! I've been worried. Why didn't you call to let me know you'd be late?'

She pushes the door closed, tosses her keys on the side, missing the artsy papier mâché bowl, and heels off her shoes.

'Where've you been?' I persist.

She looks pale and sways unsteadily on her feet.

'A few of us went out for a drink after the trial,' she mumbles. 'Sorry.'

'And you couldn't find thirty seconds to call or text?'

'Don't lecture me. I'm not in the mood.'

'I was worried, that's all.' I catch the bitter claw of alcohol on her breath. 'I've been leaving messages on your phone all evening.'

'My phone died.' Her pupils are black and her eyes bloodshot. She avoids my gaze.

Something's wrong. She bounces off the wall as she brushes past.

'What is it, Abi? What's happened?' I follow her into the kitchen where she heads for the fridge, hooks out a bottle of Sauvignon Blanc and pours herself a large glass.

I watch her carefully, trying to read her. Her shoulders are tight and her skin pallid. Her lipstick is smudged, and dirty black grains of mascara speckle the dark skin under her eyes. Her cheeks are pinched and as she lifts the glass to her mouth, her hand trembles.

'Abi? Talk to me. What's going on?'

'Nothing. I'm fine.'

'You don't look fine. You look like you've seen a ghost.'

She licks her lips, swallows, and finally looks at me. It might just be the alcohol, but it looks like she's been crying.

'You're upset,' I say, fear bubbling up from the pit of my stomach. Abi can get emotional when she's been drinking but this seems different. 'What is it? The trial?'

'No.' She shakes her head. Her hair is still pinned up from court. 'Nothing like that.'

'Then what?'

She looks to the ceiling and sucks in her top lip as if she's trying to hold back her tears. 'Don't make a big deal out of it, okay? It was nothing.'

'Abi? You're scaring me.'

'I probably imagined it.'

'Imagined what?' I say, exasperated. Why won't she just tell me?

'I think someone followed me home.'

Chapter 2

It's like a punch in the stomach that knocks the wind out of my lungs.

'What do you mean followed you home?' My head is a blizzard of questions.

'I don't know,' Abi says, shaking her head. 'There was a man —'

'What man?'

'I don't know. I didn't see his face.' She bangs the glass on the worktop and wine sloshes over her hand.

'You didn't walk home from town, did you?'

'This isn't my fault, Henry. I didn't ask to be followed by some creep.'

'You should have called a cab.'

'I thought the walk would clear my head.'

'Did he say anything? Did he try to touch you?' I know I should be comforting her, reassuring her she's safe now, but the fiery rage of anger is taking hold. I'm conscious of balling my fists and grinding my teeth. I can't help it.

'No, nothing like that.'

'What then? I want to know what happened.'

'Nothing happened,' she replies tartly. 'He followed me for a bit and then he was gone. It gave me a scare, that's all.'

Abi folds her arms across her chest and her head sags.

'We should call the police.'

'And tell them what? I didn't get a good look at him and he didn't actually do anything.'

'But who knows what he was planning. Maybe you were lucky and he got scared off.'

'Just forget it,' she says.

That's easy for her to say. I unball my fists and rub my eyes as Abi pulls up a chair at the table, glancing at the mats and cutlery I laid out hours ago.

'I cooked a lasagne for the end of the trial,' I explain. 'But it's past it now.'

'Right,' she says coolly, as if I'm trying to score points. 'That was thoughtful. I'm sorry.'

I shrug like it doesn't matter, even though it does. I wanted tonight to be special and instead, we're arguing about how Abi was nearly attacked on her way home. Anything could have happened. I can't understand why she doesn't want to involve the police. What if he attacks another woman? How's she going to feel then? I shudder at the thought. But once Abi's made her mind up about something, I know she'll dig her heels in and won't be convinced otherwise. It's a battle I'll lose.

I take a deep breath through my nose, fill my lungs, and let it out slowly, releasing the anger and tension inside. I sit at the table and push the laptop to one side.

'Where did you go after the trial?' I ask.

'Just into town with the team. It was supposed to be a thank you for their hard work on the case. I didn't realise the time until Helen and a couple of the others started ordering shots and talking about going on to a club. You're probably right, I should have taken a taxi, but it's not far to walk.' She runs a finger around the rim of her glass. 'And anyway, I shouldn't have to worry about walking alone at night.'

'I know, and we shouldn't have to worry about car thieves either, but we still lock our cars.'

'Don't be flippant.'

'I'm just saying —'

'He came out of nowhere. I thought I was imagining it at first,' she says.

'Where?'

'In the housing estate behind the train station. I heard footsteps. He was right behind me. Breathing down my neck.'

'You got a look at him then?'

Abi sighs. 'No. He had a hood on and kept his head down. I should have taken my trainers in my bag to change into, but I didn't know I was going to walk. And of course, my phone was out of charge and there was no one around.'

'Jeez, Abi, he could have —'

'But he didn't.' She forces a smile, but it doesn't mask the anxiety behind her eyes. 'I got to the main road and he was gone.'

'Are you okay?' I ask as she finishes her wine and sits back, staring blankly into space.

'I was thinking about the girls,' she says. 'And you.'

'Don't.'

'But what if — '

'It didn't.' I don't want to think about what might have been. How would I cope without her? The girls growing up without their mother.

'I know but — '

'Let's talk about something else.' I couldn't bear to hear anymore. 'Tell me about the case.'

Abi sits up straighter and wipes the corner of her eye with her thumbs. 'The jury was only out for three hours,' she says more brightly.

'Three hours?'

'Yeah, I know, it surprised us too.'

There was no doubt Jimmy and Dean Farrow were one hundred per cent guilty of Billy Bowden's murder but after three witnesses were scared off, together with the contamination of the DNA evidence in the lab, the case against them had looked flimsy and the result far from assured.

'Unanimous verdicts on both defendants too,' she adds.

'No surprise after all the long hours you put into the case.'

Her glassy eyes narrow as she lifts her face to stare at me. 'What's that supposed to mean?'

'All I'm saying is that after all your hard work, it's no surprise you won.'

'Great. I feel guilty enough as it is without you trying to make me feel worse,' she says, standing and weaving across the room to the fridge.

'I wasn't trying to make you feel guilty.'

'I know I've not been around much for the girls, but I'll make it up to them.' She empties the wine bottle into her glass and tosses it into the recycling bin. 'It's not easy juggling work and being a mother, you know.'

'I know,' I say. 'And the girls understand. They know how important this trial has been to you.'

'Of course they don't,' she scoffs. 'How could they? All they see is their mother too busy to play with them. Not around to pick them up from school. Hardly ever here for bedtime or reading stories.' Her eyes glisten as she continues to beat herself up for all the hours she's not been around.

I had no idea she felt like this. We'd agreed after Katie was born that Abi should return to work and I'd take care of the children and the house. It was a grown-up, sensible decision that made total sense, especially as she earns the lion's share of our income and I'd never been career-driven. Besides, I enjoy spending time with the girls and the reduced hours I negotiated with the council gives me more time to spend in the kitchen and on my blog. I thought the arrangement suited us, but the tears tracking down Abi's cheeks as she leans against the kitchen worktop tell another story.

'I'm never here for them,' she says. 'Nativity plays. Sports days. Carol concerts. Parents' evenings. I've missed them all, Henry, and soon they'll be all grown up and I'll have missed out on the best part of their childhoods.'

'Hey, what's brought this on?' I move towards her and lift her chin with my finger. I hate seeing her upset. 'You're a great mum and a brilliant lawyer. Don't give yourself such a hard time.'

'But it's true. I'm so wrapped up in work half the time, they hardly ever see me. What kind of mother does that make me?'

'A very good one. Now stop it. The girls worship you. I tell you what, now the trial is over, why don't we book a holiday? Just the four of us?'

Abi sniffs and smiles. 'Okay. That would be nice.'

'And you can spend as much time with the girls as you want. I'll start looking into it in the morning. Now, are you hungry? You ought to eat something.'

'I thought the lasagne was ruined?'

I think for a second or two, then reach into the fridge and unwrap a packet of manchego cheese from its waxed paper, lay it on a board and find a box of crackers from the cupboard above the toaster. 'Cheese and crackers?'

'Perfect,' Abi says, as we return to the table. She cuts herself a generous triangle of cheese.

'We're all so proud of you,' I say. 'I know you have to work hard and put in the hours but think what you did for Billy's family. You brought them justice. It's as much as anyone could have hoped for.'

'And to get unanimous verdicts,' Abi says, 'especially after losing our witnesses. I'd been half-expecting them to try to nobble the jury.'

It's pretty obvious that someone trying to protect Jimmy and Dean had interfered with Abi's witnesses ahead of their appearances in court and persuaded them to withdraw their statements, but it had never occurred to me they might try to corrupt a jury.

'You don't have to worry about it anymore,' I say. 'Jimmy and Dean aren't getting out of prison for a very long time.'

'I'm certainly not going to miss having to face the Farrows in court every day.'

I smile, but I'm worried. It hasn't occurred to me before how much Abi's job exposes her to bad people. She's surrounded by them every time she steps into court, and more often than not, she's building a case against them. Convincing a jury to convict them, often putting them away for a long time. Do all the families blame her if their sons and husbands and boyfriends are sent down because of her clever words and razor-sharp mind?

'Do you think...' I say as I push a cracker around my plate, my mind spinning with all kinds of questions. 'The man who followed you tonight, do you think he was connected to the trial?'

'Where did you get that idea from?'

'I mean, what if it had something to do with the Farrows?'

Abi snorts. 'Don't be ridiculous.'

'You know what they're capable of. God knows what they did to frighten off your witnesses.'

'That was different,' Abi says, but I can read the worry on her face. The tightness around her cheeks. The narrowing of her eyes. 'And besides, what would be the point? The case is over. The jury convicted Jimmy and Dean of murder. They'd have nothing to gain by targeting me.'

'They might be looking for revenge,' I say. 'Or retaliation.'

'Come on, it's the Farrows, not the Mafia.'

'Why not? You've been a mouthpiece for Billy's family in all the news bulletins this evening, and your picture's all over the papers. If they were looking for someone to blame, I can see why they might focus on you.'

'They might as well have gone after the judge. Or the jury. Or the police,' Abi says. 'My role wasn't any more significant than theirs.'

'All I'm saying is you need to be careful.'

'Don't be stupid. It was nothing. I told you he didn't even do anything.'

'He scared you though, didn't he?'

Abi shrugs like a petulant child. 'A little.'

'And maybe that was all he intended. For now.'

Chapter 3

Abi doesn't want to stay up talking. She's had a long day. She's tired and drunk. I tell her to go to bed while I clear up. It's an excuse to straighten out my head. I hate the thought that she was followed home. That something could have happened to her. I would never have forgiven myself. And I'm worried it was more than something random. What if she *was* being targeted by the Farrows? What if they have decided to come after her?

As Abi fumbles around upstairs, I drop our plates into the dishwasher, wrap up what's left of the cheese and scrape the burnt lasagne into the bin. I listen to her heavy, uncoordinated footsteps creaking across the floorboards, the crash of the bathroom door threatening to wake the girls and the rush of water running in the basin.

She'd been quick to dismiss my concerns about the Farrows, but she needs to watch her back. They're dangerous people. You only need to look at what Jimmy and Dean did to Billy Bowden in his own home. You can only imagine what kind of upbringing they must have had and the sort of family they've come from.

What they did was abhorrent, like something out of a horror movie. Along with their now-dead brother, George, the two men tricked their way into Billy's house and began stubbing cigarettes out on his arms and face to force him to open his safe. When he refused, they stripped him naked, tied him to a chair, and poured boiling water over his genitals. He must have been in agony in the last moments before he died when his weak heart finally gave up. And all for less than a couple of thousand pounds in cash. It was awful, and the press gleefully published every single detail.

While I'm sure most people would agree they deserve to rot in prison for the rest of their miserable lives, not everyone's convinced of their guilt. Their father, Joseph, for example, who was there every day of their trial protesting their innocence to anyone who'd listen and making wild claims about police corruption and how his sons had been fitted up. Abi had told me he'd been warned several times by the judge about his behaviour in court after making several noisy outbursts and had been close to being removed from the proceedings.

He's the one we should be worried about. Jimmy and Dean are in prison starting long sentences tonight, but Joseph, the head of the family, is out there somewhere, no doubt fuming about the result. Had he followed Abi tonight, trying to scare her? I don't know. He's not someone who easily blends into a crowd with his bushy grey whiskers, barrel chest and tattooed arms, like a short, squat Hulk Hogan gone to seed.

I'd seen him pictured in the papers and on the evening news a few times, attending court hand in hand with a younger woman with bleach-blonde hair and enormous hooped earrings. Too young to be Jimmy and Dean's mother. His girlfriend, I guess.

If it wasn't Joseph who'd stalked Abi tonight, then maybe it was another member of the family. An uncle, a nephew or a cousin perhaps. We both need to stay vigilant, at least for the next few days. Maybe when the story has blown over, the press have moved on and Joseph has come to terms with the convictions, we can relax our guard. But right now, my palms are sweating and my heart is racing. If they followed Abi home, do they know where we live? Are the girls in danger? Am I?

I'm getting ahead of myself. I don't know for sure it has anything to do with them. It could have been a random stranger for all I know, but the timing can't be a coincidence. Still, there's no point working myself up into a state until I know for certain. Even so, I'm not taking any risks. Better safe than sorry.

The dishwasher clicks and hums as it floods with water and begins its cleaning cycle. I check the oven is switched off and before I kill the lights, I lock the back door, slip out the key, and leave it on the side. I'm taking no chances tonight. I won't be able to sleep unless I'm sure the house is totally secure, especially if the Farrows know where we live. I check the window over the sink in the kitchen is shut, put the laptop back on Abi's desk in the corner and on my way upstairs, stop by the front door.

The bolt is gummed up with paint and needs a few sharp thumps with my fist to free it. I force it into its housing, grazing the skin off my knuckles, and secure the deadlock. No one's getting in short of taking a bulldozer to the door.

But as I tramp upstairs to bed, finally allowing myself to relax, I'm jarred by a sudden panic. Are the downstairs windows at the front of the house shut? I can't remember the last time we'd had any of the windows in the living room or dining room open, but I won't be able to settle until I've checked.

I steal back downstairs, step into the dining room and flick on the lights. All the windows are shut and secure and I'm relieved to find there's no hooded knifeman lurking in the shadows either. It's pathetic. Of course, there's no one in the house. My imagination is running out of control. I need to get a grip.

I cross the hall into the living room and slip behind the sofa to peer behind the heavy pleated curtains. It's pitch black outside, other than the hazy, flickering orange glow cast by the street lights. In the house opposite, the lights are on upstairs. I see a shadowy figure pull a blind closed as the moon makes a fleeting appearance from behind a thick blanket of cloud.

The window's shut, of course. Why wouldn't it be? We rarely open it, even in the summer. I test it with my fingers, just to be sure, and make sure the handle is locked. I sigh with relief, happy I'll now be able to sleep.

I'm about to step away when I notice Abi's car isn't on the drive next to mine. It takes a second or two to remember she left it in town and walked home. How could I forget? It's all I've thought about since she told me some hooded creep had followed her home. If I get up early, I can cycle in and pick it up before the school run. I don't want her walking to work after what happened tonight.

And then something else catches my eye.

Movement in the street.

I squint. Am I seeing things that aren't there?

No.

By the lamppost.

There's someone out there.

I drop the curtain and run for the stairs. I bolt up them two at a time, yelling out in panic, completely forgetting Norah and Katie are asleep.

'Abi! Abi! Quickly,' I shout, bursting into the bedroom where my wife is climbing into bed.

She freezes and stares at me like I'm insane.

'Henry? What is it?'

'Outside,' I gasp, my chest tight. 'There's someone out there.'

'Where?'

'Out the front. In the street. By the lamppost,' I gasp. 'There's someone out there watching the house.'

Abi's eyes open wide, but she doesn't move. She stays in bed, half-in, half-out, clutching the duvet tightly in one hand as if my words have cast a spell on her, turning her to stone. 'Look for yourself,' I say, switching off the main light and hurrying to the window. I yank back the curtain an inch and peek through the crack, my breath frosting the glass.

Abi creeps out of bed in her pyjamas, and pads slowly across the carpet towards me.

'It's the man who followed you earlier,' I say, my breath coming slowly back under control.

'Where?' There's a tremor in Abi's voice. 'It can't be.'

It won't settle her nerves, but I need her to see. If this is the same guy who followed her home and now he's turned up at the house, we definitely need to involve the police.

'There,' I say, pointing to the lamppost where I'd seen a hooded man loitering. Head down. Hands in his pockets. Casually leaning. Watching our house. Watching us.

But as I stare into the gloom, there's no one there. I scan up and down the street. Maybe he saw me and ran off. I pull the curtains fully open and press my nose against the chill glass. Across the road, the lights in the house opposite go out.

'He was there just a minute ago, I swear,' I say as Abi rests a hand on my shoulder.

'It's late. Come to bed.'

'Abi, I'm not making this up. I saw him. Under the lamppost, watching the house.'

'Well, he's not there now.'

She doesn't believe me. She thinks I'm seeing things. But I'm not. I can picture him clearly. Tall. Skinny. Blue jeans. Light blue hooded top. Trainers. That's not come from my imagination.

'But — '

'Henry, you're being paranoid.'

'I'm calling the police,' I say, patting my pocket, looking for my phone.

'There's no one there! You're tired. Get some sleep. Things will be clearer in the morning.'

She thinks I'm projecting my fears. But I definitely saw someone, didn't I? A thumping tension headache is building behind my eyes, but I'm not going mad. I know what I saw. But if Abi doesn't believe me, how can I possibly expect the police to take me seriously?

I slip my phone back in my pocket and reluctantly draw the curtains. Abi climbs back into bed, plumps up her pillow and pulls the duvet over her shoulders while I slope into the bathroom to wash my face and clear my head.

I know what I saw. There was someone out there in the street, staring up at the house from under the darkness of a hood. And the chances are it's the same man who followed Abi home, who now knows where we live. But what does he want? Is he just trying to scare us?

The cold water makes my skin tingle and as I stare at the stranger looking back at me, I'm shocked. My eyes are hollow and ringed with dark bags, my face pallid. I look tired and tense.

I brush my teeth, undress, and climb into bed. I can tell Abi is already asleep from the way her breathing has become slow and heavy. I don't know how she's found peace so easily. I guess it's the booze. I lay with my hands on my stomach, staring at the ceiling, my mind in turmoil.

We're safe in the house. The doors are all locked and the windows shut. No one can get to us in here, but I can't stop worrying or thinking about that man I saw under the lamppost. Is it one of the Farrows? And what does he want?

I force myself to think about something else. Work. My blog. A new recipe. But my mind repeatedly returns to the same worry. I see Joseph Farrow's beady eyes staring at me, his wiry, grey whiskers masking an evil smile. And no matter how hard I try, I can't shake that image from my head.

Chapter 4

I've barely slept a wink and at half five, wide awake and exhausted, I give up trying and roll out of bed. Despite Abi's reassurances, things aren't any clearer this morning. I'm still not sure if I saw someone outside, and the gnaw of anxiety in my gut hasn't lessened any. I pull on a pair of Lycra shorts and a cycling jersey and as I tiptoe out of the room, Abi rolls over and groans.

'What time is it?' she mumbles, without opening her eyes.

'Early. Go back to sleep.'

'Where are you going?' She raises her head off the pillow and stares at me through narrow slits, her hair a ruffled mess.

'To pick up your car.'

Abi slaps a hand to her forehead and moans. 'You're an angel. It's in the usual place behind the cinema. The keys should be in my bag. But you don't need to do that. I can walk.'

'I'd rather you took the car this morning. Anyway, I could use the fresh air and the exercise. I didn't sleep much.'

The keys are at the bottom of Abi's handbag, under the detritus of lipsticks, tissues, a brush and her purse. I creep out of the back door, roll my bike out of the shed, strap on my helmet and set off with the cool morning air chilling my cheeks. It's only a short ride into town, but it's early and the commuter traffic has yet to build. I fly through traffic lights and junctions and across roundabouts without having to stop once as if all the stars are aligned in my favour for a change. As I ride, my muscles loosening, my mind returns to the man I thought I saw outside the house last night.

It seemed real at the time and even now, with a cool breeze clearing my head, the image of him standing there casually is sharp in my mind. Last night, I was convinced it was Joseph Farrow, or someone from his family, wanting to take some kind of twisted revenge on Abi, and nothing overnight has changed my mind.

The Farrows are not the kind of people you want to cross and the idea they know where we live because one of them followed Abi home is terrifying. Why she thought it was a good idea to walk last night, I still can't fathom. I thought she had more sense.

My lungs fill with oxygen and the blood pumps hard through my veins. Gears click smoothly and tyres hiss effortlessly across the asphalt as my body becomes completely in tune with my bike. Muscle and sinew perfectly aligned with pedals and chain.

I hang my arm out to indicate I'm turning right and swing into the car park behind the old cinema. There's no smooth tarmac or pristine white lines marking out the spaces in neat rows here. It's just a patch of ground made up of broken concrete and stone chippings, tufted with weeds and wild grass, where everyone parks in a mad free-for-all. But it's cheap to park for the day, which is why it's popular with people who work in the town.

But it's still early and there are only a handful of cars parked here this morning. Among them is Abi's Mini. Her pride and joy, finished in petrol blue metallic paint, with a white roof and matching wing mirrors. It was a risk leaving it overnight in the centre of town. There are no lights or CCTV cameras, and as I roll to a halt, I'm grateful at least it's not been stolen. However, I immediately notice the damage to the windscreen. Someone's attacked it with a sharp stone or a screwdriver. It's not an irregular, random scratch, but a word deliberately etched into the glass.

The lines and curves of each letter have been gone over roughly several times until they've been gouged deeply into the glass. The letters look ragged and aggressive. At first, it makes no sense.

The word looks like 'TOR' but with the 'R' flipped and written in reverse. A graffiti tag, perhaps?

I groan as I run my fingers over it. Why are some people so incapable of respecting other people's property these days? It was probably kids hanging around the car park at night with nothing better to do. Abi's going to hit the roof. But it's her own fault. She should have paid to leave it overnight in the secure multistorey. I guess we might get the cost of the repair covered on the insurance, but it's going to mean taking it into the garage. It's all time and effort.

Angrily, I blip open the doors and push my bike around the back of the car. I'm about to flip open the boot to toss my bike in when I see the rear glass has also been defaced. Two more words etched in capital letters, similar to the graffiti on the windscreen. It's been done by the same person.

'IN HELL', it says.

A cold shiver runs from the back of my neck to the base of my spine. Stunned, I glance around as if whoever did this might still be hanging around, watching for my reaction. But the car park's empty. They've long gone.

How am I going to tell Abi? I can't hide it from her. She's going to notice it as soon as she sees the car.

Hastily, I remove the front and back wheels from my bike and shove them in the boot, wrapping them in an old sheet with the frame. And then, with my heart still pounding, I jump in behind the wheel and slot the key in the ignition.

The word scratched into the windscreen is directly in my eye line. I gasp. The word isn't 'TOR' as I first thought. And I'm pretty sure it's not a graffiti tag. It's been written in reverse to be legible to anyone sitting in the car.

When I glance up, the words etched into the rear glass fill the overhead mirror. Only now does it become obvious that the words are intended to be read together and deliberately scratched into the glass where they can't be missed. I try to swallow the lump that's formed in my throat, fighting the panic like fire rushing through my veins.

'ROT IN HELL'

A message. Not random graffiti.

This isn't good. This isn't good at all.

Chapter 5

Abi sits behind the wheel of her car on our drive staring at the letters etched menacingly into the windscreen.

'Oh my God, my poor car. Who could have done something like that?'

'It's worse. Look in the mirror.' It's better to show her than to try to explain.

'Rot in hell? What's that supposed to mean?'

'I don't know,' I say, 'but don't worry, I'll get it sorted for you. It'll probably need replacement glass front and back.'

'How much is that going to cost?'

'The insurance should cover it, but I'll need to report it to the police to get a crime number.'

Abi hauls herself out of the car and slams the door shut. She's erased any evidence of a hangover behind a perfect layer of make-up. 'Bloody kids,' she mumbles.

'Maybe it wasn't kids.'

She frowns.

'What if it was the Farrows?' I heave my bike out of the boot and reassemble it on the drive.

She shakes her head, but I can see the doubt in her eyes.

'It's not random vandalism', I say, but I don't think she wants to believe it's anything more sinister than that.

'Why would they? What would be the point?'

'I don't know. The same reason you were followed home from town last night? The same reason there was someone loitering outside the house? They're trying to scare us.'

'This isn't the Wild West, Henry. People don't go around behaving like that.'

'The Farrows do.'

'For God's sake, will you stop going on about the Farrows. This probably has nothing to do with them. It's just bad luck, that's all.'

'But —'

'We'll talk about it later. I was going to take Norah and Katie to school today. I haven't taken them for ages. But can I borrow your car? I don't want them seeing mine.'

Inside the house, the girls are fighting over a plastic toy horse. Norah's considerably stockier and taller than her sister, but Katie is putting up a good fight. Norah screams and releases the toy as Katie stamps on her foot. I suspect Norah's tears are born more out of indignation than pain.

'That's my horse', Norah howls when she sees me coming through the front door.

'Isn't!' Katie hisses.

'That's enough', I shout as Norah throws herself at my legs.

'It's not fair, Daddy. She took it from me. It's mine. I was playing with it first.'

'It's my horse!' A smug smile curls across Katie's lips as she holds the horse up triumphantly.

'If you can't agree, then perhaps it's best if I look after it today,' I say, holding out my hand to my youngest.

Katie reluctantly hands the toy over, her bottom lip stuck out sulkily. 'Now, have you had breakfast? Mummy's going to take you to school today.'

'Mummy?' Norah's brow furrows.

Abi appears at my side. 'That'll be a treat, won't it, girls?'

'But Daddy always takes us to school.'

I wince. Abi's desperate to reconnect with the girls, but we've established a routine. We're always out of the door by half eight. I let Norah sit in the front seat of the car and we sing along to Little Mix songs all the way to school. We park on one of the side roads and walk to the playground playing games or chatting about their day ahead. We repeat the same routine in reverse on the way home.

'But Mummy wants to take you today,' I say. 'Won't that be lovely? All the girls together.'

'Not fair,' Katie harrumphs.

'Don't be silly. You'll hurt Mummy's feelings.'

'It's nice to be so popular,' Abi says, bristling.

They're only kids. She should know better than to take anything they say seriously, but I remember what she said last night when she was drunk. She feels like a failure because she doesn't spend as much time as she'd like with them.

'Don't take it personally. It's only because they're used to me being around.' I kiss her on the cheek, inhaling the scent of her perfume.

'Get off, you're all sweaty.' She pushes me away. 'Go and have a shower.'

I check my watch. 'You need to have them out of the house by eight-thirty.'

'Yes, yes, I know. Right, girls, kitchen. You need to have breakfast, otherwise you're going to be hungry.'

Norah wipes away her tears and takes Abi's hand, following Katie, who's run ahead.

'Oh, and don't give Katie toast,' I say. 'That bread brings out her eczema.'

'Right,' Abi says. 'I think I can manage now. Thanks.'

I shouldn't have said anything. Now she thinks I don't trust her to look after her own children. I can't help it. I've spent so much time with them, I could write the operating manual on how to keep them alive. What they like to eat. What they won't eat. What they can't eat. What they pretend they don't like to eat but will if given the right persuasion. What time they need to go to bed. How to treat their fevers. And crucially, when they have after-school activities and when they need picking up. It's all logged in my brain, but with Abi so preoccupied with work, I worry she doesn't have the same level of knowledge.

After I've showered and shaved, the girls race past me on the stairs on their way up to their bedrooms to grab their jumpers and ties for school. Abi's sitting at the kitchen table looking at her phone.

'Work?' I ask, as I fetch Norah and Katie's packed lunch boxes from the fridge and slip them into their bags.

'Hmm? No, it's Flick,' she says.

Felicity Woodgate. One of Abi's oldest school friends. She's okay, although her husband's a bit of a prick.

'How is she?'

'She wants to meet up tomorrow night.'

'Sounds good. You could do with letting your hair down a bit after the last few months,' I say.

'I was going to suggest they come over to ours. What do you think?' She stands and sidles up to me, biting her bottom lip.

I know that look. She puts her arms around my waist and presses her body close to mine.

'That's fine.' I kiss the soft skin on her neck below her ear.

'Would you cook?'

'Dinner?'

'I know how much you like to show off in the kitchen.'

I groan. 'Tomorrow night? That's not much notice, Abi.' I love to cook but I also like to have time to plan things properly and to think about menus and ingredients. It's a creative process that can't be rushed.

'You don't have to do anything special, but we haven't had the gang around for ages.'

'The gang?' That meant she also wanted to invite Felicity and Colette's awful husbands, and I couldn't stand them, especially after the last time we'd all been out. That had been a fiasco of epic proportions. But how could I say no? After all the stress Abi had been through in the last few months, it was the least I could do. If it meant keeping Abi happy, I'd have to bite my tongue.

'We've not been together since *Meld*,' Abi says.

'Don't remind me.'

'Come on. Put it behind you. You can't stay cross with Johnny and Ralph forever.'

I would never forgive them for what had happened that night, but she was right. It was petty to hold a grudge.

'Fine,' I say. 'Invite them. I'll have a think about what I can knock up.'

Her face cracks into a wide, beaming smile as her fingers tap on the screen of her mobile. 'Great, I'll let them know.'

Chapter 6

Without the hassle of the school run, I arrive at the office ten minutes early and use the time to brew a strong coffee before making it to my desk and firing up my computer. I'm so tired, my eyes gritty and sore, that I need something to keep me awake through the morning. My ancient PC chugs and whirrs and eventually springs to life with a welcoming chirruping chorus.

Fifty new emails since I last logged on. Where the hell have they all come from? I close my inbox down again, my mind distracted. I can't focus on work this morning. I have bigger things to worry about, like the attack on Abi's car and what, if anything, the Farrows have to do with it. I glance over my shoulder but no one's paying any attention to me, so I open an internet browser and search for news items about Abi's trial. I'm surprised by how many articles there are, many with the same or similar headlines.

Sadistic brothers who tortured man to death guilty of murder

I run a cursory eye over a few of the stories, but I'm not interested in the details of the case. I know it inside out. Abi and I have talked about little else in the last few weeks. It's taken over her life and so, by extension, mine. What I'm looking for is background information on the convicted men, Jimmy and Dean Farrow, and the wider family. The Farrow name was vaguely familiar to me before the murder. I know they're a notorious criminal family, but that's as far as it goes. I guess if I can find out something about their past, I'll better understand what they're capable of, although part of me wonders whether I really want to know.

A few reports carry pictures of Jimmy and Dean's father, Joseph, flicking two fingers up at the camera. At least I think that's what he's doing, as that part of the image has been pixilated. When I run a search on his name, a long list of historic court and crime stories comes up. He's like a one-man crimewave. He has convictions for assault, possession of offensive weapons, burglary and extortion. Plus, interestingly, several convictions for intimidating witnesses. The man's been in and out of prison more often than I've been to the supermarket.

It makes me think it's more and more likely that Joseph Farrow was behind the damage to Abi's car. At the very least, he sanctioned it. Looking at his past, it's exactly the nasty, vindictive kind of thing he'd do.

'What are you looking at?'

The voice over my shoulder makes me jump. I snap the webpage closed as Zena, one of our junior assistant planning officers, sits on my desk, swinging her legs.

'Nothing,' I say, sounding as guilty as Adam in the Garden of Eden.

'Reading up on your wife's case?'

Zena joined us straight from university but is stuck in that awkward transitional phase between being a student and an employee. Her clothes are more bohemian than professional and she has striking raven-black hair cut in a severe fringe just above the arch of her eyebrows. She always wears bright, letterbox red lipstick and heavy eyeliner. She thinks it makes her look alluring. Kooky, like a wild siren. But it's a front. She's timid and easily damaged, so she puts on this bold front to keep unwanted male attention at bay. Her friendship with me is just another extension of that armour.

She sees me as some kind of father figure. Safe. Non-threatening. Very much married. But someone who can guide her through the peculiarities of working in a council planning office. I should be flattered, but with my fortieth looming in a matter of days, she just makes me feel old. Christ, she probably can't even remember the Millennium.

'Just checking the coverage,' I say.

'You okay? You look terrible.'

'Thanks. Didn't sleep much last night.' I run a hand over my face.

'Oh,' she says, but doesn't ask why. She's more interested in what other people are saying and thinking about *her*. It's an age thing. Another one of the Instagram generation more interested in her likes and follows. The modern-day yardstick of popularity. 'Are you coming to this meeting?'

I look at her blankly for a second, my sleep-deprived brain working in slow motion.

'God, yes! I'd almost forgotten,' I say, glancing at my watch. The rest of the office is already shuffling towards the conference room. I was so focused on the Farrows that the departmental meeting has slipped my mind.

I jump up as the phone on my desk rings. It'll have to wait or I'm going to be late. I ferret through a drawer in my desk for a notebook and after four rings the phone diverts to my voicemail. A recording of my nasally voice cuts in, announcing I'm unavailable and giving out my mobile number to try. It reminds me to switch it to silent.

Zena and I take seats at the back of the conference room together, next to the window overlooking the car park. At least it's something to look at. These meetings are as dull as counting sheep and about as soporific. It doesn't help that Roger Heathfield, our principal planning officer, has a tone and manner that can cure insomnia.

As he stands at the front, clears his throat and mumbles through an introduction, my mind wanders back to the Farrows. What do they want? Are they planning anything else? And what do they possibly hope to achieve? As Abi said, the trial is over. Jimmy and Dean have been convicted. Targeting her makes no sense, but I guess these aren't people who think and act in the same way as the rest of us.

Roger drones on about budgets and overspends. I glance out of the window and watch a white van swing into the car park. It pulls up outside reception directly below me and by craning my neck I can see the driver jump out, remove a stack of boxes from the back and wheel them inside on a sack barrow. It's marginally more interesting than what Roger has to say. He's moved on to health and safety matters and a new set of procedures the council has introduced for all staff.

I stifle a yawn, my heavy eyelids fluttering, and pick out Abi's Mini. A mobile windscreen fitter is due out early afternoon to replace the glass.

I thought Abi would go berserk when I showed her the damage, but she's been remarkably calm. She loves that Mini, but it's only a lump of metal and plastic. Funny how people attribute such powerful emotions to inanimate objects. I joke sometimes that she loves that car more than me. She's never denied it. She's always taking it off to have it cleaned and valeted. It costs a small fortune. But I don't really mind. If Abi's happy, I'm happy.

'Henry?' I'm vaguely aware of Roger calling my name, but at the same moment, I spot a lone figure standing in the car park, looking up at me. Hood over his head. Hands in his pockets. I narrow my eyes and snatch a shocked breath, wondering again if I'm imagining things. I rub my tired eyes, and for a fleeting second, I think I'm going to faint as the blood rushes from my head to my toes.

'Henry? Are you alright?' Zena touches my arm.

He's still there. Staring up at the window. His face obscured. It's the same man who was outside the house. I'm sure of it. Same build. Same height. Same hooded top. Or at least it looks the same. He's followed me to work. But why? What does he want? Why can't they leave us alone?

'I'm sorry —' I gasp, jumping out of my seat, aware of the growing sweat patches under my arms. 'I need some air.'

I push past Zena's outstretched legs, stumbling. Clumsily brushing past people in my haste to get out of the room. I mumble an apology as I stand on someone's foot, my hand grasping for the door handle. Then I'm spilling out into the office, my head spinning. I run past my desk, into the corridor and shoulder my way into the men's toilets.

I'm going to be sick.

I barge into a cubicle and slam the door shut, then pull out my phone, and with shaking hands, call Abi.

Chapter 7

'Henry? What's wrong?' There's a note of alarm in Abi's voice. 'Take a deep breath and talk to me.'

'He's here. The man who followed you home. The one I saw outside the house,' I gasp, my words tumbling from my mouth.

'Alright,' she says, but I hear the scepticism in her tone.

Why does she never believe me? She has this habit of treating me like an idiot, as if I don't know what I'm talking about. I'm sure she doesn't mean to, but the condescending tone she takes, as if she's superior to me, is like fingernails down a chalkboard. It's bad enough that she's the main breadwinner, without her belittling me.

'Did you get a good look at him?' she asks.

'He was too far away and he had a hood up.'

'So it could have been anyone?'

'It was him!' I hiss.

'But why would he follow you to the office?'

'I don't know.' I don't mean to raise my voice but I wish she'd listen to what I'm saying. I'm not making it up.

'It just seems... unlikely, don't you think?' Now she sounds like a lawyer cross-examining a witness. That's the problem with being married to a barrister. It's not only impossible to win an argument with her, but she takes on this patronising tone when she thinks I'm wrong about something.

She has a point though. If the Farrows' grievance is with Abi for her role in convicting Jimmy and Dean, why come after me?

Oh God, it's so obvious.

'Because they followed the car, thinking it was you!' It makes perfect sense. 'It's because I was driving your Mini this morning.'

'You don't think they might have noticed I wasn't driving?'

'Obviously not.' I can't understand why she's trying to shoot holes in my logic. Does she think I'm going crazy or does she just not want to believe they're coming after her? Coming after us?

'How much sleep did you actually get last night?' Abi asks.

'Not much. A few hours at most. I know what you're thinking, but I didn't imagine it, Abi. I wish you'd believe me.'

'I do believe you, but if you don't calm down, you're going to make yourself ill.'

My heart's beating so fast and my whole body is slick with sweat. My eyes sting and the muscles in my shoulders ache. But it's hardly surprising. It's like being back at school, hiding from the bullies. Taking the long route home rather than risking running into Tommy Peters and his boorish mates. But I'm an adult now. I shouldn't have to spend my days looking over my shoulder, worrying, wondering what trouble is around the corner. I hate it. And I hate that there's nothing I can do about it.

I called the police before I left the house to report the attack on Abi's car and told them about the stranger who'd followed her home. But they couldn't have cared any less. They took the details, gave me a crime number and that was it. I guess they have bigger fish to fry.

'Why are you being so chilled about this, Abi? Aren't you worried?'

'Of course I am, but what good is worrying going to do?' she says. 'There's no point both of us getting worked up, imagining every face in the crowd is out to get us.'

'Is that what you think I'm doing?'

'No, I'm just saying one of us needs to keep a level head.'

'If this is Joseph Farrow, we need to be worried. You know what that family's like. They nobbled three of your witnesses for a start,' I say.

'You know what Joseph Farrow looks like, right?' Abi asks. 'You've seen pictures of him. You wouldn't be able to miss him if you saw him in the street.'

'Yeah,' I say, thinking of the pictures I've seen in the papers. 'Of course. Why?'

'So you'd recognise him if he was standing in the car park?'

I shuffle my feet anxiously. I know where she's going with this. 'It wasn't him,' I mumble. 'But he might have put someone else up to it. It could be a cousin or a nephew...'

I hear Abi's high heels clatter across the wooden floor of her office. 'I tell you what, is he still out there?'

'I don't know. I can't see from here.' I let myself out of the cubicle, but the window in the gents' toilets has frosted glass which I can't see through.

'Why don't you go outside and speak to him? Find out what he wants.'

'What?'

'Talk to him. Put your mind at rest,' Abi says, deadpan.

She's serious.

'I can't do that.'

'Why not?'

'It could be dangerous.'

Abi sighs. 'What about seeing if you can take a picture of him?'

Typical of Abi to be so practical. I'd have never thought of that. I could probably snatch a picture on my phone if I could get close enough without scaring him off. Then we might at least be able to identify him. We could even go back to the police. It's evidence we're being harassed. 'Okay, I'll give it a go.'

'Let me know how you get on. Listen, I've got to go. I'm supposed to be in court. I'll speak to you tonight.'

Abi hangs up without even a goodbye and I'm left holding a silent phone to my ear.

Trying to get a picture of the guy outside isn't a bad idea though. At least it's something practical I can do. And if I can get the picture, maybe Abi will take me more seriously.

I wash my face with cold water and take a moment to compose myself before returning to the office. I'm dismayed to see the meeting hasn't finished yet and I creep back into the conference room with an apologetic nod to Roger, who's still going strong, even though I can see he's totally lost the room. Everyone's slumped in their seats looking bored.

'Everything okay?' Zena asks as she tucks in her knees to let me past.

I glance furtively out of the window, but there's no one out there. The man's gone. For now, at least.

'Did you see that guy out there earlier?' I ask.

Zena follows my gaze out of the window, frowning under her perfect fringe. 'What guy?'

'A guy in a hooded top, watching us. It doesn't matter,' I say as I retake my seat.

'Are you sure you're okay? You look like you've seen a ghost.'

'Is there a problem back there?' Roger has stopped talking and is staring at us with eyebrows raised.

'No, sorry, Roger,' Zena answers before I can speak.

'Then perhaps you could show a little courtesy and not talk all the way through my meeting please, Miss Edwards. There'll be plenty of time over lunch to catch up on the latest *Love Island* gossip.'

The room titters. What a patronising prick. My skin prickles with irritation as Zena stiffens, embarrassed. Fancy speaking to her like that in front of everyone.

'That's out of line, Roger,' I say before I can stop myself. I'm in no mood for it today. I'm tired, irritable and stressed. 'It's my fault. I'm not feeling so good. Zena was only asking if I'm okay.'

'I wouldn't mind Zena checking if I was okay,' Conor, another junior member of the team, who really ought to know better, quips. He's always fancied himself as the class joker, the smart kid at the back with the witty put-down and an over-inflated opinion of his own importance. The smart-arse who always writes offensive rather than amusing comments in people's birthday and leaving cards, and who loves to come in on a Monday morning bragging about his weekend 'conquests'. Desperately trying to be loved. Hopelessly ill-equipped for office life. I'm fed up with his sexist bullshit, especially when it's at Zena's expense.

'What did you say?' I ask, fixing him with a stare.

Conor shrugs, his boyish cheeks turning rosy. 'Nothing', he mumbles.

Not so smart now as all eyes in the room turn on him and he squirms uncomfortably.

'Apologise', I demand.

'What?' He looks horrified.

'Apologise to Zena for being a male chauvinist pig', I say.

'Alright, Henry, that'll do', Roger says, trying to diffuse the situation.

'Not until he's apologised.' I keep my eyes fixed on Conor, enjoying his obvious discomfort.

'Conor, just apologise will you', Roger says, rolling his eyes. 'Then we can get on.'

Conor folds his arms defensively across his chest. 'Alright. I'm sorry. Happy now?'

'Watch your mouth in future', I tell him.

'Thank you, Henry. That's enough. Leave the discipline to me.'

That's it. I've had it. I can't concentrate on work anyway. I shouldn't be here. I pinch the bridge of my nose to relieve the pressure behind my eyes.

'You know what?' I say, standing. 'I'm going to take the rest of the day off. I'll be on my mobile if anything urgent crops up.'

Chapter 8

The letter is lying on top of a pile of bills, pristine white against the mud-coloured coir mat. There's nothing ominous about it, other than it has no name or address on it and no stamp, which means it's been hand-delivered. I don't even give it a second thought as I let myself into the house, sweep it up with the other post and put it on the side while I make myself a cup of tea.

My head's pounding and I'm nauseous with exhaustion. My neck is knotted with stress and my energy has dipped. Maybe I'm coming down with something. There was a nasty bug going around the office a few weeks ago and it would be just my luck that I've picked it up. I'd have been useless if I'd stayed at work. Better to take the day off to rest and recuperate. And with Colette and Felicity coming to dinner with their dreadful husbands tomorrow, I need to be fighting fit. Otherwise, I'll never cope, especially as I'm supposed to be cooking. Which reminds me, I need to think about menus.

Maybe seafood to start. Nothing too heavy. Oysters or scallops perhaps. Something oozing with taste that leaves them wanting more. And for the main, a twist on a classic. I could do steaks with a celeriac puree. Simple. Elegant. Classy.

I don't need their approval, and yet I crave it. And of course, all the talk will be about how amazing Abi was to win her court case and how she was all over the news. Nobody could be prouder of her than me. She pulled that result out of the bag even with her case falling apart. She deserves a bloody medal. But honestly, I could do without an evening of Colette and Felicity fawning all over her, telling her how simply wonderful she is. I already know.

I sit at the kitchen table with my tea, open my phone and write a shopping list of ingredients. I'll probably swing past the farm shop. It's a bit more expensive, but I know they'll have everything I need. And it's good quality. Better than all that pre-packaged rubbish from the supermarket. I should probably feature the shop on the blog as the site is supposed to be all about the best of local food, and anyone who's anyone around here knows that it's the place to go.

I set up the blog at Abi's suggestion. The original plan was to provide honest, no holds barred reviews of the best, and worst, restaurants in the area. We called it *Nosher Bites Back* and kept the reviews anonymous so they could be genuinely critical without fear of comeback. I intended Nosher to become a trusted online food critic who lifted the lid on the restaurant scene around here, in the same way Belle de Jour had once revealed the seedy underbelly of prostitution in London. A combination of acerbic wit and uncompromising truths.

But in recent months, I've expanded the blog's content to include recipes of my own. It's given me a renewed focus, and seems popular with my followers, especially when I post pictures of the final dish. It doesn't mean I've given up on the restaurant reviews, especially as new establishments are popping up all the time, like the new Spanish tapas bar that's opened recently in Whitstable. Maybe Abi and I could go for my birthday. We could make it into a special treat. After all, it isn't every day you turn forty.

As I finish my tea, my gaze falls on the stack of letters I'd put to one side. I sift through them one by one. A glossy brochure in a transparent plastic wrapper addressed to Abi. An electricity bill. The offer of a new credit card from a bank I've never heard of. And a charity begging letter seeking donations for a new animal sanctuary, complete with the obligatory pictures of sad-looking dogs.

Lastly, I open the plain white envelope, imagining it's one of those clever marketing campaigns to trick you into thinking you've received an actual letter from a real person. Inside is a single sheet of milk-white paper. Curious, I unfold it and smooth it out on the table. There are four printed lines of text. No company name or logo. No sales pitch. No fancy marketing copy. I turn the sheet over, but it's blank on the other side. It's weird. As I read, my breath catches in my throat.

One death was too much.

Two is unbearable.

An eye for an eye seems only fair after what you've done.

So now I have nothing left to lose, I'll see you in hell.

I read it over again twice more with my hand trembling and the sensation that the ground is falling away under my chair.

One death was too much?

Whose death?

And two is unbearable?

I immediately think of the Farrows. I bet this is their work. Its exact meaning isn't entirely clear, but the sentiment is obvious. I was right. They blame Abi for Jimmy and Dean's convictions. And now they want revenge.

An eye for an eye?

I'll see you in hell?

It chimes with the message etched into the glass on Abi's Mini. I flush hot and cold. This feels serious. Is it a death threat? What else can it possibly be? And whoever wrote it must have been to the house to deliver it. That means they came right up the drive and stood on the doorstep.

I should call Abi. But what about the girls? Are they in danger? Should I collect them from school early, just in case? Or am I overreacting? It's only a letter. Words on a piece of paper. But the tone and the language are deeply disturbing.

Perhaps I should call the police. Or is it better to ignore it?

I have absolutely no idea what to do.

❖

I resist the urge to call Abi at work because she'd only worry and there's nothing she can do about it. But the moment she walks in, I sit her down and slide the letter across the table.

'What's this?' She eyes me warily.

'Open it.'

She slips the sheet of paper out of the envelope and gingerly unfolds it. Her lips move as she reads the four lines to herself, her eyes opening wide. She glances at me.

'Where did you get this?'

'It was on the mat when I got home,' I say. I tell her I'd taken the day off sick and after finding the letter, I picked up Norah and Katie early from school as a precaution.

She puffs out her cheeks as she reads the letter again, then drops it on the table and folds her arms. 'I wouldn't worry about it.'

'What? Why? They're threatening us. Can't you see?'

She shrugs. 'The world's full of weirdos who get a kick out of sending shit like this. We get loads of these in the office.'

'You're not worried?'

'No.'

I've spent most of the day pacing up and down the house, my mind in turmoil, unable to think about anything else. The only brief distraction was the arrival of the windscreen repair technician to fix Abi's car. Why's she being so relaxed? Isn't she worried?

'But what if it's from the Farrows?'

'Look, people get fixated on big cases, especially when there's been so much media coverage. It'll be some sad little man who still lives with his mother, cloistered away in his bedroom on his computer with nothing better to do.'

I can't believe what I'm hearing. 'But it was hand-delivered. Whoever wrote it knows where we live and has been to the house. Doesn't that concern you even a bit? Aren't you worried about the girls?'

Abi carefully folds the letter back into its envelope and pushes it my way.

'The best place for it is the bin,' she says. 'It's a letter from a crank. Ignore it.'

'But the threat,' I say, wanting to shake her to her senses. 'An eye for an eye? I'll see you in hell?'

'It doesn't mean anything. It's gibberish.'

'One death was too much. Two is unbearable. That has to be a reference to the court case. Billy Bowden's death first, followed by George's death in custody.'

Three brothers, Jimmy, George and Dean, had all been part of the plot to rob Billy Bowden. They were all in the house on the night he died, and as far as anyone could tell, they all played a part in torturing Billy to his death. But George had taken his own life while on remand awaiting trial. Somehow he'd laid his hands on a razor, cut his own wrists and bled out before anyone found him. That must be the second death mentioned in the letter.

'You're twisting the facts to fit your own narrative,' Abi says, a crackle of irritation in her voice. 'Why would the Farrows be concerned about Billy Bowden's death when they caused it?'

'I don't know,' I say, running my hands through my hair. All I know is that someone with a grudge against us is doing their best to unsettle our comfortable lives. I've barely slept in the last twenty-four hours and now I'm worried sick about my family's safety. 'I think we'd better let the police know.'

'What's the point? They won't do anything,' Abi says. She's probably right.

They didn't seem at all interested when I reported the damage to Abi's Mini and explained she'd been followed home by a stranger. They were hardly going to call in the Flying Squad because someone had pushed an anonymous letter through the door.

'So we're just going to ignore it?' I say, throwing up my hands in despair.

'That's exactly what we're going to do.' Abi reaches across the table for the envelope, screws it up theatrically and tosses it in the bin under the sink. 'There. It's gone,' she says, rubbing her hands as if she's cleaning them. 'Now, I suggest you forget all about it and stop stressing.'

'I'd feel better if we reported it. At least the police would have a record if something happened,' I say. I'm not ready to forget it as easily as Abi, and I won't bury my head in the sand.

'I told you, it's a waste of time.'

'You're a bloody criminal lawyer. There must be someone in the police you can talk to.' I immediately regret raising my voice. I shouldn't be taking it out on Abi, but her flimsy grasp on how serious this might be is so frustrating.

'There's no need to take that tone with me.'

'I'm sorry, but we shouldn't be dealing with this on our own,' I say, following her across the kitchen. I grab her wrists and hold her hands in front of her chest. 'We need help.'

'We're fine.'

'For the girls' sake.'

'Henry, stop it!' She wriggles free from my grasp and turns to stare out of the window over the sink.

'Please, Abi. Do it for me. For us. Talk to someone.'

She bows her head. It's a sign of surrender. She doesn't want to fight with me.

'Fine,' she snaps. 'There are a couple of people I know from court who I could speak with, but I wouldn't hold your breath. They have a lot on their plates and I'm not sure there's anything they'll be able to do.'

Chapter 9

I sleep better knowing Abi's going to talk to one of her police contacts. If nothing else, they might give us some advice, even if there's nothing they can do.

She steps out of the en suite wrapped in a bath towel, drying her hair. 'You won't forget to make that call today like you promised, will you?'

I pull on a pair of grey suit trousers and button up my shirt, conscious that it's a little tight around the stomach these days. I need to get out on my bike more, but exercise is the last thing I can think about right now with everything that's happening.

'Please, Henry, stop going on about it. I said I'd speak to someone and I will.'

'When?'

'As soon as I get into chambers.'

'Okay.' I don't know why she can't just phone someone now. Or why she didn't want to do it last night. 'Remember, you promised.'

Abi sighs as she sits at her dressing table and runs a brush through her hair, staring at her reflection in the mirror. 'Yes, I know.'

'And you'll let me know what they say?'

'Yes!'

At last, it feels like we're doing something positive and I don't feel anywhere near as stressed as I did yesterday. My head's still a little foggy even after catching up on sleep, but it's Friday. I only have to get through the day and then we have the weekend ahead of us. Perhaps we'll go out and try to put all this behind us. We've been promising to take Norah and Katie to the zoo for weeks.

'What time are your friends getting here tonight?'

'*Our* friends,' Abi corrects me. 'I've told them to be here for half seven. Do you know what you're cooking yet?'

I stand behind Abi and kiss her bare shoulders. 'If I told you that, it wouldn't be a surprise, would it?' I smile into the mirror. 'Don't worry, you're going to love it.'

When it comes to my food, Abi's my number one fan but also my harshest critic. I hope I don't disappoint her tonight.

As usual, she leaves the house first, grabbing a dry slice of toast on her way out while I cajole the girls to finish their breakfast, clear away the dishes, pack their lunches in their school bags and yell at them to get their shoes on.

I may have over-reacted taking them out of school early yesterday. That letter came as a shock. I really didn't know what to make of it. Plus, I was tired and on edge and the girls' safety is always at the forefront of my mind.

Would parenting have been easier if we'd had boys? Maybe I'd be more relaxed, but a father is always going to worry about his daughters, no matter what age they are. And it's not as though they missed much. Norah had a PE lesson and Katie was practising her reading with a volunteer teaching assistant.

This morning I have no qualms about sending them in. They're as safe at school as they would be at home. Probably more so with all the security measures in place these days. You can't just walk in anymore. Now you either need a key code or have to wait for the office to buzz you in. Things have moved on since my time.

Thankfully, I make it through the day with no major dramas or crises, which is just as well, as I don't think I would have had the emotional resilience to deal with anything remotely stressful. Instead, I spend most of my time going through a backlog of planning applications for garages, extensions and the odd conservatory, while hiding behind my computer monitor and periodically checking my phone for a call from Abi that never materialises. I guess despite her promise, she's not had the chance to speak to any of her police contacts yet. I resist the urge to call for fear of being accused of pestering her. I'll have to wait to find out what's happened when she gets home.

As usual, I leave work at three to collect the girls from school and drag them moaning around the farm shop while I pile a trolley high with everything I need for what's turned out to be quite a complex menu.

Back home, I feed them spaghetti bolognese and leave them to play while I crack on with prep for the meal.

Abi arrives home early for once and I'm grateful that she takes over bath and bedtime while I busy myself in the kitchen. I'm so preoccupied and there's so much to do that I forget to ask if she spoke to anyone about the letter.

When she finally joins me in the kitchen, she's showered and changed. She's styled her hair in loose ringlets, re-done her make-up with smoky dark eyes and is wearing a sleeveless, flowing black dress. It's only friends for dinner, but Abi never misses an opportunity to dress up. I don't hold it against her. She deserves to have fun tonight, to celebrate after a long and tough few weeks.

'I spoke to one of the detectives I know,' she says nonchalantly as she pops open a bottle of champagne from the fridge, the cork flying across the room and bouncing off a wall.

I'm at the sink, up to my elbows in suds, trying to make the kitchen look presentable before our guests arrive.

'And?' I try not to sound too keen, to let her tell me in her own time, even though I'm desperate to know what he said.

'He was really helpful, actually. I told him about the car and the letter and that you thought it might be connected to the Farrow case.'

I dry my hands on a tea towel and lean against the counter, watching as Abi pours herself a glass of champagne, the fizzy foam of bubbles shooting up the inside of the glass and almost spilling over her hand. 'And what did he say?'

'As a favour to me, he was going to send someone out to have a word with the family,' Abi says. 'It's not something they'd normally do, but I laid it on about how worried you'd been.'

'Thanks. Blame it on me, why don't you?'

'You were the one who insisted I should raise it.'

'No, no,' I say. 'That's good. That's really good.'

I toss the tea towel on the side and put my hands on Abi's hips, pulling her towards me. It feels like we've turned a corner. If the police are prepared to warn the Farrows off, we shouldn't have anything more to worry about.

'Happy now?' Abi asks, raising an eyebrow.

I move to kiss her on the lips, but she offers me a cheek instead and pushes me away. 'You'll smudge my lipstick.'

'Thank you,' I say. 'You see, it was the right thing to do.'

'So can we stop with all the talk now about threatening letters and strangers loitering around in the dark?'

I shrug.

'And please, don't say anything tonight. Colette and Flick will only worry.'

'Fine by me, but I thought you never keep secrets from them?'

'Let's just try to enjoy tonight, shall we? I can't wait to see what you're cooking.'

She tries to lift the lid on one of my pots on the hob, but I slap her hand away. 'All good things,' I tell her as there's a sharp knock at the front door.

'That'll be them.' Abi checks her watch. 'They're early.' But there's no hiding the delight on her face.

She strides off, tottering on dangerously high heels. A moment later, I hear the door click open and the sound of voices on the doorstep. I recognise Felicity's demure giggle and her husband, Johnny's booming laugh. I steel myself. I've not seen either of them since the disastrous night we'd all eaten at *Meld*, a newly opened Euro-Asian restaurant I'd been dying to try for months. It had been the most embarrassing night of my life, and after the humiliation of being thrown out, I'd not forgiven them yet. But I suppose I can't hold a grudge forever, especially as they weren't entirely to blame.

Johnny wafts into the kitchen in a cloud of potent cedarwood aftershave, his shirt gaping open to reveal too much of his smooth, waxed chest, his long grey hair slicked back fashionably behind his ears. He heads straight for me with arms wide open as if he's going to hug me. I can't stand it. All this mock friendliness. This faux metro-sexual bonhomie. I plaster a fake smile on my face. It's as if that night in *Meld* never happened.

'Johnny, good to see you,' I say with as much enthusiasm as I can muster. I'm only doing it for Abi's benefit. She deserves to have a good night and I don't want to be the one to spoil it.

I hold my arm out to shake Johnny's hand, but he nudges it aside and pulls me into a bear hug. My face presses into his muscular shoulder as he slaps my back with stinging blows. He's in annoyingly good shape for a man in his forties. Must be all the time he spends sculpting himself in the gym. I can just imagine him standing there with heavy weights in both hands, admiring himself in the floor to ceiling mirrors.

Behind him, Felicity, a blonde waif with porcelain skin who can't look anyone in the eye until she's at least two glasses of wine into the evening, steps into the room with Abi, hanging back like she's a little embarrassed, cast in the shade by her husband's over-friendly enthusiasm.

'I brought you a gift,' Johnny says, grinning with big Hollywood-whitened teeth. He produces a bushy potted plant from behind his back.

'Thanks,' I say. 'There was no need.' I immediately recognise the wrinkly orange fruits hanging from curled stems under the leaves.

'It's a chilli plant,' Johnny says.

'Yes, I know.' I'm not an idiot. I can recognise a chilli plant when I see one.

Johnny's grin grows broader as he glances over his shoulder at Abi, making sure he has her attention. 'And not just any chilli,' he says. 'It's a naga plant because I know you like your food spicy.'

'Naga?' Abi says, heading for the fridge. She fetches the bottle of champagne, pours two glasses and hands them out to our guests.

'Henry knows, don't you, mate?' Johnny grips my bicep and gives it what I guess is supposed to be a friendly squeeze.

I wince. Why does he have to call me mate? 'It's a really hot chilli.'

'*The* hottest.' He looks so pleased with himself, I'm almost loath to correct him. It's actually a really thoughtful gift. Something practical I can use.

'Not quite the hottest, but still pretty potent,' I say. I can't help myself. It's a rare chance to put him in his place, not that he even seems to notice. 'Put it this way, you wouldn't want to touch one and then rub your eyes. You'd be screaming for your mother to put you out of your misery.'

Johnny finds this hysterical. 'Yeah, good one, mate.'

I cringe. 'Why don't you take Felicity and Johnny through to the lounge while I crack on?' I say to Abi.

Anything to avoid small talk with them.

Another knock at the door.

I make a space on the kitchen windowsill for the naga plant as Abi trots down the hall. My jaw tenses when I hear Ralph's braying laugh, followed by Colette simpering over Abi's hair and how wonderful she looks in her dress.

I can't put off seeing them by hiding in the kitchen. They'll think I'm being rude, so I reluctantly trudge into the lounge where Ralph and Johnny are sharing a manly embrace like two bear cubs, almost knocking each other off their feet. Felicity and Colette exchange less demonstrative air kisses, avoiding smudging each other's make-up.

'Hey, big man,' Ralph says when he sees me in the doorway. 'She got you chained to the stove again?' He winks conspiratorially at Abi. It's the same old hackneyed put down every time he comes to dinner as if the cooking should be left to the women and the more time I spend in the kitchen, the less of a man I become.

He and Johnny are the same. They've never said anything to my face, but I'm sure they think less of me because Abi has a better job, brings in more money and leaves the childcare and household chores to me. As if that's somehow emasculating rather than a progressive solution to a modern lifestyle problem, which is how Abi and I see it. I don't think they have an idea how tough it is to look after kids and hold down a full-time job. Johnny and Flick farm their two kids out to a nanny, even though Felicity doesn't work, and Ralph and Colette don't have children. So neither of them is in a position to judge.

My life is a constant merry-go-round of school pickup and drop-off, feeding, bathing, dressing, playing, reading, helping with homework and preparing packed lunches, even before I think about my job at the council. It's a never-ending, thankless roller-coaster. And on top of all that, there's the food blog that takes time and effort. Johnny and Ralph might both run their own companies, but I reckon that would be easier in comparison to what I do.

As Ralph shakes my hand, he grips it so tightly it feels like he's going to crush it. He grins. Does he share the same orthodontist with Johnny? They have the same impeccable white veneers. It's the kind of smile only money can buy.

'I brought some of the decent stuff,' he says, handing me a bottle of red wine.

I give the label a fleeting glance. I won't fall into the trap of sounding so grateful that he launches into a long monologue about how he discovered the vineyard in a secret corner of Burgundy on his travels to find himself and now has a personal supply flown in twice a year. I've made that mistake before.

'Great, I'll open it and put it on the table.' It's a good excuse to get away.

I return to the kitchen, stopping only briefly to kiss Colette's cheek. I like Colette, despite her choice of husband. She's the most down-to-earth of all of them, and with her Boden-chic pale pastel loose-knit sweaters and sensible shoes, there's nothing pretentious about her. She's also a bloody good head teacher.

Time to finish the starter. I pop the wine on the table in the dining room and hurry back to the kitchen.

Bringing all the elements together onto the plate at the right time is the most stressful part of the meal for me. And I want this to go well, to prove a point to Johnny and Ralph. I'm heading for the fridge to retrieve the apple salsa I'd made earlier when I hear a loud buzzing.

Abi's phone is snaking its way across the worktop as it rings on silent, the screen lit up with an incoming call. She must have left it there when she was pouring the champagne. I can't help but glance at who's calling.

It's a name I don't recognise.

Steve Hicks.

Means nothing to me. But why's he phoning on a Friday evening? Must be important. I'm busy. I should ignore it. If it's that important, he'll leave a message.

The phone stops ringing. But almost immediately starts buzzing again.

'Abi! Your phone,' I shout, but she doesn't hear me.

So I pick it up and answer it.

'Hi, Abi's phone.'

'Is Abi there? Can I speak with her?'

'Who is this?' I ask, wedging the phone between my shoulder and my cheek as I light a flame on the hob.

'It's DI Steve Hicks. She asked me to look into something for her. I have an update I thought she'd like to know about.'

I immediately stop what I'm doing. 'Just a minute.'

I jog into the lounge, where Abi is talking animatedly with Colette and Felicity.

'Abi,' I say, holding my hand over the phone's microphone.

She shoots me an irritated look.

I hold the phone up. 'It's DI Steve Hicks. He has an update about the Farrows.'

She snatches the phone, makes her excuses to her friends, and steps into the hall. I stand close behind her, trying to hear what's being said. I trust it's good news. Hopefully, they've confessed and the police have warned them to leave us alone.

'Right. Uh-uh. Okay,' Abi says as she listens. 'Well, thanks very much, Steve. I appreciate it.'

'Well?' I ask as she hangs up.

Abi turns around with a haunted look on her face, her eyes dull and emotionless. My stomach flips.

'He said one of his team spoke to Joseph Farrow this afternoon.' Abi stares at her phone, unable to look me in the eye. 'He wanted to let me know what he had to say for himself.'

'And?'

'He denied everything.'

'Everything? Shit.' An empty hollowness opens up inside me and my legs go weak.

'What did you think he was going to say? Did you really think he'd make a full confession? It doesn't mean he didn't do it,' Abi says. 'But if it was him or someone in the family, their cards are marked now. They'd be idiots to try anything else now they know the police are involved.'

'You think?' I'm not convinced.

'Trust me, there won't be anything else to worry about.'

'But what if it wasn't the Farrows? What if none of this had anything to do with them at all?' I say, my mind a sudden maelstrom of doubt and confusion. I'd been so convinced it had to be them because of the court case and the timing of everything so soon after it ended, but now I'm not so sure. 'What if it's someone else?'

'Like who?'

'I don't know,' I say. And that's what worries me the most.

There's only one thing worse than fighting a war, and that's fighting a war with an invisible enemy.

Chapter 10

As I return to the kitchen to begin on the scallops, my mind drifts. My head's spinning and I can't concentrate on what I'm doing. If the Farrows weren't responsible for vandalising Abi's car, hanging around outside the house and my office, or sending that threatening letter, who was? And why? I suppose Abi's right. The Farrows might have lied. They were hardly going to admit to harassing the barrister who prosecuted Jimmy and Dean, but it's put doubt in my mind and the niggle of worry has returned to my stomach.

With a slight tremor, I produce six perfect plates with what I hope is food that will blow their minds. The scallops are sensuously crusted with a caramel glaze and should be complemented beautifully by the tartness of the watermelon rind and apple salsa. The chilly fried oysters give the dish a pungent kick.

Abi's corralled everyone into the dining room and filled their glasses with wine. As I walk in, they fall silent and there's a ripple of expectation when they see and smell my food.

'This looks bloody amazing,' Johnny says, bowing his head over his plate as he inhales the aromas, murmuring his appreciation.

'So, to start,' I say, standing at the head of the table, 'we have seared scallops topped with watermelon rind, miso puree, sesame and chilli fried oyster and a green apple salsa.'

A tingle of pride prickles my skin as Colette and Felicity give me a polite round of applause and Abi shoots me an appreciative wink while toasting me with her glass. I feel my lips curl into a satisfied smile and, for a moment, all my worries evaporate. I don't think about Joseph Farrow or the damage to Abi's car or the anonymous letter I found on the doormat. I'm lost in the moment.

And as our guests start to eat, momentarily silenced as they savour the flavours, I'm reminded of why I put myself through the stress of cooking such complicated dishes. It's because there's something magical about good food that brings universal happiness.

Soon, the chatter picks up again and the room comes alive with conversation and laughter, drowning out the clatter of cutlery on porcelain.

'Oh Abi, we haven't even asked you about the trial yet,' Colette says, picking up her wine glass. 'You were all over the news. I thought you were amazing.'

Abi lowers her head and looks suitably humble, even though I can tell she's loving it. We all like to be appreciated for the good things we do.

'Yeah, well done, Abs,' Johnny chimes in. 'We wondered whether those scumbags were going to get off when you lost those witnesses. Bloody bad luck, but fair play to you for getting the result. You must be chuffed to bits.'

'It was my case to lose, really,' Abi says, batting the compliment away. 'It would have been a weak jury not to have found those two guilty.'

'Don't be so modest,' I say. 'She worked damned hard on that case. We've hardly seen her for the last few months.'

'You must be so proud of her,' Ralph says.

Of course I'm proud of her, but it's not what he means. I can tell from the way his lip curls fractionally upwards on one side of his face. It's a dig at me. He's never liked me. Never thought I was good enough for Abi. They've known each other since university and he can't understand what a hotshot lawyer like her is doing married to a guy who works for the council and looks after the kids. He wonders why she couldn't have married someone like him. A guy who owns his own business and drives a Porsche.

'She deserved to win,' I say.

'I hope those two men never get released after what they did.' Felicity finishes a forkful of scallop and pushes her plate away, screwing up her pretty freckled nose. 'The horrible things they did to that poor man. It was disgusting. They should be strung up.'

'Steady on, Flick.' Ralph throws up his hands in mock outrage. 'You can't go around hanging common criminals. You'll give all those snowflakes a heart attack.'

'Leave her alone.' Colette chastises Ralph with a tap on his arm.

'I'm serious,' Felicity continues. 'I don't suppose they'll serve their full sentences and before you know it, they'll be out again. It's not right. If you take a life, you should lose your life. Simple as that.'

Abi stands and reaches for a bottle of wine. 'Anyone for anymore?' she asks. She's trying to subtly change the subject. I don't blame her. A full-on debate about the merits of capital punishment is an unsavoury topic for the dinner table.

'How's that new car of yours, Ralph?' I ask, pouncing on the first thing that comes to mind to help her out. I vaguely remember him talking about it when I last saw him at *Meld*. A big sports utility vehicle, as I recall.

'Yeah, it's good,' he says. 'What are you driving these days? Not still that hairdresser's car, are you?'

I ignore the jibe as Abi catches my eye and gives me a thankful smile.

'I can't drink too much tonight,' I hear Colette tell Abi as she tries to top up her glass. 'I need to keep a clear head. We have the inspectors in next week, so I'm going to have to spend the weekend working. It's going to be a total nightmare and I need to be on top of my game.'

I look around. Everyone's plate has been virtually licked clean in a fraction of the time it took me to prepare the dish. I take it as a sign they've all enjoyed it.

Abi jumps up to clear the table.

'I can manage,' I say. 'You're supposed to be having fun. Sit and chat.'

I collect plates from Felicity and Johnny first, then glide around the table towards Ralph and Colette. But as I step behind Ralph's chair, he throws his arms up and makes a loud noise. Startled, I almost drop the plates. Ralph laughs uproariously.

'What the fuck, Ralph?'

'Steady on, those plates almost ended up on my lap.' This amuses Ralph no end. He looks around the table at the others, as if he's waiting for them to get the joke.

'It's funny,' he says, 'you know, like that silly waitress in *Meld*.'

The table falls quiet in awkward silence. No one looks at Ralph, finding more interesting things in their laps or on the table. Everyone knows what he's talking about, but only Ralph's crass enough to mention it.

'What?' he asks, looking genuinely perplexed that no one else finds it funny. 'Come on, you remember. That waitress in the restaurant who dropped the plates down my front. My shirt's still got a grease stain on it even though it's been through the wash like a dozen times.'

'It's not funny, Ralph,' I say. He's killed the good vibe. Even I was beginning to enjoy myself before he opened his big mouth.

'It was only a joke.'

'It wasn't very funny,' I repeat. Nothing about that night at the restaurant is remotely amusing. I can't believe he brought it up. Actually, it's Ralph. I can.

'Alright, I'm sorry. I shouldn't have mentioned it.'

'No, you shouldn't,' I agree as I collect his and Colette's plates.

'What's your beef, Henry? I was only messing.'

'It's been a stressful few days if you must know,' I say. I can feel the virtual daggers flying across the table from Abi. She thinks I'm going to tell them about the letter and the attack on her car when she specifically asked me not to.

'The school run getting a bit much for you, is it?' Ralph looks to Johnny, who obliges by laughing at his stupid joke.

'Parents in the playground giving you a hard time again?' Johnny retorts. Apparently, this is hilarious as both men fall about laughing.

I glance at Abi. She's watching me with a steely expression, willing me to keep my cool. Not to blurt out what's really on my mind.

'So what is it?' Ralph asks. 'Why's your week been so stressful?'

I hate the challenge in his tone, that nothing I've been through could compare to anything he's had to deal with. Or does he just think I'm weak and pathetic?

'It doesn't matter.'

'Come on, tell us,' Ralph presses.

'Henry.' There's a warning in Abi's tone. She really doesn't want me to tell them, but if they knew, perhaps they'd be more understanding.

'Someone sent us a death threat,' I say, the words tripping carelessly off my tongue. 'That's what we've been having to deal with this week, okay?'

Chapter 11

Matunde Yeboah had made the semi-finals of a popular TV cookery talent show with his uniquely flamboyant style, model good looks and a devil-may-care attitude. He'd been the hot favourite to win the whole thing until a disaster with a lemon souffle had seen him crash out one show short of the final. Eight months later, he announced he was opening *Meld*, his first restaurant. Not in London, but in rural Kent, at a location by the sea and a twenty-minute drive from our house.

Thanks to the huge amount of press coverage, it had become *the* place to eat. Obviously, I had to review it for the blog. Abi booked the table months in advance because of the long waiting list, but for some reason invited Felicity and Colette and their husbands.

'It'll be fun,' she promised.

'As long as they don't get drunk and ruin the evening.'

'They won't. They'll be on their best behaviour.'

I should have known better.

The evening started on the wrong foot when Abi arranged for us to meet at a nearby pub for a few drinks. Johnny and Ralph were already two pints down when we arrived, and by the time we left for the restaurant, they were boisterously drunk.

We turned up on the dot of seven thirty, but I guess it was bad luck our table wasn't ready. The maitre d' couldn't have been more apologetic, but Johnny hit the roof, ranting like an entitled arsehole about their lack of respect and professionalism. It wasn't a big deal, but Johnny being Johnny had to make a scene in front of everyone.

When we were finally seated thirty minutes later, Ralph decided whatever Johnny could do, he could do better and louder, turning his ire on the poor waitress who'd been allocated to our table.

She was only young, with mousy brown hair and a nervous manner, like she was afraid someone was about to jump out and shout boo in her face. Her nails were chewed to the tips of her fingers and the backs of her hands were inflamed with eczema. She wasn't the most engaging waitress I'd ever met and her smile was hard won, but she didn't deserve the way Ralph spoke to her, even if she hadn't come running to take our drinks order the moment we'd sat down.

'No, no, no,' he'd yelled when she began pouring water from a jug. 'We don't want fucking water. We need wine. And lots of it. Now run along and bring us three bottles of your most expensive red.'

I cringed, not only at the dismissive way he'd spoken to her but because Abi had promised them it was our treat and we'd be picking up the bill.

Eventually, the waitress, Sally-Anne (I found out because I actually took the time to talk to her), came with our starters. It was another stroke of bad luck that there'd been a mix-up in the kitchen.

'The roasted miso celeriac?' she asked, skilfully balancing six plates.

We all looked at her blankly. Nobody had ordered the celeriac. Sally-Anne flushed with embarrassment. 'What about the crispy sesame squid?'

Colette and Felicity put their hands up. 'Should be two of those,' Colette said.

'I only have one,' Sally-Anne said, flustered. 'I'll have to check with the kitchen.'

'What a fucking shambles,' Ralph muttered, as she scurried away.

'Give her a break. She's doing her best,' I said. We were supposed to be enjoying the food, not stressing about the service.

Ralph grumbled something under his breath I didn't hear.

'It is a fucking shambles,' Johnny agreed, knocking back half a glass of wine in one mouthful. 'Frankly, I expected better given the prices they charge.'

It wasn't even as if he was paying.

A couple at the next table shot us a look that could have cut diamonds. Johnny and Ralph had become louder and louder the more they'd drunk, egging each other on. They were spoiling the evening not only for me but for everyone within a ten-metre radius of our table, which was most of the restaurant.

I tried to distract myself from their loutish behaviour by watching Matunde working in the kitchen, directing operations like a drill sergeant. The building had been designed with open-plan kitchens so diners in the restaurant could observe the chefs preparing the food. It was all part of the theatre of the experience and a big lure for me.

Matunde was every bit as impressive in the flesh as he'd been on TV. A towering presence in the kitchen. His chef's whites dazzled against his dark skin and he never stopped for a second. He was constantly on the go, orchestrating dishes and giving his final approval before anything left the pass, all while remaining ice cool and unflappable.

He'd shot a couple of sour glances at our table as the evening progressed and I could see he was becoming increasingly annoyed by the noise and general rowdiness. It wasn't a nightclub after all. It was where people were paying good money for a sophisticated evening out.

'I can't believe it, he's coming over,' Colette screamed with excitement, pointing towards the kitchen.

Sure enough, Matunde had abandoned his post and was heading across the restaurant towards our table with long, languorous strides. He rested a meaty hand on the back of Ralph's chair and leaned in.

'I'm Mat,' he said. 'The owner. How are you enjoying your evening so far?'

'As soon as your stupid waitress pulls her finger out and gets her act into gear to bring us some food, I'm sure we'll enjoy it,' Johnny said. He didn't suffer fools - or celebrity chefs - gladly.

Matunde stiffened. I doubt anyone had ever had the front to be so rude to his face before. 'I'm sorry to hear not everything's to your satisfaction this evening. We do our best to make sure everyone has a good time at *Meld*.' He pointedly stressed the word 'everyone' and I had the impression he was holding himself in check. Not letting his irritation with us show.

'It's fine,' I said. I didn't want him to think we were disrespecting him or his restaurant, although it was a little late for that. And there was no need to be rude.

'Actually, it is a problem,' Ralph slurred, swaying on his chair. 'If you want my honest opinion, this place is a shitshow. We had to wait over half an hour for our table - even though Abi booked it more than four months ago - and then the waitress totally fucked up our order. And now she's disappeared altogether. If I was to run my business like that —'

'I'm afraid we've had a few staffing issues this evening,' Matunde said, cutting him off. 'We've been hit by a sickness bug and I've had to send half of the staff home and call in some agency staff. The rest are doing their best. So my apologies that you've had to wait a little longer than we'd normally like, but I hope you'll bear with us.' His lips peeled back into a forced, gappy smile.

'Let's hope the food's worth the wait then,' Ralph mumbled into his glass.

'And while we want you all to have a good time, please be mindful that there are others dining with us tonight and your behaviour is upsetting a few people.' He picked up one of the empty bottles of wine from the centre of the table and gave an appreciative shrug. 'And maybe go easier on the booze? I'd hate to have to ask you to leave.'

Leave? My cheeks flushed with embarrassment.

'Are you threatening us?' Johnny asked, his jaw tightening.

'Not at all. All I'm asking is that you remember where you are and that people are paying a lot of money for a fine dining experience in peace.'

And as unexpectedly as he'd arrived, Matunde withdrew, his point made. I hung my head in shame as he walked off.

'That was uncalled for,' Colette said.

'Bloody rude, if you ask me,' her husband added.

I glanced across the table at Abi for support, but she'd resumed chatting with Felicity as if nothing had happened.

'What a total prick,' Johnny complained in my ear. 'Imagine if I'd talked to one of my clients like that.'

'What? Yes, I suppose,' I said. I didn't want to get into an argument with him, but Matunde had a point.

Eventually, the correct starters arrived and we all dived in hungrily. Sadly, after all the hype and expectation, I was left disappointed. I'd ordered sea bass tartare with pickles and white currants, but it was underwhelming. The fish hadn't been seasoned at all well and the pickles were so tart they overpowered the rest of the dish. There was no balance between the elements. I'd expected better but said nothing as the others seemed to be enjoying their food. I guess I just chose the wrong thing.

'How is it?' I mouthed to Abi.

She scrunched up her nose. She'd ordered the halibut, served with smoked cream and heritage radishes. 'It's okay,' she mouthed back.

Hardly a glowing endorsement. It wasn't just me then. The food simply wasn't up to the high standard we'd expected. Maybe it was because of the staff shortage and the kitchen was stretched. At least on a positive note, Johnny and Ralph had toned down their behaviour, obviously feeling suitably chastened by Matunde's warning, despite their bravado.

Unfortunately, there was another long wait for our mains, which gave Johnny and Ralph more cause for complaint, sniping increasingly bitterly about the service with every passing minute, while they continued to sink an ocean's worth of expensive wine.

When Sally-Anne did arrive with the next course, her face pinched with the strain of a busy evening's service, I was relieved there was no repeat of the mix-up with our starters. No mistakes this time. Everyone was happy. Or so I thought. My sous vide grouse with beetroot was adequate without being mind-blowing and was served lukewarm, but I bit my tongue and kept my disappointment to myself. Nobody else took issue with their dishes, so I didn't make a fuss.

Felicity was the last to finish. She always picked at her food, taking tiny morsels on her fork as if she was worried every mouthful was going to pile on a pound of fat to her emaciated frame.

Eventually, we were all done, but what happened next, I'm still not sure.

Sally-Anne was clearing the table behind ours and whether Ralph tried to grab her arm or made some inappropriate comment, I don't know, but she spun around, startled, and lost her balance. A dirty plate slipped from her hand and the remains of someone's meal ended up down the front of Ralph's shirt and in his lap.

The poor girl froze in horror, her mouth gaping in shock as Ralph jumped out of his chair, a pulsing vein on his temple throbbing, his face flushed puce.

'You stupid fucking girl,' he screamed with a poisonous snarl. A total overreaction.

'I'm so, so sorry,' she said, attempting to wipe his shirt clean with a napkin.

'Leave it!' he bellowed.

A stunned hush fell over the restaurant as Sally-Anne hurried away in tears.

The maitre d' rushed over with some damp cloths and tried to placate Ralph. But there was no pacifying him. He was fuming. It wasn't so much a red mist descending as a tropical monsoon. He was physically shaking. Even Colette couldn't calm him down.

'What was she thinking?' he shouted.

'Come on, Ralph, she didn't do it on purpose,' Colette said.

'Didn't she? She's been a fucking liability all evening.'

Abi shrank in her chair, looking as mortified as I felt. She caught my eye and we stared at each other in silent solidarity.

'Sit down and stop making a fuss,' Colette continued, in the head teacher voice I'd only ever heard her use at school. 'You're spoiling everyone's evening.'

Eventually, Ralph's temper cooled and he finally sat back down at the table, but with a face like thunder.

I'd had enough. I couldn't sit there with everyone watching us, thinking I was friends with a loudmouthed idiot like Ralph.

'I'm popping to the gents,' I announced as I stood. I folded my napkin on the table and walked away, my legs shaking. I needed some space. A timeout from the madness.

The toilets were located down a poorly lit corridor next to a door into the kitchen marked 'Staff Only'. As I approached, it swung open and a waitress dashed out. I caught sight of Sally-Anne in the kitchen, doubled over, sobbing. At least she wasn't on her own. A young guy in chef's whites was with her, rubbing her back. He stood her up and threw his arms around her.

She'd been timid from the moment we'd been shown to the table. Now she looked totally broken. Her fragile spirit crushed. All because Ralph was an arsehole.

As the door began to swing closed, the young chef looked up and caught me staring. I looked away and hurried on with the shame of a voyeur caught peeking at something I wasn't supposed to have seen.

I pushed open the toilet door, but a hand clamped on my shoulder, spinning me around.

I turned to find myself nose-to-nose with the chef who'd been consoling Sally-Anne. His eyes were speckled red with tiredness, his jacket stained with gravy smears. He stood so close, studying my face, that I could smell the vinegary tartness of his breath. I braced myself for an earful, expecting him to tear strips off me for Ralph's unforgivable behaviour. I'm sure he must have recognised me from the same table.

Instead, he stuck out a hand, grasped mine, and clasped it tightly.

'I'm Marcus,' he breathed, tight-lipped. 'One of the sous chefs.'

'Hi,' I mumbled, my heartbeat hastening.

'Sally-Anne's a bit upset.'

'I'm sorry. I —'

'We're short-staffed tonight. She's doing her best. All the waitresses are having to double up. It's a nightmare.'

'Yes, I —'

'So cut her some slack, okay? And tell your friends.'

He slapped me on the shoulder to emphasise his point.

'Of course. Sorry.'

'How's the food?'

'What?' His manner had changed in a beat.

'The food. Is it good?'

I nodded enthusiastically. 'Superb.' For a moment, I couldn't recall what I'd even had. 'It was...' I floundered.

'Yes?'

'Amazing,' I lied. 'The sea bass tartare was divine,' I continued, as it came back to me. It didn't seem the moment to get into a debate about how to season fish properly. 'And the grouse was perfection.'

The chef sighed. 'I'm glad you enjoyed it.'

We stood for what seemed like minutes, staring at each other, until my mouth was desert dry.

'I need the —' I said, nodding to the toilet door.

'Right, yes. Hope you enjoy the rest of your evening,' he said. And then he was gone, disappearing back into the kitchen, leaving me to wonder what the hell had just happened.

I stepped into the toilets and composed myself. I washed my face with cold water and inhaled a deep breath. But I couldn't stay in there all night. I had to go back eventually, so steeling myself I stepped back into the corridor as the staff only kitchen door crashed open and a looming figure emerged. Matunde, his arms swinging, a determined lope to his stride. Timidly, I followed. He marched straight up to our table and banged his fist down, making all the glasses jump.

'That's it, I want you all out,' he boomed, as I slipped back into my seat. 'I've never met a bunch of ruder, more ungrateful, privileged people in my life.'

'Now hang on a minute —' Johnny jumped up, but Matunde cut him short with a raised hand and he was left goldfishing.

'You've been disruptive from the moment you walked in and now you've reduced one of my waitresses to tears on a night I told you we were short staffed. It's unforgivable.'

People booked tables at the restaurant for the theatre of the kitchen, but that night they got more drama than they'd bargained for. As I looked around, everyone was staring at us. What must they have thought?

'You can't talk to us like that. Do you know who I am?' Ralph said.

'No, and I don't care. This is my restaurant and I won't stand for it. You're going to pay your bill. You're going to leave Sally-Anne a big tip as an apology for the way you've treated her, and you're going to leave.'

'But —'

Matunde waved a finger at Felicity, stopping her protestations.

'This is bullshit.' Johnny pushed Matunde in the chest.

The chef stumbled back, his expression twisting in anger, before he came back at Johnny, getting right up in his face. For a moment, I thought they were going to come to blows.

'You'll leave now or I'll call the police,' Matunde said, lowering his voice.

'So that's it, you're throwing us out?' Abi balled up her napkin and threw it on the table. She was on the verge of tears.

'Yes, and don't come back. Ever.'

'Fine,' Ralph said. 'The food was shit anyway. I wouldn't come here again if you paid me.' He pushed his chair back and stormed off with Johnny, Colette and Felicity following behind.

'I'm so sorry for all the trouble —' I began.

'Just pay and get out.'

The maitre d' appeared with the bill. I didn't check it. I just shoved my credit card in the reader and paid. All I wanted was to get as far away as possible from *Meld* and everyone who'd watched us being humiliated. I shrugged off Abi's attempts to take my hand, put my head down, and followed the others out as some diners applauded.

It was the most demeaning experience of my life. What made it worse was that by the time we'd caught up with the others, Johnny and Ralph were laughing about it. It was a big joke to them. The blood boiled in my veins. I couldn't look at them. Couldn't stand to be breathing the same air. The evening had been a disaster from beginning to end, and they were primarily to blame.

So when I saw a line of taxis waiting outside a pub, I pulled Abi away and jumped in the first one in the queue. We drove home in silence, neither of us saying a word. I was too angry to speak, physically shaking with rage.

'Well, that went well,' Abi finally said, as we pulled up at home and I paid the driver.

'I never want to see or speak to Johnny or Ralph again,' I said, as I stormed up the drive, fishing for the house keys in my pocket. 'I mean it. I never want to set eyes on them again.'

Chapter 12

'A death threat?' Colette's mouth drops open, while Felicity glances at Abi and back to me, the glass in her hand frozen in mid-air.

'What are you talking about? What death threat?' Ralph screws up his face.

'Henry's joking,' Abi says. 'You know what he's like.'

'I'm not joking. I can show you.' I'm glad now I hooked the letter out of the bin after Abi went to bed last night. I don't know why I felt the need to hold on to it, but it seemed important.

'Henry, no,' Abi says, sternly. But it's too late. The cat's out of the bag. Anyway, I'm sure it's a good thing to share what we're going through.

I grab the rest of the plates and hurry into the kitchen. The letter's in the drawer where we keep all the junk we don't know what else to do with. Old batteries. Packs of playing cards. Unused mobile phone protective screens. Birthday candles melted down to half their size, as if we're ever going to use them again. The envelope is crumpled and smeared with jam. I pull it out, smooth it against my leg and march back into the dining room.

'It was a silly crank letter,' Abi's telling them, 'but Henry's got all worked up about it. It's nothing. Honestly.'

All eyes fall on me as I walk in. 'Did you tell them about your car?'

Now she's really going to be mad, but I don't care. If someone's targeting us, we need the support of friends, even if the friends are Colette, Felicity and their stupid husbands.

'Your car?' Colette asks.

Everyone's staring at Abi now, totally focused on her, waiting for her to explain. She sighs and shoots me a look that tells me I'll probably be sleeping on the couch tonight.

'I went out for a few drinks after the court case and left the car in town,' she says. 'Someone vandalised it overnight.'

'They wrote "Rot in hell" on the windscreen and the rear glass,' I elaborate. 'And then yesterday I found this pushed through the door.' I hold up the letter.

Colette reaches across the table and takes it from me.

'You don't need to read it,' Abi says.

'Why didn't you say anything before?' Felicity's alabaster face is even paler than usual.

'There's nothing to tell. Henry thinks my car and the letter are connected, but I'm sure it's just a coincidence.'

I raise my eyebrows. Does she really still think that?

'And the man who followed you home and was loitering around outside the house?' I say.

Felicity clamps a hand over her mouth. 'Abi? What the hell?'

I sit down. The main course will have to wait.

'Honestly, it's all in Henry's head.'

'What, even the damage to your car and that letter?' I nod at Colette, who's pulling the single sheet of paper out of the envelope and squinting to read the small typed print in the glow of the candles on the table.

'What's it say, Col?' Johnny asks, leaning forwards, his hands clasped together as if in prayer.

Colette reads it out slowly, in the same tone she might read out a clue to a treasure hunt or a riddle, which I suppose in a way it is. 'One death was too much. Two is unbearable. An eye for an eye seems only fair after what you've done. So now I have nothing left to lose, I'll see you in hell.'

When she's finished, she looks up at me over the top of her glasses. 'What's it mean?'

'Who knows?' I say.

'Any idea who sent it?' Ralph takes the letter from his wife and reads it to himself. 'I mean, it's obviously someone with mental health issues.'

'Exactly. That's what I said.' Abi steeples her fingers and presses them to her lips. 'Henry thought it might have something to do with the court case. Jimmy and Dean's father upset his sons were convicted and looking for someone to take it out on, but the police don't think it has anything to do with them.'

'That's not exactly what they said, is it? They said they've spoken to Joseph Farrow and he denied having anything to do with the letter or your car,' I remind Abi. 'It doesn't mean he didn't do it.'

'But why would he?' Colette asks. 'What's the point?'

'Precisely,' Abi says.

Ralph fills his glass and rocks back in his chair. 'Well, if not him, who?'

'Could be anyone, I suppose,' Felicity says. 'Is there anyone you've upset recently? A neighbour perhaps?'

'No, nothing like that.' Abi shakes her head.

'What are these two deaths it talks about?' Ralph's passed the letter to Johnny, who's spread it out on his placemat and is scrutinising it line by line. 'One was too much and two is unbearable?'

'We thought it might be a reference to Billy Bowden's death,' I say.

'And the second one?'

'George Farrow, the third brother who died in police custody.'

'Ahh, makes sense,' Johnny says.

'No, it doesn't,' Abi snaps. 'First, Joseph Farrow doesn't care about Billy Bowden, and second, why would he blame me for George's death? Surely, if he had a grudge against anyone, it would be the police.'

'Is that why you took the girls out of school early yesterday?' Colette's eyes narrow as she looks at me across the table.

'I probably overreacted,' I say. 'I panicked. To be honest, we've both been a bit on edge since this all started a few days ago.'

'Speak for yourself.' Abi folds her arms and leans them on the table. 'Anyway, enough about our silly issues —'

'They're not silly,' I protest. 'We need to take it seriously.'

But she ignores me. I thought she'd be keen to chat it through with her friends, but it's clear I've overstepped the mark. 'Oh, Flick, Colette, you've not seen our new bathroom yet, have you? Why don't I show you while we're waiting for Henry.' She glances at me briefly. A warning to drop it now and to get on with cooking. 'Will you boys be alright here on your own for five minutes if I take the ladies upstairs?'

Builders had recently put in a new shower and retiled our en suite. I thought Felicity and Colette had already seen it. Maybe not.

As the three women leave the room and climb the stairs, I take my cue, returning to the kitchen, leaving Johnny and Ralph on their own, chatting in the dining room. I need to get on with the steaks if we're going to eat tonight. I've said my piece. I'll have to deal with the consequences later when everyone's gone home and it's just me and Abi, although what's she saying to the girls upstairs?

I bet she's telling them I've blown it all out of proportion. I wish I could be a fly on the wall. Without me there to correct her, she'll be convincing them black is white by now and that there's nothing to worry about. I wish it was true, but I don't believe it. Ever since Abi told me she was followed home and I saw that man outside the house, I've been anxious with worry. And I can't shake the feeling there's more to come. That this is merely the appetiser ahead of the main course.

As I slosh a healthy slug of oil into a frying pan and it begins to smoke, Johnny and Ralph appear, glasses in hand.

'Are the girls still upstairs?' I ask through tight lips, irritated at the invasion of my space. Why couldn't they wait in the other room? I don't like anyone watching while I'm cooking, especially these two.

'Steak?' Ralph asks, stating the obvious as he sees the raw meat on the side, still in its waxed paper from the butcher.

'Wagyu,' I say. I've pushed the boat out. I don't want anyone leaving the house tonight saying the food wasn't up to scratch. My reputation is at stake.

'Fancy.'

He means expensive, and yes, it was, but it'll be worth it. I'm serving it with oxtail-topped onion, aubergine and walnut compote, a celeriac puree and blackberry jus. It's an extravagant dish but it should impress, if I can get on in peace.

'Sounds like you and Abs have been through a tough few days,' Johnny says, watching as I toss the steaks into the pan. They hiss and spit, sizzling satisfyingly. 'What with the letter and the damage to Abi's car. And didn't you say someone followed her home the other night? The question is, what are you going to do about it?'

'I'm not sure,' I say, puzzled. What does he think I'm going to do? What can I do? I don't even know for sure who's responsible, and that's the worst thing.

'Abi's playing it down, but I can see she's worried,' Johnny continues, as if he can read my wife better than me. 'You've got to look out for your family, right?'

'Of course.' Like I don't know that. But it's not that easy.

Ralph dips a finger into the oxtail simmering on the hob and licks it clean. I have the overwhelming urge to slap his hand, but I let it go.

'You know what they say about bullies?' he says. 'You need to stand up to them. Let them know you won't be pushed around.'

'But I told you, I don't know who's doing this to us.'

'What about this guy, Farrow?'

'Joseph? He was my first thought but —'

'What do you know about him?' Johnny asks.

'Only what I read online. He's a thug who's spent most of his life in trouble with the police. Not a nice guy.' I take the steaks off the heat and put them to one side to rest.

'Even more reason to stand up to him.' Johnny finishes his wine and puts his glass down. 'Guys like that, you give them an inch and they'll wipe the floor with you.'

'Talk to him in a language he understands.' Ralph thumps his fist on the counter. 'You can't let him threaten your family. He needs to know you can't be intimidated. You've got to think about the girls too. How would you feel if something happened to them?'

It's my worst nightmare. If Farrow so much as touched a hair on their heads, I'd happily kill him with my bare hands. 'But what am I supposed to do?'

'Think like a street fighter,' Johnny says, taking a boxer's stance and punching the air with a series of rapid jabs. 'Go in hard and fast and land a knockout blow. What you can't afford to do is trade punches with him. A guy like that is always going to win a slug-fest. But if you can surprise him, and hit him hard enough, he'll go down and stay down.'

He's talking in riddles. I'm certainly not going to get into a boxing match with Joseph Farrow. 'I don't understand what you think I should be doing.'

'Come on, Henry,' Ralph says. 'What's the knockout blow he can't come back from?'

'I... I... ' I stammer. 'I don't know. I'm sorry, I don't know what you're trying to say.'

Johnny sighs and hangs his head, as if he's disappointed with me. 'It's simple. Go after something or somebody precious to him. Something he'd hate to lose.'

'Have you lost your mind?' I switch off the gas under all the pans on the hob. I really need to start plating up or we'll never eat. Johnny and Ralph are talking drunken nonsense, and frankly, I wish they'd leave me alone to get on with it.

'Alright, let me put it another way,' Johnny says. 'You need to grab him by the bollocks and squeeze until he's blue in the face and decides you're not worth the bother anymore. Do you get it?'

'Not really.'

'Swat him like a mosquito,' Ralph says. 'If it was me, I'd go for the easy option. A can of petrol and a box of matches.'

'What the hell, Ralph? Are you insane?' Is he really suggesting what I think?

'Why not? It would be a big statement. A couple of glugs of petrol through the letterbox while he's asleep, light a match and it's goodnight Vienna. Boom!' Ralph throws his hands out wide, making the gesture of an enormous explosion going off.

It's madness. The booze talking. They're drunk and they don't know what they're saying. Or they're teasing me. Either way, they can't be serious. They can't really be advocating setting fire to Joseph Farrow's house. I might be desperate, but I'm not an idiot. Or a criminal.

Chapter 13

Abi and her friends traipse back down the stairs in a conspiratorial huddle as I carry the plates through to the dining room.

'Just in time,' I smile, my chat with Johnny and Ralph still rolling around in my mind. 'What've you been talking about?'

'Never you mind,' Abi says, tapping the side of her nose. 'Women's stuff.'

Why do I feel she's hiding something from me?

They retake their seats around the table and start raving about the food.

'Oh, Henry, this looks amazing.'

'It's like a picture on a plate.'

'Smells sooooo good.'

But I hardly take in their compliments, nor do I get that usual frisson of satisfaction from all the positive comments. There's an atmosphere in the room hanging heavy like smog. It's infected everyone. They're pretending as if nothing has happened, but everyone's subdued, even Abi. And the conversation's become stilted and awkward as they all make an obviously conscious effort not to mention night stalkers or death threats.

'I love your dress,' Felicity tells Abi.

'Thank you. It's Roksanda. How are the kids?'

'Martha's learning the violin and Victor's started rugby on a Saturday morning,' Felicity says.

It's the staid, dull conversations of the middle classes who have nothing better to talk about. And when Johnny asks me, 'How's work?' I know the evening's hit rock bottom.

'Yeah, it's fine,' I tell him. What else can I say? He has no more interest in my job than I do in his or Ralph's. Best to kill the conversation stone dead before it starts, even if I do come across as rude.

The evening doesn't get any better after that and as I sit back, listening to the inane, pointless chatter around the table, all I can think about is what Ralph said earlier.

He was joking, right? He had to have been. You can't go around setting fire to people's houses just because you don't like how they've behaved towards you.

I watch him as he chats, his easy confidence and charm like sticky treacle, retelling the same anecdotes I've heard before. Mocking the patients who flock to his ophthalmic surgery and who pay for his extravagant lifestyle. Moaning about the roadworks on the A2. Telling everyone about the amazing fuel consumption of his new car. Nobody else seems to notice how vacuous he sounds. They all laugh and smile, encouraging him. I wish he'd just shut up. Johnny's as bad, always with a better story than Ralph up his sleeve. I've never noticed the raw rivalry between them before, like Johnny can't stand Ralph outperforming him in anything, whether it's in business, sport or socially. It's all quite exhausting.

While the chit-chat continues to flow, the conversation is more muted than usual. It's as though the evening's good humour has been sucked out of the room by my stupid decision to tell everyone about the death threats and the stranger outside the house.

And just after eleven, Felicity announces they need to leave, apologising that she and Johnny have to get back for the babysitter. It's early for them, but Colette and Ralph follow soon after. We've had evenings with the four of them that have gone on into the early hours, but tonight it's as if they can't get away fast enough.

'Think about what I said,' Ralph says, stepping outside and turning to shake my hand. He winks at me and I shrink away. 'Don't let the bastards get you down.'

'Thanks for a lovely evening,' Colette says, pulling her husband towards the taxi waiting in the road.

I leave Abi at the door waving her goodbyes, grateful we have the house back to ourselves. The evening wasn't as bad as I'd been expecting, especially as everyone seemed to appreciate the food and they all left early. In fact, I'm glad they came. I've been holding onto this bitterness and anger ever since that night in *Meld.* We haven't exactly cleared the air and Ralph and Johnny would never be close friends, but for Abi's sake it's better we are at least able to be in the same room together. I've not completely forgiven their behaviour, but at least I'm able to put it behind me.

I return to the kitchen to finish clearing up. Most of the dishes had fitted in the dishwasher, but I hand-wash the glasses and some of the dirtiest pots. Nothing worse than coming down to a messy kitchen in the morning. Abi joins me, grabs a clean tea towel from a drawer and dries up the glasses as I line them up on the draining board.

She's tense and silent. Now I know I really am in trouble.

'Did you have a nice time?' I ask, testing the water.

'It was fine.' She can barely bring herself to speak, let alone look at me.

'They seemed to like the steak.'

'Yes, it was very nice.'

I can't stand it when she sulks. I wish she'd shout or yell, but when she sends me to Coventry, shutting me out, I don't know how to cope with it. If she has something to say, we should talk about it.

'Look, I'm sorry —' I begin.

'I'm going to bed.' She cuts me off as she drapes the damp tea towel over the handle of the oven door.

'Okay. I'll be up in a minute. I'll just finish up here and lock up.'

Abi sighs as she walks away.

My security routine before I retire for the night is much more thorough since I spotted that man hanging around outside. I take about ten minutes every night, double and triple-checking all the doors and windows, but it's worth it for the peace of mind. I wouldn't be able to sleep otherwise.

Abi is in bed, reading, when I finally make it up to our bedroom. She doesn't look up from her book as I walk in, sit on the edge of the mattress and peel off my socks. I don't want to go to sleep on ill-feelings. That's how resentment breeds.

'I'm sorry if I spoke out of turn,' I say. 'Are you still cross with me?'

I hear her put down her book. I glance over my shoulder and see she's fiddling with the arm of her reading glasses.

'I asked you not to mention the letter, but you did anyway,' she says.

'Only because I'm worried about you. Colette and Felicity are your best friends. It's good they know, isn't it? Did you have a chat with them about it when you came showed them the bathroom?'

I suspect she played it down.

'A bit,' she says. 'They think you did the right thing bringing it up.'

'There, you see?' I don't want to sound triumphant. It's not a game.

'But that's not the point. I asked you not to say anything.'

'I said I'm sorry.'

'You only brought it up to score points,' she says.

That's brutal, although there may be an element of truth in what she says. It certainly put Johnny and Ralph back in their boxes for the evening. 'I thought you didn't keep secrets from your friends,' I say.

'It's not a secret, but you made it sound like something it's not.'

'Someone's threatening us, Abi. I don't know why you don't seem to take that seriously.'

'It's a bit of mindless vandalism and a crank letter,' she says. 'But our friends are now under the impression someone's sent us death threats, thanks to you.'

I shrug. There's no point arguing. We have a different view on it and I doubt anything I say is going to change her mind. I only wish I could dismiss it so easily. Instead, it weighs heavily on my shoulders.

'What were you talking to the boys about? I could hear you from upstairs chatting in the kitchen,' Abi says.

I glance away. I'm a terrible liar and she can always spot when I'm not telling the truth. 'Nothing much.' I clear my throat. 'Boys' stuff really.'

When she doesn't immediately say anything, I know she doesn't believe me. How can I tell her what Ralph said? I stand up and unbutton my shirt.

'It's good that you're all getting on again, at least,' she says.

'They're still arseholes.'

'Henry!'

'What? It's true. And they're both as bad as one another.'

'They're my friends. Don't speak about them like that.' Abi folds her arms defensively across her chest.

'You can't see it, can you? The way they've always got to get one over the other, like a pair of silly schoolboys. It's pathetic.'

Abi shakes her head. She knows what I mean, but thinks it would be disloyal if she agreed with me. She's known Ralph since university and for some inexplicable reason they've remained close, and not only because he's married to one of her best friends.

I fold up my trousers, hang them in the wardrobe, and pull on a pair of pyjama bottoms.

'What are we going to do?'

'About what?'

'The Farrows.'

NOTHING LEFT TO LOSE

'Not this again.' Abi groans. 'Do you really still think they sent that letter? I thought you'd seen sense.'

'I don't know what to think.'

'You worry too much. Come on, come to bed.' She pats the duvet and throws it back, inviting me in.

At least it looks as though I've been forgiven. Maybe I worry too much. Am I taking it all too seriously? One thing that struck me earlier was what Johnny said about looking out for my family. It's my role to protect them, no matter what. And if someone is sending death threats, surely I'm duty-bound to be concerned?

I slip into bed and lie staring up at the ceiling with my eyes wide open.

Abi kills her light, rolls over to face me and throws an arm across my chest.

'Goodnight. Sleep tight,' she says.

But I'm not sure if I can. My mind's too active and every creak, pop and scratch I hear from the walls, the ceiling, the roof, the garden, the trees, is an intruder trying to break in. I listen to Abi's breathing slowing and deepening as she tumbles towards sleep. I'm envious it comes so easily to her while my mind is a jumble of worry and anxiety.

'Abi,' I whisper into the veil of darkness.

'Mmmm,' she mumbles.

'Do you feel safe here? I mean, in this house?'

'Yes, of course.'

'It's just I was thinking about Joseph Far —'

'Henry, stop! We've talked about this. Stop dwelling on it.'

'What if he doesn't stop?' I say.

'Henry, please. I can't go on like this. You're becoming obsessed. We don't know who sent that letter or vandalised my car, but you're going to make yourself ill if you keep dwelling on it,' she says.

'I can't help it. I keep wondering what he's going to do next.'

'You're being ridiculous.'

'Am I?' I ask. Is it ridiculous to worry about your family and to want to keep them safe? It seems perfectly reasonable to me.

'Yes. Please stop.'

'But you know what Joseph Farrow is capable of. He's a thug. I wouldn't put anything past him.'

Abi switches her light on again and blinks at me as her eyes become accustomed to the brightness. 'If it is Farrow, he'd be an idiot to try anything after the police spoke to him.'

'And what if he does? What if we need to take matters into our own hands?'

Abi stares at me blankly. 'What do you mean?'

'Exactly that. If Joseph Farrow keeps coming for us, maybe we need to think about retaliating,' I say.

'Jeez, would you listen to yourself? Retaliation? Have you completely lost the plot?'

'It might be what it takes,' I say. 'I don't want to be looking over my shoulder for the rest of my life.'

'I don't believe I'm hearing this. You stay away from the Farrows, do you understand me?'

'I was just saying —'

'Promise me, Henry. Whatever's going through your mind, you won't go near Joseph Farrow or his family. They're not to be messed with.'

I'm shocked by the ferocity in Abi's tone. I guess she knows what Joseph Farrow's capable of better than me.

'Okay, calm down,' I say. 'It was only an idea.'

Actually, it was Ralph and Johnny's idea, but I don't tell her that.

'Well, it was a stupid idea,' she says. 'And I don't want to hear any more about it.'

Chapter 14

A loud thudding crashes into my dreams, jarring me awake. It sounds like a sledgehammer breaking rocks and is followed by the unmistakable crack of shattering glass. My heart pounds as hard and as fast as if I've been plunged into an ice bath. Yobs smashing beer bottles in the street? A recycling bin knocked over by foxes? No, it hadn't sounded like either of those things. It sounded as if it had come from inside the house.

I sit bolt upright, my breath in my throat, ears straining.

Please, not a window.

'What was that?' Abi mumbles from her sleep.

I slip out of bed with every muscle and sinew tightly wound. In the dark, I look for a weapon and spot the silhouette of Abi's hairdryer on her dressing table. It's not much, but it'll have to do. Simply having something in my hand makes me feel better.

As I creep across the room, listening, I picture a man in a balaclava, round, gaping holes for his eyes and mouth, stealing up the stairs. Heading for the bedrooms. For the girls. For us.

'I'm going to look', I whisper to Abi as she sits up in bed with the duvet clutched to her chest. There's a quiver in my voice I hope she hasn't noticed.

I edge to the window. Yank back the curtain. Peer outside. The street's deserted. A tangerine glow from the street lamps casts angled shadows across the tarmac. I'm not sure what I thought I'd see. A van waiting with its engine running? A getaway car idling? What I don't expect to see is the figure that darts out from behind my car.

He runs into the road. Arms pumping. Head hooded. Along the pavement. Away from the house. Not looking back.

He disappears into the night as I stand frozen, hardly able to breathe.

'Did you see something?' The duvet rustles as Abi climbs out of bed.

'Stay there', I hiss, holding up my hand to stop her. 'And call the police. Tell them there's an intruder. I'm going to check on the girls.'

With sweat-slick palms, I slip out onto the landing. The hammering in my chest is so loud it echoes around my skull. I push open Norah's door. She's sleeping soundly, oblivious. Next door, her sister has her duvet knotted around her legs, fast asleep. I pull their doors closed and tiptoe towards the stairs.

My fingers flex around the handle of Abi's hairdryer.

'Is there anyone there?' I call out into the dark.

I don't want to disturb whoever's down there. I want them to know I'm awake. I want them to run away. I have no desire to play the hero. I only want my family to stay safe.

The stairs creak and moan like I've never noticed before as I make my way down one step at a time. When I reach the hall, my hand snakes across the wall, finds the switch, and flicks on the light. The brightness is reassuring. Even as an adult, I find nothing is as scary in the light as it is in the dark.

The sweaty tang of garlic and sourness of pickled vegetables hangs in the air from last night's meal. A reminder the house was full only a few hours ago. Now I feel very alone.

I start with the lounge, nudging open the door and immediately sensing something's wrong. The hairs on my arms lift. My skin prickles. And a cool breeze grazes my face. That's not right, unless I left the window open, which I categorically know I did not.

My stomach lurches. I turn on the lights and the curtains billow as if caught in a draught. I rush to the sofa and behind the drapes find a jagged hole the size of a football. And on the carpet, behind the couch, an ornamental rock from the garden, sitting in a pool of glass shards.

I peer through the window, horrified. But there's something else. Something I didn't immediately notice. What looks like dark rivers running down the undamaged panes. It's obscene. Even more disturbing than the broken window.

I rush into the hall and unbolt the front door. Outside, I stumble over a discarded tin pot. It clatters down the drive and disappears under my car.

From the lawn, I stare back at the house. I can see now the cause of the rivers down the window. It's all over the white render too. A scarlet explosion, like blood, in ugly splatters that drip in thick tributaries.

Red paint.

Everywhere.

I suck in a breath, my knees weak.

So much for Joseph Farrow leaving us alone after being warned off by the police. The letter was a notice of intent, but this is something much worse. Tangible. Visceral. A direct attack on the house. On us. A deliberate escalation of hostilities. But why?

I still don't understand.

What does he want?

As I stagger back into the house, nausea blooming in my stomach, Abi appears at the bottom of the stairs, pulling on a dressing gown.

'What's going on?'

I lead her into the lounge and point to the smashed glass and the streaks of red paint running down the window like tentacles.

'I've called the police,' she says, mobile phone in her hand and her face blanching. 'They're sending a patrol car.'

'It's a bit late for that. I think he's gone. I saw someone running away from the house.'

'Did you see his face?'

I shake my head and fall into the chair by the TV set. I stare at the window and the paint, my throat tightening as tears pool in my eyes. I can't remember the last time I cried, but suddenly it's all too much to take.

'What are we going to do, Abi?' I ask. 'What the fuck are we going to do?'

'Hey, come on, it's only a broken window and a bit of paint,' she says. She perches on the edge of the chair and takes my hand. So typical of her to be the stoic one, putting a positive spin on a bad situation. But I can read in her face that she's as shaken as I am.

'It's more than that. Farrow wants us to know how easily he can get to us.'

'Don't be silly. Look, the police are on the way. They'll sort this out.'

I shake my head. The police have been next to useless until now. They didn't care when I reported the damage to Abi's car and their attempts to caution Farrow to stay away from us have ended in this. 'They won't do anything, Abi. Don't you see? We're on our own. We're going to have to deal with this ourselves.'

Abi's face darkens. 'What are you talking about?'

'We can't rely on the police.' Now I've decided, I'm enveloped by an unexpected calm. My heart rate slows and my mind is crystal clear. 'I'm going to sort this out, but in the meantime, I think it's best if you and the girls move out for a few days. For your own safety. At least until I get the house cleaned up.'

'No', Abi says, forcefully. 'We're not leaving. We'll stay together as a family.'

I squeeze her hand. 'It's not safe. Not yet.'

'We're not leaving you.'

'Just for a few days, Abi. Please', I implore her. I know she doesn't want to leave, but it's best if they're out of the way.

'What about you? What are you going to do?'

'I'm going to put an end to this.'

'Henry, you promised you wouldn't go near the Farrows.'

I hold up my hand in a gesture of submission. 'I know. You're right. They're dangerous. But I don't plan to go anywhere near them.'

'What then?'

'You'll see.'

Abi jumps up and starts pacing the room. 'I don't like this, Henry.'

I heave myself out of the chair and hold her tightly. 'It's going to be okay. Trust me.'

She pulls away and looks me in the eye, trying to read my expression. 'Where would we go?'

Now she's coming around to the idea. She's seen it makes sense, that the girls aren't safe here. I really don't want them to leave, but I have no choice.

'We'll find somewhere,' I say. 'Maybe a hotel. And then in a few days when this is all over, you can come home and we can get on with our lives.'

'I still don't like it,' she says.

'I know, but do you trust me?'

She stares at me for a moment. I'm asking a lot, I know. But I'm not sure she'd go along with my plan if I told her what was I was planning.

'Of course I trust you,' she says, eventually.

'Good. Then pack your things and wake up the girls.'

Chapter 15

We don't need to rouse the girls. With all the noise and commotion in the house, first Norah appears at the top of the stairs, followed a few moments later by Katie. They hover on the landing, yawning and staring at us with sleepy eyes.

We rush up to reassure them, but they sense our anxiety.

'Daddy, what's happening?' Norah asks. 'Why are all the lights on?'

I can't lie to them, but I can't tell them the whole truth either. I settle on a sanitised version instead.

'The window downstairs got broken,' I say, as Abi tries to steer them back into their rooms. But they're having none of it.

'Where? I want to see,' Norah says.

Abi glances at me and I shrug. We can't hide it from them.

I take Norah's hand and lead her into the living room. Abi follows, carrying Katie on her hip. She's clutching a rag doll and her pyjama top rides up over her tummy.

I pull back the curtain and show them the hole in the glass that's letting in a chill stream of air.

'Did a bad man do it?' Norah asks, her brow knotting with worry.

'It was just an accident,' I say. I've always vowed not to lie to my children, but there are some truths they need protecting from.

Norah tries to climb onto the sofa for a closer inspection, but I grab her and pull her away. 'Careful,' I say. 'There's broken glass everywhere. You wouldn't want to cut yourself, would you?'

A wash of pulsing blue lights sweeps across the room, bathing our faces, the walls and the carpet. Norah stands on the tips of her toes to peer out of the window and Katie stirs from Abi's shoulder.

'What's that?' Norah asks.

I'm not sure how I'm going to explain to an eight and a six-year-old why a police car has turned up without troubling them.

'It's the police,' Abi says. 'They're here to look at the window to see if they can work out what happened.'

'Oh,' says Norah, still staring outside, apparently satisfied with this explanation.

'I'll go. You stay here with the girls.' I rush outside to meet two police officers as they climb out of a patrol car parked at the end of the drive.

'Mr Hutton?' a female officer with blonde hair tied back in a ponytail asks. 'Reports of an intruder?'

'Yes, but I think they've gone now. I saw someone running off, but one of our windows has been smashed where I think they tried to get in and as you can see, they've thrown paint over the front of the house.'

The officer casts a glance at her male colleague. He's tall and athletic-looking with bright eyes and a kind face.

'Is everyone out of the house?' he asks.

'No, my wife and kids are inside.'

'Mind if we take a quick look around?' the female officer says. 'Then we can take a statement.'

'Be my guest.'

As the two officers head for the door, a voice calls out over the low hedge to my left. 'Is everything okay, Henry?'

Our elderly neighbour, Paul Lamb, is standing in his dressing gown, hands in his pockets, looking concerned.

What am I supposed to tell him? I don't want him to worry, but he's seen the paint and the broken glass.

'Everything's fine,' I say.

He raises a bushy eyebrow.

'Sorry, if we woke you,' I add. He's still staring at me, waiting for me to elaborate. I sigh. He might as well know. 'Someone put a rock through the window. We've been having a bit of trouble lately, but it's nothing to worry about.'

'Are you all okay? Abigail? The girls?'

'We're all fine. It was a shock, that's all. We thought we'd better call the police, you know, to be on the safe side.'

'You can't be too careful,' he says. 'Is there anything I can do?'

'No, thank you.' I watch the two police officers nosing around in the lounge through the window. They'll have to take us seriously this time. I can show them the letter and they'll have a record of the report I made about Abi's car. At least they're here and can see the damage for themselves. 'Actually, there is something, if you don't mind.'

'Anything,' Paul says. 'Name it.'

'Would you look after Katie and Norah while we speak to the police? They're wide awake wondering what the hell's going on and I don't want them listening in. We told them it was an accident.'

'Of course. They can spend the rest of the night here if you like. They can sleep in the spare room. No problem at all.'

❖

Abi and I sit at the kitchen table with the two officers and explain everything that's happened over the last few days. They nod and diligently take notes as I tell them about Abi's stalker, the man who was loitering outside the house and my office, the damage to Abi's Mini and the letter that was hand-delivered to the house. I retrieve it from the junk drawer and give it to the female officer. It's been passed around so much now I doubt there's any realistic chance of pulling any fingerprints from it.

The officer removes the letter from its envelope and reads the four lines of text before handing it to her colleague and making a note in her book.

'Does this make any sense to you?' she asks.

'Not really, but Abi's a barrister,' I explain. 'We think this might be connected to a court case she was involved in.'

'The Billy Bowden murder case,' Abi adds.

The female officer's mouth forms an 'O' of surprise. 'I thought you looked familiar,' she says. 'I think I saw you on the news.'

Abi bows her head, embarrassed.

'We think —'

'*You* think; Abi corrects me.

'I think it might be the Farrow family, angry at Abi after the two sons were found guilty of the murder.'

'I spoke to DI Steve Hunt, and he said he sent someone around to speak with them. Of course, they denied everything; Abi says. She's leaning across the table, fiddling nervously with her fingers, her knuckles white.

The female officer smiles sympathetically. 'I see. Is there anything else that makes you believe this might be connected to the court case?'

Here we go. The same old fob off because we can't prove anything.

'For example, did you get a good look at the man who followed you? Or the one who was outside the house?' she asks.

'No, but —'

'And you said you saw someone running away from the property tonight?'

'Yes; I say. 'But it was dark, and I only saw them briefly.'

'So you wouldn't be able to identify them if you saw them again?'

'No.'

The male officer scratches his face. 'Is there any CCTV footage that might help us identify them?'

'No, we don't have cameras; I say.

'Are you aware of any witnesses?'

Isn't finding witnesses their job? 'No.'

I knew it was going to be like this.

The officer closes his notebook and clasps his hands on the table. 'We'll send a forensics team around when it's light, but I should warn you that cases like these are difficult to solve. We may not be able to identify the perpetrator. As a lawyer, I'm sure you'll appreciate the difficulties, Mrs Pilkington-Hutton.'

'What about the Farrows?' I ask, as Abi nods in agreement. She's always said it was a waste of time involving the police, and now I can see why.

The male officer holds up a hand. 'We'll look into that possibility,' he says, but I don't have any faith in his promises. 'And in the meantime, if anything else comes to light, let us know.'

He passes a business card across the table. Abi picks it up, studies it briefly and slips it into the pocket of her dressing gown.

'Thank you, officers,' she says. 'I'll show you out.'

Abi goes back to bed, but I don't bother. I know I won't sleep. I'm far too wired. Instead, I spend my time trying to locate an emergency glazier and when I fail, take matters into my own hands. I find an old off-cut of chipboard in the shed, roughly saw it to size and board up the window so at least the house is secure and watertight.

The physical exertion takes my mind off Joseph Farrow and when I'm done, I sit at the kitchen table and pull up the laptop. If I'm not going to sleep, I might as well make good use of the time, even though I know I'm going to feel like death for the rest of the day. At least it's the weekend and I don't have to worry about making it through a day at work.

The clock on the wall strikes half four as I open my food blog and retrieve my notes for the pecan and maple dessert I'd been meaning to write up. I already have the photos on my phone, so it's just a case of typing up the recipe. Even my frazzled brain can cope with that, but the words don't exactly flow through my fingers. It's like wading through mud as I try to break the recipe down into easy-to-follow steps that match the pictures I've taken.

An hour later, I'm done. I hit publish, check it's gone live and post an Instagram story with the looping video I made of the final dish as I pulled it out of the oven and served it on a plate. It's probably about time we posted another restaurant review. The problem is we've not been out to eat since *Meld*. I need to find somewhere new. Maybe I'll suggest it to Abi when all this trouble with the Farrows has blown over.

Abi joins me in the kitchen just before six. She looks terrible. Her hair's a mess, she has dark rings around bloodshot eyes and her face is taut with worry. She heads straight for the kettle, fills it and flicks it on.

'Did you get back to sleep?' I ask.

'Not really. My mind's all over the place. I couldn't switch off.'

'We'll get you booked into a hotel this morning,' I assure her. 'You and the girls will be better off there. At least you'll be able to get some sleep.'

'Is that really a good idea?' she asks, leaning against the counter. 'Don't you think we should all stay together?'

'Not until I can guarantee we're safe here.'

'What are you going to do, Henry?'

'A few improvements to the house. That's all,' I say. 'Nothing to worry about.'

'And you're definitely not going to go near Joseph Farrow?'

'Of course not,' I say, looking shocked that she could even suggest such a thing. 'I made a promise and I intend to keep it.'

Chapter 16

When we collect Norah and Katie from the Lambs', they're both still in their pyjamas, tearing around the house screaming as Paul chases them, pretending to be a monster. It's good to see them so carefree. I was worried how they might react to the window being smashed. But that's the great thing about kids. They don't dwell on stuff like we do as adults. Knowing the girls, they've probably completely forgotten about it already, caught up in the excitement of a late-night adventure.

Abi dresses them upstairs while I chat with Paul and Linda in the kitchen.

'What's going on, Henry?' Paul perches on a stool, wheezing. He doesn't have much hair, and what is left sprouts wildly, little wispy strands that seem to have a mind of their own.

I take a deep breath and tell them everything. Neither of them says anything, but Linda, a frail old lady with a curved spine and a shuffling gait, pats my arm sympathetically. She's never been tall, but in the years we've known her, she seems to have shrunk. Her head now barely comes up to my chest, but there's still a sparkle behind her milky eyes.

'What are you going to do?' she asks.

'I'll check Abi and the girls into a hotel for a few days and then I'm going to make sure they can't touch us again.'

Paul nods sagely. 'You know they're welcome to stay with us for as long as you need.'

'You've done enough already. I want them somewhere they can't be found and anyway, Abi didn't sleep much last night. A hotel bed will do her good,' I say.

'And what about you?' Linda asks. 'You look tired, Henry. You need to look after yourself.'

'My family's my priority.'

We find a cosy hotel on the outskirts of town. After Abi and the girls check in, I return home to begin work to make the house safe. I don't want to be apart from my family a minute longer than necessary, so there's no time to lose.

The outside of the house looks worse in the daylight. The splatter of paint has dried in dark, angry streaks and the ugly chipboard square I put up over the window does nothing but draw attention to the damage.

A police forensics officer arrives mid-morning and asks me to stay out of the way while she dusts the window frame for prints and checks the rest of the garden for footprints and any other clues.

I remember the tin of paint I kicked under the car last night. She drops it into a clear plastic bag and, together with the rock that was used to break the glass, she stows it in the back of her van. When I ask if she's found anything else, she shakes her head and tells me that in most cases like these, conclusive forensic evidence is hard to find.

No sooner has she left, and with impeccable timing, the emergency glazier arrives. He takes less than thirty minutes to replace the broken glass and clean up the mess.

Later that afternoon, after I've scrubbed the worst of the paint off, leaving only a faint pink stain on the white render, an engineer from a home security company I called turns up. He'd agreed to come out at short notice on a weekend after I poured my heart out over the phone and convinced him it was an emergency.

I immediately warm to Sanjay. He has a sunny smile that seems permanently fixed on his face. I tell him about the rock through the window and the tin of paint that was thrown at the front of the house, but I don't elaborate. I don't tell him about the letter or the vandalism to the car. Or my suspicions about Joseph Farrow and his vendetta against my wife. He sucks in air through his teeth and shakes his head.

'Nasty business,' he says.

He asks to look around so he can make a detailed assessment and roams through the house with a clipboard, studying all the windows and doors with a knowing nod. Finally, we sit at the kitchen table to discuss his recommendations.

'I don't want to turn the house into a fortress,' I say, 'but I need to know my family is going to be safe.'

He nods as if he understands perfectly. 'Absolutely,' he says.

'I was thinking a few extra locks on the doors, some locks on the windows and maybe some CCTV cameras front and back,' I say.

Sanjay nods and makes another note on his clipboard. 'We can do that, sir. We can make you secure and fit a few gadgets too, so you can monitor the house remotely if you wish.'

'There's one other thing. I'm worried how easily they smashed the glass in the window at the front of the house —'

'I doubt it was easy,' Sanjay says. 'It's double-glazed. It would have taken a big effort to smash it because of the cushion of air between the panes, you see.'

That explains the loud banging I heard before the sound of shattering glass.

'But they did it,' I say. 'And if they did it once, they can do it again. If they want to get into the house, the windows are a weak point.'

I need peace of mind if I'm going to allow Abi and the girls to return home and if I'm ever to get a decent night's sleep again.

Sanjay tilts his head. 'I wouldn't exactly say a weak point.'

'I want bars fitted to all the windows.'

For the first time, Sanjay's smile slips and his jaw drops. 'Bars?'

'Yes, on all the windows. I want the house totally secure.'

A shadow of a smile creeps across his lips as if he thinks I might be joking. 'I would suggest your best bet is triple locks on all the doors and maybe even an alarm system to complement the cameras. If anyone tries to break in —'

'I don't care about the doors. They're solid enough. It's the windows that concern me', I say.

'But really, bars? On all the windows?'

'That's right. Can you do it?'

'Of course I can do it, sir', Sanjay says, 'although it's a little unusual.'

'It's an unusual situation.'

'Of course. I understand.' He chews the end of his pen while he studies his clipboard. 'So to confirm, you want me to fit bars to all the windows in the house?'

'Yes.'

'Like in a prison?'

'That's right', I say. 'I don't want anyone to threaten my family while they're in this house again.'

❖

That night, I sleep fitfully. The house feels empty without Abi and the girls. It's too quiet and every time I hear a car rumble past or the sound of the pigeons on the roof or the creak of a tree branch, I snatch a breath and hold it, fearing the Farrows are back. I try to tell myself it's an irrational fear, but my subconscious won't let it go.

Last time, it was a rock through the window. The next time, it'll be something worse. I'm sure of it. I try not to think what it might be, but my mind runs riot. The thought of someone breaking into the house intending to hurt us, hurt my family, leaves the blood running cold in my veins.

I must fall asleep eventually but wake early to the sound of birdsong and the first light of day spilling through the curtains. My brain is foggy with tiredness and the bedsheets are rucked up where I must have been restless in the night.

It's a relief to see Sanjay again. He's been incredibly accommodating, agreeing to do the work on a Sunday morning. I'm sure he has a family of his own he'd rather be spending time with, but he must have seen how desperate I am.

He turns up just after eight and immediately begins work on the new locks for the front and back doors. He works quickly and efficiently, a master of his trade, and by mid-morning he's finished. He's about to start on the windows when I suggest a quick coffee break.

'Are you sure you still want to go ahead with putting bars on all the windows?' he asks as we stand in the kitchen with steaming mugs. 'It seems such a drastic measure.'

'I can't risk someone getting into the house while we're asleep or not here,' I say. 'I'm doing it to protect my wife and my daughters.'

'It's your choice, of course.'

'I've made up my mind.'

'Very well.' Sanjay puts his mug down and folds his arms. 'Do you play any musical instruments?'

I frown. It's an odd question. 'No, I'm not at all musical,' I say. 'Why do you ask?'

'I play classical guitar,' he tells me. 'I can play to a fairly high standard. I might even have been able to make a career out of it if I'd been brave enough. It might have worked out, but it might not. The point is, I'll never know because I didn't have the guts to try. I was afraid of failing. Instead, I stuck with what I knew. Security systems. Locks, bolts, cameras, alarms.'

I nod, confused. I don't know why he's telling me this. I guess he's just trying to make polite conversation.

'What I'm saying is fear has a funny effect on people's behaviour. It's like glue that gums up their heads. In my case, it stopped me from following my dreams. I was afraid I would fail. That I wasn't good enough. You see, fear stops a lot of people from doing the things they know will make them happy. Do you see what I mean?'

I nod. 'I wanted to be a chef when I was younger.'

'There you go.' Sanjay throws up a hand as if to say, I told you so. 'What happened?'

'My father didn't approve. He didn't think it was a proper job and I was too scared to go against his wishes,' I say, the bitterness and regret rising from the deep recesses of my memory.

'What did you do instead?'

I laugh bitterly, thinking about what might have been. 'I became a planning officer,' I say. 'It's a steady job and the pay's not bad,' I add, as if I need to justify it not only to Sanjay but to myself.

'I see a lot of scared people in this business. People call me all the time because they want more locks or CCTV covering every angle because they're scared of something. Their fears might be real or not, but in my experience, more security is rarely the answer.'

It's another odd thing for Sanjay to say. 'You'll do yourself out of business if you go around telling people that.'

'Do you really want to turn your house into a prison because a couple of thugs smashed a window? What does your wife think?'

'She doesn't know.'

'I see.' The air whistles as he draws it in between his teeth. He tilts his head to one side.

'She'll be fine,' I say, 'as long as the girls are safe. Anyway, it's not only the smashed window. Other things that have happened too.'

And I tell him everything, starting with the threatening letter, letting it all out in a flood, hardly stopping to draw breath. I tell him how it made me feel angry, fearful and anxious. I tell him about the Farrows and Billy Bowden and the court case. How I suspect they've been responsible for everything. And I tell him how worried I am that at some point soon, they're going to come back to finish what they've started. I'm sure he has no interest in hearing it, but he listens patiently.

'Nasty business,' Sanjay says. He says it so often, it's almost become a catchphrase. 'And if I was in your shoes, I'd be worried too. But if you put bars on the windows, it won't only stop people from getting in, it could stop you from getting out too. What if there was a fire?'

'My mind's made up. Maybe in time, when this is all over, we can remove them. But for now, it's the right thing to do, for the sake of my family.'

'Alright, if you're totally sure, let's get started.'

The noise of drilling, as Sanjay starts on the windows, is obscenely loud for a Sunday morning. Worried it might be disturbing Paul and Linda, I leave him to it and head next door to apologise.

I knock and wait. Paul answers and immediately invites me inside. 'Is everything okay?' he asks.

'Everything's fine. I just came around to say sorry about the noise.'

Paul waves his hand dismissively. 'Don't worry about it. Nothing else has happened, has it?'

'No.'

Linda shuffles into the hall holding a bundle of wool and a pair of knitting needles. She smiles when she sees it's me.

'Hats and gloves for the grandchildren,' she says, holding up the wool. 'But I'm not as fast as I used to be.'

They usher me into their lounge and I sit on the edge of an old green floral sofa. The television is on, the volume painfully loud. Paul switches it off and sits in an armchair by the window. Linda joins me on the other end of the sofa and continues knitting.

'I was lucky to find someone who could come out at short notice to look at the locks,' I say.

Paul nods. 'I saw the van outside.'

'I found him online,' I explain. 'He's putting some more locks on the doors and making the windows secure. I've also asked him to put up some CCTV cameras. I'm not sure what else we can do. We'll be safer than the Bank of England by the end of the day.'

Paul chews his lip. He looks worried. 'Actually, I'm glad you popped in, Henry. With all the trouble you've been having, it's made us think about how safe we are here.'

'What do you mean?'

'Well, I was reading about that court case Abigail was involved in. You know, the old man who was attacked in his home.' Paul folds his leathered, liver-spotted hands in his lap.

'That was a highly unusual case, Paul,' I say.

NOTHING LEFT TO LOSE

'But if someone tried to break in here, I'm not sure how protected we are.'

Linda's knitting needles click-clack in my ear with the monotony of a slow-moving train.

'I could ask Sanjay to look and make some recommendations if you like,' I say. I don't want to worry them unnecessarily. Ours is a uniquely peculiar situation. Paul and Linda shouldn't be concerned.

'Could you?' Paul looks up, his eyes bright. 'The problem is, even the security light we had fitted at the front has stopped working.'

'It probably just needs a new bulb.'

'I can't get up there, Henry. Not with these knees.' He taps his legs and gives a throaty laugh. 'Besides, Linda would never let me up a ladder.'

'I don't mind having a look,' I say.

'Oh no, you don't have to do that.'

'It's the least I can do after you took in the girls. I think I have some spare bulbs at home. Let me get my ladder and I'll be right back.'

I jump up from the sofa before Paul can protest. They've always been so good to us. It's nice to do something in return for a change. I'm sure it's a simple job.

I hurry back to the house. Sanjay has almost finished the living room window. Maybe it does look a little like a prison, but at least we're going to be secure. I grab my ladder from the shed, pick up a screwdriver, find a couple of spare bulbs, and head back to Paul and Linda's.

Paul's waiting for me outside and holds the ladder while I climb up to inspect the broken light which is attached to the wall high under the eaves. I don't like

125

heights, but I try not to think about falling as the ladder wobbles under my feet.

I unscrew the front glass plate, carefully remove the old bulb, and replace it with a new one. But when I cover the light sensor with my hand, it stubbornly refuses to come on.

Not the bulb then.

'Is it working?' Paul shouts up to me.

'Not yet.'

It might be the sensor that's packed up, in which case it's probably sensible to replace the entire unit. But I've not given up yet. A thick black electrical cable runs up the wall and disappears into the roof space. I wonder if that might be the issue.

'Can I get into your loft and check the cabling?' I ask Paul as I carefully descend the ladder on watery legs.

I carry the ladder inside and set it up under the loft hatch. I use the torch on my phone to peer into the attic and haul myself up into the dark.

There's hardly room to move. The loft is full of a lifetime's worth of belongings spilling out of cardboard boxes. Books are stacked up in piles. Paintings in gilded frames are propped up against the rafters. And there's even a table and set of wooden chairs stacked up.

I scramble into the eaves where I guess the cable from the security light must enter the house. I dig around under a thick carpet of insulation, holding my breath against the tiny fibre-glass particles, and finally locate the electrical lead. The problem is immediately apparent. Something has chewed through it, exposing the coloured wires inside.

Probably mice. And now I look harder, I can see telltale black droppings everywhere, gnawed holes in the bottom of boxes and shredded piles of foam and plastic. I've no idea how they've managed to get in, but the whole place looks infested.

Paul sticks his head up through the loft hatch, holding up a mug of tea.

'Any luck?' he asks.

I crawl towards him on my hands and knees, careful not to brush against the dusty cobwebs hanging from above like feathery stalactites.

'You've got a mouse problem, I'm afraid,' I say. 'They've gnawed the cable. Look.' I shine the torch on my phone around the loft, picking out some of the damage.

Light bounces off a white plasterboard wall at the far end of the loft where our two houses are joined. At the base of the board, where it meets the ceiling joists, I spot another semi-circular hole, its edges roughly gnawed by tiny teeth.

It looks as though they've broken through into our side. I'm going to have to check our attic too. I think about all the junk we've tossed up there over the years - the girls' baby clothes, toys, books, Christmas decorations and who knows what else. I wonder how much is ruined. It's the last thing I need right now.

'Looks like we're both going to need to put traps down,' I say with a sigh.

'I guess it's a good job you found it when you did,' Paul says.

Chapter 17

Although Sanjay finishes the windows late on Sunday afternoon, he returns the next day to install the CCTV cameras. I'd already decided to take a few days off work. I can't focus on anything right now, beyond getting to the bottom of who's been terrorising us. They can cope without me in the office for a few days, I'm sure. And there's plenty I can get on with at home and on the blog.

I call Abi first thing but don't tell her about the mice. She'd freak out if she knew, and anyway, one crisis is enough.

'How are Norah and Katie?'

I can hear them chattering in the background. It's only been a couple of days, but I miss them so much.

'They're fine. Ready to come home though,' Abi says.

'What did you do yesterday?'

'I took them to the park and we met up with Colette and Felicity. I couldn't stand to be stuck in the room all day. I was going up the walls.'

I chuckle at the thought of the girls confined to a hotel room, jumping on the beds and leaving their dirty clothes strewn across the floor.

'How did you sleep?' I ask.

'Better. You?'

'It was weird being in the house on my own. It'll be nice to have you back.' I hesitate, fearing the answer to the question I need to ask. 'And has everything been okay?'

'You mean, has anything else happened? No, it's been quiet. We're fine. Anything at the house?'

'No, but I've had a guy here fitting new locks and stuff most of the time.' I deliberately don't elaborate on all the work I've had done. I want it to be a surprise.

'I'm looking forward to getting back.'

'Listen, I'm taking a few days off, so I'll pick up the girls from school tonight and bring them back here. I'll see you when you've finished work.'

'Okay. I shouldn't be too late. I love you,' Abi says.

'I love you too.'

The rest of the morning is taken up working with Sanjay on where best to fit the cameras to eliminate any blind spots around the house. Then he shows me how to access the live feeds and historic footage through an app on my phone.

'So even if you're away,' he says, 'you can check on the property, and the servers will store all the old footage for seven days before it gets wiped.'

It's the last piece of the jigsaw and finally, the house feels secure. While we're inside, the Farrows, or anybody else, can't touch us. I can sleep easy in my bed and hopefully, in time, they'll lose interest. I can't wait to see Abi's face.

When Sanjay's gone, I call a pest control company who promise to send someone out later in the week to sort out our mouse problem. I don't want them chewing through electrical cables or anything else in our loft. It's a shame they can't send anyone sooner, but at least it's in hand.

Norah and Katie come screaming towards me when they're let out of class at the end of the day. I pull them close and drink in their familiar scent.

'I missed you, Daddy,' Katie says, pushing her rucksack into my chest.

Norah is less demonstrative, but I can tell by the way she clasps my hand as we walk back to the car that she feels the same.

'Are we going home to our house now?' she asks.

'Yes, back to your own room and all your toys.'

'And Mummy too?'

'Yes, when she finishes work.'

The girls clamber into the back seat of the car and I make sure they're securely strapped in. My precious cargo. I throw their bags on the front seat as I hop in behind the wheel and spot a brown padded envelope sticking out of the top of Norah's satchel. With curiosity getting the better of me, I pull it out for a closer look.

I don't know how long I sit with it in my lap while the girls bicker in the back. It could be a minute. It could be ten. But I can't tear my eyes away from my name scribbled roughly on the front in capital letters and black ink. I instantly think about the letter that was pushed through our door, even though that was in an unmarked plain white envelope and this is a padded package.

Just Henry.

No surname. No address.

I shudder as a chill coils down my spine.

'Norah, where did you get this?' I ask, holding the package up.

'A man gave it to me,' she says, like it's the most natural thing in the world to have happened.

'What man?'

I watch her in the rear-view mirror, my mouth dry.

'Just some man. He gave it to me at lunchtime.'

I force myself to stay calm. There's no point in losing my temper with her.

'What man, honey?'

'I don't know,' she says. 'He said I had to give it to you. He said it was important.'

My heart flutters. 'Did you recognise him?'

She shakes her head violently, sending her long hair flying.

'And he came into the playground, did he?'

How has this happened? I thought the school had staff on duty during lunch to keep the kids safe. And yet apparently, someone has walked up to Norah and handed her a package unseen.

'He was standing outside and passed it over the fence,' Norah explains.

'Did he say anything else?'

'No.'

'Did you get a good look at his face?'

She howls in pain as her sister pinches her arm and, after a fleeting moment of indignation, flings an arm out at Katie in retaliation.

I've lost her.

'Stop that! Both of you!' I yell.

'She started it,' Norah wails.

'You're both as bad as one another. Norah, listen to me. This is really important. The man who gave you this parcel. Did you see his face?'

'No,' she shouts at me.

'Alright, I'm not cross with you, but I thought you knew better than to talk to strangers.'

She pretends to cry, making loud howling noises, rubbing her eyes with her knuckles.

'That's enough,' I say. She can't tell me any more.

I weigh the package in my hand. It's feather light. And yet I can feel something inside. Small and rectangular. No bigger than my thumb. I tear the end of the package open and tip it out in my hand.

A silver USB stick drops into my palm. Metallic. Unmarked. My heart misses a beat and restarts hard and fast. What the hell is this?

I stare into the empty package, expecting to find a note or a letter. Some kind of explanation. But there's nothing in it other than this small sliver of metal.

My imagination goes into overdrive. If it's come from the Farrows, it won't be early birthday best wishes. And the manner in which it's been delivered is telling too. Using Norah. Making the point that they know where my kids are. How to get to them. They know my weak point and this is another message. I don't like it one bit.

I shove it in my pocket and move off into the school traffic that's moving frustratingly slowly. I tap the steering wheel in agitation as we creep forward, with cars trying to pull out in front of me and parents and children dodging precariously between the vehicles.

Eventually, we reach the main road. I put my foot down and accelerate out in front of a lumbering articulated lorry that flashes its lights. I don't care. All I care about is getting home and onto my computer.

All the way home, Norah pesters me for ice cream after dinner. It's usually a weekend treat, but as we pull onto our drive, I cave in. Anything for a quiet life.

As I struggle with the keys for the new locks, Norah stares at the outside of the house.

'What's happened, Daddy?'

'It's so no more windows get broken,' I say, shepherding the girls inside with a cautious glance over my shoulder. The hairs on the nape of my neck prickle and I have the feeling we're being watched. But there's no one there. It's all in my imagination.

'The girls are home tonight then? Back to a full house?'

Paul's standing on his drive, tossing a black sack into the wheelie bins. I groan inwardly. He's angling for a chat, but I don't have the time. All I want to do is get inside and investigate what's on the USB stick in my pocket.

'Yup, home again,' I say with a polite wave.

'And is Abigail coming home tonight as well?'

'Yup,' I say, curtly. 'She'll be here.'

'Right, and did you get hold of anyone about the mice?'

'They're coming later this week. Sorry, Paul. I can't stop. I need to feed the girls before they have a complete meltdown.'

'Right you are,' he says. 'Catch you later.'

I slip inside the house, shut and lock the door and gather up Katie and Norah's shoes, which they've abandoned in the hall. I shouldn't have been so dismissive. I think Paul's lonely. I know he has Linda, but since their own children left home, they don't see many people. Maybe I'll pop around later and check in on them. Right now, I only have one thing on my mind.

The girls have vanished upstairs. They've only been away a couple of nights, but I can hear them turning out their toys, the rustle of hands sifting through dressing-up costumes and boxes of Lego. It's like everything's new to them, just like when we returned from two weeks away in Provence last summer.

As they seem to be playing happily and not griping about being hungry, I snatch the opportunity and flip open the laptop on the kitchen counter. It boots up annoyingly slowly and I jiggle my foot in anticipation, watching a white logo morph onto the black screen, blinking at me as if it's been woken from a deep sleep. Eventually, the black dissolves and my desktop appears, littered with countless icons.

I pull the USB stick from my pocket and plug it into a spare slot. With a calming deep breath, I click on the one folder it contains, which has been labelled 'Watch Me'.

What is this? Alice in Fucking Wonderland?

The folder contains a single video file which has been named 'Exhibit A'. A passing nod to Abi's job? It's too much of a coincidence.

I glance across the room to check Norah and Katie haven't sneaked back downstairs, and click on the file.

The screen goes blank for a second or two before a video player opens to reveal a single frozen frame, blurred and out of focus, like the camera was in motion when the footage stopped. There's green foliage at the edge of the shot. And a meandering path. At a guess, I'd say it was filmed on a mobile phone. It has that grainy, hand-held feel about it.

My finger trembles as it hovers over the trackpad.

I click play.

The footage jerks into shaky movement as the camera bobbles around for a few seconds and then stabilises. It reminds me of secretly recorded footage I've seen in undercover documentaries exposing dodgy businessmen accepting backhanders and unsuspecting criminals trading guns or fighting dogs. It has that same unpolished rawness.

I continue to watch, transfixed, as it becomes clear whoever is filming is in a park. There are children playing on swings, a slide and a roundabout. But as the camera moves closer, I see it's not just any children. It's Norah and Katie.

Acidic bile burns the back of my throat.

Then the camera pans left and picks out three figures sitting on a bench. Abi's in the middle, clasping a cup of coffee. Felicity and Colette sit on either side of her, their knees touching. Felicity has Abi's free hand in her lap. They look cosy in their huddle. Conspiratorial.

The cameraman zooms into their faces until they're blurred and fuzzy, apparently oblivious that they're being filmed.

And that's it. The film stops and the computer resets to the first indistinct frame again. I don't need to see any more. It doesn't need subtitles or a commentary. I can see it's another message.

I'm coming for you.

I know where to find you.

I can hurt you and your family at any time I like.

I slam the laptop closed and bury my head in my hands. He's taunting me. A cat pawing a cornered mouse.

It's also a reminder that no matter how safe we are in the house, we can't stay inside forever. And when we leave, we're vulnerable. All of us.

How has he got so close without Abi spotting him? It must have been obvious they were being filmed. How could she have not noticed?

My immediate thought is to call Abi. But what's the point in worrying her at work? There's nothing she can do, and the chances are she's in court, anyway. At least Norah and Katie are home and safe.

❖

It's early evening when I'm startled by a loud banging on the front door. The girls have already eaten and I was working up to begin their bedtime routine, steeling myself for the battle ahead. I look up from my laptop with my heart racing. It's late for visitors and I'm not expecting anyone.

Joseph Farrow?

Don't be stupid. Why would he be knocking?

I creep into the hall with my hands balling into fists, wishing whoever it is would go away. I don't want to open the door.

Another three loud knocks echo through the house.

I don't know what to do. If I ignore it, will they go away or keep knocking until one of the girls comes down to investigate and I have to explain to them why I'm not answering?

And then I remember the security cameras Sanjay has installed. There's one right above the front door. I can't believe I've forgotten already.

I pull my phone from my pocket and call up the app that lets me access the live feeds. I select the camera over the door and stare at the figure on the doorstep. I'd expected to see Joseph Farrow or one of his cronies, so it takes me a second to realise it's Abi, looking agitated.

I fly at the door, releasing all the new locks and bolts. I'd forgotten she doesn't have a set of keys yet.

When I peel open the door, Abi's standing with her arms folded, her face dark and brooding.

Something's wrong. Something else has happened.

'What is it?' I gasp, glancing over her shoulder into the street, half expecting to see someone loitering. But there's no one there.

'Henry, what the hell have you done to the house?'

Chapter 18

'How could you think this was a good idea?' Abi shoves me in the chest as she barges her way inside.

'But —'

'It's an absolute eyesore.'

'The house wasn't safe,' I say, stunned by her reaction. I thought she'd be pleased I'd taken steps to protect her and the girls. She's totally overreacting. 'No one's going to get in now, short of bulldozing through the front door.'

'It's too much. We can't live like this, like... prisoners. It's absurd.'

'I want you to feel safe.'

'I want them taken down. All of them,' Abi says, tossing her briefcase and handbag down and shrugging off her coat.

'I've only just had them put up,' I say. I can't believe she's being so unreasonable. 'What if Farrow comes back and tries to break in again?'

'Henry, I won't say it again. I'm not living like this. We're only a length of razor wire and a guard tower away from having our home turned into a maximum security jail. I mean, what must the neighbours think?'

'I don't care what they think. I only care about my family,' I say.

'I should never have gone away. It was a mistake. What else have you done?'

'Nothing.' She's made me all defensive, questioning myself. I thought I was doing the right thing to protect us all.

'You've obviously changed the locks.' Her eyebrows shoot up.

'Sorry, yes, I've had new locks put on the front and back doors.' I pluck a new set of keys from the papier mâché bowl on the side. 'Here. These are for you.'

She snatches them and loops them onto her keyring. 'Is that it?'

'I've had CCTV cameras installed around the house as well. You can view the footage on your phone. I can show you.' I hold up my phone, but she doesn't seem interested.

'Where are the girls?'

'Upstairs, I was about to start bath —'

'I'll do it,' Abi snaps.

I can't believe she's getting this worked up about a few bars on the windows.

'They've had their tea,' I say.

Abi turns away from me, heading for the stairs, but stops and spins around, her eyes narrowing.

'What if we need to get out in a hurry? What if there's a fire? What are we supposed to do then?'

I scratch my head. As Sanjay pointed out, there's no way out through the windows in an emergency. 'It won't be forever,' I explain. 'And when this all blows over, we can have them removed.'

Abi shakes her head like she can't believe what she's hearing. 'No, Henry. Get them taken off tomorrow.'

'I can't! Not just like that.'

'I mean it.'

I hang my head. There's no arguing with her when she's like this. And she's not going to see sense, unless...

'Maybe this will change your mind,' I say, striding into the kitchen.

If she wants persuading that we're not safe while Joseph Farrow is out there looking for some kind of twisted vengeance, maybe what I discovered on the USB stick will make her think again.

'I found this in Norah's schoolbag,' I say, holding up the empty brown package. 'She says a man handed it to her over the playground fence at lunchtime.'

Abi has followed me into the kitchen and glances suspiciously at the envelope I've ripped open at one end.

'Who?'

'She didn't recognise him.'

Abi shakes her head in disbelief.

'This was inside,' I say, holding up the USB stick. 'You're going to want to watch this.'

I plug it back into the computer and pull up the video file. I hit play and stand back so Abi has an unobstructed view of the screen.

'What is this?' she gasps as the footage focuses on Norah and Katie chasing each other up a playground slide, down again, and onto a roundabout.

I say nothing, letting her take it all in as the camera pans around and zooms in on Abi and her friends.

'Turn it off,' she says. 'I don't want to see any more.'

'He was there,' I say. 'Joseph Farrow was in the park with you, filming. I can't believe you didn't see him.'

Abi puts a hand to her forehead and runs it over her hair. 'I didn't see him,' she says. 'I didn't see anyone.'

'Are you sure? He must have been right there in front of you.'

'I didn't see anyone,' she repeats, raising her voice. 'If it was Joseph Farrow, I would have recognised him. He doesn't exactly blend in.'

It's exactly what I thought. I'd have recognised him anywhere with that bushy beard and all those tattoos. 'It could have been an accomplice,' I suggest.

'But why were they filming us? And the girls?'

I shrug. 'They're playing mind games. Letting us know how easily they can get to us.' It's the only reason I can think of.

'I don't like this, Henry.'

'No, neither do I. I'd better let the police know. Do you still have that officer's contact details?'

'Somewhere.' Abi disappears into the hall where she left her handbag and comes back with the business card the police left with us.

'I'll call him,' I say. 'The problem is there's nothing to link the footage to the Farrows, just like the letter and the vandalism to your car. But maybe they'll be able to pull some prints off that stick.'

'After you've had your hands all over it? I dount it.' Abi pulls out a chair at the kitchen table and slumps down, raking her fingers through her hair. 'I can't stand it.'

It's the first time I've seen her get properly upset since the night she was followed home. She doesn't easily let her guard down, but I can see now it's getting to her. She's always been so strong. So composed. I'm not used to her being like this, and I'm not sure how to handle it.

'Why are they doing this to us?' When she looks up, she has streaks of mascara running down her cheeks. 'What are we supposed to have done? If this is the Farrows, why me? Why us? Why not the police or the judge? There were twelve men and women on the jury. Why not them? It's not fair.'

I kneel at Abi's feet and take her hands, pulling them away from her face.

'Hey, we're going to get through this. We're in it together,' I say. 'Everything's going to be fine.'

She shakes her head. 'It's not though, is it? And what if it's not the Farrows? I've prosecuted hundreds of cases. It could be something to do with any one of those. I just can't see a way out of this. It's going to go on and on - and how does it end?'

'That's why I wanted us to be safe inside the house, at least. Whatever they do, they can't touch us here. I know the windows are a bit much, but I don't want to take any chances, not until we've sorted this out.'

Abi sits back and puts her fingers to her lips. 'I don't know what we're going to do.'

'Neither do I. But we're going to get through it. I promise.'

❖

Abi puts the girls to bed and we eat in silence, distracted by our thoughts. What is there to say that hasn't already been said? We're being held hostage by an invisible enemy with no discernible motive. I can't see what else we can do but batten down the hatches and wait for the storm to blow over.

After we've eaten, Abi announces she's going to have a bath and an early night. I listen to the sound of water running in the bathroom upstairs, make myself a peppermint tea, and retire to the lounge. I have a whole batch of cookery shows I've been meaning to catch up on, but I can't focus on watching anything tonight. Instead, I open the app on my phone that allows me to access the CCTV cameras around the house and I flick through them one by one, looking for anything suspicious.

As well as the camera above the front door, there are two covering the back garden, as well as a separate one pointed towards the shed where I keep my bike. There's another covering the side return, and one directed towards the drive where our cars are parked.

Watching the feeds is strangely addictive, even though there's not much happening outside. A few cars trundle past, their tail-lights a white-hot glow in the monochrome images. A fox with an extraordinarily bushy tail steals through the garden and I catch the flittering glimpse of a pair of bats outside the kitchen window.

I don't know how long I spend staring at my phone, but eventually, my eyelids droop as exhaustion creeps up on me after the last few stressful days and sleepless nights.

When I wake with a start, it takes a moment to remember I'm slumped in the armchair in the lounge. The house is silent and in darkness and my phone is buzzing on my chest.

I rub my eyes, sit up, and check the screen.

There's a message from a number I don't recognise.

Want to know a secret about your wife?

I blink twice, my eyes fading in and out of focus. Is this a joke? Someone trying to prank me? Or worse, one of those scam texts that tries to lure you into clicking a link that downloads a virus onto your phone?

But there is no link to click. Just eight discomforting words.

I should ignore it. Delete the message and block the number. It's someone trying to cause trouble, maybe even Joseph Farrow, although I've no idea how he's found my number.

I put my phone face down on the arm of the chair. I don't want to know. There's nothing Abi would keep from me. We don't have secrets. We've always agreed that's the basis of a solid marriage.

And yet, the niggle of curiosity and doubt bubbles and ferments in my brain. As much as I try to think about something else, anything else, I can't. Does Abi really have a secret she's keeping from me? And then I think about the kinds of secrets a wife would keep from her husband.

Surely not. Abi's not like that. I trust her.

Maybe I trust her too much. I don't know where she is or who she's with half the time, but it's never occurred to me to worry before. We both agree infidelity is the worst kind of betrayal.

And yet I know I'm punching above my weight. She's way out of my league. If she's my Nicole Kidman, then I'm her Keith Urban. She's beautiful like a nineteen-forties Hollywood starlet, poised and elegant. A natural red-head with a smile that melts my insides and piercing coral-sea blue eyes that can be both fierce and kindly, and change in the beat of a hummingbird's wing. And she's just as beautiful inside, with a brilliant mind and a youthful spirit that seems to keep her forever young.

I'm just a bloke who sifts planning notices for the council. My hair is greying at the temples - although I'm grateful I've held onto it at all given my father was bald by the time he was thirty - and the beard I grew to hide a weak chin is more homeless vagrant than designer chic these days.

We're an unconventional couple in that respect. Even the way we met was unusual, in a bar where she was supposed to be on a blind date with a guy who failed to show. Someone she knew vaguely from work who'd asked her out. I didn't care. It was his loss. She was nervously twiddling an olive-speared cocktail stick around her martini glass with one eye on her phone and the other on the door.

I smiled when our gaze met, embarrassed I'd been caught staring, but I guess she was used to that. Even after ten years of marriage, I see men watching her. It's always given me a thrill of excitement that she's on my arm and not theirs. It's never occurred to me to be jealous before.

When she smiled back, my legs turned to jelly. Without a hint of reticence, she pulled up a stool next to me, and as I'd been stood up by a friend, we started chatting. Nine months later, I chanced my arm with a marriage proposal, expecting she'd laugh, but to my eternal surprise she said yes and the following year we were married.

We're as strong today as we were back then, except now with two beautiful girls and an amazing house. I just can't imagine Abi cheating on me, any more than I could envisage me cheating on her.

But if there is something going on, I need to know. And like an angry mosquito bite itching to be scratched, I can't ignore the message on my phone any longer.

I snatch it up and type a hurried reply with my thumbs.

Who is this? How did you get my number?

I hit send.

And wait.

Holding my breath, I stare at the screen as the message vanishes into the ether.

Seconds tick by slowly.

Eventually, a tick appears showing the message has been delivered.

Come on, come on.

Three dots. My mystery messenger is typing a reply.

A message pops up.

Do you want to know or not?

Of course I want to know. You can't dangle a crumb like that in front of a man and expect him to shrug and move on. Whoever is texting me knows this full well. I know they're playing with me but I'm hooked.

It's probably nothing.

But my neurosis doesn't know that.

I think back to all those nights in the last few months that Abi's stayed late at the office. She said it was to prep for the Billy Bowden case. Was she lying to me? Using it as an excuse to carry on behind my back? My gut turns to mush.

No, she'd never do that.

Would she?

I squeeze my eyes shut as an image of Abi on her back with another man between her thighs pops into my head. I push it away. There's nothing to suggest she's been anything other than faithful, other than this anonymous text that's come out of the blue.

And why would I believe that?

I type another message.

Yes. Tell me.

Again, I watch the message spiral off and wait anxiously for a reply with my heart cantering like I'm on amphetamines.

I tap my foot impatiently on the floor.

But I don't have to wait long.

My phone buzzes in my hand as another message pops up.

No, not a message.

A photo.

I stare at it, wondering if I dare to open it, fearing what I'm going to find. A picture of Abi that I'll never be able to unsee? But now I have it, I can't ignore it.

With a sick feeling in my stomach, I click on it.

It shows a busy open-air restaurant. Chairs and tables on the pavement under maroon parasols. A small queue of people waiting to be seated. I know where this is. It's that place in town serving what's supposed to be authentic French cuisine if steak frites and moules marinière are your idea of authentic French cooking.

I shake my head, confused. What am I supposed to be looking at? Whatever it is, it doesn't appear to be evidence of Abi's infidelity. I sigh with relief and send another message back.

What is this?

A second photo arrives. It seems to be the same image but enlarged on a small section of the dining area. It's a little pixilated because of the zoom, but there's no mistaking what I'm looking at. My heart sinks and my guts twist.

'Oh, Abi,' I mutter under my breath. 'What have you done?'

Chapter 19

I study the photo, shaking. Abi is sitting opposite Ralph, leaning in towards him, their faces too close, like lovers on a first date. But it's his hand on top of hers that's most crushing. It's such a tender gesture. Skin on skin. A public display of affection.

My mind is driven to places I don't want it to go, imagining Ralph's clammy hands all over my wife's naked body. Their limbs entwined. Seedy hotel rooms. The back of Abi's Mini. A horrific montage of their infidelity. How could she do this to me? Haven't I always been there for her? The embodiment of loyalty and devotion? And this is how she repays me, with Ralph of all people.

How have I missed it? And how long has it been going on? I'd never had the faintest suspicion.

My throat tightens and my stomach wrenches with nausea.

How could they do this to me?

And what about Colette? I presume she doesn't know either. They've played us both for fools. It's the most complete betrayal I can imagine. A husband and a wife stabbed in the back with the same filthy knife.

How am I going to explain it to the girls? They're too young to understand. Too innocent. It's the sort of thing that could damage them for the rest of their lives. A legacy that will probably taint their relationships for years to come.

How could Abi have been so selfish?

I click away from the image and tap out another message, my hand trembling with shock and anger.

How did you get this?

And when was it taken? It looks recent but I can't be sure.

So many questions tumble around my brain. I need answers or I'm going to lose my mind.

The message has been delivered and read, but there's no response. This has to be Joseph Farrow's work. He must have known this would rip us apart. Is he sitting at home laughing at me? Revelling in my world collapsing? Well, I hope by destroying our lives, he's happy now.

In frustration, I type another message.

Just tell me

This time, it's not delivered. Now he's dropped the grenade, the bastard's probably switched off his phone.

In desperation, I try calling the number. A hollow silence echoes in my ear and the blood hammers through my veins. Eventually, I get an automated response, a robotic voice telling me the person I'm calling is not available.

I slam the phone down on the arm of the chair.

How have I been so blind?

The last time I saw Abi and Ralph together was when everyone came to dinner on Friday night. After everything that's happened since, it seems a long time ago. I didn't notice anything going on between them that night. Certainly nothing to arouse my suspicion. In fact, they barely exchanged a word while I was in the room. Perhaps that in itself should have given me cause to suspect something was going on. But I was so focused on the meal and anxious about seeing Johnny and Ralph again. Maybe I'd been blinkered to what was really going on.

As I stare into space, my mind and body numb, the door creaks open.

'Henry?'

I'd not heard Abi come down the stairs. Her sudden appearance makes me jump.

'What are you still doing up? Come to bed,' she says.

I swallow the bile that rises from my stomach and burns my throat. How can I share a bed with her, knowing what she's done?

Have they been in our bed?

I can't pretend I don't know. I have to say something.

'I know about you and Ralph,' I croak.

She flinches. Only slightly. But I see it.

'What?'

She does a great job of looking innocent. All those years of drama in court are paying off. Could I be mistaken? No, I have evidence. I hand her my phone and show her the photo.

'You should have taken more care,' I say. 'It wasn't exactly the most discrete location.'

Abi uses two fingers to pinch the screen, zooming in on the image.

'What's this?' she demands.

'The evidence of something going on right under my nose, apparently.'

'Evidence of what exactly?' Abi's tone is sharp. Defensive. 'That Ralph and I had lunch together?'

'You never told me you were meeting him. If you had nothing to hide, why didn't you say anything?'

'I didn't know you were keeping tabs on me. Where did you get this?'

'It's not important,' I say. It'll only complicate matters if she knows Farrow's sent it.

'Of course it's important.' Her eyes blaze. She's furious.

I thought she might have the decency to at least be contrite. Beg for my forgiveness. Tell me it was a one-off and will never happen again. But she's not sorry. She's only angry that she's been caught.

'If you must know, it was an anonymous tip-off.'

Abi throws the phone angrily back at me. It bounces off my chest and lands on the floor.

'You mean it's come from the same person who filmed me and the girls in the park and sent that letter?'

'Possibly. But that's not the point,' I say. 'The point is you and Ralph have been carrying on behind my back, making a fool out of not only me but your so-called best friend.'

'Huh! You seriously think I'm cheating on you?' The way she says it, it's like it's the most preposterous idea she's ever heard.

I've had enough of being lied to.

'Well,' I say, 'are you?'

Abi stands rooted to the spot. I can't hold her gaze. I reach down and pick up my phone, the first inkling of doubt creeping into my mind. Her reaction isn't one of guilt.

'Of course not,' she says through clenched teeth.

'But you met him for lunch behind my back.'

'He was worried about me,' she says. 'Obviously you'd told them all about the letter and the attack on my car —'

'So it's my fault?'

'No! But when he then heard our window had been smashed, he was concerned about me.'

'Hang on,' I say, the cogs in my head turning slowly. 'So this was taken today?'

'I don't really see what the big deal is. Sometimes Ralph and I have lunch together if we're both free. It doesn't mean I'm screwing him.'

'Keep your voice down,' I hiss. 'You'll wake the girls.'

'And frankly, I'm disappointed you think I'd do something like that to you.'

'So why's he holding your hand?'

'I told you, he was concerned. There's nothing more to it,' she says.

'Does Colette know?'

'For pity's sake, Henry, there's nothing to know.'

'So she's aware of these cosy little lunch dates the two of you have been sharing?'

'Can't you see what's going on here? Someone's trying to get inside your head and make you believe something that isn't true, purely to destroy us. Are you really going to let them win that game?'

This has Joseph Farrow's fingerprints all over it, but it doesn't mean she's not having an affair with Ralph, although I'm feeling less sure than I was.

'If you seriously think I could cheat on you, then you don't know me at all,' Abi says.

'What am I supposed to think?'

'You're supposed to trust me.' Abi breathes out heavily through her nose, her demeanour softening. 'I promise there is nothing going on between me and Ralph.' She comes closer and perches on the arm of my chair, taking my hand. 'I could never hurt you like that.'

I want to believe her, I really do.

'Now, more than ever, we need to be strong,' she continues. 'We can't let Joseph Farrow, or whoever this is, come between us. Ralph and I are friends and that's all. You have to believe me.'

I'm so confused. I don't want to be played for an idiot. I don't want to be that guy who lives in happy ignorance while his wife's screwing behind his back. But I can't let Farrow sabotage our marriage if she's innocent.

'I don't know what to think anymore,' I say.

'I guess it comes down to whether, after ten years of marriage, you still trust me.'

Chapter 20

I really want to trust her. But how can I ignore that picture? There's something about the way they're looking at each other, how Abi appears to be hanging on Ralph's every word. And of course, there's his hand on top of hers in the middle of the table that leaves me feeling queasy.

But it is only one photo, and photos can be deceptive or staged. I should know better than to put my entire trust into a single image. I can't throw my marriage away that easily. What I need is more proof.

'I need to be by myself for a bit,' I say.

'Fine. Suit yourself. But you think long and hard about exactly what you have to lose if you continue to accuse me of something I haven't done.'

She shuffles out of the room and into the kitchen. I hear the drawer where we keep the medicines slide open. The rattle of pills in a bottle. The chink of a glass and water running. I guess she needs some help sleeping.

'I'm going back to bed,' she grumbles as she passes the lounge door.

I can't bring myself to wish her goodnight.

Her footsteps fade as she trudges up the stairs. Our bedroom door clicks shut and the floorboards creak as she climbs into bed.

I know what I have to do, but I need to bide my time.

I give it the best part of an hour, pacing up and down, thinking through everything Abi said and picking over the details of that photo.

Eventually, I creep up to the bedroom in the dark and crack open the door. I can just make out the outline of Abi on her side, cocooned under the duvet, her breathing slow and deep.

'Abi,' I whisper. 'Are you awake?'

She moans as she stirs, but rolls over and falls back into a peaceful slumber.

Do I really want to do this? Is this how husbands behave, even if they do think their wives are cheating? Probably not, but my trust in Abi has been severely tested tonight. This is the only way I might restore it or...

I can't think about the alternative. It's too painful.

Abi's phone is on charge on her bedside table. I tiptoe to her side of the bed, carefully lift the duvet to expose her arm, and gently grab her wrist. Wincing, I pull her hand out, spread her fingers and press her thumb onto the fingerprint sensor on her phone.

It instantly unlocks to reveal a home screen crowded with icons. If there's any evidence of her infidelity, this is where I'm going to find it.

I place her hand back under the duvet and steal into the en suite bathroom, locking the door behind me. If she finds me snooping through her mobile, she'll go berserk.

Sitting on the edge of the bath, I explore her text messages first. Many of them are from me. A few from her bank with access codes for her online account, one from the garage reminding her the Mini's service is due and another about a forthcoming doctor's appointment. Nothing from Ralph.

There's much more of interest in her WhatsApp account. Messages from all sorts of people, some of whom I recognise, like Colette, Felicity and Abi's clerk, Helen. But many I don't. I can't believe how many people she knows. My contact list stretches to maybe fifty people, but Abi has what looks like hundreds of contacts.

But I only care about one.

Ralph's name appears high on a long list of exchanges, showing they've been communicating recently. This is where I'm going to find proof of their relationship if it exists, but once I've read it, there's no turning back. I never imagined I'd be the sort of husband who checks his wife's phone behind her back, but here I am. I need to know for sure.

I hesitate, but only briefly.

I click open their chat history, preparing myself for the worst. I half expect to find a long series of messages detailing sordid rendezvous and intimate declarations of love. But there are less than a dozen exchanges.

Abi isn't stupid. She'd have deleted anything incriminating. But as she's often pointed out to me, an absence of something isn't proof it didn't happen.

The oldest message appears to have been sent last week, after the Farrow trial had ended. I work my way through them, starting with the oldest.

~Ralph

Congratulations, Abs. So proud of you x

I try not to read too much into the kiss. It doesn't necessarily mean anything.

Abi had replied a few hours later.

~Abigail

Thanks - relieved to have secured a result. It was never certain x

Another kiss, I note.

~Ralph

Let me take you for a drink to celebrate

~Abigail

Definitely! That would be great x

~Ralph

Actually, what about lunch next week?

~Abigail

Even better - Monday?

~Ralph

Perfect! Let's say 1pm at the usual place.

The usual place? So their lunch dates *are* a regular occurrence.

But that's it. No proclamations of undying love. No details of secret trysts in out-of-town hotels. No promises that one day they'll both leave their spouses to be together. Nothing at all to suggest there's anything untoward going on between them.

I'm partly relieved, but not entirely convinced. They might be being careful not to leave any evidence. At best, it's inconclusive.

My shoulders slump and I rub my tired eyes. It's almost two in the morning and here I am, locked away in the bathroom, scrolling through my wife's phone for evidence of an affair. What am I thinking? Now I've looked, I'm tinged with guilt and the tawdry grubbiness of a peeping tom.

I should put the phone back and get to bed. Forget I've seen that photo. But I can't. I've gone this far. Crossed a line. I might as well check her other messages. If Abi is having an affair with Ralph, it's possible she's confided in a friend.

And before I know what I'm doing, I've clicked on a string of messages between Abi and Felicity, the one person she never keeps secrets from.

Mostly it's inconsequential chatter and gossip. Congratulations from Felicity after Abi won her case. A brief discussion about plans for the dinner we hosted on Friday and polite thanks afterwards. A fleeting mention of the threatening letter I'd brought up and Felicity checking how Abi was coping. Nothing earth-shattering.

Apart from one message that stops me in my tracks as I scroll down.

~Abigail

Lie to him. Whatever you do, DON'T TELL HENRY!!

My heart almost stops.

Don't tell Henry what exactly? That she's screwing Ralph behind my back?

I hear the bed creak as Abi rolls over. I'll have to be quick. I flick back through the previous messages, trying to make sense of the conversation.

~Felicity

Henry won't know what's hit him. When are you going to tell him?

~Abigail

Not yet. It's a secret for now.

~Felicity

I can't imagine the look on his face. What if he asks me about it?

~Abigail

He won't.

~Felicity

But what if he does?

~Abigail

Lie to him. Whatever you do, DON'T TELL HENRY!!

They don't mention Ralph by name, but it must be what they're talking about.

A sharp knock on the bathroom door scares the life out of me.

'Henry, are you in there?'

Shit. Shit. Shit.

I switch off the phone and shove it into my back pocket.

'Yeah, just coming.'

'What are you doing in there?' Abi rattles the handle, trying to open the door.

'Nothing. Just cleaning my teeth.' I grab my brush and squeeze a dollop of toothpaste onto it.

'Let me in. I need the loo.'

I hurriedly run the brush over my teeth and spit out the foam before unlocking the door. Abi stumbles in, bleary-eyed.

'It's late. Why are you still up?'

It's almost as if she's forgotten about our argument. She pushes me out of the door and shuts it behind her. Hopefully, she was so groggy she didn't notice her phone was missing.

I sneak around to her side of the bed and plug it back in before peeling off my clothes and climbing into bed with my heart thumping.

The bathroom door clicks open and I hear Abi's bare feet pad across the bedroom floor. As she hops into bed and the mattress rocks, I pretend to be asleep.

But sleep isn't going to come easily now.

I lay there wide awake, my mind turning circles on itself with torturous thoughts. All I can think about is that photo of Abi and Ralph, and the message Abi had sent to Felicity.

Lie to him. Whatever you do, don't tell Henry.

Chapter 21

Abi is already up and dressed when I wake. I can hear her downstairs with the girls. The clatter of dishes and cutlery signals she has breakfast in hand. Just as well as I've overslept and if I don't hurry, we'll be late for school.

I take a quick shower, but don't bother to shave. There doesn't seem much point. I spent the night tossing and turning, wondering how I could have been so stupid not to have realised Abi has been cheating on me. The photo of her with Ralph at an intimate lunch was compelling enough, but the text exchange with Felicity has confirmed my worst fears.

It's probably been going on for months. How have I missed the signs?

I don't want to face Abi this morning, but I can't put it off. I'm going to have to look her in the eye at some point.

I lumber down the stairs feeling like I'm carrying heavy weights on my shoulders. Abi is in the kitchen stacking the girls' bowls and plates in the dishwasher.

Katie rushes past me with crumbs and raspberry jam plastered around her mouth. Norah is still at the table with her head buried in a book.

'You'd better clean your teeth or we'll be late for school,' I tell her, ruffling her hair. It's not been brushed, I notice.

She reluctantly climbs down from her chair and weaves out of the room, still reading. I ignore Abi, not sure what to say. There are so many emotions fizzing around my brain. Anger. Betrayal. Confusion. Shame.

'We need to talk,' Abi says, shutting the dishwasher door and folding her arms across her chest. 'I'm not apologising for something I didn't do.'

I grab a carton of juice from the fridge, pour a glass, and gulp it down in one mouthful.

'Henry, for God's sake, talk to me!' she shouts.

'What's the point?'

'The point is you've as good as accused me of having an affair with Ralph and I've told you it's not true. So where does that leave us?' she says.

'I don't know.' I shake my head sadly. I've not really thought it through. Where *does* this leave us? We can't go on as we are.

'It was one photo. Taken from a distance by someone we don't know to make it look like something it wasn't. To cause trouble between us. I don't know what more I can say to make you understand.' She throws up her hands. But she's only angry because she's been caught. 'And frankly, if you don't trust me, then I don't know where this marriage is heading.'

'You want a divorce?' I ask. Is that what she's trying to say? Does she want out so she can be with Ralph?

'Of course I don't want a divorce. I want you to believe me when I tell you I haven't cheated.'

'How can I trust anything you say when everything that comes out of your mouth is twisted?'

'One photograph, Henry. It was one photograph.'

She looks genuinely upset, but it's her job to win arguments, and I'm not a jury that can be manipulated at her will.

'It doesn't mean it's not true though, does it?' I say. 'Just be honest with me, Abi. Admit that you're sleeping with Ralph.'

'Is that what you want to hear?'

I shrug, with a suspicion I might be coming off a bit like a sulky schoolboy. 'I want to hear the truth.'

'I've told you the truth! Why are you being like this? I've never given you any reason to doubt me, so why now?'

It was pointless arguing. She would never admit what was really going on. I sighed. 'Forget it. I need to get the girls to school or we're going to be late.'

I spend the rest of the morning stewing over Abi's betrayal, my mood darkening by the minute. I even end up taking it out on the girls, angrily switching off their music in the car even though we always sing along to Little Mix on the way to school. Not today. I'm not in the right frame of mind.

Norah sulks and Katie tells me she hates me.

If we ended up divorcing, what would happen to the girls? There's no way I'm letting Abi have full custody after what she's done. She's the one in the wrong, not me. Why should I be punished?

After dropping off the girls in the playground, I sit in the car, lost in my thoughts. My world has been torn apart. Everything I'd taken for granted has been pulled out from under my feet. Nothing's going to be the same again.

There's no way Abi and I can come back from something like this. But she hasn't admitted to the affair, even after I confronted her with the evidence, and that's left me with a nagging doubt. What if she is telling the truth?

Maybe there's another way I can find out for sure. Or at least try.

I pull away and head for the outskirts of town to a faceless, modern commercial park where Ralph's ophthalmic practice is based. If Abi is having an affair with him, maybe Ralph will be man enough to admit it. At least I can look him in the eye and see how he reacts. If he lies to me, I'm sure I'll be able to tell.

I park at the front of the practice and walk into a cavernous reception. It's one of those industrial buildings with exposed block work and no ceilings, just metal joists and air conditioning ducting left on show. It's cold and echoey. Even the furniture is minimalist and uncomfortable-looking. Typical of Ralph to pay more attention to style over the needs of his patients.

The receptionist on the front desk continues to type without looking up as I approach. It's a little power play. She knows I'm here, but she's making me wait. Putting me in my place. But I don't have time for games.

'I need to see Mr Hornstein,' I say. 'It's urgent.'

The woman stops typing and looks up at me over the top of her glasses with a startled expression, as if she can't believe I've interrupted her.

'Do you have an appointment?' she asks, snottily.

'No, just tell him Henry Hutton is here.' I won't be given the brush off by the receptionist. 'I'm a friend of his.'

'I'm afraid Mr Hornstein's diary is completely full today. I can make an appointment for you in —'

'I need to see him now.'

'Perhaps I could take a message?' She shoots me a steely eyed, thin smile.

I can see why Ralph's hired her. She's the perfect gatekeeper to keep all those needy patients off his back.

'I don't want to leave a message.' I feel my irritation levels rising. 'I need to see Mr Hornstein and I need to see him now.' I slap my hand on the counter for emphasis, making the receptionist jump.

An elderly woman sitting with a magazine in the waiting area glances up.

'We don't tolerate abuse against staff,' the receptionist says stiffly. 'Do you want me to call the police?'

'No,' I sigh. 'I just need to see Mr Hornstein.' The forceful approach isn't working. I need to change tack. 'Look, I'm sorry, I didn't mean to raise my voice, but there's an important personal matter that's come up that I really need to speak to him about. I only need five minutes of his time.' I force a friendly smile.

The receptionist stares at me for a moment or two and thaws a little.

'I can't promise anything,' she says, 'but give me your name again and I'll pass it to him before his next appointment. It's the best I can do.'

'Henry Hutton. Tell him it's about Abi.'

'Alright, take a seat.'

Twenty long minutes tick by before a door opens at the end of a gloomy corridor and Ralph appears with a wizened old man walking with the aid of a stick.

I vault out of my seat before the receptionist has a chance to warn him.

'Ralph!'

If he's surprised to see me, he doesn't show it. Maybe Abi's already spoken to him.

'Henry, what are you doing here? Is everything okay?'

Ralph guides the old man to the reception desk. The receptionist is already out of her seat.

'I'm so sorry, Mr Hornstein. I told him you were busy but he wouldn't take no for an answer.'

'It's okay.' Ralph waves her away.

'Can we go somewhere quiet? I need to talk to you,' I say.

Ralph glances at a faceless clock on the wall and nods. He takes me into a compact consulting room and sits at a desk. I remain standing.

'I know about you and Abi,' I say. There's no point beating around the bush.

He stares at me blankly. It's a pretty good poker face. 'What do you mean?'

He sits up straight and clears his throat. It's not much of a tell, but I think he knows exactly what I'm talking about. I continue to look at him, watching his face, saying nothing.

An awkward silence hangs heavily between us. He can't stand it. I know he'll feel the need to fill it.

I'm right. He sighs. 'Look, it was a long time ago, okay? I honestly thought you already knew. It meant nothing. We were both young and it really didn't amount to much. I'm sorry, I assumed Abi had told you.'

I take an involuntary step backwards like I've been punched in the face. I hadn't expected him to admit it so readily, but it's not the confession I'd expected.

'What do you mean, a long time ago? When?'

'At university. Seriously, it was nothing, mate.' Ralph frowns. 'How did you find out?'

I wish he wouldn't call me mate.

Abi had mentioned nothing about being in a relationship with Ralph while they were students. I knew they'd been friends, but I thought that was it. The idea of the two of them together, now I know it's true, sends spiders crawling over my skin.

How many times had they slept together? Where? And when? Part of me wants to know all the gory details, but I also know that once they're in my head, they'll be forever nibbling at my fragile ego. I'll never be able to forget. Maybe it's better I don't know.

'And more recently?' I ask.

Ralph's eyes narrow behind his expensive designer glasses. 'Recently?'

'Enough with the games. You're still seeing her, aren't you?'

'Of course not!' At least he has the decency to sound affronted.

I show him the photo on my phone.

'This was sent to me yesterday.'

His head wobbles. 'Who sent it?'

'It doesn't matter.'

'You mean, you don't know.'

I won't let him derail me. I didn't come here to talk about who sent the image or why. I'm only interested in getting to the truth about him and Abi.

'Are you sleeping with my wife?' I ask, with what I hope is a hint of menace.

'Of course I'm not! God. How can you even think that? I wouldn't do that to you, or Colette for that matter. We had lunch together. What's the big deal? I thought it might cheer her up after everything you guys have been through recently.'

It's exactly what Abi told me. Their stories match, but they could have colluded. She could have called him on her way to work. I really want to believe him, but it's not just the photo. There are the text messages between Abi and Felicity as well.

'Just lunch?'

'Just lunch,' Ralph says. 'Look, Abi's an amazing woman. She loves you and you're lucky to have her. I'd never come between the two of you. I respect you both too much.'

Respect? Huh!

'Someone's trying to fuck with you, mate. I don't know who or why, but you can't let the bastard screw up your marriage. You and Abs are great together, and you have two amazing daughters. It would be a terrible shame if you threw that all away because of a stupid photograph. Take my advice. Delete the picture and move on. I'm guessing you've already spoken with Abi?'

I nod.

'And how did that go?'

'She denied it too.'

'Because there's nothing going on.'

He would say that, wouldn't he? But what about the way he's looking at Abi in the picture? His hand on top of hers. And now I know they have a history. They were clearly attracted to each other once and you can't just turn your feelings for someone on and off, can you? Plus, there's that WhatsApp message.

Lie to him. Whatever you do, don't tell Henry.

Had Abi confided in Felicity about the affair?

I've heard enough from Ralph. I can't stand to spend another second in the same room with him. I turn on my heel and reach for the door, but hesitate with my hand on the handle.

'Does Colette know?' I ask.

'Does she know what?'

'That you're sleeping with Abi?'

'Didn't you hear me? I'm not sleeping with her,' Ralph says, jumping up.

But I'm already halfway out of the door. I've heard enough of his lies. I don't believe a word he's said.

I need some air and some space to think.

I've always thought Abi and I had a solid marriage and that nothing could come between us. I thought we were happy. But it's terrifying how quickly it's unravelled. And although I might not know the whole truth yet, I'm building a clearer picture of what's been going on.

If Abi's relationship with Ralph had only been casual when they were students, why had she never mentioned it before? I can only think of one reason. She still has feelings for him. What if they're like one of those couples in romantic comedies who tell themselves they're not supposed to be together and yet somehow keep returning to each other's beds until they finally realise they were always meant to be together?

Of course, it's not only *our* marriage this is going to destroy. I suspect Colette is still in blissful ignorance like I was before I saw that picture. But she deserves to know the truth about her husband.

And if he won't tell her, then I will.

Chapter 22

The school is on the other side of town and the traffic moves frustratingly slowly. As I crawl along, tapping the steering wheel, I plan how to break the news to Colette. People tend to blame the messenger when it's bad news. I only hope she's not angry with me. At least I'll be able to empathise with her. We're in the same boat. They've made fools of us both.

I park in the staff car park adjacent to the main school building in a flagrant breach of the rules. Parents aren't supposed to park on the school grounds. We're expected to park in the street. But screw the rules. What are they going to do? Sue me?

At the main entrance, I jam my finger on the door buzzer until someone lets me in. I throw the door open and march to the reception desk where the office secretary is sitting behind a plastic security screen, presumably to protect her from angry parents. I can't think of any other reason for it.

She recognises me when she looks up and smiles.

'Mr Hutton,' she says. 'Is everything alright?'

'I need to speak to Colette – I mean Mrs Hornstein.'

'Of course, I'll see if she's available.' Her manner couldn't be any more different than Ralph's receptionist. She doesn't ask if I have an appointment or question my right to see her.

I step back and watch as she picks up the phone, dials a number and waits for Colette to answer. She turns and smiles at me again.

'Mrs Hornstein, I have Norah and Katie Hutton's dad here asking if you're free to have a word,' I hear her say. 'Yes, of course. Right. Yes. Thank you.'

I raise an eyebrow as she hangs up.

'If you'd like to take a seat, she'll be right out,' she says. So helpful.

There are six chairs lined up along a wall decorated with a seascape collage of dolphins, whales, fish, octopus and even a mermaid, painted in rich blues and greens by the children. I take the chair closest to a door with Colette's name on it.

Two minutes later, the door opens and Colette steps out into the corridor with a beaming smile. She's plaited her hair into a neat, single braid that falls down her back and is wearing mushroom-coloured trousers and a taupe sweater. The poor woman has no idea of the devastating news I'm here to bring.

'Henry, what a lovely surprise. Come in. What can I do for you? Is it the girls? Problem?'

She sits behind a large oak desk in front of a casement window with views over the playing fields.

'No, it's not about the girls,' I say, pulling up a chair. 'They're fine.'

'I'm glad to hear it.' She laces her fingers together and rests her elbows on the desk, her head hung to one side, waiting for me to elaborate.

There's no point prevaricating. So I come right out and say it. 'Did you know about Abi and Ralph?'

Her eyebrows shoot up like I've flicked the end of her nose. 'What about them?'

'Did you know they had a thing going at university?'

'Oh, yes, that,' she says, sounding relieved. 'Absolutely. Water under the bridge. All happened a long time ago. Why?'

'Oh,' I say. 'You did?'

Am I the only one who's been kept in the dark?

'Of course. I don't think it was ever serious. Didn't Abi ever mention it?'

I shake my head. What an idiot I am. 'No,' I say. 'She didn't. I think they still have feelings for each other.'

I show her the photo on my phone.

'What do you make of this?'

Colette studies the picture through round spectacles that reflect the light so I can't see her eyes. Her brow furrows.

'Where's this come from?' she asks.

'It's Abi and Ralph, together,' I say, somewhat unnecessarily.

'Yes?' she shrugs. 'They're old friends. They meet up for lunch in town from time to time if they're free. It's what friends do.'

Colette hands the phone back to me.

'And it doesn't bother you?'

'Not really. Why, does it bother you?' she asks.

I sigh. 'I think they're having an affair.' I didn't want to be so blunt, but Colette's missing the point.

She stares at me for a second or two and then laughs.

'What's so funny? Don't you believe me?'

'I'm sorry, Henry, but I've known Abi for a long time. There's no way she'd cheat on you, especially not with Ralph.'

'But the photo? Did you see how he was looking at her? He's even holding her hand.'

Colette waves in the air, dismissively. 'You're reading too much into it,' she says. 'I can't believe you'd even think it. Is that why you came here? To tell me that?'

I hang my head. Have I really got it so wrong? Colette doesn't even seem open to the idea that there could be anything going on between them. Which would have been my reaction until last night.

'You never told me where the photo came from,' she says.

'It was sent to me anonymously.'

'Ah, I see. That makes sense.'

'What do you mean?'

'I guess it's come from the same man who sent that horrible letter and who damaged Abi's car? What's his name? Farrow?'

'Probably, but so what? The point is, Abi and Ralph have been carrying on behind our backs and you don't even bat an eyelid.'

'Oh, come on, Henry. You don't believe that any more than I do. It's absurd.'

'Is it?'

'Yes, of course it is. You need to ask yourself why the photo was sent to you. What were they hoping to achieve?'

'Yes, I know, but it doesn't mean it isn't true.'

'But you can't jeopardise your marriage because of one photograph that's clearly been sent intending to cause a rift between you and Abi.'

'There's something else,' I say. I'm on the verge of telling her about the text messages between Abi and Felicity. The proof that Abi's hiding something from me. If I tell her, it means admitting I've been going through Abi's phone and raises the spectre that she's been betrayed by not only Abi but Felicity too.

She arches an eyebrow. 'Yes?'

'It doesn't matter.'

'Have you talked to Abi?' Colette asks.

'She denied everything.'

'There you go then.'

'But she would, wouldn't she?'

'Then she can't win. You won't believe her, no matter what she tells you. I think you'd be better off finding out who's behind all this nonsense, Henry, rather than worrying about Abi's fidelity. It strikes me your priorities are all wrong. Now, I'm sorry, you'll have to excuse me. I'm supposed to be talking to the chairman of governors at eleven.'

She stands, walks out from around the desk, opens the door and steps to one side.

'That's it?'

'I'm sorry, Henry. I think you're behaving like a child. I suggest you go home, have a good think about everything you're about to throw away and then make peace with your wife. I only hope for your sake it's not too late.'

'Fine,' I say, getting up and brushing past Colette angrily. I'm not one of her pupils she can patronise. 'But don't say I didn't warn you when the truth comes out.'

I stomp down the corridor and rattle the main doors until the office secretary buzzes me out. The bloody school is more like a prison these days. I hurry to the car and sit with my head on the steering wheel and Colette's words hammering around my brain.

They meet up for lunch sometimes in town from time to time if they're free. It's what friends do.

If Colette knows they're meeting up regularly and doesn't worry, why should I? Ralph and Abi are friends. They've known each other for years. Is it that Abi's not keeping secrets from me, but her lunch dates with Ralph are so regular she doesn't feel they're worthy of mention? In which case, I've overreacted and maybe been too quick to cave in to my paranoia, nearly hitting the nuclear button on my marriage.

It's not as though Abi has been sneaking off for unexplained weekends away. I haven't stumbled across any mystery payments from our bank account. As far as I'm aware, she doesn't have a secret second phone and there's been no sudden loss of interest in sex. The more I think about it, there have been none of the warning signs I would have expected if Abi was cheating on me.

Just the photograph.

And the messages.

I suppose it's possible Abi and Felicity were talking about something entirely unrelated to Ralph. I'm still uneasy that Abi asked her to lie to me, though. But have I jumped to the wrong conclusion? And if that message wasn't about Ralph, then what?

I would have been a lot less suspicious if Abi had told me she and Ralph had had a fling when they were students. Maybe she was too embarrassed or didn't think I'd want to know. She's never been remotely interested in my love life before we met. It's a subject we simply don't discuss.

And so what if she enjoys the odd lunch with Ralph? It's not a crime. They're old friends. Just friends. Nothing else. Like Colette said, going for lunch together is what old friends do. There's nothing sinister about it. And as for that picture, who knows how many Farrow took before he settled on the one that makes it look like there's more going on than meets the eye.

Maybe it's not Abi who's making a fool of me. Maybe it's Joseph Farrow, leading me to doubt my own wife. Trying to drive us apart.

I should trust her more. Colette's right. My focus should be on the person who sent the photo in the first place and how to make it stop. Not looking to lay blame on Abi.

I'll phone her and apologise. I'll blame it on the stress. She'll understand, I hope. The sooner I do it, the better. It can't wait until tonight. I need to clear the air before she gets home.

I try her number, but it goes straight to voicemail. She's probably in court.

'Hi, it's me,' I say. 'I just wanted to say I'm sorry. I've been doing a lot of soul-searching today and I've realised I've been...'

I've been what? Rude? Judgemental? Distrustful? Dismissive? Probably all those things and more.

'... stupid. I shouldn't have accused you of cheating with Ralph. But I realise now I was wrong and, umm, I hope you can find it in your heart to forgive me. That's all. See you tonight. Love you.'

I drop my phone in my lap and bang my head with my hands.

Idiot!

I don't fancy spending the rest of the day cooped up on my own in the house, and it's too early to pick up the girls, so I go for a drive instead. I have nowhere to be, but driving always helps me to think.

I head out into the countryside, through lush green lanes and rolling hills, letting my mind drift. I hate fighting with Abi. It's not good for the girls either, to see their parents at each other's throats.

My phone on the passenger seat buzzes. I glance over. It's a message but I can't see who it's from. Hopefully, it's Abi letting me know she's picked up my voicemail.

I pull over in the entrance to a cow field to check.

My stomach twists. It's not Abi. It's from the number that sent the photo of Abi and Ralph together.

What now? Why can't he just leave us alone?

It's another photo.

I think about deleting it and blocking the number. That's the sensible thing to do.

But I can't.

My curiosity is an invisible force that drags my finger to the screen and taps in the unlock code.

I don't want to see what he's sent me now.

But there's a part of my brain that has to know.

I can't help myself. I click on the icon and open the image.

Chapter 23

The photo has been taken through the chain-link fence around the grounds of the school. It shows dozens of children running and playing with their coats hanging off their shoulders and socks bunched around their ankles.

And there, in the centre of the image, are my two beautiful girls. Norah, in a huddle with two others showing them something in her palm. And away to her left, Katie, chasing after a boy, her arms outstretched like she's about to catch him.

What the hell?

I clench the phone so tightly, my hand hurts.

The phone buzzes with a follow-up message.

Such pretty girls. Just like their mother.

A sickly burn scorches the back of my throat. Please, not the girls. Whatever this is, don't involve them. They're only children. I type a rapid reply. The first thing that comes into my head.

I'm warning you, stay away from them.

I wait anxiously for a response. A confirmation at least that Farrow's read and understood my message. That I won't stand for the girls to be involved in this.

When there's no response, I try again.

Do you understand? Whatever this is about, leave the girls out of it.

I grind my teeth as I watch and wait for confirmation the message has been delivered and read.

Another minute passes before my phone buzzes again. Finally. It's a single emoji.

A laughing face.

Bastard.

If he lays a finger on my daughters, I'll kill him. I'll hunt him down and break every bone in his body until he's begging for mercy.

It must be Joseph Farrow, although I still don't know for sure. He's the only one with any real motive. He's targeting me to get to Abi, but he's been careful not to reveal himself. Maybe I can get him to confirm his identity if I can string him along a bit.

I compose another message.

I know who you are and you don't scare me.

I wait with sweaty palms.

I think I do and you're terrified of how easily I can destroy your family.

I stab at the keyboard in frustration.

I know it's you, Joseph. Game's over. This ends now.

His reply makes me shudder.

This ends when I say it ends.

The message is accompanied by an angry face emoji, as if we're engaged in a teenage spat. I lower my phone and glance out of the windscreen with a stalking sense of dread. I'm in the middle of nowhere, so why do I feel as if I'm being watched? The hairs on my neck lift and my skin crawls. Has he been following me?

No, I'm being stupid. Of course he hasn't. He's at the school, watching the girls. I slam the car into gear and aggressively pull away, plotting the shortest route back in my head. It's nearly pickup time anyway.

I race back to the school, ignoring all the speed limits, and find a parking space on a side road. I sprint towards the playground, weaving around the early arrivals, young mothers ambling along with pushchairs and screaming toddlers. Everyone is a potential threat. Joseph Farrow or one of his cronies could be here right now, waiting for Katie or Norah. Plotting to snatch them.

I scan the playground, looking for a glimpse of a hooded top. Someone lurking in the shadows. Someone who's not supposed to be here. The problem is, I recognise some of the parents' faces, but not every one. And as more and more parents arrive, it's clear how easy it would be someone to hide in plain sight.

If he's here, I'm going to find him and I'm going to confront him. I've had enough of this. It's time to end it. Now.

Slowly the playground fills up, a broiling mass of parents chattering, the hum of small talk growing louder. It was bad enough that he approached Norah and handed her a package during school time, but he's crossed a line now and I won't let him get away with it.

A snaking line of children emerges from the rear of the school, accompanied by a teacher. The reception class is always first out. The children in the line look so young, hardly old enough to be in school, with their oversized uniforms hanging off their tiny frames and bags bigger than their bodies.

Two more classes follow, processing out in single file. The children wait until they've spotted a parent and only then are they allowed to run off. It's an excellent system to keep them safe.

Soon the playground is a chaotic shamble of children, coats, bags, and parents. Like a swarming mass of ants, everyone heads for the gates to leave.

Norah and Katie's classes always seem to be the last to be let out.

While I wait, I continue to scan the playground for someone who shouldn't be here.

And then I spot him.

He's by the gate with his back to me. A dark hood pulled over his head. Scruffy jeans. It looks like the same figure who was loitering outside our house a few nights ago. The same man I saw in the car park at work. Probably the same man who followed Abi through the estate.

He's got some nerve coming here.

I don't want to make a scene in front of everyone, but I have to tackle him. There's no point in calling the police. He'll be long gone before they get here.

I step out from the shadow of an oak tree and walk towards him, my eyes fixed on his back. When I lose sight of him for a few seconds among the milling throng, I panic and break into a jog.

There are so many people in my way. Parents, pupils and toddlers. Pushchairs. Bags. Coats. All holding me up. I slalom through the crowd, hurrying, panic and fear squeezing my chest.

I spot him again. He's leaning against a wall now, casually trying to blend in. Hands in his pockets. I almost trip over a rucksack abandoned on the ground, but catch my balance, bumping into a heavily pregnant woman.

'I'm so sorry,' I gasp, but I don't have time to stop.

I have a far bigger concern.

As I draw closer, I'm surprised he doesn't move. If he was here watching me, he isn't doing a very good job.

I reach out, grab him by the shoulder. At last, I'm going to face him eye to eye. I spin him around, my fists clenched.

'Hey! What are you doing?'

'I - I'm sorry,' I stammer, as a woman stares back at me, horrified. Her hair's scraped back from her face and tucked into her hood.

A boy runs up to her, swinging a bag. 'Hey, Mum,' he says.

'Hey, babes. Did you have a good day?' She leans down to kiss his cheek, glowering at me.

'I thought you were someone else,' I mumble.

'What do you think you're playing at?' she hisses at me, big gold hoops swinging from her ears. Her son runs off and she prods me in the chest with a bony finger, her fake nail digging through my shirt. 'That's assault, that is.'

Several other parents have fallen silent and are watching, horrified.

'I didn't mean —'

'What are you, some kind of pervert, grabbing women like that? I should report you.'

I back away with my hands up in apology.

The phone buzzes in my pocket. Grateful for the distraction, I pull it out and read the new message.

Tut. Tut.

It's followed a second later by another photo.

It's a picture of me with my hands on the woman I've just accosted. It looks like I'm about to punch her. But that's the least of my worries. It's proof that he *is* here, somewhere. Watching.

I look up and around, desperately hunting for his face in the crowd. But it's like he's a ghost, invisible but omnipresent.

'Daddy! Daddy!' Katie screams, running up to me from nowhere and grabbing my arm. 'I won an attendance certificate.'

But I'm not listening. I'm looking. All my energies focused on hunting out the man who's made it his mission to terrorise my family.

Now Norah arrives, barely acknowledging me as she walks past, chatting with her friends. A group of eight-year-olds going on twenty-eight.

I stand frozen to the spot, my limbs heavy and my heart pounding.

'Come on, Daddy, let's go home.' Katie's pulling me away. 'I'm hungry.'

I put a protective arm around her shoulder and pull her close. Then I give one final, quick look around the playground, hoping to spot something I've missed. But wherever he was, he's gone.

'Alright, I'm coming,' I say, letting my daughter tug me towards the gates.

I can't get out of the playground fast enough.

Chapter 24

Abi's home by six. I greet her in the hall with a chilled glass of chenin blanc. I have a lot of making up to do if she's going to forgive me.

'How was your day?' I ask cheerily as she slips her jacket off and hangs it on one of the pegs with the girls' coats.

'It was okay,' she says.

'Did you get my voicemail?'

'Yes.'

'And?'

'And what, Henry? What do you want me to say?'

'Am I forgiven?' I peel off my apron, scrunch it up and toss it onto the counter as I follow her into the kitchen.

'For what? Accusing me of trashing our wedding vows and cheating on you or for accusing me of an affair with one of my best friend's husband?'

'I said I'm sorry.'

'It's going to take a bit more than sorry. I would never cheat on you, but you were so quick to believe that stupid photo,' she says, finishing most of the glass of wine and topping it up from the bottle in the fridge.

'I've cooked Thai-style chicken wings.' Good food's always been my way of winning Abi around, whether it was when we were first dating or just to cheer her up after a bad day in court.

'How are we supposed to trust each other if you think that little of me?'

'I do trust you, but I wasn't thinking straight.' I run my fingers through my hair and massage the back of my neck. She's hurting badly and I'm not sure what to say to make it better. I desperately want to ask her about the WhatsApp message she sent to Felicity, but that would mean revealing I've accessed her phone without her knowledge. That probably would be grounds for divorce.

'How can I make it up to you?'

'I don't want you to make it up to me. I want you to trust me. And no more running off to Ralph and Colette with your wild accusations.' She fixes me with a penetrating glare as she leans across the counter like I'm a defendant in the witness box. She can be quite terrifying when she wants to be.

'You know I went to see them?'

'Of course I do. Colette called me as soon as you'd left the school. She was worried about me, which is more than I can say for you.'

'It won't happen again.' I lower my gaze to the ground and rub a patch of the linoleum with my toe. I'm ashamed I was so quick to jump to conclusions. Of course, Abi wouldn't cheat on me. I hope.

'I've never given you any reason not to trust me, have I? And yet, at the first sign of trouble, you immediately think the worst. How are we supposed to move on from that?'

'Why didn't you tell me you and Ralph had a thing at university?'

'What?'

'Ralph told me. He said you'd been in a relationship with him when you were students.'

Abi rocks back, her eyelashes flickering. 'It wasn't exactly a relationship,' she says, sounding defensive. 'It was more of a fling. And it was never serious. It was such a long time ago, I didn't think it was important.' Abi turns away to look out of the window, her glass hovering at her lips.

'If you had nothing to hide, why keep it a secret?'

'It wasn't a secret!' she says, spinning back around to face me.

'What else do you call it?'

'I know nothing about *your* previous girlfriends.'

'You never wanted to know,' I say. It's not a defence.

'I assumed you wouldn't want to know about me and Ralph.'

'You're still close friends. Can't you see how I might be suspicious?'

Abi chews on her lower lip. 'I guess.'

'Colette knew about it and I'm betting Felicity did as well.'

Abi shrugs. I think she's beginning to understand why I jumped to conclusions. 'I don't know. Maybe I should have said something. But really, there wasn't much to tell.'

I step closer, take her wine glass and put it on the side so I can hold both her hands. I stroke a stray strand of hair away from her face and look her in the eye. 'No more secrets?' I say.

She nods. 'No more secrets.'

'And I promise I'll never doubt you again.'

'Can't you see that's more important than ever, right now?' she says. 'I hate all these horrible things that have been happening to us, but we need to fight it together. That means being strong for the sake of Norah and Katie, if nothing else.'

'I agree.' I throw my arms around her and we hold each other, swaying like we're caught in a gentle breeze.

When she pulls away from me, her eyes red-rimmed.

'I love you,' she says.

I kiss her lips. 'And I love you.'

'So what are we going to do?'

'About Farrow?' I ask.

'Assuming it is him.'

'I don't know. Sit tight and hope it all blows over? What else can we do?'

'And if it doesn't?' Abi asks.

I breathe out through my nose. I don't have the answer. 'I had another message from him today.'

Abi's eyes open wide. 'What now?'

'Another photo.' I show Abi the picture of Katie and Norah in the school playground.

She snatches the phone out of my hand and holds it close to her face, her expression twisting in horror.

'When was this taken?'

'I'm not sure. Today I think.'

She grasps the edge of the counter as her knees buckle. 'Please, no,' she gasps. 'Not the girls.'

'They're okay. They're safe. He's not touched them,' I reassure her.

'What the hell was he doing at the school again?'

'It's just another way to frighten us. He knows he can get to us through the girls.'

'Did you warn Colette?'

'To be honest, I went straight to school, picked the girls up and brought them home where I know they'll be safe,' I say. 'I wanted to speak to you first.'

'I'd better let her know.' Abi staggers off to look for her phone.

'We ought to let the police know as well,' I say when she returns. 'In fact, I suppose we should also let them have the number it was sent from. Maybe they can trace the phone or something.'

Abi nods as she taps at her mobile, typing out a message, I assume to Colette.

'I thought I spotted him this afternoon, while I was waiting for Katie and Norah,' I say. 'Turned out to be the wrong person, but then he sent me another picture of me and this woman in the playground.'

'He was in the school?'

'He must have been. He could have been hiding among the other parents. Who's to know it's not someone with a child at the school? I don't recognise everyone.'

'He could have taken the girls,' Abi says.

'I don't think so,' I say, although I'm not so sure. In the confusion of pickup, it wouldn't be that difficult to snatch a child, although I'd like to think neither Norah nor Katie would go off willingly with a stranger. 'But it won't harm to talk to them again about stranger danger.'

The thought of someone taking either of the girls was too horrible to imagine.

'I don't like this,' Abi says, putting her phone down and folding her arms. 'He's got us running around in circles, first trying to split us up and now threatening the girls. What's he going to do next?'

'Perhaps we should try to get away for a few days,' I suggest. 'Just the four of us. Somewhere he can't find us. It would give us a chance to plan what we're going to do.'

'I don't know. It's a nice idea but we can't really justify taking the girls out of school and I have so much work on at the moment.'

'I'm sure if we explain to Colette, she won't object to the girls missing a few days of school — '

I was going to suggest Abi could find someone to help with her caseload, but I'm interrupted by an intrusive knock at the door.

'Who's that?' I hiss.

'I don't know. Check the cameras. I thought that was why you had them installed.'

'Yeah, good point.' I open the app on my phone and inspect the feed from the camera over the door. 'It's Johnny. What's he doing here?'

Abi relaxes like she's been deflated.

'I'm not psychic. Why don't you find out?'

Johnny's the last person I need to see tonight. Well, maybe not the last person. It would be worse if it was Ralph. I slowly unbolt and unlock the front door. Johnny's standing on the doorstep with his hands in his pockets, chewing gum.

'Hey, Henry,' he says, like I'm a long-lost friend. He grabs my hand and slaps my upper arm. He's far too over-friendly. 'Do you fancy a beer? I thought we could hit the town and let our hair down for a bit. What do you say?'

I narrow my eyes and stare at him suspiciously. Johnny has never asked me to go for a drink with him. I'm so surprised, I'm lost for words.

'Grab your coat. I'm sure Abs can cope without you for one evening.'

'Um, I'm not sure,' I say. 'It's not really a good time. We've not eaten yet, and it's not fair to leave Abi to cope with bedtime.'

'Come on, she won't mind. Let me talk to her.' He pushes past me into the hall and swaggers into the kitchen like he owns the place.

By the time I catch him, he's hugging Abi and kissing her on both cheeks.

'Johnny, what a pleasant surprise,' she says. From the smile on her face, she's more pleased to see him than I am.

'Johnny wants to go for a beer but I explained that we've not eaten yet and the girls are still up.'

'Abs, you can cope on your own for one night, right?' Johnny says.

'Of course. You should go. Have fun.'

I try subtly shaking my head at Abi, but she either doesn't see, or she ignores me.

'I was going to get an early night,' I protest. 'It's been a trying few days.'

'All the more reason to come out and blow off some steam. Come on, don't be a wet blanket.'

'Maybe just for an hour,' I say. He won't take no for an answer.

'That's the spirit. Don't wait up,' he says to Abi.

And the next thing I know, I'm pulling on my shoes and coat and heading out of the house.

Chapter 25

The bar is hot, noisy and full of students. I thought we'd be going to a quiet pub where we could talk, but the place Johnny's chosen is more like a nightclub, a basement dive with ornate arches supporting a curved brick ceiling. Garish neon signs decorate the walls and there's even a DJ playing pumping music that's so loud I can hardly hear Johnny when he asks me what I want to drink.

I lean casually on the bar, trying to look like I fit in, but it feels as though everyone's looking at me, wondering what an old git like me is doing in a place like this. I'm like a fish on a bike.

Johnny doesn't seem to share my discomfort in the slightest. He blends in better than I do with his designer jeans, crumpled linen shirt open halfway down his chest and his hair styled and waxed in a fashionable tousled rough crop.

I'd have made more of an effort if I'd known where he planned to take me. I'd have put on a clean pair of jeans for a start. And I'd definitely have left my jumper and waterproof at home. Not cool at all.

I hop up onto a barstool and try to relax with the throb of a banging dance tune ringing in my ears.

Johnny picks up his pint with a practised nonchalance and raises it to a group of young women who approach the bar.

'Evening ladies,' he says, with a smarmy smile.

What a creep.

They giggle, order drinks and move away.

'Tough day?' he says, returning his attention to me.

'I've had better.' I sip my Coke. I can't risk a fuzzy head drinking alcohol. I need to keep my brain focused until we've resolved our problems with Joseph Farrow.

Johnny nods sagely, like he understands exactly what I've been going through. But how can he understand how impotent I feel? How completely helpless, vulnerable and emasculated it's left me? What would he have done in my shoes? I'm sure a man like Johnny wouldn't have let things spiral out of control in the way I have. He'd have confronted it head-on, like a bull defending its calf. I doubt he'd have put bars on his windows and ended up feeling like a prisoner in his own home. It's not his style.

'I heard about the photo,' he says.

'Abi and Ralph?'

He nods. 'You still reckon it's this guy, Farrow?'

'I can't think who else it could be.' It's disconcerting to have to shout to be heard.

'Poor Abi.'

What? Poor Abi? What about me? I'm the one he's been messaging with creepy texts and photos.

'You must be worried about the girls too?' he says.

'You heard he was at school taking pictures of them?'

'What a sick bastard.' Johnny checks his watch. It's the third time in less than three minutes.

'Waiting for someone?' I ask.

But he's already climbing off his stool. I follow his gaze and spot Ralph sidestepping through a crowd on the dance floor.

What the hell is he doing here?

He heads straight towards us as if he knew we'd be here, which clearly he did. I've been set up.

'I didn't realise Johnny had invited you too,' I say.

'He thought it would be a good idea for us to meet on neutral territory to clear the air.'

I groan inwardly. Clear the air? And Johnny had chosen this place? What was he thinking?

Ralph holds out his hand. 'No hard feelings?'

What could I do other than accept his olive branch, beyond storming out and making a scene? Abi would never forgive me.

'No hard feelings,' I say, as he grips my hand and nearly crushes my fingers. It's his way of reminding me who's the alpha male.

'Did you really think Ralph was shagging Abi?' Johnny slaps us both on the back and laughs.

I wince at his crassness. I'm still not entirely happy that Abi hadn't mentioned they'd been together romantically at university or that they were meeting regularly for lunch.

'It was a misunderstanding,' I mumble. 'I've had a lot on my plate.'

'No harm done, eh?' Johnny yells. 'All friends together again.'

Friends? That's pushing it. I have next to nothing in common with Johnny or Ralph. They are both as loud and boorish as each other, not to mention self-centred, arrogant, egotistical, self-absorbed and image-obsessed. I only put up with them because they're the husbands of my wife's best friends.

And I've still not forgotten how their behaviour got us kicked out of *Meld*. Their sense of entitlement ruined the evening for us all. Just because you have money and run a successful business doesn't give you the right to behave like you're better than everyone else. I still cringe at how they reduced that waitress to tears. It was unforgivable. No wonder the owner had thrown us out. And yet Johnny and Ralph thought it was all one big joke. A funny anecdote to share.

What they didn't seem to get was that people's feelings had been trampled on. And when people get hurt, it leaves scars.

'You know I'd never do anything to come between you two, don't you?' Ralph says, standing with a pint of lager in one hand and the other hand in the pocket of his chinos. 'We're just good friends.'

So why does the thought of them together leave me feeling so queasy? I wish I hadn't found out about their past. Now when I see Ralph, all I can think about is his sweaty hands pawing my wife's body, his mouth tracing the curve of her neck. Needles of jealousy prick my insides.

'What you really need to worry about is that someone was following Abi and watched us have lunch,' he says. 'And if it is this scumbag Farrow, you need to do something about it.'

'I don't know it's him for sure, but I can't think of anyone else who'd have it in for us. He sent me a picture of the girls today.'

Ralph's eyes widen. 'That's not good.'

'But what can I do? I've made the house secure, but I can't watch Abi and the girls twenty-four hours a day.'

'Like we said before, you're going to have to confront him,' Johnny says. 'You need to make him see he's messing with the wrong man.'

Not this again.

'I can't,' I say. 'You don't know what he's like.'

'We could have a word with him,' Ralph says. Johnny nods like this is a plan they've worked out in advance, dismayed I've not sorted it out myself.

'I wouldn't go near him,' I say. 'He's a total psycho. He's spent most of his adult life in and out of prison.'

'He's just a bully,' Johnny says, 'who needs putting back in his box.'

'I told you before, you need to fight fire with fire,' Ralph adds.

Fire? Now I'm nervous. The last time we had this conversation, Ralph suggested I should torch Farrow's house.

'It's the only language they understand,' Ralph continues.

'It's fine, thank you,' I snap. 'I can protect my family. I'll deal with it.'

'Will you though?' Ralph asks. 'Abi's a good friend. I'd hate to see anything happen to her.'

Chapter 26

It's still dark when I wake with a dry mouth, my nose blocked and my ears ringing from the loud music in the bar. I roll over and reach for my phone. The screen lights up my hand and through the crack of one eye, I read that it's only four twenty in the morning.

I put the phone back and collapse into the pillow with a silent groan. Waking up far too early is becoming an increasingly regular occurrence, particularly since the trouble with the Farrows started.

I'd wanted to leave the bar by about half nine, but Johnny and Ralph had persuaded me to stay for one more drink at a quieter cocktail bar where they were playing chilled jazz rather than thumping club tunes. Fortunately, there was no more talk about what I should do to protect my family, and they both seemed far more interested in talking about themselves than my problems. So I stayed and even shared a whisky with them, which to be fair, did wonders at knocking off the edge of my anxiety.

Abi was asleep when I arrived home and didn't stir when I climbed into bed.

Now I'm awake, I roll my head to face her. She's tucked up under the duvet with only the top of her head poking out, facing towards the window, away from me. From the way she's breathing, I can tell she's still sound asleep.

I close my eyes and imagine lying on a sun-kissed beach somewhere in the Caribbean, soft golden sand between my toes and a cool breeze wafting off the sea. But sleep is beyond me. I'm wide awake, although my eyes feel like they're swollen inside my head.

Eventually, I get bored with lying there chasing sleep, prop myself up on my pillow and pick up my phone again. Ten minutes of scrolling through some social media might be all I need to send me off.

But the more I look, the wider awake I become.

If it was lighter, I'd consider getting up and going for a bike ride while the traffic's light, but I can feel how cold it is outside the warmth of the bed and it's easier to lie here scrolling through endless reams of rubbish than to force myself to get up.

I flick aimlessly through some recipes of vague interest, watch a video of a cat pulling silly faces and get worked up over a story someone's posted about plans for another two thousand homes to be built on the outskirts of the town.

And then I find something that makes me stop scrolling and snatch my breath.

It's a news article from the local paper about a house fire. The details are scant, but there's enough to make my pulse race.

Breaking news
Firefighters are dealing with a serious fire at a house in Ashford.

It's reported that the blaze broke out at a property in Kepple Street at around 1am after the alarm was raised by neighbours.

There are unsubstantiated reports that two bodies have been found in the house which locals have confirmed belonged to Joseph Farrow, whose sons were recently convicted of the torture and murder of Billy Bowden.

Police and fire crews are expected to give an update later.

I stare at the name. Joseph Farrow. And swallow down the lump that's grown in my throat. A million thoughts race through my mind.

I click on a video attached to the story and watch dramatic footage of a house engulfed in fire. Flames lick out of the windows while mushrooming black clouds of smoke pour from under the eaves of the roof into the ink-black sky.

It looks like it's been filmed on a mobile phone, shot in portrait mode on a blurry background, wobbling as whoever's filming moves around with an unsteady hand. Pulsing blue lights illuminate the backs of half a dozen heads belonging to what I presume are neighbours who've come out to watch. People in T-shirts and dressing gowns, staring in muted shock. The indistinct shadows of firefighters moving back and forth in front of the house and a jet of water being fired from a long hose.

The footage only lasts for a minute or two and when I've watched it, I hit play and watch it all over again.

'Abi,' I hiss, rocking her shoulder.

'Mmm,' she mumbles from the depths of sleep.

'Abi, wake up. You need to see this.'

'What time is it?'

'Early. Look!' I hold the phone to her face as she rolls over onto her back.

She grabs my wrist and pushes it away to a distance she can see.

'What is it?'

'A fire at Joseph Farrow's house.'

'What?' Suddenly she's wide awake, propped up on her elbows, holding my hand steady as she watches the video. Then I read out the report and we stare at each other in silence.

I've never wished anyone dead, but if it's true, and one of those bodies is Farrow's, it could be the end of our nightmare.

Of course, we don't know for sure that it's Joseph Farrow who's been making our lives a misery, but all the evidence points in his direction.

'Bloody hell,' Abi says at last.

'I know. It's unreal, isn't it?'

My stomach shamefully fizzes with excitement. It's so insensitive to feel like that about someone's tragic death, but my body can't disguise my true feelings. Farrow has made our lives a living hell and if he's dead, well, I won't be losing any sleep.

'What a horrible way to die,' Abi says, 'trapped in your own home. I can't imagine how terrifying that must have been.'

'If they were asleep, they might have been overcome by smoke and knew nothing about it,' I say. The alternative, that Farrow was awake and confronted by an inferno with no way out, is unimaginable. He might have been a psycho, but it was a horrible way for anyone to die.

It's a bit of a coincidence that only a few hours earlier, Ralph and Johnny had been talking about dealing with Farrow for me.

What was it Ralph had said?

I told you before, you need to fight fire with fire.

Was he being literal? He'd been more to the point when he'd been here for dinner.

Petrol through the letterbox while he's asleep. Light a match and it's goodnight Vienna. Boom!

Surely he couldn't have been that stupid, could he? I didn't ask him to do it. In fact, I'd explicitly told them not to interfere.

'There's something I need to tell you,' I say, pinching the bridge of my nose. We'd only promised each other yesterday that we'd keep no more secrets. I have to tell Abi what Johnny and Ralph had said.

'What?'

She knows I'm about to drop a bombshell. Did she pick it up in the tone of my voice?

'I'm not really sure how to tell you this, so I'm just going to come right out and say it.'

'For Christ's sake, Henry, spit it out. What is it?'

'The fire,' I say, fiddling with the phone in my lap. 'I think Johnny and Ralph might have had something to do with it.'

For a moment, I think Abi's going to laugh. Does she really think I'm joking?

'What?'

'It was something they said last week when they were here for dinner. They were telling me I needed to stand up to Farrow and not be bullied. Ralph then sort of suggested the easiest way to do it would be to start a fire. I didn't think he was serious, but he said something similar again last night.'

Abi shakes her head, deep furrows appearing across her forehead. 'He said what?'

'He suggested I pour petrol through the Farrows' letterbox and put a match to it,' I say.

'Don't be ridiculous. Why would Ralph say that?'

'I guess he was trying to help. I don't know, he was drunk. I didn't take it seriously, but now, this...'

'No,' Abi says, like she can't or won't believe it. 'He would never do that. It's insane. He just wouldn't.'

She wrings her hands, her knuckles turning white.

'How can you be so sure?' I ask gently. I never thought he'd be capable of it either, but the coincidence is too stark to ignore. Within hours of Ralph offering to help me deal with Joseph Farrow, a house fire appears to have caused his death.

'Because I know him!'

'You certainly do,' I say, flippantly. The words trip off my tongue before I can stop them. I shouldn't have said it, but I'm still wrangling with the revelation that they slept together as students. That they share a secret history.

'What's that supposed to mean?'

'Nothing.' I wonder if she'd be so quick to defend me?

'I can't believe you could think he could have anything to do with something so heinous,' she says.

'But I can't ignore what he said. And if the police are investigating...'

'What are you trying to say, Henry?' She turns to me, her eyes burning with indignation.

She knows what I'm thinking, but she wants me to say it. Challenging me to see if I have the balls.

'If Ralph started that fire and people have died, I have to tell the police what he said.' I lower my gaze, unable to look her in the eye. She's going to hate me for it, but how can I not say anything? That would make me complicit.

'Absolutely not. No way, Henry. I won't allow it.'

'So you're asking me to cover it up?'

'I'm telling you there's no need to inform the police.'

'I see, and if he did it? Then what? What if it emerges that we knew all along and said nothing? What do you think that's going to do for your career?'

'He was drunk. You said it yourself. He didn't know what he was saying.'

I can't believe what she's asking.

'I think the police would be the best judge of that,' I say.

'So you'd happily ruin Ralph's reputation because of one drunken conversation,' she says. 'Because once the police arrest him, his reputation will be tarnished, whether or not he did it.'

'But it's the right thing to do,' I insist.

She stares at me, her steely eyes boring into my skull.

'I know what this is really about,' she says. 'This isn't about the fire. This is about getting one over on Ralph, isn't it? You're jealous of him. Of us. And this is your petty way of getting back at him.'

'No,' I protest. The thought hadn't even occurred to me. 'It's not like that.'

'Isn't it?'

'Of course not.'

'Then don't do it. Don't say anything to the police.' She takes my hand and strokes it. 'Please, Henry. Do it for me, if you love me.'

I'm damned if I do and damned if I don't. But I can't afford to fall out with Abi again, not after we've only just made up.

'Fine,' I say.

'Thank you.'

'But I'm not happy about it.'

Neither of us gets back to sleep, our thoughts consumed by the fire, Joseph Farrow and the suspicion Ralph may have been involved.

Eventually, we give up, get up early and have breakfast with the girls. It's rare that we all sit down to eat together, but I can't enjoy it. Not until we know more about what's happened to Farrow. We put the TV on in the kitchen and keep half an eye out for the local news, hoping there'll be an update.

Sure enough, it's their top story on the seven-thirty bulletin. They show the same grainy footage of the house in flames I'd seen online, but there's no further information about bodies. They don't even mention that there have been any deaths.

Abi and I tiptoe around each other, barely speaking while trying to maintain the appearance of normality in front of Katie and Norah. Abi drops her mug in the sink and pulls on her shoes, balancing with one hand on the back of a chair.

'I'd better get going,' she says.

'Let me know if you hear anything.'

She grabs her briefcase and is about to leave when her phone rings. She answers without checking who's calling.

'Oh hi,' she says, glancing at me and arching her eyebrows. The way her whole body goes rigid suggests it's someone important.

'Who is it?' I mouth, but she turns away to concentrate on the call.

'Yes, we saw,' she says. 'Right, I see. Are you sure? Okay, thanks for letting me know.'

She hangs up and stares at the phone, the colour draining from her cheeks.

'Abi?'

She looks up, startled, as if she's forgotten I'm in the room. 'That was Steve Hicks, my police contact. He was calling about the fire.'

I slowly put down the bowl I was carrying to the dishwasher. 'And? What did he say?'

'He confirmed they've found two bodies.' She hesitates for a beat, sucking in her bottom lip. 'They're still waiting for formal identification but they think it's Joseph Farrow and his partner.'

I release the breath I'm holding. My legs go limp and a rush of jubilation spreads from my stomach. Joseph Farrow dead. Gone. Out of our lives forever. I shouldn't be so thrilled about someone's death, but it's as if a switch has been flipped and all my worries and anxieties are fading away. I grab the counter for support and shake my head in disbelief.

'That's it then,' I gasp. 'It's over.'

'Who's Joseph Farrand?' Norah asks, looking up from the book I thought she was immersed in, her mispronunciation bringing a smile to my lips.

'Nobody, sweetheart. Nobody we have to worry about.'

Abi stares at me, blinking rapidly. She licks her lips and swallows. She doesn't look as relieved as I feel. She's probably in shock. This calls for a celebration. Maybe I'll pop a bottle of bubbly in the fridge for later.

'They're treating it as arson,' Abi says. 'Steve said someone poured an accelerant through their letterbox in the early hours while they were asleep upstairs. They found the bodies in their bed.'

We stare at each other for a yawning age, neither of us sure what to say, but I guess we're thinking the same thing.

'Don't say it,' Abi says as I open my mouth to speak. She waves a stiff finger at me, her eyes pricked with tears.

'We need to discuss it,' I say.

She darts a glance at Norah and Katie. 'Not now. We'll talk tonight.'

There's little point arguing. She doesn't want to hear it right now. Better I let her process it for a while. Maybe she'll see sense when she thinks it through. But we can't sit on our hands and say nothing. If there's any chance Ralph was involved in starting the fire, we're duty-bound to report it. Especially as it's now murder. She, more than anyone, must know that.

Abi picks up her briefcase and marches out of the house without uttering another word. She doesn't even say goodbye to the girls. Her mind must be in absolute turmoil, which makes me wonder about the depth of feeling she still has for Ralph.

I hurry the girls upstairs to clean their teeth.

It's funny to think that I'd been worried about sending them to school today after receiving that photo of them in the playground, but now there's nothing to fear. The threat's gone. Snuffed out like a candle.

I recall the words etched into the glass on Abi's Mini and smile at the irony.

Rot in hell.

Well, exactly. We never asked Farrow to come into our lives. It was his choice to start something. Not mine. And not Abi's. I guess it's true what they say. You reap what you sow.

Chapter 27

On the way to school, the girls and I sing our hearts out. It's worrying how many Little Mix lyrics I know off by heart. I crank up the stereo and hammer out the beat on the steering wheel, not caring who hears us. The sun is shining, there's hardly a cloud in the sky and I'm feeling good. The heaviness I've been carrying on my shoulders for the last week has been lifted and I feel as light as air.

'Shall we have pizza for tea?' I suggest.

'Yes!' Norah and Katie chorus.

I only usually let them have pizza as a special treat, on birthdays and on holiday. But today feels special. We'll wait until Abi gets home and eat together around the table. Or even better, in front of the TV, as it's a celebration.

When I get home, I might call Sanjay and see if he's free to remove the bars on the windows. I can smile about it now. Who the hell fits bars on the windows of their own home? The neighbours must think we're insane. I can't wait to get some normality back into our lives.

I drop the girls off in the playground, carefully avoiding the woman I mistakenly confronted yesterday when I see her dropping off her son. I kiss the girls' heads, tell them I love them and when the bell rings, watch with a swelling heart as they run off to class.

I deliberately avoid switching on the radio on the way home. I don't want to hear any more about the fire or the Farrows for the time being. I want to savour this moment of freedom and relief.

When I pull up onto the drive, a supermarket delivery van is parked outside Paul and Linda's house. Paul's on the doorstep taking bags of shopping in from the delivery driver. It reminds me, I need to chase up the pest controller.

Paul sees me, smiles and waves. I wave back. I might pop in later and tell them our news. I'm sure they'll be pleased to hear our troubles are over. But as I'm about to climb out of the car, my mobile rings. It's Ralph. The last person I expect to hear from.

Curious, I answer. 'Hey, Ralph.'

'I take it you've seen the news?' he says. 'There's been a fire at Joseph Farrow's house.'

He sounds shocked, but is he feigning it?

'Yes, I saw.'

'And they've found two bodies.'

I unclip my seatbelt and sit staring across our lawn at the bars on the lounge window, remembering the night Farrow put a rock through it. I can still see the pink stain of the red paint he threw across the front of the house. I don't care that he's dead. I feel no remorse. No sadness. Only relief.

I pray Ralph's not about to confess his involvement. There's no way I can avoid reporting it to the police if he does, not without risking being charged with perverting the course of justice.

'I mean, you must be so relieved,' he continues. 'It's terrible, of course, if anyone has died, but I imagine you and Abi are feeling pretty content right now?'

'Yeah,' I say. 'We're glad it's all over.'

'And how's Abi?'

'Good,' I say. 'Shocked.'

'Of course. Stands to reason. It's weird though, isn't it? Wasn't I only saying the other day that the best way to tackle the problem was head-on? I think I even suggested torching the bastard's house.' He chuckles a nervous laugh.

Is he accusing me?

There's an uncomfortable silence as he waits for me to say something.

'I mean, you didn't, did you?' he eventually asks.

'Seriously?'

'Right, no, of course not. Absolutely,' he says. 'But it's a bit of a coincidence.'

'It was your suggestion, Ralph,' I say, incensed that he could even think I could do something like that. 'Perhaps I should ask you the same question.'

'I was joking.'

'Joking?'

'Yeah.'

'Right,' I say. 'It wasn't very funny.'

'No, you're probably right.'

I start work on the pizza dough as soon as I get in and I've made myself a coffee. As I measure out the flour, Ralph's accusation still rattles around my head.

How could he think I'd have anything to do with the fire? If anything, it makes him look even more guilty, like he's trying to deflect the blame. I still have a hard time believing he'd have it in him. He's an optician after all. Not a member of the Mafia. Unless Johnny egged him on. No, it was crazy. One of those strange coincidences. I'm sure a man like Joseph Farrow had lots of enemies, people he'd crossed who wanted him dead. Live by the sword. Die by the sword.

I sprinkle flour liberally over the counter and knead the dough until it's smooth and elastic. Then I wrap it in clingfilm and leave it to prove in a warm cupboard.

The bars on the kitchen window cast long shadows across the floor as the sun rises to its midday peak. I might as well try Sanjay and see if he's free to come back this week. There's no point waiting. And the sooner the bars are off the window, the happier Abi will be.

I find his number in my phone but it goes straight to voicemail. I leave a brief message asking him to call back and toss the phone on the side.

I'm about to fetch the laundry basket to start on the washing when it buzzes. It's probably Sanjay calling back. I snatch it up and freeze. It's not a call. It's a message.

Did you read about the fire?

An icy shiver runs down the length of my body and I almost drop the phone. I glance up, as if there's someone in the room with me and shake my head, trying to understand, to make sense of what I'm seeing. It's impossible. The message has come from Joseph Farrow's number. The same number that sent me the photos of Abi and Ralph and the girls in the playground.

What the hell is going on?

Farrow is dead. The police as good as confirmed it to Abi. So how the hell is he sending me a message from the grave?

Unless I'm losing my mind, there's only one logical explanation.

It isn't Joseph Farrow.

It was never Joseph Farrow.

Does it mean all this time we've been looking in the wrong direction? I can't think of any other explanation, which means something infinitely worse. It means a stranger is terrorising us. An unknowable menace like an indistinct shadow flitting behind the heroine in a haunted house. Or a dark silhouette sliding beneath a stranded boat in the middle of the ocean.

If it isn't Farrow, then who? Someone with a grudge? No, it's more than a grudge. A vendetta. Someone who feels so strongly, they've taken the time and effort to make our lives a living hell.

But I can't think of anyone we've upset, at least not to the extent that would warrant this. Yes, there have been a few occasions when I've lost my cool behind the wheel and may have angrily exchanged cross words with another driver. But nothing to explain this kind of behaviour.

Something to do with work then? A disgruntled applicant who's had their plans for an extension or conservatory rejected? But I can't think of anyone. No one who's made a complaint at least.

The most likely explanation is still that it's someone who's been prosecuted by Abi. Someone who thinks they're the victim of a miscarriage of justice, perhaps?

The fact is, I don't know. And that's terrifying.

With trembling hands, I compose a reply.

Who is this?

The response is almost instant.

You really don't know?

It's accompanied by a laughing face emoji, like this is some kind of game. But it's not a game. It's sick.

My phone buzzes again.

Didn't you think the flames were pretty?

I take an involuntary step back, almost as if I've been punched square in the chest as I'm struck by a terrible realisation. It's worse than I ever thought it could be. Slowly, I type out a reply.

Did you start the fire at the Farrows' house?

An instant response.

Do you think I did?

My head spins. If they did, I can't see any reason for it. Whoever this is, they're completely and utterly criminally unhinged.

I don't know what to think anymore. Who is this? And why are you doing this to us?

I hit send, but it's met with cold, hard silence. I stare at the screen, willing a response to appear. I desperately need answers to make sense of this all, but they don't come. I guess whoever this is doesn't want to give me the satisfaction of any easy answers. All part of the mind games they've played with us from the moment we received that first anonymous letter.

One death was too much.

Two is unbearable.

An eye for an eye seems only fair after what you've done.

So now I have nothing left to lose, I'll see you in hell.

I still don't know about the letter's meaning. What are these two deaths if not a reference to the Billy

Bowden court case?

With my anger and frustration building, I toss the phone across the room. It smashes against the wall and tumbles to the floor as my legs give way and I slump to the ground, sliding down a cupboard door. I sit with my head in my hands, defeated.

How the hell do I make this stop?

It's driving me insane and I can't see any way to make it end. I can't bear the taunting, the constant need to look over my shoulder, the unrelenting fear of what's going to happen next.

Unless...

Could it be a case of mistaken identity? If there's no obvious motive to target me and Abi, then that has to be the logical conclusion. They either think we've done something we haven't. Or they've confused us with someone else.

Yes, that has to be it.

Although there was that message on Abi's phone I wasn't supposed to have seen.

Lie to him. Whatever you do, don't tell Henry.

Did that have something to do with this? What's the secret Abi's keeping from me? The only way to find out for sure is by confronting her and asking her outright. I'd have to confess I'd been looking on her phone, but the fallout from that has to be better than the purgatory we're going through. Anything would be an improvement on this continued torment. It's like being locked in a dark room with no windows and realising you're not alone, but with no idea who or what is locked inside the room with you.

I thought by making the house more secure, I'd feel safer. I thought we could shut out all the bad things and ride out the storm. But I was wrong. The walls of the house feel like they're closing in on me, suffocating me. I've spent a fortune on locks and cameras and bars on the windows, but we're still being tormented.

On the other side of the room, my phone buzzes and rattles across the floor with another incoming message.

I hesitate to look, fearful of what's coming next.

But I can't ignore it. Maybe it's finally an answer to one of my many questions.

I drag myself across the floor. A spider's web of cracked glass obscures the phone's screen, but I can still read the message clearly.

You know

What the hell does that mean? What am I supposed to know? Who is this? What do they want? I don't have a clue. I type a hurried reply.

I don't know what you mean.

But I get the same response.

YOU KNOW

'The point is, I don't fucking know,' I scream at my phone. My head feels like it's been clamped in a vice. My whole body shakes.

And then there's a knock at the door.

Chapter 28

The knock echoes through the empty house, sharp and businesslike, snatching the breath from my lungs. A crazy thought percolates into my head. What if it's them, outside? Here at the house.

I'm being paranoid.

It's the middle of the day. They wouldn't come here.

I check the CCTV feed on my phone. There's a man standing outside the door in a scruffy navy-blue linen jacket and creased trousers. His tie hangs loose, and a leather satchel is slung across his back. He's studying the front of the house, no doubt wondering why anyone would put bars on their windows. I don't recognise him. A salesman?

I watch him curiously for a moment or two. When I don't answer the door, he knocks again. Louder.

I might as well see what he wants. At least it's a distraction from my anxieties.

I unlock and unbolt the door and peel it open just wide enough to peer out.

'Whatever you're selling, I'm not interested,' I say.

The guy ignores my stony reception and smiles broadly, his eyes sparkling. He's not easily put off, which suggests he's used to cold calling.

'I'm not trying to sell anything,' he says. 'I'm a reporter from the local paper. It's Henry Hutton, is it? I wondered if I could have a quick word?'

A journalist? That's all I need.

'If it's about the fire, I don't know anything,' I blurt out. Why would he be here about the fire? There's nothing to connect me with the Farrows unless he's here to talk to Abi because of her involvement in the court case?

The guy frowns. 'It's nothing to do with a fire. It's about your blog, Nosher Bites Back.' He throws me another disarming smile.

I'm momentarily thrown. Hardly anyone knows about the blog and all the reviews have been written anonymously. My name shouldn't be linked with it at all.

'How do you know about that?' I ask, taking a step back and letting the door open wider.

'Everyone's talking about it,' the journalist says.

'What?'

The blog has a small but dedicated following of a couple of hundred people. As far as blogs go, it's a minnow.

'Especially that fantastic piece you wrote about *Meld*.' He grins so widely, I think his face might split in two.

I wasn't particularly happy with Nosher's review of *Meld*. I wonder in retrospect if it was overly harsh, our experience tainted by the humiliation of being thrown out and the way we'd been treated by the celebrity chef who ran it. It could probably do with a rewrite now we've all had time to calm down.

'You've read it, then?' I ask sheepishly.

'Read it? I've got a copy printed and framed above my desk. It's hilarious.'

I'm surprised by his enthusiasm. It wasn't that great, as I remember.

The reporter cocks his head and narrows his eyes. 'You know it's gone viral, right? It's all over social media. You're famous.'

'I don't know what you're talking about.' I scrutinise him, trying to work out if he's being serious or just mocking me.

'This is priceless,' he laughs. 'You don't know, do you? Here look.' He pulls his phone from his pocket, stabs at the screen, and holds it up for me to see.

I stare at an unfamiliar Facebook post someone has created, reproducing elements of the *Meld* review, with phrases pulled out and highlighted.

'See, this post alone has had five hundred thousand likes. People are going mad for it. It's like when that woman left a review for her leggings after she slipped down the side of a mountain and they didn't rip.'

I look at him blankly. I don't know what he's talking about.

'Anyway, people love it,' he continues. 'There are even copycat spoof reviews doing the rounds.'

I'd never posted the review on Facebook, but I guess someone had seen it and shared it. I can't get my head around it. The last time I checked, which was probably a few months ago, the viewing figures for the blog hadn't miraculously jumped. This must have all happened in recent weeks, while I'd been completely oblivious.

'People have been sharing their favourite lines,' the reporter says. 'My favourite is where you said it takes less time for a forty-year-old virgin to get laid than it does to get a table at *Meld*. I love that,' he says, smirking like a love-sick puppy.

I wince. That was definitely harsh.

'How did you find me? The blog's anonymous,' I say.

'It's my job. I figured it had to have been written by someone local and so I've been doing some digging.'

It's not much of an explanation. I'm curious to find out how he did it. Abi and I haven't mentioned it to anyone, not even Felicity or Colette.

'Alright,' he says, 'I'll tell you. I worked out there was a link between Nosher's Instagram page and your personal account. It didn't take a rocket scientist.'

And it was hardly Watergate.

My worry is that if he's worked it out so easily, how many other people have done the same? If I'm unmasked, I'll never get a table at a restaurant again.

'Well, thanks for letting me know,' I say, pushing the door closed.

The reporter's arm shoots out and he shoves the door open again.

'It's not the blog I want to talk to you about. At least not directly,' he says, assuming a more serious expression. The charming smile has slipped. 'I'm writing a piece on *Meld* and I wanted to get a reaction from you as you're intrinsically tied up with the story. Obviously, I'm happy not to reveal your real identity, if you'd prefer. I'm happy for a quote attributed to Nosher.'

'Hang on,' I say, 'what story?'

His brow furrows. 'Don't you know? Man, you really are out of touch. The restaurant's closed down.' He pulls a pen and notebook from his satchel. 'It was very sudden. Loads of staff have been laid off and people are complaining because they'd been waiting months for a table. The speculation is that it's because of the negative publicity generated by your blog. So I wondered if you had a comment to make?'

He might as well have smacked me around the head with a baseball bat. I had no idea.

'When?'

'We only found out last week,' he says, 'after a few disgruntled customers contacted the newsroom. The owner, Matunde Yeboah, posted an apology on social media. Do you know him? He's the celebrity chef off that TV show.'

'Not personally.'

The reporter shrugs as if it's of no relevance. 'Well, anyway, he didn't specifically mention your blog as a factor for the closure, but I figured it's been read by so many people, it must have had some impact on business. I mean, you described it as shambolic. And to be honest, after what you wrote about it, I don't think I'd have wanted to eat there.'

The reporter chuckles, but I can't see anything remotely amusing about it. I'm horrified that a review on my blog could have had such devastating consequences. All those poor people out of a job. And God knows how much money Matunde had sunk into the venture. Surely, nobody could seriously blame the blog though. They must have had underlying problems.

I scratch my head, trying to recall exactly what the review had said that was so damning. 'The blog piece never said it was shambolic.'

'Not in so many words.' The reporter flicks back a couple of pages in his notebook. 'What you actually said was that the restaurant was massively overpriced, the waiting staff were a joke and the food overly simplistic and lacking flavour.'

'You're taking it out of context,' I say.

The journalist glances up briefly before continuing, 'I quote, "Even the decor was tawdry and uninspiring. It reminded me of a cross between a cheap Amsterdam brothel and a Peckham bedsit."'

'It was a joke.' Admittedly, a poor one. 'An amusing observation.'

I flushed with shame.

'You even had a few words to say about the owner. Let me jog your memory. You said the open plan dining area provided an innovative opportunity to watch the kitchen staff at work and was one highlight in an otherwise pitiful experience, particularly as it gave you the chance to witness the owner and TV celebrity, Matunde Yeboah, dripping fat globules of sweat into your starter at the pass.'

Yeah, I could see how that might look.

'Not exactly a glowing endorsement, is it?'

I squirmed. What could I say? He was reading the words directly from the blog. I could hardly deny them.

'So do you accept your blog must have been, at least in part, responsible for the premature closure of the restaurant?' He asks so innocently, like a hangman asking if a noose is comfortable around your neck.

I panic, not sure what to say. 'Yes. No. I don't know,' I mumble, struggling to think straight as I try to imagine how my response might be interpreted in print. How's it going to make me look? I wish he'd just go away and leave me alone.

The reporter scribbles something down.

'What are you writing?'

'And what would you like to say to Mr Yeboah?'

'What?'

'Would you like to apologise to him? This is your opportunity.'

'But I didn't —'

The reporter's pen is poised, his eyebrows raised. 'Go on,' he says.

'I don't think I have anything to apologise for.'

'Really? Interesting.' With a flick of his wrist, he scribbles down some unreadable hieroglyphics, his pen scratching unnervingly loudly across his pad.

'Wait! Stop! That's not on the record,' I say. I can see how it's going to look. 'Don't write that down.'

'And do you have any words of regret for all the staff who've lost their jobs? Your waitress on the night, for example. You mentioned her in your review. You said Sally-Anne exhibited all the training and customer service skills of someone recruited from the local fast-food burger joint. You added she had all the charisma of a floundering wet fish.'

Fuck.

Poor Sally-Anne didn't deserve that on top of the way she'd been treated on the night. I should never have posted the review. What a massive mistake. But it was too late now. The damage was done. *Meld* had gone out of business and everyone was going to think it was all my fault.

'Do you have a comment for our readers?' the reporter presses.

My mouth opens and closes silently like a guppy fish. Behind the reporter, a man with a camera and a long lens appears from nowhere and snaps a picture. Instinctively, I hold up a hand to hide my face. But that's only going to make it look like I have something to hide. I'm screwed.

'Can we get a quick picture?' the reporter asks, a bit late. 'It would be nice to have a shot of you at your computer working on the blog.'

'Fuck off!' I yell at him, slamming the door shut.

I want to crawl into a deep hole and never show my face again.

What the hell have I done?

'Mr Hutton?' The reporter fingers open the letterbox and shouts into the house. 'Just a couple more questions, please. Mr Hutton? Are you there?'

I slump to the floor in a heap of despair and clamp my hands over my ears.

Chapter 29

When Abi returns home, I'm pacing up and down the kitchen, chewing my nails.

'Henry, what is it?' she asks, dropping her bags on the floor.

'We have a problem. We have a very fucking big problem.'

'Okay, talk to me,' she says, the calm voice of reason. 'Whatever it is, it can't be that bad.'

'Which do you want first? The bad news or the really bad news?' I'd spent most of the day fretting about what the journalist had said, turning it over and over in my mind.

Now she looks worried. Katie comes racing into the room, still in her school uniform.

'Daddy, can I watch TV? Please?'

I wouldn't normally allow the girls to watch television this close to bedtime, but I need Katie and Norah out of the way so I can have Abi's undivided attention.

'Yes, but only for twenty minutes and then it's bedtime.'

'It must be serious,' Abi says, pouting as Katie runs off without even acknowledging her mother's presence.

Abi knows how strict I am about the girls' nighttime routine and letting them stay up to watch television. I close the door and we sit at the kitchen table. I blow air into my hands, not really knowing where to begin. How do I tell Abi all our worst nightmares aren't over? They've only just begun.

'I got it completely wrong,' I say. 'It wasn't Joseph Farrow harassing us. I was so convinced it was him, but I couldn't see the truth.'

'What do you mean? What's happened?'

'I had another text message this morning from what I thought was Farrow's number. But it couldn't have been him, could it, because he's dead.'

Abi goes still, her eyes darkening.

'The message asked if I'd heard about the fire.' I take my phone and show her the texts. 'And whoever sent it pretty much admitted they started it.'

'Bloody hell, Henry. Why didn't you call me?'

'I thought you'd be in court. Anyway, there was nothing you could do.'

'You could have left a message.' She frowns. The cogs in her head are turning slowly, trying to piece together what I'm telling her. 'Why would they start a fire at the Farrows?'

'I don't know. I haven't worked that out yet.'

'There has to be a reason.'

'Abi, there's more,' I say. 'I also had a visit from a journalist earlier. He came to the house to talk to me about the blog.'

I explain the accusations he made and how he's going to write a piece, blaming the sudden closure of *Meld* on the harsh review I'd posted on the blog.

'It's been read by tens of thousands of people. He as good as accused me of stitching up Matunde and all the staff who've lost their jobs,' I say.

I keep thinking about our waitress. We'd not only ruined her evening, thanks to the way Ralph and Johnny had treated her, but we'd also unwittingly cost Sally-Anne her job. Who knows how many others there were. Twenty? Fifty? I'd counted at least half a dozen chefs working in the kitchen. There were probably another ten or fifteen waiting staff. Plus cleaners and pot washers. That's a lot of people out of work because of one poorly considered review.

'Restaurants fail all the time,' Abi says, trying to be the voice of reason. 'It's a tough business. You don't know the review had anything to do with it.'

'Not according to the journalist who was here.'

'Critics criticise restaurants,' Abi says. 'It's what they do. It happens all the time, and even the famous places get critical reviews. The whole point is they're supposed to be subjective. One person's point of view.'

'But the review of *Meld* wasn't fair, was it?'

'Of course it was,' Abi says.

'The restaurant's overpriced, the staff are a joke and the food's lacking in flavour? It was a bit harsh.'

'It was a fair reflection of our experience.'

'Coloured by the fact we were thrown out,' I say.

'I don't think so.'

'The decor was tawdry and looked like a cheap Amsterdam brothel?'

Abi smirks. 'It was supposed to be funny.'

'It should have been more objective. The problem was it was written in the heat of the moment. I should have waited before posting it. Let tempers cool. It was a big mistake,' I say, shaking my head.

'Come on, Henry. You're being melodramatic, don't you think?'

'No, Abi, I don't. You don't see it, do you?'

'I can understand this has upset you, but honestly, you need to put it into perspective. What's the worst that's going to happen? A piece in the local rag outing you as Nosher and a column that no one's going to read pointing a vague finger in your direction,' she says.

I sit stunned as she talks, hardly able to believe how someone so sharp in a courtroom can be so obtuse.

'There are two options,' she says. Now she sounds like a lawyer. 'You either say nothing and keep your head down, hoping the story blows over in a day or two. Or we issue an apology taking full responsibility. We start by saying sorry to Matunde and all the staff who've lost their jobs but explain it was an honestly held view and that we sincerely regret any offence taken or harm caused. I can help you draft it if you like, and we can stick it on the blog.'

'An apology won't make this go away, Abi.' I spring out from my chair and slam my hand on the table, making her jump. You don't get it at all, do you? This is what the last week has been all about. The threatening letter. The vandalism to your car. The rock through the window. The paint on the walls. The text messages. It all comes back to this.' I'm shouting now, but I have to make her understand.

'What are you talking about, Henry?'

'It's obvious, isn't it? It's Matunde Yeboah. He blames me for destroying his business and his reputation. He's lost everything because of that bloody review. And now he's taking his revenge by trying to destroy us.'

Chapter 30

'Matunde Yeboah? Are you serious?'

I don't know why Abi finds it so hard to believe. It's absolutely clear in my mind that Matunde is behind the campaign of hate against us because of the review on the blog which he blames for the closure of his business.

'Why not?'

'It seems extreme, that's all,' Abi says.

'The man's lost his livelihood and his reputation because of the review. Now he wants us to suffer the same way he thinks he and his staff have suffered. You know what chefs can be like. They're arrogant and hot-headed. It's obviously him.'

Abi shakes her head. 'I don't know, Henry. It doesn't feel right.'

I stop pacing up and down the kitchen and stare at her, confused. 'What's that supposed to mean?'

'I don't know. It's just a gut feeling. You said he's issued an apology to his customers. Have you read it?'

'I didn't see the point,' I say.

'It might at least give us some idea of his state of mind. Let's have a look.' She scrolls through her phone while I continue to pace. When she finds it, I watch her lips flicker while she reads it to herself.

'What's it say?'

'Apology to all my customers, blah, blah, blah. Difficult financial conditions. It's been an exciting journey of discovery. One day, he hopes to be back. Looking forward to bringing joy to everyone with his food again. That's it.' She looks up at me over the top of her phone. 'Nothing about the blog at all.'

'Let me see.'

I scan the brief statement he's posted on his Instagram feed. There's not even an oblique reference to the blog or the review.

'It doesn't mean he doesn't blame us,' I say.

'But going to all that trouble to get back at us? What would it achieve?'

'Revenge isn't a rational behaviour, Abi.'

'No need to patronise me.' She takes her phone back and puts it face down on the table, folding her hands on top of it. 'And if you really think it was Matunde, then how do you explain the letter? One death was too much? Two is unbearable? Why would he write that?'

'I don't know. The guy's unhinged. Who knows what's going through his head right now. Maybe it's a reference to the death of his restaurant?'

Abi raises a perfectly manicured eyebrow. 'Seriously?'

'I don't know,' I say, irritated at being cross-examined. 'All I know is that Matunde Yeboah has got it in for us and I need to make him stop.'

'Fine,' Abi says, rocking back in her chair. 'So what are you planning to do?'

'Burying our heads in the sand and hoping it will go away hasn't worked, so I don't see I have any choice other than to confront him. I'll have to talk to him and make him come to his senses. What else can I do?'

'He could be dangerous.'

'You've changed your tune. Just a minute ago, you didn't believe this had anything to do with him.'

'I didn't. I mean, I don't. But if by some miracle it is him, you should be careful, that's all.'

'I just want to talk to him and explain,' I say.

'If you're that convinced Matunde is behind all of this, don't you think you should call the police? You've not even told them he's been texting you. You could start by giving them the number to trace.'

I shake my head. 'It's a waste of time. They're not interested.'

'They will be if he's started the fire at the Farrows.'

'The only way this is going to end is if I can make him understand how sorry we are. I need to apologise to him face to face. If he can see we're genuinely remorseful, that might be enough to persuade him to leave us alone.'

A night sleeping on it doesn't change my opinion. Matunde Yeboah is the most likely suspect for everything that has happened to us in the last week. The letter. The damage to Abi's car. The smashed window. The threatening texts and pictures. It all points to him. And at least now I know I can do something about it.

His behaviour has been completely irrational, bordering on psychopathic, but it's a different prospect dealing with a vindictive chef than tackling a career criminal like Joseph Farrow. I would have never gone near Farrow. He was dangerous and unpredictable. Best left to the police.

It was confirmed publicly overnight that Farrow died in the fire at the house, alongside his partner, Bridget, but even though I now know he had nothing to do with the harassment against us, I still don't shed a tear for his death. I've read too much about the pain and suffering he's caused throughout his pitiful life. It's better he's dead.

I'm confident I can look Matunde Yeboah in the eye and make him see sense. The only problem is, I don't know how or where to find him. The obvious place to look is at his restaurant. It closed several weeks ago, but there's a possibility he might still be around while he's winding up the business and so, as I have no other way of finding him, after dropping the girls at school, I don't go home. I drive back to the restaurant I vowed never to visit again.

I park on a street of terraced Victorian houses and approach on foot with my nerves jangling. Matunde isn't Joseph Farrow, but it still won't be an easy conversation. He's a big man. Tall, broad and muscular. If he gets physical, I don't stand a chance. Plus, I haven't been in a fight since school when Gary Robertson got me in a headlock and bundled me to the floor in front of the whole of Year 9. I can't even remember why.

There's an air of desolation hanging over the building. You can tell it's empty even from a distance, partly because the windows are screened with sheets of newspaper and all the lights are out.

Coming back stirs unwelcome memories. I have a flashback of Johnny and Ralph stumbling out onto the pavement so drunk they could hardly stand. The embarrassment of a roomful of eyes fixed on my back as I was marched out into the rain-drenched night. My blood boiling. Humiliated and close to tears. Too angry to speak as I grabbed Abi's arm and led her towards the nearest taxi. Johnny and Ralph's laughter ringing in my ears. Still thinking it was all one big joke. My fury split between Johnny and Ralph, who'd behaved like asses, and the staff in the restaurant who should have handled the situation better. They'd overreacted when they'd thrown us out. It wasn't our fault they'd been short-staffed. And it didn't excuse the poor standard of food or the way they treated us.

It's funny, I had no idea that night it would end like this.

I cross the road and stroll casually up to the building, my hopes of finding Matunde fading. One of the sheets of newspaper taped to the window has come loose, flopping away from the glass and providing a peephole inside. The rows of bottles that had decorated the shelves behind the bar have been cleared away, chairs are stacked on tables and the floor is littered with cardboard boxes.

It's a sad sight. Although it's still early, a busy, functioning restaurant should be coming to life at this time of the morning with preparations for the lunch service getting underway. To see it locked up and abandoned is heartbreaking. Although we had an awful night here, there's nothing worse than witnessing first-hand the shattered dreams of someone's failed business. All those chefs and waiters out of a job. A pang of guilt pinches my insides.

I put my hands to the window to shade my eyes as I peer through the gap in the newspaper screen. It's bigger inside than I remember. More cavernous, but maybe that's because the tables and chairs have been stacked up and pushed to one side. A string of red fairy lights hangs limply from the ceiling and a pile of leather-bound menus is gathering dust on the edge of one of the tables.

I step back and notice a letter signed by Matunde has been stuck to the inside of the window. It looks like the same statement he's posted on his social media feeds, with an additional apology to anyone who's turned up with a table reservation and wasn't aware of the restaurant's closure.

Unfortunately, there's no contact number or email for Matunde, but on the bright side, there's no mention of the blog or the review either.

I'll have to find Matunde some other way. He's clearly not here. I step back and almost tread on the paws of an elderly Labrador sniffing my calves. I ruffle his head and he looks up at me with sad, rheumy eyes.

'He likes you.' A woman with unruly grey, wiry hair and a flowery patterned raincoat stands close by, holding a dog lead looped behind her back.

'He's very handsome.' Norah's always trying to talk us into getting a dog, but they're a lot of hard work and it wouldn't be fair to keep it cooped up in the house all day while Abi and I are at work.

'It's a shame it's closed,' the woman says, nodding at the restaurant. 'Did you have a table booked?'

'Oh, no,' I say. She's mistaken me for a disgruntled customer, which I suppose in a way I am. 'I was just looking.'

'It's a shame for the town. So many people have been turning up not having heard the news and been left disappointed.'

'I ate there a few weeks ago,' I say.

'Lucky you. It was a bit out of my price range.' She laughs.

'I'm not sure it was worth all the hype.'

The dog has lost interest in me and is wandering off to investigate a curious smell at the base of a lamppost further up the road.

'Pictures on plates, was it? Nice if you like art, but not if you have an empty stomach.' Her chuckle turns into a nasty hacking cough.

'Unfortunately, the night we came they were short-staffed, and it wasn't as good as we'd been expecting.'

'Oh,' the woman says. 'The only time I've been in there was after everyone else had gone home, to clean the toilets.'

'You used to work here?' I say, my interest piquing.

'Until they laid everyone off with no warning,' she says bitterly. 'Rumour has it someone wrote a nasty review and loads of people cancelled their reservations. That's what I heard, anyway.'

I glance at my feet, my cheeks burning, hoping the woman doesn't notice. I'm still not convinced the review, gone viral or not, could have had such a significant impact on business. Even Matunde admitted in his statement of apology that he was facing a tough economic climate.

'Did you know the owner?' I ask.

'What, Mr Yeboah? Not really. I saw him a few times when he stayed late.'

'I was hoping to talk to him,' I say. 'I don't suppose you know where I can find him? Does he live around here?'

'Sorry, no idea.'

'Okay, not to worry. Thank you anyway.'

The woman glances up the street. 'Come on, Bert, you don't want to be eating that.' Her dog has found a pile of soggy chips dumped by a litter bin. She heads off after him, ambling stiffly.

'It was nice to meet you,' I say.

She smiles and nods. I stuff my hands in my pockets and turn to head back to the car when she calls after me.

'Actually, your luck might be in,' she says, nodding over my shoulder. 'That looks like Mr Yeboah now.'

I follow her gaze and see a green BMW, its engine burbling, pulling up in an on-street parking bay a few doors down from the restaurant. The engine dies and the familiar, imposing figure of Matunde Yeboah steps out of the car.

My heart leaps in my chest. I've come here to find him, but now he's here, panic strikes. What am I going to say? How's he going to react to seeing me?

I need a minute to compose myself and get my thoughts straight in my head. I'd been rehearsing what I'd say on the drive over, but now my mind's a blank. I shrink away, taking refuge in the shadow under a tree as the woman and her dog meander away.

Matunde leans into his car, grabs an iPad, and tucks it under his arm. He's taller than I remember. Well over six foot. And really broad across the shoulders. Or maybe it's the tight white T-shirt that emphasises his lean physique. He looks like a man who keeps himself in great shape. One of those guys who's totally at ease in the gym, pumping weights, all rippling abs and popping muscles.

He skips up the steps to the restaurant with an athletic spring in his legs while sifting through a bunch of keys.

My palms are sweating. It might be the only chance I get to confront him, but my legs are suddenly as heavy as concrete. If he's the man who's been taunting us all this time, he could be dangerous. What was I thinking? Abi was right, I should have gone to the police, not tried to deal with this on my own.

Too late now.

I force myself to step out from under the tree before I change my mind. Matunde's already slipped inside the restaurant and the door's closing behind him.

I bound up the steps and catch it before it shuts, pushing it open again.

'Excuse me, Mr Yeboah,' I say, breathlessly.

He turns, surprised. 'Yes?' He peels off a pair of expensive-looking aviator sunglasses and perches them on top of his head.

'I'm Henry Hutton.' My mouth is sandpaper dry. I expect at least a flicker of recognition when he sees me, but he stares at me blankly. He either has a hell of a poker face or I'm barking up the wrong tree. Whichever it is, I'm completely wrong-footed. 'I mean Nosher, from Nosher Bites Back. Can I talk to you for a moment?'

'Nosher, right,' he says, nodding as he looks me up and down.

He doesn't punch me in the face. Or call me every name under the sun. He doesn't even blink. To my immense surprise, Matunde invites me inside like I'm an old friend, not someone he blames for single-handedly destroying his business.

'Come in,' he says. 'You want a coffee?'

He flicks on the lights and I follow him into the stripped out kitchen. He busies himself with a chrome coffee machine while I hover, taking in the sad sight of what was once a busy restaurant. He grinds some beans. The machine hisses and belches steam and he produces two strong espressos. He invites me to sit at the bar under bright spotlights suspended from the ceiling.

'I'm surprised to see you here. What do you want?'

It's unnerving how relaxed he is. If he blames me for the closure of *Meld*, he's keeping his cards close to his chest. Maybe he wants to lull me into a false sense of security. With the windows covered, there will be no witnesses to whatever happens in the next few minutes. But strangely, I don't feel afraid now I'm sitting here with him, sharing a coffee, our knees virtually touching. He's an enormous guy, but he's not behaving in a threatening manner. I don't feel unsafe, even if I should.

I try to read his expression. Does he look like a man capable of orchestrating such hatred against me and my family? In all honesty, no. He's calm and composed. Unflustered to see me. But then, if he's a psychopath, maybe I shouldn't be surprised. I just need to keep my wits about me.

'I wanted to apologise,' I say, toying with my fingers in my lap. 'I'm sorry if you felt the review had anything to do with the closure of the restaurant. I didn't know it was going to take off like it did.'

I'd practised the apology in my head on the drive over, but hearing it out loud, it sounded pathetically inadequate. I wasn't conveying the depth of my regret. But then, I'd never been that good with words.

I'd done a bit of research before I went to bed last night. According to the papers, Matunde had sunk around a million pounds into opening *Meld*, convinced his TV fame and the area's "unquenched desire for a high-end restaurant experience" would as good as guarantee its success. He clearly hadn't factored in a vitriolic food blogger shattering his dreams.

'You're a great chef and you deserved the restaurant to be a success,' I say, squirming on my stool. I've never been good at apologising. It's a weakness. I've always found it easier to blame someone or something else, but there's no getting out of it this time, not if I'm going to persuade him to leave us alone and end his vendetta against us.

Matunde raises a crooked eyebrow. 'Funny, that's not what your review said.'

I flush with embarrassment. The review was supposed to have been flippant and witty, but somehow it ended up sounding spiteful and malicious. It had become too much of a reflection of the unfortunate events of the evening, rather than focusing on the food. It was personal and nasty, ridiculing people who'd been trying to do their best on a tough night.

I wish I could change what was written. But it was too late. The words were out there and thanks to the internet, they could never be retracted.

'The review was... a mistake,' I mumble.

Matunde finishes his coffee and places his cup on the bar. He takes a deep breath and folds his arms over his bulging chest. 'You know, I can take criticism of my food. That's fair game, even though I'm good at what I do. Critics critique and I've developed a thick skin. You have to when your dishes are being pulled apart on TV in front of the nation. But you crossed a line when you criticised my staff. That's what I'm struggling to forgive.'

He takes a breath and studies me before continuing. 'I remember the night you came in with your friends. We'd been hit by a sickness bug and were struggling with a staff shortage. Maybe I should have shut the restaurant for the evening, but I didn't want to disappoint people who'd been on a waiting list for months. Instead, we pulled together and did our best. And this was the thanks I got.'

'I'm sorry, we —'

'The last thing we needed that night was a drunken mob causing problems and being difficult.' Even though he's clearly upset, Matunde keeps an even tone and doesn't raise his voice. The way he's able to maintain his cool while he's laying into me is unsettling. 'You made a scene and spoilt the evening for everyone else. It's why I had to ask you to leave and why you'll never eat in one of my restaurants again.'

Why do I feel like a schoolboy being reprimanded by the headteacher?

'I guess I was embarrassed by the way you threw us out and some of that came out in the review. I know it was wrong but...'

But what? There really was no excuse for the tone of the review nor for insulting his staff.

Matunde looks into my eyes with an intense gaze that I can't hold. I fiddle with my coffee cup, concentrating on lining up the handle so it's precisely parallel with the edge of the bar.

Eventually, he says, 'You didn't need to come here today to apologise. That must have taken balls.' He leans back and sucks in the air between his teeth. 'You know what? Life's too short to hold grudges. In my experience, they don't do anyone any good. They just eat you up from the inside. I appreciate you coming to talk to me.' He shoves out a meaty hand. 'Apology accepted.'

'Seriously?' I take his hand and shake it vigorously. 'That's very good of you,' I say with a wide grin.

'The ban remains, though,' he replies with a glint in his eye. He's not joking.

'You don't know what a weight this is off my shoulders.'

I can't believe how easy it's been. Abi didn't believe me when I said all it might take was for me to look him in the eye and tell him I'm sorry, but that was exactly what was needed. He just wanted me to come and admit I'd been wrong and to beg his forgiveness. If only I'd known that a week ago, we could have saved ourselves so much stress and anxiety.

A fizz of excitement and relief swells from my stomach. This is amazing news. I can't wait to tell Abi. She's going to be so proud of me.

'Returning hate for hate only multiplies hate,' Matunde says. 'Martin Luther King. I think in this age of hate we all need to show each other a bit more compassion, don't you?'

'Totally,' I agree. 'So that's it? All's forgiven? That's an end to it now?' I feel almost as if I'm floating. It's the most incredible feeling. Better than sex. Better than any drug.

'It's all cool with me.'

'Great. No more rocks through the window, then?' I laugh nervously.

'What?'

'And no more threatening letters?'

He shakes his head, his expression blank, but I guess he's being coy. He doesn't want to admit to it in case I go to the police.

'Can you clear something up for me, though, just for my curiosity?' I persist. 'You said one death was too much, but two was unbearable. What did you mean?'

'I don't know what you're talking about.'

'Please? It's been driving me nuts trying to work it out.'

'I'm sorry, man, you've completely lost me,' Matunde says.

'You know, the letter you put through the door?'

He stares at me like he really doesn't know what I'm saying, and I don't think he's faking it. A numbing chill slowly descends over my body. 'The paint over the front of the house? The text messages? The pictures of Abi and Ralph? The girls in the playground?'

Matunde keeps shaking his head.

'I know it was you. Come on, there's no need to deny it. I won't take it any further.'

'I think you've confused me with someone else.'

It has to be him. Who else could it be?

'I'm begging you,' I say. 'I've apologised. But I really need you to tell me you did all those things.'

'I've done nothing. I told you, I don't know what you're talking about.'

He spins his mobile phone absentmindedly on the top of the bar. I watch it go through three complete rotations before it comes to a stop. Is that the phone he's been using to text me? To send me those photos?

'I can prove it,' I say.

I pull out my own phone and find the number that's been texting me, the number I thought belonged to Joseph Farrow. I hit dial and hold the phone to my ear, waiting for the ring tone.

Matunde looks at me like he thinks I've lost my mind. The phone crackles and hisses in my ear. Eventually, the number connects and rings. I glance at Matunde's phone and wait for the buzz from my call.

But nothing happens.

It doesn't ring, and it doesn't buzz.

Chapter 31

I hang up. I must have mis-dialled. I dial again. I listen to the ringing in my ear. But Matunde's phone stays silent.

'Is everything okay?' he asks.

I open my mouth but I can't form any words. I was so convinced I'd finally solved the mystery. But it's not him.

My stomach cramps and I flush with a prickly, sweaty heat.

If not Matunde, then who?

Oh God, Abi and the girls. An image flashes through my mind of Norah and Katie at school, running around the playground, watched by a faceless, hooded figure lurking in the shadows.

He could be anywhere. At the school. At the house. At Abi's chambers. I need to call and warn her. She needs to be on her guard until I can work this out.

'I thought it was you,' I gasp. 'But you know nothing about it, do you?'

Matunde shakes his head. I try dialling Abi's number, but as usual, it goes straight to voicemail. If I leave a message, she's only going to freak out. I'll have to try her again later. Maybe I should let the school know though. But what are they going to do? The police then?

'Has someone been causing you trouble?'

I scratch the back of my head and suddenly I'm telling Matunde everything, as if he cares. He's probably secretly pleased. Karma for what he thinks I did. 'I thought you blamed me for the closure of the restaurant and were trying to take some kind of revenge. I thought that if I made my peace with you, you'd leave us alone.'

'You really think I'm capable of all that? Threatening behaviour? Criminal damage?'

'I couldn't think of anyone else who had a motive. It's not like we're in the habit of upsetting people.'

'There must be something you've done to upset someone.'

'Trust me, I've been through it a million times in my head, raking it over, trying to work it out.'

'That's tough. Especially when you have a young family. What are you going to do?'

'I honestly don't know.' I feel like running away, packing the girls and Abi up in the car and driving to somewhere no one will ever find us. I can't think of any other way of making this stop. And if I can't find out who's behind it, it could go on and on. I don't even know what they want from us. 'I am sorry about the restaurant,' I say. 'I'm not sure what's worse, the dreadful review or accusing you of all that stuff.'

Matunde smiles kindly, showing off a perfect set of white teeth. 'Listen, I need to be honest with you. The review hurt, especially when so many people were sharing it online and we started to get cancellations, but it's not the reason the business failed. I'd overstretched myself and miscalculated the costs. Because I could cook and I'd been on TV, my ego was convinced I knew how to run a restaurant. But it's a lot tougher than I thought. And a lot more expensive. The margins are so tight, but I was so focused on the food, I took my eye off the bottom line. I could never make enough money and ultimately that's the reason it failed.'

I frown. 'But you had people literally queuing up to eat here. We were on a waiting list for months before we got a table.'

Matunde shrugs. 'I was still bleeding money and when the bank stopped lending me cash... Unfortunately, that was around the same time as your review was gaining some interest.' He bites his lip and glances down. 'The staff didn't know I had cash flow problems, but they knew all about your review, so I let them think it was the reason for the closure because it was easier than admitting I'd fucked up. You handed me a scapegoat on a plate. I probably owe you an apology too.'

I can't believe what I'm hearing.

'So you knew the review had nothing to do with the closure of the restaurant, but you sat there and let me grovel for your forgiveness anyway,' I say, my anger rising.

'I didn't ask you to come here and I've never publicly blamed the failure of the business on the review.'

The implications of Matunde's confession filter slowly through my brain. He might not have blamed me, but there were other people who clearly did.

'Let me get this straight,' I say, my grip tightening on my phone. 'Everyone who lost their job here thinks it's my fault the business folded?'

'I wouldn't say —'

'You let everyone believe it was my fault,' I repeat.

Matunde sighs, his shoulders slumping with defeat. 'Some of them believed that, yes. And some of them took it hard.'

'Like who, exactly?' My heart is racing.

'There was the waitress who served you the night you were here, for a start,' he says.

'Sally-Anne?'

'You named her in the review and said some pretty horrible things about her. She didn't take that too well.'

I bet she didn't. Ralph had reduced her to a quivering wreck on the night and the review had no doubt compounded her distress.

Sally-Anne, the waitress who was supposed to be attending our table, exhibited all the training and customer service skills of someone recruited from a fast-food burger joint and possessed slightly less charisma than a floundering wet fish.

Why had I published that? It was cruel and insensitive and wasn't even funny. 'We shouldn't have used her name,' I say, embarrassed. 'That was wrong.'

'I'm sorry, but you probably ought to know, a few days after we had to let her go, she took her own life.'

I blink at Matunde, not sure I've heard him correctly. 'What?'

There are tears in Matunde's eyes.

'I had to go to her funeral and watch her parents trying to come to terms with their daughter's death, knowing I was partly to blame. Can you imagine how hard that was?'

'I... I...' I stutter, words failing me.

'She was a bright girl, but quite shy. She was coming out of her shell but losing her job after being vilified in your review was, I guess, too much for her.'

I'm consumed by a dark cloud of shame. We as good as killed her. First, there was the way we treated her on the night, and then the review. This is going to live with me for the rest of my life. The guilt. The shame. The regret. If only I could turn back the clock and change everything.

'She was engaged to one of my sous chefs. A guy called Marcus Arquette. I had to let him go too, so the restaurant closing hit them twice as hard as everyone else. They both lost their jobs with a wedding to pay for. It was horrible having to tell them,' Matunde says.

Marcus? The name sounds familiar. And then I remember. I met him briefly. He was the chef I'd seen consoling Sally-Anne in the staff room after Ralph had upset her. The guy I thought was going to hit me.

'He found her hanging from a door in their flat,' Matunde says, swallowing hard. His eyes flick to the ceiling as a tear snakes down his cheek. 'I only found out afterwards she was two months pregnant.'

'Pregnant?' His words are a sucker punch.

Matunde nods. 'No one knew. Not even her parents. They were planning to tell everyone after the first scan. Such a senseless waste.'

My phone slips from my fingers and falls to the floor. I stare at my cold, numb hands as if expecting to see them covered in blood.

'As you can imagine, Marcus was beside himself,' Matunde says. 'His whole life was destroyed in a flash. The future he had planned, all his hopes and dreams, gone.'

'I don't know what to say.'

'There's nothing you can say. Sally-Anne's gone and there's nothing either of us can do or say to bring her back.'

I sit in the car and repeatedly hit redial until Abi finally answers. I need to talk to someone. I can't deal with this on my own. The sadness and the guilt are too heavy for my shoulders alone.

'Henry?' she says breathlessly when she finally picks up. 'What is it? Did you speak to him?'

I tell her about Sally-Anne and the baby and Marcus and the wedding. It pours out of me in a torrent. I hardly pause to take a breath. I have to get it out of me, expunge it like it's a soul-destroying poison.

'It's all our fault,' I cry. 'We killed her, and we killed her baby. She should never have been named in the review.'

Abi is silent for a second or two. She's trying to take it in. 'You can't blame yourself,' she says.

'If it wasn't for the blog, she'd probably still be alive,' I say, surprised she's trying to downplay our role in all of this.

'You don't know that for a fact. She and her boyfriend both lost their jobs. That would have had a much bigger impact on their lives than a few words in a review, especially if they were supposed to be saving up for a wedding and a baby.'

'But she'd been humiliated by the blog,' I say. 'And she knew tens of thousands of people had read it.'

'And it's awful. It's a horrible, horrible thing that's happened. But you can't blame yourself,' Abi repeats.

I couldn't imagine the depths of despair into which Sally-Anne had fallen to feel the only way out was to take her own life and that of her unborn child.

'But I do,' I sigh. 'I can't help it. I feel responsible, Abi. We all should. But at least everything is starting to make sense now.'

'What do you mean?'

'The letter. The texts. Your car. The smashed window. It wasn't Matunde. It was Marcus.'

I hear Abi exhale slowly. 'Henry...'

'No, listen to me. Think about the letter. One death is too much, but two is unforgivable. Remember? We didn't know what that meant before. But now we do. He's talking about Sally-Anne and their baby. That's why he wants revenge. He blames us because Matunde let the staff believe the restaurant had to close because of the blog and the bad publicity. It didn't, but they don't know that. Marcus thinks we're to blame. That's why he's been coming after us.'

'Look, we've been down this road before when you've convinced yourself you're certain what's going on. Maybe it's time we involved the police again?'

'Not yet. I can't prove any of this. I need more time.'

'So what do you want to do?' Abi asks.

It's so obvious now, like the fog of confusion has lifted, but I can hear Abi still needs convincing. This time I'm certain I'm on the right track. I just need to find Marcus Arquette before he does something stupid. He's obviously desperate. And desperate people do desperate things. Like going after my daughters because he thinks I'm responsible for the death of his child.

'I'm going to find him and I'm going to stop him,' I say.

'How?'

'I'm not sure. Matunde refused to give me his address.'

'Didn't you tell him what's been going on?'

'Of course I did. He says it's against privacy laws to give out the information and I need to go through the police.'

'And you're sure it's him? You've been wrong before.'

'A hundred per cent, Abi. It's Marcus Arquette. He's behind everything.'

'Well, it can't be that hard to track him down. We know his name, where he worked and what he was doing for a living.'

'I don't even know where to start looking,' I say.

'I have an idea. Leave it with me.'

Chapter 32

The flat is on the top floor of a shabby terrace on a busy road, its frontage soot-blackened and its wooden-framed windows cracked and peeling from neglect. It has its own front door painted in faded duck-egg blue and a mottled brass knocker and matching letterbox.

Abi found the address. She created a fake social media profile and reached out to Sally-Anne's friends, telling them she'd only recently heard about her untimely death and wanted to send her fiancé a condolence card.

I wouldn't know where to start doing something as devious, but Abi knew exactly what she was doing and eventually, one friend responded with the address and a cryptic warning.

Be careful of Marcus. Don't trust him.

What was that supposed to mean? After everything he'd put us through, I'm well aware of what he's capable of. But I have to remind myself he's a man in turmoil. He's lost everything he loves. Anyone could go off the rails faced with such a tragedy.

I'd considered messaging him again, to tell him I was onto him and that I wanted to meet up. But I feared he would disappear and then I'd never find him. Better to tackle him face to face, and besides, he's been remarkably quiet since the fire that killed Joseph Farrow. He's not even responded to the missed calls I made to his phone when I was with Matunde in *Meld*. It's like he's gone completely off the radar. It's possible he's lost interest in us, but I don't think so. He's playing a game. The problem is, we have no idea of the rules.

I check up and down the street and compose myself, rehearsing what I'm going to say. Marcus is a man in grief. It won't do either of us any favours going in with all guns blazing. I need to listen to him and sympathise.

He's lost his fiancée and his unborn child. He must be going through unimaginable heartache. I have to find a way to connect with him and make him understand the damage he's doing to my family. That it won't bring Sally-Anne back.

I'm confident he'll see sense. He's not a criminal like Joseph Farrow. He's a chef who had a good job. He can't really want to throw away his future on some misplaced vendetta.

Maybe we can bond over our love of food. It's an area of common ground at least and has to be worth a try. The prize, if I succeed, is that our lives can go back to normal. There's no need to involve the police. If Marcus calls a halt to hostilities, that's an end to it, as far as I'm concerned. I won't take any further action. There'll be no stain on his reputation. No criminal record. Nothing to stop him from moving on, getting another job, and rebuilding his life.

But it has to end today. No more letters or texts or threats against my daughters or my wife. He leaves us alone, and never bothers us again.

I step up to the door and reach for the brass knocker. This is it. Make or break. Do or die.

I'm about to knock when the warning from Sally-Anne's friend pops into the forefront of my mind.

Be careful of Marcus. Don't trust him.

I push away the niggle of uncertainty. I *don't* trust him. At least not yet. Not until I've looked him in the eye and we've squared away our differences. Who knows, we might even end up as friends. Stranger things have happened between two people going through adversity together.

I strike the knocker three times.

And stand back, the seconds ticking slowly in my head, as I wait on the pavement, oblivious to the passing traffic, listening for footsteps on the stairs. The click of a lock. The creak of the door opening.

And I wait.

A minute passes. And then two.

I shuffle from one foot to the other and check my watch.

After all the trouble we've gone to to find him, I hope he's in.

I knock again, striking the knocker more forcefully in case he's asleep or watching TV with the sound up too loudly.

Nothing.

I crouch down and peer through the letterbox at a threadbare carpeted staircase.

'Marcus? Hello? Are you there? It's Henry. We need to talk.'

Silence. No TV blaring. No radio. No footsteps padding across the floor.

There's no one in. I'm fairly sure of that now.

A neighbour might know when he's due back.

Or I could wait.

Or...

I should walk away and come back later, but I have an uncontrollable urge to look inside. There could be something to help me understand Marcus's motivation, or more to the point, what he's planning next.

It's something I'd never normally consider, but he's pushed me to the edge. I won't touch anything. Just look. He never needs to know I've been here.

There's no way in through the front, so I wander around the back of the terraced row of houses and find a stinking narrow alley where the bins are kept. A gate at the back of Marcus's flat is hanging open between two crooked fence panels. It opens up into a neglected garden with knee-high grass, a tumbledown shed and a couple of abandoned children's push-along toys bleached by the elements.

A metal fire escape spirals up to Marcus's flat on the first floor. You never know, he might have forgotten to lock the door. I sneak across the garden, praying no one is watching, and take the fire escape two steps at a time, grimacing every time my foot makes the metal clang or the whole structure creaks.

I make a fist and hammer on the dirty plastic door at the top of the steps. I'm sure Marcus isn't in, but it's best to knock. Imagine if I barged in and bumped into him coming out of the shower or something. How would I explain that away?

When there's no response, I reach for the handle. I'm sure it's locked, but now I'm here, I have to try. I hold my breath and twist my wrist. To my surprise, the door opens a crack.

'Hello?' I call. 'Anyone home?'

It's not too late to walk away. This isn't why I came. But now I'm here I can't leave. An invisible force is pulling me inside. I check over my shoulder and slip into the flat, silently closing the door behind me.

Be careful of Marcus. Don't trust him.

It's okay. He's not here and anyway, the urge to take a peek into his life is too strong to resist.

I'm in a small kitchen cluttered with pots and pans, an extensive collection of herbs and spices in glass jars and a set of sharp-looking chefs' knives on a magnetic board screwed to the wall. I make a mental note of those knives, just in case I need them.

At the back of my mind, I'd pictured Marcus so stricken with grief that he'd succumbed to a life of squalor, too miserable to bother taking any care of himself or the flat. But it's not like that at all. Everything looks clean and tidy. The kitchen is small, but it's perfectly appointed with everything in its place. There are no dirty dishes in the sink or trails of toast crumbs dusting the worktops.

Sweat pools in the small of my back as I tiptoe through a narrow hallway and into a dingy living room with heavy curtains pulled across the window. A grubby velour button-backed three-seater sofa that's seen better days dominates the space. There's a TV in the corner, a gas fire attached to the wall and an upturned fruit box being used as a coffee table. It's stacked high with piles of cookery books, but it strikes me how few other personal touches there are. No ornaments or paintings. No posters or photographs, potted plants or candles. It's sterile and not at all homely.

Through a door leading off the hallway, there's a bathroom with a mould-stained plastic shower curtain hanging over a chipped white ceramic bath, a mirrored cabinet over a basin, and a toilet squeezed in behind the bath. But there are no shampoo bottles, bars of soap, toothbrushes or paste. It's weird, almost as if the room isn't used.

I pull the door shut and push open another on the opposite side of the hall.

It's a bedroom in semi-darkness with heavy blue curtains diffusing an indigo blush across a double bed that takes up most of the floor. There's the slightest hint of perfume in the air, the first and only hint I've picked up that a woman lived here.

A juddering image of Sally-Anne hanging from her neck from one of the doors steals into my mind, making me shudder. I squeeze my eyes shut and when I open them again, the image has gone.

I study the rest of the room, noting the pine wardrobe pushed up against the wall, a white desk under the window and a teddy bear with a lopsided grin propped up on the pillows. Sally-Anne's? It doesn't seem like something that would belong to Marcus. It's the only non-functional item I've seen in the flat so far, almost as if he's cleared out anything else that belonged to her, erasing all the memories.

I straighten the bear's tie and lift him to my face. He smells of sweet, cheap perfume, like an olfactive echo of the past. A reminder of Sally-Anne. Definitely not

Marcus's soft toy. I put him back, making sure he's in exactly the same position I found him, and walk around the end of the bed.

There's nothing on the desk other than a pile of white paper, neatly stacked. Under it, there's a laserjet printer. Without a forensic examination, there's no way of knowing if the paper and the ink from the printer are the same as were used in the threatening letter sent to us, but I strongly suspect it. It's hardly definitive proof, but I'm certain Marcus wrote and delivered that letter.

It was Marcus who followed Abi home from town and was loitering outside the house. It was Marcus who vandalised Abi's car and smashed our front window with a rock from the garden. And it's Marcus who's been sending me all those texts and photos of Abi and the girls.

He's torn our lives apart, left us frightened and anxious and dreading what's coming next. I've even fitted bars to the windows at home. That's how paranoid he's made me. I know he's been through a lot, losing Sally-Anne and the baby, but I can't forgive how he's terrorised us. We didn't deserve any of it. We weren't to blame for Sally-Anne losing her job or taking her own life, and yet he holds us responsible. God knows what kind of sick revenge he's planning. But if he goes anywhere near my girls, I will kill him.

The buzz of my mobile in my back pocket startles me. It's eerily loud in the silent flat. I expect it's Abi checking up on me.

But it's not. It's a message from a number I now know belongs to Marcus.

Found anything interesting?

What the hell? Does he know I'm in the flat? Is he watching me?

I edge out of the bedroom, pulling the door closed, and creep back into the living room, half expecting to see him standing there with a cruel grin on his face.

He's not, but he definitely knows I'm here. Somehow. Security cameras? I glance around the walls and the ceiling, but can't see anything obvious.

I type a hurried reply.

Marcus?

An immediate response.

So you've finally worked it out. What are you looking for?

I won't dignify that question with a reply. I've had enough of dancing to Marcus Arquette's tune. If he wants answers, then he needs to meet me face to face.

We need to talk.

I watch the three dots pulsing on my screen as he types.

It's a bit late for talking. Now it's payback time. You took everything from me. An eye for an eye is only fair.

I sigh. Nothing's changed. He's still plotting some kind of twisted revenge. I want to scream and rage at him about how wrong he is to come after us, but I can't do that over text message. Instead, I remember the lines I rehearsed on my way over here and how it's important I try to connect with him.

I'm sorry about Sally-Anne, but I'm not responsible for her death.

His response is virtually instant.

There's no one else to blame. My pain will be your pain.

My pain will be your pain? This guy is seriously unhinged. But if he thinks I'm going to stand by and let him hurt Abi or the girls, which is what he's implying, he has another think coming.

I've had enough. This has to end. And if he won't let it go, I guess I'm just going to have to find him and let him know he's picked on the wrong family. I've had a gutful of this bullshit.

My thumbs fly across the screen, tapping out a furious message.

Screw you, asshole

I switch off my phone and shove it in my pocket.

Let him stew on that for a while and see how he likes it.

Chapter 33

Marcus could be anywhere, planning anything. I need to find him, to stop him, but my priority is my family and keeping them safe, especially the girls who have no idea of the danger they're in.

I race out of the flat, sprint down the fire escape, out of the garden and back to my car. I'm in such a panic, I drop my keys in the gutter as I fumble with them. My hand shakes as I crouch to pick them up.

I need to calm down. Keep a level head.

Traffic's typically slow through town, but finally I make it to the girls' school. I scan the pavement outside for any strangers, but it's all quiet. At least I know what Marcus Arquette looks like. It was only a few weeks ago that I'd encountered him in *Meld*, and I'll never forget his face. Wild, staring eyes. Hooded brows. Square jaw. Lips lifted on one side in a permanent sneer.

Satisfied he's not here, I find a parking space in the street opposite the school and kill the engine. I'm not taking any chances. I'll wait and watch until the end of the day, if that's what it takes. And if Marcus is here, I'll find him and...

I'll deal with that if the situation arises.

I call Abi to explain Marcus's flat was empty and to warn to stay vigilant.

'He's building up to something,' I say, catching her on her way into court. 'And he knows we're onto him. I only wish I knew what he was planning.'

I watch as children spill out into the playground at lunchtime, their screams and laughter filling the car with joyful noise as I try unsuccessfully to spot Norah and Katie. And an hour later, I watch them all filter back inside.

A short while after that, I'm startled by a knock on the window.

My eyes snap open and my head jars back. I must have briefly nodded off.

I recognise one of the male teachers crouching by the side of the car. He indicates for me to wind the window down.

'Hello, sir,' he says, with the officiousness of a traffic warden. 'Is everything okay?'

'Yes, fine, thank you,' I say, sitting up straight and rubbing a hand over my face.

'It's just that you've been parked up now for a few hours watching the playground. Some of my colleagues wanted to call the police, but I said I'd come and have a word first.'

'It's nothing like that,' I say. I feel my cheeks burning. He thinks I'm child molester. 'I'm Henry Hutton. Norah and Katie's dad. I had nowhere else to be, so I thought I might as well turn up early and wait for them to finish.'

'Four hours early?'

I could hardly tell him the truth, that we were being stalked by a psychopath for some perceived injustice he'd suffered and that I was worried about the girls' safety.

'Mrs Hornstein knows me,' I say, as if that explains everything. 'She can vouch for me.'

'Right,' he says, drawing out the syllables like he's trying to decide whether I'm a predatory paedophile or simply deranged.

'There's nothing to worry about, honestly,' I add. Although that's not strictly true. They have nothing to worry about from me, is what I mean.

Eventually, the teacher nods and walks away. I watch him lope across the road, through the playground and back into the school, casting one final distrustful glance in my direction.

Where was he when Marcus Arquette was taking pictures through the fence and handing Norah a package during playtime? Typical of these do-gooders to always be looking in the wrong direction at the wrong time.

Eventually, three-thirty rolls around and I make sure I'm first in the playground for pickup, even if the girls' classes are predictably the last ones to be let out. I bundle them into the car, never letting them out of my sight and on the way home keep a close eye on my mirrors for any cars that might be following us. Suddenly, every vehicle and every unidentified figure is a threat.

My heart rate only levels off when I have Norah and Katie safely inside the house and I've locked and bolted the front door. Here, at least, Marcus Arquette can't get to us. We're safe.

I sweep up a pile of post from the mat, tidy away the girls' shoes they've kicked off in the hall and head into the kitchen, thinking about what I can cook tonight.

But there's something wrong.

I can't immediately put my finger on it. It's just a niggling feeling in the pit of my stomach. A sixth sense that someone's been in the house. But it's impossible. All the doors are locked and secured. It's just my paranoia playing tricks on my brain.

And then I see it.

My 'I Love New York' mug on the counter.

My blood runs cold. I distinctly remember clearing all the breakfast dishes away this morning before I left with the girls. And even though I did the same thing every morning, I could recall wiping down the surfaces and sweeping away the crumbs and smears of jam and butter. I remember because I'd had to find a clean cloth under the sink as the old one had a big hole in it.

So what was the mug doing out? Abi hadn't mentioned popping home from work and I don't believe in ghosts.

I drop the post on the table and take a few tentative steps closer, like it's a bomb liable to explode with the slightest disturbance. I reach out to touch it and recoil like I've been stung. It's still warm and half-full of tea.

I gasp and spin around, expecting to see someone standing behind me.

Marcus?

But there's no one there.

I hear a thud from upstairs. The girls giggling. Suddenly, I don't feel safe anymore. Someone's been here.

Are they still here, inside the house?

Fuck.

I grab a carving knife from the block by the sink and sprint for the stairs.

The girls are playing in their rooms. Norah is building something elaborate out of Lego and Katie is treating her soft toys to a tea party.

What do I do?

'Stay in your rooms,' I tell them. 'I'll be back in a minute.'

I pull their doors closed and check each of the other upstairs rooms, starting in the family bathroom, and methodically working my way through our bedroom and en suite, the spare room and the airing cupboard, gripping the knife tightly, praying I won't have to use it.

Satisfied there's no one upstairs other than the girls, I dash back down and check all the rooms downstairs, the living room, the dining room, the utility. I check behind the curtains and in all the cupboards.

Nothing.

There's no one else in the house.

But what about the mug? How did it get there? It didn't magically appear. It was still warm, so someone must have been in the house within the last hour. But there's simply no explanation for it. I shudder with fear. I hate mysteries, especially when my family's lives are in danger.

If it was Marcus, the only way he could have broken in was if he'd stolen a set of keys and had a second set cut. It seems unlikely. But someone has been in the house while we were out.

There's one way to confirm for sure.

I put the knife back in the block and call the girls downstairs, luring them with the promise of watching some TV before tea. I don't want them out of my sight.

We all settle on the sofa, Norah on one side of me, Katie on the other, and the laptop open on my lap. If Marcus let himself in with a set of keys, he'll have been picked up on the cameras. It's just a matter of scrolling back through the footage to find out when.

I start with the camera covering the front door, but I immediately discover a disturbing issue. Somehow it's pointing upwards so all it's captured is candyfloss-white clouds floating across the sky. You can't see if anyone has approached the house from the road at all. It's unlikely the camera's been knocked. It must have been moved deliberately.

But if it was Marcus, as I suspect, the camera will have captured him tampering with it. So I scroll back an hour. And then another. And another.

Eventually, the time code shows just before 10am.

This is crazy. Has he been in the house all day? If so, what's he been doing all this time?

And then something weird happens.

There's a blip, like a digital glitch, and suddenly the position of the camera is back to how it was before, showing the approach to the front door and the drive. But the time code has jumped to 7:19am. Almost three hours of footage is missing.

I scratch my head, confused. The only way the footage can disappear like that is if there's been a fault with the system or someone has manually deleted it. Has Marcus hacked my account? Maybe he's cleverer than I'd given him credit for.

I check the footage from the other cameras around the house, but there's no sign of Marcus or any further glitch.

I have a terrible feeling about this and until I've worked out what's going on, I don't want Norah and Katie in the house.

'Right, come on, girls. Put your shoes and coats on. We're popping out,' I say, slamming the laptop closed and jumping up.

'But we're watching this,' Norah moans, pointing at the inane cartoon on the TV.

'You can watch it later.' I stride across the room and switch the TV off.

Katie bursts into tears.

I don't have time for this nonsense. We need to get out. I grab their hands and pull them into the hall.

'Please, put your shoes on,' I beg them.

'Where are we going?' Norah says with a huff, half-heartedly pulling on her coat.

'Let's see if Paul and Linda are in.'

'I don't want to!' Katie screams, stamping her foot.

I kneel so we're eye to eye and help her on with her coat. 'I know, sweetie. But it's only for half an hour. They might have a treat for you.'

I shouldn't be bribing them with sweets. It's not good for their teeth, but it seems such a trivial concern when Marcus Arquette is out there somewhere planning who knows what. And it seems to do the trick. Katie's tears dry up almost as quickly as her tantrum began.

'Are we allowed them before tea?' she asks.

'Yes,' I say. 'As a special treat.'

I don't bother locking the door behind us. There doesn't seem much point if Marcus has his own set of keys and can come and go as he pleases. For now, Paul and Linda's will have to suffice as a temporary refuge until I can work something out.

I hurry them up the Lambs' drive, clutching their hands. It's not dark yet, but strangely, all the curtains are drawn and I can't see any lights on in the house. It's not like them to go out. Linda's not particularly mobile these days. It's an effort for them to go anywhere. And besides, their car is still parked on the drive.

I hammer on the door and wait impatiently, tapping my foot on the ground.

When no one answers, I knock again.

Still no answer.

'Right, change of plan,' I say.

'Where are we going now?' Norah asks innocently.

'In the car.'

'Where?'

I don't have a clue. All I know for sure is that I have to get them away from the house until I can be one hundred per cent sure it's safe for us all. I'm going to have to call in a favour with Felicity and Johnny. At least there'll be other children at the house for them to play with.

'Why don't we see if Martha and Victor are around for a play date?'

'Yay!' Katie cries as I blip open the car doors. She loves playing with Martha. She's two years older and way cooler than any of her school friends.

I call Felicity hands-free from the car, relieved when she picks up.

'I'm sorry to ask, Flick, but can you have the girls for a couple of hours please?'

'Sure,' she says. 'What's wrong?'

'I can't really talk right now, but you know I wouldn't ask if it wasn't an emergency. I hope it's okay, I'm on my way over to yours right now.'

Chapter 34

Felicity, who I'd never thought of as particularly maternal despite having two children of her own, welcomes Norah and Katie into the house like a favourite auntie, ruffling their hair and making a fuss of them. Martha is waiting at the bottom of the stairs and the three girls charge off without a backwards glance.

'You're a lifesaver,' I say, loitering on the doorstep.

'It's no problem. Do you want to come in?'

She's desperate to find out what's going on, but if I agree to stay, she'll spend the next half an hour interrogating me until she's drawn every detail out, and I don't have the time.

'I need to get back. I think someone's been in the house.'

Felicity's mouth drops open. 'Really? How awful. Did they take much?'

'No,' I say, shaking my head. 'You don't understand. It wasn't a burglary.'

She cocks her head and narrows her eyes.

'It's complicated,' I say. 'I think it's the same guy who sent us that threatening letter.' I sigh. I wasn't going to

NOTHING LEFT TO LOSE

tell her, but she might as well know. 'It's one of the chefs from *Meld*. He's... He has some mental health issues. I'll get Abi to call you later and she can explain.'

Felicity looks like I've told her I have three heads.

'Jeez,' she gasps. 'Is he dangerous?'

I hesitate. I actually have no idea what Marcus Arquette is capable of, nor how dangerous he might be. All I know is that he blames me for the deaths of his fiancée and his unborn child and he's spoiling for some kind of revenge.

'Yes,' I say. 'That's why I don't want the children in the house until I know what he's planning.'

On the way home, I call Abi and tell her I think Marcus has found a way into the house and that I've dropped the kids off with Felicity for their safety.

'The house?' she asks, sounding incredulous. 'How?'

'I don't know.'

'Right, I'm leaving chambers now. I'll be back in twenty minutes.'

While I wait, I search the house again, looking for more proof Marcus was here. He must have come for a reason, other than to scare us, but I'm not sure what exactly I'm looking for. Signs he's been through our belongings? Our clothes? He could have been doing anything while he had the house to himself.

I climb the stairs slowly, listening for movement. I'm fairly confident he's gone now, but I'm not taking any chances. I picture him jumping out of a cupboard or springing out from under the bed with a maniacal grin on his face. Sometimes I wish I didn't have such an active imagination.

As I reach the landing, I spot a couple of marks on the carpet outside the girls' bedrooms. When I stoop down on one knee to inspect them further, I see it's dried mud. The girls always take their shoes off downstairs, so I don't think it's come from them.

There's something else. A dark ball of fluff. No, not fluff. It sticks to my fingers when I pick it up. It's old spider yarn blackened with dirt, the sort of thing you find in dusty cardboard boxes that have been left in the shed.

In our bedroom, I go through our wardrobes and drawers, but I can't see anything's been tampered with or removed. I check our bedside tables, starting on my side, and then Abi's. There's an unopened green envelope in her drawer. Curious, I pull it out.

It has my name scribbled on the front in Abi's looping handwriting. For a second, I'm confused, until I remember it's my birthday tomorrow. How could I have forgotten? It might be my fortieth, but I hope she's not planning to make a fuss. I'm not in any mood to celebrate while Marcus Arquette is stalking us.

I put the envelope back and head into Norah and Katie's room, but it's almost impossible to tell if anything is out of place as both floors are covered in toys, dressing-up costumes, paper, pens and dolls. It's like an explosion in a toy factory.

I head back downstairs and inspect the dining room, lounge and kitchen, but find nothing else to suggest an intruder has been in the house. The mug of warm tea remains the most conclusive proof.

When Abi gets in, I'm sitting at the kitchen table staring at the mug. If Marcus left it on the side to deliberately freak me out, it's working.

'Hey.' Abi comes up behind me and kisses my cheek.

'I found this on the side when I came home with the girls,' I say, nodding at the mug.

'So?'

'I didn't leave it out and there was still warm tea in it.'

Abi pulls out the chair opposite and sits down. 'Maybe you forgot to put it away this morning.'

'Forgot? Didn't you hear me? It was still half-full with warm tea.'

'You think it was Marcus?' she asks.

'I can't think of any other explanation, can you? He's toying with me, letting me know no matter what I do, he can get to me any time and any place,' I say. 'Even in our home.'

'I just don't understand how he could have got in. I mean, this house is better protected than the Vatican secret archives. You'd need a tank to break in.' Abi reaches across the table and strokes the back of my hand.

'Or a spare set of keys.'

'And where would he have got those from?'

'He could have stolen yours or mine and had a set cut.' It sounds more far-fetched when I say it out loud than it did in my head. 'There was also some mud on the landing that looks like it's come from a shoe.'

'Could have been one of the girls,' Abi suggests.

'I don't think so. It's Marcus. He's been here. I'm absolutely certain of it. There was something else. It's weird.'

I tell her about the CCTV camera above the front door that had been moved and the mysterious missing footage.

'Don't you think that's strange?' I ask.

But I'm not sure she does. Instead of answering my question, she jumps up and puts the kettle on.

'Abi?'

'Could have been a technical hitch. Want one?' she asks, holding up a mug.

I shake my head. 'You don't think it's odd? Marcus must have moved the camera, but how the hell did he delete the footage?'

'Well, look, he's gone now. I suggest we bolt the doors from the inside tonight and maybe get your man back to change the locks again?'

'He was only here a few days ago. He's going to think I've totally lost the plot,' I say. I can imagine Sanjay's face when I see him.

Nasty business. Very nasty business, Mr Hutton.

'At least Marcus won't be able to get in again.'

'True. I'll call him in the morning. See if he can come out tomorrow. I'll tell him it's an emergency,' I say.

'Tomorrow?' Abi looks crestfallen.

'He won't come out tonight.'

'But tomorrow's your birthday.'

I groan. 'Don't remind me.'

'Don't be like that. I've taken the day off work. I was hoping we could have one day at least not worrying about threatening letters and rocks through windows.'

'I wish it was that easy,' I say.

'We can't let Marcus rule our lives, Henry. He's trying to frighten us, that's all. And if we give in to that, he's won.'

I fear Marcus has something much worse in mind than trying to scare us. His last text message was unambiguous about that.

There's no one else to blame. My pain will be your pain.

But for Abi's sake, I'll do my best. Anything for a semblance of normality around her. And it'll probably do us good to spend the day together. We haven't had much time for each other lately.

'Fine,' I say. 'We'll try to forget Marcus Arquette for a day. I'll see if Sanjay can come later in the week. Just promise me there won't be a cake with forty candles on it.'

'Perfect!' Abi's face lights up. 'Now, why don't you start on dinner and I'll pop over to Flick's to pick up the girls.'

I drag myself up as Abi skips into the hall. I can probably throw together some pasta for us all. Unusually, I'm not in the mood for cooking tonight. I'm too distracted, feeling like a stranger in my own home. I still can't believe how calm Abi's been tonight. I thought she would have properly lost the plot if she suspected Marcus had been here, but she played it down, almost to the point of nonchalance.

I guess she's putting on a brave front for me. Anchoring me. Always the lawyer, plotting things through with logic and reason while I run around flapping with hysteria. It's a good thing. If we were both like me, we'd end up winding each other up into a total frenzy.

In the salad tray at the bottom of the fridge, I find a red pepper and some overripe tomatoes which I can use for the base of a pasta sauce, but I've forgotten we're out of garlic. Maybe Abi can pick some up on her way back.

I trot into the hall, hoping to catch her before she leaves.

'Abs, could you pick up —'

She fumbles guiltily with her phone and tries to hide it behind her leg. She was texting someone. I saw her thumbs flying across the screen.

'What?' she asks, a mottled flush rising up her neck.

'Can you get some garlic on your way home?'

'Sure.' She smiles and slips the phone in her bag as she pulls on her jacket.

'What were you doing?'

'Nothing,' she says.

She's hiding something. It's written all over her face. My stomach flips and the walls crash in around me.

Lie to him. Whatever you do, don't tell Henry.

'Who were you texting?' I would never normally ask. I never wanted to be that husband who checks up on his wife. But I've never had cause to be suspicious before.

'No one,' she says, and then adds, 'Flick. I was letting her know I'm on my way.'

She's behaving really oddly tonight.

'Abi?'

'What?'

'Is there something going on?'

She pulls a silly smile and narrows her eyes like she doesn't know what I'm talking about.

'Like what?'

'I don't know. Anything you want to tell me?'

'No.'

'You hardly batted an eyelid when I told you Marcus had broken into the house, made himself tea, and tampered with the CCTV cameras,' I say.

Of course, the one other person who has access to the feed is Abi. She could have easily deleted those missing three hours on her phone while sitting at her desk at work.

But why? What reason could she possibly have?

'That's not true, but there's no point in both of us running around like we've lost our heads,' she says.

'Is that what you think I'm doing? I'm trying to protect our family!'

'Alright, there's no need to raise your voice.'

'What are you hiding, Abi?'

She looks at me, horrified. 'What?'

'Let me see your phone.'

'Don't be ridiculous,' she says.

I hold out my hand and stare at her. 'If you have nothing to hide, let me see.'

'No, I'm not giving you my phone. If you don't trust me, that's your problem. I'm going to get the girls. I'll be back in an hour.'

She storms out of the house and slams the door, rattling the pictures on the walls in the hall.

If she had nothing to hide, why wouldn't she let me see her phone? She's definitely lying to me. She swore there was nothing going on with Ralph, but has he been here today with her? Is that why she had to destroy the camera footage so I wouldn't catch them out? Did she make the mistake of leaving a mug of tea on the side? It would certainly explain a lot.

All this time I've been worried about Marcus Arquette, but the real threat to my family has been from that weaselly scumbag, Ralph. It has to be him. It all makes sense now. The feeling I had that someone had been in the house. The lost CCTV footage. Abi's guilty behaviour. It's Ralph.

The question is, what am I going to do about it?

Chapter 35

It isn't a conversation I want to have in front of the girls, so I don't raise the subject when Abi returns home. It's going to be one of those ugly, undignified chats that will inevitably end in raised voices, indignation, denials and tears. But I want the truth. I need the truth.

Abi's infidelity is the last thing we need right now with a crazed psychopath hellbent on destroying us, but I can't ignore it. I've spent the last hour chewing it over in my head, working myself up and imagining the worst. I can't believe they were together in our house, in our bed. The thought of it makes me want to puke.

As I hear the front door open and click shut, my body tenses. The girls come racing into the kitchen, bubbling with excitement, their faces glowing.

'Did you have a nice time with Martha and Victor?' I ask.

But they've already run off, chasing each other up the stairs, laughing and giggling. I love that sound.

'Hey,' Abi says. 'Something smells good.'

'It's only pasta.'

She places a bulb of garlic on the counter.

'It was the last one,' she says.

'I made it without. I couldn't wait.'

'That was a waste of a journey then.'

I shrug, stirring the sauce vigorously, taking my boiling rage out on the pan while I wait for the pasta to cook.

Abi sets the table in silence. If I say something now, it's all going to come out in a torrent and it's not the time with the girls in earshot.

I serve up four bowls and we sit around the table together. The girls chatter non-stop about their day at school and the afternoon they spent at Felicity's house.

'Martha has her own pony,' Norah says nonchalantly, like I don't know her game.

For the last year, horses have become a bit of an obsession. So far I've resisted caving into riding lessons, worried it's an expensive fad she'll quickly grow out of. I can tell she's about to up her demands. But it's Katie who beats her to it.

'His name's Rocket,' she says, spearing two cones of penne pasta on the end of her fork. 'Can we have a pony?'

'Maybe,' I say. 'One day.'

Abi shoots me daggers across the table. She knows as well as I do, we don't have the land or the money for a horse and stables.

'Martha also has a TV in her room,' Norah says.

'You're not having a TV in your room,' I say. 'You're too young.'

'Martha's the same age as me.'

'I don't care. It's not going to happen.'

And that's how the meal goes on. The girls are overtired and I'm stressed. Going to Felicity's house has opened their eyes to a treasure trove of material things they think they need or deserve. Felicity and Johnny spoil their kids, buying them things out of guilt because neither of them spends enough time with them.

Meanwhile, Abi looks like she doesn't have a care in the world. How can she sit there so calmly, knowing what she's done? That she's ripping this family apart. I've been so distracted with this business with Marcus, I've not been able to see what's been staring me in the face.

Who knew my wife could be so duplicitous? The gall of the woman, bringing Ralph back to the house while she knew I was hunting down the man who's been terrorising us. And then to cover it up so casually. If I'd not found that mug on the side, I might still be in blissful ignorance. And to think I believed her the first time she denied it.

I've been such a fool. I even apologised for doubting her!

Abi looks after bath and bedtime while I wash and clear up, my anger and resentment fermenting. When I've finished, I try to distract myself by working on my blog, trying to think of some new recipes. I might as well take advantage of the site's newfound popularity and fame. But I struggle to concentrate. There's too much spinning around my head.

Marcus. Ralph. My wife's infidelity.

The scariest thing is that I don't know how any of it ends. I'm not losing my girls, though, that much is certain.

'Think I might go up and read my book,' Abi says, as she appears at the door.

I flip the laptop closed with my heart drumming. 'Are you having an affair with Ralph?' I ask.

Abi rolls her eyes and lets her head loll to one side. 'Not this again, Henry, please.'

'Yes or no?'

'Of course I'm not having a fucking affair with Ralph. I told you before!'

'Did you bring him back to the house today while you were supposed to be at work?'

'You really want me to answer that?'

'Is that why you deleted the CCTV footage?' I ask.

'What do you want me to say? Yes, Ralph and I have been screwing behind your back for years? Yes, he regularly pops over when you're out and likes to take me from behind over the kitchen table? For fuck's sake, Henry. Would you ever listen to yourself?'

'Who were you texting tonight before you went out to pick up the girls?'

'Henry, stop! I don't know where this is coming from, but maybe we need to get some help. Some counselling. I didn't realise this whole thing with Marcus was affecting you quite this badly.'

'This has nothing to do with Marcus.'

'Doesn't it? He's inside your head, messing with your mind. Can't you see? I've never given you any reason to doubt me, so why, after ten years of marriage, are you being like this?'

So typical of her to turn this on me, like this is my fault.

But maybe she has a point.

My head's all over the place. I don't know what to think or believe anymore. Whichever way I look at it, it feels like the entire world is conspiring against me.

'Because if you weren't here with Ralph today and you didn't tamper with the cameras, there's only one other explanation,' I say. 'It means Marcus was in the house. That somehow he broke in, hacked the CCTV system and vanished into thin air. And if he's done it once, he can do it again.'

Chapter 36

I'm woken by the sound of the bedroom door crashing open and the thud of tiny feet. I crack open one eye just in time to see Katie launch herself onto the bed and land on my legs with a yelp of delight.

'Daddy! Daddy! It's your birthday!' she yells at the top of her voice, shattering the morning peace. 'Are you having a party today with all your friends?'

'And a cake with lots of candles?' Norah has sneaked up beside me and is standing next to the bed in her pink unicorn pyjamas.

I struggle to sit up and scratch my head. I've had another restless night worrying about Marcus Arquette, punctuated with dreams in which I'm drowning as Abi drifts off oblivious in a wooden rowing boat with Ralph at the oars.

'I don't know', I say. 'Grown-ups don't really have parties with cake. I'll probably just have a quiet day.'

It's the day I've been dreading. Goodbye to my thirties. The best years of my life already a distant memory. How can I be forty already? And still only feel twenty-one? It's not fair.

'No, you won't,' Abi says, leaning over to kiss me. 'It's all planned.' She grins with delight.

'What's all planned? I hope you've not gone to any trouble. I told you I didn't want any fuss.'

'But it's your fortieth. Of course I'm going to make a fuss.'

She seems to have forgiven me this morning, despite the accusations I threw at her again last night. Maybe not forgiven, but at least temporarily forgotten. Abi loves birthdays, especially other people's. She wouldn't want anything to ruin my big day.

'What is it?'

'I can't tell you. It's a surprise, but I know you're going to love it.'

I groan. 'Really?' If there's one thing I hate more than a fuss being made on my birthday, it's surprises. All that expectation to look equally shocked and excited. I'd rather just go to the pub for a quiet meal and a drink.

'Don't be such a sourpuss.' Abi punches me on the arm. 'It's going to be amazing. I can't wait.'

Katie shoves a present into my chest. She's obviously wrapped it herself. All the paper's scrunched up and she's used far too much tape, but I love it all the more for the effort she's made. I make a big show of prodding and shaking it, trying to guess what it is.

'Is it an aeroplane?' I ask, frowning quizzically.

'No, silly,' she giggles.

'A dragon? A sword? A tree? Africa?'

With every guess, Katie laughs harder until she's in near hysterics and almost falls off the edge of the bed and I have to catch her.

'Just open it,' she instructs.

I rip open the paper and admire the stuffed grey kitten poking its head out of a colourful cardboard box. I suspect she had herself in mind more than me when she chose it.

'Call him Snoopy.'

I glance at Abi, who's smirking. 'Sorry,' she says. 'She picked it out herself. Insisted that's what she wanted to give you.'

'I love him,' I say. 'But do you think you could look after him in your room for me?'

Katie beams with delight.

Norah shoves a homemade card under my nose, showering the duvet in a cloud of silver glitter.

'To the best daddy ever,' I read out loud. 'All my love and kisses, Norah.'

'I made it myself,' she says.

'And I love it. Thank you.' I wrap my arms around Norah's shoulders, kiss her on the head, and hug her tightly.

Abi reaches into the cupboard beside her bed and hands me the green envelope I'd stumbled across yesterday, together with a small box wrapped in silver paper and topped with a bow. I rip it open. It's a Tissot watch. The one I mentioned I wanted months ago. She remembered.

'Thanks,' I say, and put it on my bedside cabinet.

'Don't you like it?' Abi looks wounded.

'No, yeah, it's great.'

I know she denied there was anything between her and Ralph, but I'm still having a hard time accepting it. There's a twinge of doubt that persists at the back of my mind I can't shake. It's like an aching chasm between us that's going to need time and effort to bridge.

'Is everything okay?' she asks, taking my hand.

'Yeah, of course.' I force a smile and pull my hand back. 'I'm going to take a shower. Thanks for the watch, it's perfect.'

'The girls wanted to make you breakfast in bed.'

I screw up my nose. 'All those crumbs in the sheets? Why don't I make pancakes for us all instead?'

'It's your birthday,' Abi says. Now she looks really pissed off.

I don't want to ruin the day before it's even started.

'Sorry, it's a lovely idea, but I'm sure the girls will have just as much fun making pancakes instead.'

They don't seem to mind in the slightest, especially when I let them use the hand mixer and they end up spraying the kitchen with batter. Today I don't care, especially as they seem to be having so much fun. They help me cut up lemons and pour sugar into a bowl and we all sit at the table together to eat.

As it's my birthday, Abi insists on taking the girls to school. I'd almost forgotten it was a school day.

'Be careful,' I say, as they're getting ready to leave. 'Keep an eye out for any cars that follow you and watch for anything suspicious in the playground. Any trouble, call me.'

I can see Abi thinks I'm being over protective.

'What? I just want the girls to be safe,' I say.

'Nothing's going to happen, okay. Now relax. It's your birthday.'

After they've left, I find I can't relax. I should have taken the girls. What was I thinking, letting Abi go off with them on their own when Marcus is out there somewhere?

I sit on the edge of a chair at the table, tapping my foot on the floor, chewing my nails and counting down the minutes until Abi's home safely. I make tea to distract myself and try to read the news headlines on my phone.

When the postman arrives and I hear the letterbox spring open, followed by the thud of mail landing on the mat, my heart skips. But it's only a few birthday cards and some junk mail. Nothing threatening. Nothing from Marcus, but I know he's not gone away. He's out there plotting something right now. I only wish I knew what.

I push him out of my mind. I've promised Abi I won't stress about him today. She wants us to enjoy my birthday together and it's what I'm determined to do. I'm itching to know what she has planned. Hopefully, it's something that will involve just the two of us. God knows, we could do with the time together to patch things up.

When she returns from the school run, I try to tease it out of her.

'Come on, just tell me', I say. 'You know I hate surprises.'

Abi shakes her head. 'You won't hate this one.'

'Then tell me.'

But she remains stubbornly resolute, drawing her fingers across her lips.

'Do I need to wear anything special?' I ask, trying a different tack.

'Not really.'

'Will there be other people there?'

Please, don't let it be a surprise party.

'Maybe.'

But before I can quiz her any further, there's a knock at the door.

'I wonder who that can be,' she says.

I groan when the camera footage on my phone reveals Johnny and Ralph standing on the doorstep.

'What are they doing here?'

'They've come to get you out of the way while I prepare your surprise,' Abi says cryptically. 'It's what I was sorting out when you caught me texting last night. That's why I couldn't tell you. I didn't want to ruin it.'

'So you weren't texting Ralph?'

'Of course I wasn't. Don't start that again, not today.'

I guess that makes sense. Not all secrets have to be bad ones. Maybe that was what the other message to Felicity had been all about, too.

Lie to him. Whatever you do, don't tell Henry.

Had I jumped to the wrong conclusion? What if Abi wasn't conducting an affair behind my back, but was plotting a birthday surprise? I hang my head. If I've been wrong, I'm lucky our marriage is still intact.

'Are you going to let them in or leave them standing there?' Abi says. 'They're going to take you out for the day while I get ready. I know they've upset you in the past, but you seem to be getting on better with them lately. And I didn't know who else to ask.'

'You're kidding?' My heart sinks. Not again.

'Why not?'

'They're idiots. The pair of them.'

'Come on, Henry. Don't be like that. They're really excited.'

What choice do I have? They're literally here on the doorstep, waiting for me to let them in.

'Fine,' I say resigned. It's not exactly what I had in mind when Abi said she had a surprise for my birthday.

'You'll have fun. I know you will.'

'Happy birthday, old man,' Johnny says, shaking my hand in a crushing grip as I throw open the door.

Ralph hands me a card and a bottle of wine. 'You'll enjoy that one,' he says, tapping it with his finger and winking. 'One of my special cabernets.'

'Great, thanks.' I'm conscious of Abi loitering behind me. I don't want to appear rude as she's obviously put time and effort into planning the day.

'So, I'll see you boys later,' she says. 'I'll call when we're ready for you. Have fun!'

I can't believe I'm actually going to spend my fortieth birthday with two of my least favourite people in the world. But what can I do? I can hardly refuse to go.

I bundle into the back of Johnny's Porsche, my neck contorted under the low roof. He accelerates away like he's on a racetrack. If he's trying to impress me, it isn't working. It's a thirty mile-an-hour limit along our street. There could be small children or someone elderly trying to cross. I grip the edge of the seat tightly.

'So where are you taking me?' I ask, as Johnny slips on a pair of sunglasses and cranks up the stereo. It pumps out some dreadful American rap that I'm sure he doesn't really like but thinks makes him look cool.

'A morning at the movies,' Ralph says, twisting around in his bucket seat.

I'm impressed when he tells me they've booked tickets for a sci-fi thriller I've been wanting to see for ages. It's the sort of film Abi hates and I doubt I'd have gone to see it on my own. It's a pretty thoughtful gesture.

'Good choice, thanks.'

Johnny glances at me in the rear-view mirror and grins. 'And that's just for starters,' he says. 'This is going to be the best birthday you've ever had.'

'Any idea what Abi's planning?'

Johnny and Ralph exchange a look. 'Can't say, mate,' Ralph says.

I really wish he wouldn't call me mate.

'It's not a party, is it?'

'You'll find out soon enough,' he says. 'Listen, really sorry to hear about this chef who's causing you and Abi grief, by the way. Anything we can do?'

The last time we'd talked about it, when I still thought it had something to do with Joseph Farrow, they'd both advocated I take the fight to him. And look how that ended. I'm not interested in their advice this time around. I'll deal with Marcus in my own way and in my own time.

'No, thanks,' I say. 'I'm handling it.'

The cinema car park is less than a quarter full at this time in the morning. It's an odd time to be watching a film, but what the hell. It's my birthday. It also means we get the choice of the best seats and have the theatre virtually to ourselves. There's less than a dozen other people spread around. Ralph buys bags of popcorn and fizzy drinks and as the lights go down, I finally allow myself to relax.

I deserve this. It's been a hellish few days. A couple of hours without worrying about Marcus Arquette and his petty vendetta will do me the world of good. Johnny props his feet up on the seat in front, rustling a bag of popcorn on his lap while Ralph checks his phone. It reminds me to switch mine to silent.

As I twist to hook it out of my pocket, it buzzes with an incoming message. Maybe more birthday wishes or Abi checking up on how we're getting on.

But it's neither.

It's a text from Marcus.

I sit bolt upright with every muscle in my body tense.

How's the film?

What the hell? How does he know I'm here? I turn in my seat, staring into the darkness, looking for the telltale blue glow of a mobile phone. Is he here? In the cinema? Surely I would have seen him. But how else does he know what I'm doing?

'Everything okay?' Ralph whispers as I turn the other way.

I can't see him anywhere.

The only cold crumb of comfort is that if he is here, he's not hanging around Abi or the girls.

My phone buzzes again.

Happy birthday, by the way. The big 4-0. Getting old, Henry.

Incensed, I jump up. Someone behind me tuts.

'What are you doing?' Johnny hisses.

'He's here! Marcus Arquette is in the cinema.'

'What?' Johnny puts his feet down and stares at me, wide-eyed.

If he's in the cinema, I'm going to confront him. I don't particularly like Johnny and Ralph, but for once I'm glad they're here as back-up.

I ease my way out of our row of seats, onto the steps that divide the theatre. Slowly, I walk up and down, studying every face.

'Sit down!' someone shouts out from the back, but I hardly register it.

There's a young couple at the front in matching tracksuit bottoms and puffer jackets. An older, balding man on his own a few rows behind them. On the other side, two lads with buzzcuts and tattoos. A middle-aged couple, probably retirees a few seats further back. Up and down I go, studying all their faces, looking for Marcus.

But after a few minutes and the odd look, it's clear he's not here.

In which case, where the hell is he and how does he know I'm at the cinema?

It ruins the entire film. I can't concentrate now. I'm constantly checking over my shoulder and watching the entrance, looking for Marcus. He's here somewhere. I can sense it, but I just can't see him.

As the credits roll, the lights come up and everyone leaves.

'Hey, are you okay?' Ralph taps my shoulder.

'He was here. I'm sure of it. Look, he was messaging me.'

I show Ralph my phone. He shrugs.

'If he was, he's not here now. Come on, let's get you out of here. We're supposed to be celebrating.'

They take me to a country pub for lunch and we spend the afternoon at a golf driving range, which isn't exactly my idea of fun. I've never seen the point of golf. It's made worse when Johnny and Ralph reveal themselves both to be accomplished golfers who hit the ball hundreds of yards in a straight line. When I try, I either miss the ball completely and nearly fall flat on my arse, or slice it so badly it loops off into the long grass, much to their amusement.

Johnny tries to show me how to stand properly, with my knees slightly bent and my elbows tucked in while keeping my head over the ball. But it's hopeless and they both end up laughing at me like I'm the class idiot.

I'm just about ready to call it a day when I'm saved by Ralph's phone ringing.

He steps away from us to take the call, his jaw tightening. He looks off into the distance as he listens. It looks like bad news.

Johnny and I glance at each other. He shrugs. He has no better idea than me.

'Ralph?' I ask as he hangs up. 'What is it?'

'We need to get you home,' he says. 'Now.'

Chapter 37

Felicity's sporty little BMW is parked across the end of our drive, so Johnny pulls up in the road outside Paul and Linda's. He cranks on the handbrake, kills the engine and I clamber out from the back of the Porsche, my shoulders stiff and aching from the golf. I've used muscles I didn't even know I had.

As I stretch my back and roll my neck, I notice something odd about the Lambs' house. All the curtains are drawn again, even though it won't be dark for another couple of hours. I have a sudden bad feeling. The curtains were drawn yesterday when I knocked on the door with the girls and they didn't answer. I try to recall if they were open this morning when we left the house, but if they were, I didn't notice. My mind was fully focused on where Johnny and Ralph were taking me.

Come to think of it, I can't remember the last time I saw either Paul or Linda. I usually spot one of them during the day, pottering in the garden, sweeping the drive or putting the rubbish out. They've been conspicuous by their absence.

'Give me two minutes,' I say, holding up two fingers to Johnny and Ralph as they head up our drive towards the front door. 'I just want to check on our neighbours.'

But Ralph intercepts me, snatching my elbow and guiding me towards my own house.

'I've not seen them for a few days and they're quite elderly,' I protest, but he's having none of it.

'No, you don't. I promised Abi I'd have you back on time. Everyone's waiting.'

I anchor my feet to the ground, my heart sinking. 'It's not a party, is it? You promised it wasn't be a party,' I say, shrugging off Ralph's hand.

'I never promised anything, mate. Come on, time for your big surprise.'

Johnny is already at the door, knocking. A moment later, Abi appears with a huge smile on her face. She's changed into a sparkly top and a pair of skinny white jeans and is wearing dusky eyeshadow and bright fuchsia lipstick. She looks amazing.

'Did you have a good time?' she asks, beckoning me inside. 'Did the boys look after you? Come on, come in.'

I shoot a rueful glance at the house next door, hoping my fears about Paul and Linda are unfounded. I'm sure they're fine. I'll make some excuse to pop round later to make sure.

'What's going on, Abs?' I ask as she drags me inside and helps me off with my jacket.

'You'll see.'

As she kisses Ralph on the cheek, an unwelcome stir of jealousy swirls in my stomach.

'You look stunning!' Ralph says, holding her at arm's length and giving her the once over.

No matter how many times Abi tells me there's nothing going on between them, the seed of doubt has been sown and I'm finding it hard to kill it off, especially as I now know they were lovers as students.

'Johnny, thanks for taking him off my hands. How was the film?' she asks.

Johnny pushes his sunglasses onto the top of his head. 'It was good', he says, 'apart from Henry thinking —'

'You'd have hated it', I say, quickly cutting him off. I don't need him telling Abi about Marcus and setting her fears running again. Not today.

Felicity and Colette are standing in the kitchen clutching glasses of champagne. They've started early. They're both wearing expensive-looking dresses and have done their hair and make-up for the occasion, whatever the occasion is. I suddenly feel under-dressed.

'Happy birthday, darling', Felicity says, draping an arm around my shoulder and showering me with air kisses.

I put my hands on her waist and notice how skinny she feels. Is she eating properly?

'Can't believe you're forty.' Colette hugs me tightly. 'You don't look a day over thirty-five.'

It's nice of her to say, even if it's not true. I'm sure I've aged about ten years in the last two weeks. This business with Marcus has definitely taken its toll.

'Surprise!' Abi shouts. She stretches out an arm towards the kitchen counter, which is completely covered in all kinds of fine ingredients, as if they've been laid out for an elaborate meal. Bags of lentils, pulses and beans. Fresh herbs. Exotic vegetables and spices.

'I don't understand,' I say.

If Abi's planning to cook for us all, that would be a bombshell. By her own admission, she struggles not to burn toast. A meal for six is definitely out of her league unless she's been taking secret lessons.

She glides across the room, slips an arm around my waist and runs her fingers up and down my chest. 'You know how you've always talked about taking some cookery lessons, not that I think you need them.' Everyone's watching closely for my reaction. I feel myself wilt under their scrutiny. 'Well, I've arranged for a private chef to cook us all a fabulous meal tonight, and to give you a bit of a lesson, too. I know it's not Tuscany or the south of France, but I thought this was the next best thing. What do you think?'

Actually, it's a really thoughtful gift. All my cookery knowledge has come from books or the internet. I've had no formal training. I've been talking for years about taking some lessons abroad and combining it with a holiday to France or Italy, but the time has never seemed right or the girls were too young, and I didn't like to go off on my own. Bringing a chef into the house is a genius compromise.

'That's awesome,' I say, taking Abi's face in my hands and planting a tender kiss on her lips. 'Thank you.'

'And the great thing is, we all get to enjoy your present with you!'

I guess for most people, the idea of cooking your own birthday dinner would be no kind of gift at all. But Abi's thought this through. She knows I'm happier in the kitchen than being the centre of attention at a party. It's perfect.

'I thought my watch was my gift,' I say with a pang of guilt that it's still sitting by my bedside and I've not put it on. 'I hope you've not spent too much.' A personal chef offering tailored tutoring must have cost her a small fortune.

'Well,' she says, grinning at Felicity and Colette, who have clearly been in on the planning, 'I wasn't going to tell you this, but you're going to find out at some point. I actually won it as a prize.'

Abi looks like she's going to burst. She's so pleased with herself.

'How? When?'

'Facebook,' she says. 'A local chef was looking to promote his new business. All I had to do was like and share his post to win an evening's cookery lesson and a meal for six. I couldn't believe it when I won. You know I never win anything, and of course, I immediately thought it would make a brilliant birthday present for you, although it seems mean asking you to cook your own birthday meal.'

'No, no, I love it,' I say. 'It's a brilliant present.'

'It's been a nightmare keeping it secret. I had to rope in Flick and Colette to help me. But after everything that's been going on over the last two weeks, I thought it would help take your mind off things.'

So the text message to Felicity wasn't asking her to keep quiet about an affair. It was about keeping this evening a secret. I've been such a fool, so blinkered to any other truth than the lies Marcus Arquette wanted me to believe. I should have known better. I should have trusted Abi. But I was far too quick to accept

Marcus's twisted narrative as he tried to destroy our marriage.

'I have another confession,' Abi says, looking coy.

What now? I prepare myself for a bombshell.

'You know you thought someone had been in the house yesterday? I'm sorry, Henry. It was Felicity. I gave her a set of keys, but I couldn't tell you because she was dropping around some ingredients for Tim.'

'Tim?'

'The chef,' she says. 'But then I remembered the CCTV cameras and I was worried you might log onto the system, see her letting herself in and the surprise would be ruined. So I had to move the camera before I left for work. But then you got yourself all worked up, convinced it was Marcus, and of course, I couldn't say anything.'

'Felicity? Seriously? Thank God for that.' The relief feels physical, like a blanket of iron has been lifted from my shoulders.

Again, I'd jumped to conclusions and assumed the worst. Of course Marcus Arquette hadn't broken into the house. He hadn't stolen a set of keys and let himself in while we were out. It was ridiculous I'd even thought it was a possibility, but he'd had me willing to believe anything by that point.

'Mind you, I couldn't believe she left a mug of tea out on the side and nearly gave the whole game away. Flick, what were you thinking?'

Abi laughs, but Felicity is staring at her, shaking her head.

'I didn't have tea,' she says.

Abi's laugh dries up and the humour in her eyes vanishes. 'But Henry found it when he got home.'

'I promise, Abi, I was in and out. I didn't stop for tea. I didn't have the time.'

Abi catches my eye, her brow furrowing. The room falls silent.

'Well, if Felicity didn't leave that mug on the side, who did?' I ask.

Five pairs of eyes stare blankly at me. No one has any answer.

My skin prickles and there's an uncomfortable tightness in my chest. Someone other than Felicity has been in the house. But no one else has a set of keys.

'Hey there, you must be Henry.' The voice startles me.

A tall figure in chef's whites appears from the utility, clutching handfuls of coriander, mint and basil I assume he's been foraging from the garden. A winning smile lights up his face as an icy chill runs down my spine.

'I'm Tim,' he says. 'Happy birthday. Now, I hear you're a half-decent chef yourself, but let's see if we can't teach the old dog a few new tricks.'

The blood rushes from my head down to my toes as the room spins and I'm momentarily thrown off balance. This can't be happening.

My mouth opens and closes, but no words come out.

'Henry,' I hear Abi saying distantly. 'What's wrong?'

But I can't speak. The words are stuck in my throat and all the air feels as though it's been sucked from my lungs.

How could Abi have been so stupid?

Has she completely lost her mind? What was she thinking, inviting Marcus Arquette into our home?

Chapter 38

I've lost the ability to move. My limbs are frozen and I can barely breathe. My first thought is that my eyes are deceiving me. But no, it's definitely him. Marcus Arquette is here in my house. In my kitchen. And Abi and the others have absolutely no idea.

Of course, they never met him. He was working in the kitchen on the night we ate at *Meld*. He accosted me, but never spoke to the rest of the table. They're all in blissful ignorance. And terrible danger.

What the hell am I going to do?

My phone's in the back pocket of my jeans. Maybe I could make my excuses, nip outside and call the police. But I'm sure he's not going to allow me to do that. At the very least, I should try to warn the others.

'Henry?'

Abi's staring at me with a crooked frown. She must have seen the sheer horror that clouded my face when Marcus walked in. What am I supposed to say? Thanks for the lovely birthday gift and for inviting a total psycho into our home?

'Is everything okay?' she asks again.

'Where are the girls?'

I haven't heard them since I've been home, but if they're here, I need to keep them well away from Marcus until I can figure out what to do.

'Upstairs, playing. Why?'

'No reason.'

'I can call them down if you want to see them.'

'No! I'll see them later,' I say.

If I tell her what's going on, I risk escalating the situation. What if Marcus is only here to show how close he can really get to my family? If I back him into a corner or call him out, there's no telling how he'll react or what he'll do. I can't take that chance. I have to treat him like a wild animal and do nothing to provoke him.

'You do like it, don't you?' Abi asks.

'Of course I do. It's a wonderful gift.' She knows something's wrong, but I have to go along with this stupid charade until I can work out what Marcus is up to. The last thing I want to do is endanger everyone else.

'Anyone for champagne?' Marcus asks, grabbing a bottle of Veuve Clicquot from the fridge like he owns the place.

The pop of the cork makes me jump, startling me out of my reverie.

I force a fake smile as Marcus circles the room, filling glasses. As long as he thinks I'm playing along, we should be fine.

He claps his hands to get everyone's attention.

'Ladies and gentlemen,' he says. 'Make yourselves comfortable. Have a drink. Relax. Henry and I will start on dinner shortly and in a few hours we hope to serve you a meal fit for royalty.'

'What are we eating?' Colette asks. Her pupils are big and black and she's swaying slightly in her high heels.

'To start, we'll be serving wild mushroom consommé with herb gnocchi and confit tomatoes, followed by octopus salad with mango and apple vinegar, brown shrimp jelly, a fennel and white onion sauce, served on a banana leaf with baby carrots and baby beetroot.'

To be fair to Marcus, it's a sublime menu.

'Sounds bloody delicious,' Johnny says. I can almost see him salivating, despite the enormous plate of fish and chips he's eaten at the pub at lunchtime.

I don't know how Marcus has tricked Abi. Didn't she say something about winning a competition on Facebook? He's obviously targeted her and manipulated the result. I don't know how. All I care about is how I'm going to get him out of the house again.

Our eyes finally lock and his mouth turns up with the hint of a knowing smile. He must be loving this, charming everyone into thinking he's something he's not. Look at them all, hanging off his every word. They don't know what he's capable of. But then again, neither do I. Not really.

A trickle of sweat runs down my back and I shiver, my galloping heart threatening to burst free of my chest. Is this his ultimate plan? The moment he's finally come to take his revenge for Sally-Anne's death?

One death was too much.

Two is unbearable.

An eye for an eye seems only fair after what you've done.

So now I have nothing left to lose, I'll see you in hell.

'What about dessert?' Ralph asks.

'Panna cotta with dark chocolate and salted caramel foam,' Marcus replies with a sickly smile. 'Now shall we get started, Henry?'

He reaches into a cardboard box on the floor and pulls out a chef's jacket that matches his own. He holds it up to let everyone see that he's had my name embroidered in blue thread across the breast.

'Happy birthday, Henry,' he says.

It's greeted with a polite round of applause and smiles all round.

My rictus grin makes my jaw ache.

Act normally, Henry. It's down to you to keep everyone safe.

As Marcus helps me to slip the jacket on over my T-shirt, his hand brushes my shoulder and I recoil like I've been stung. His touch repulses me.

'I can tell this is going to be a perfect night,' Abi says, grinning from ear to ear.

'I hope so,' Marcus says. 'I certainly intend to make sure it's an evening you'll never forget.'

I fear he's right. No one's going to forget tonight in a hurry, least of all me.

'You're welcome to stay and watch,' Marcus says, 'but feel free to amuse yourselves. Henry and I have a lot of work to do. Shall we start on the mushroom consommé ?'

The only hope of surviving this is to play along, so as the others form a tight group and begin chatting, I shuffle with leaden legs to Marcus's side. He hands me some shallots from a basket on the side and instructs me to peel and chop them, while he puts a pan on the hob, lights the gas and tosses in a nob of butter.

My sweaty hand wraps around the handle of one of my small knives. The blade is only a few inches long, but it's still a vicious weapon. I pride myself on keeping all my knives razor-sharp. Maybe I could slip one into my pocket while Marcus isn't watching…

But his eyes are on me like a hawk. I'll have to wait until his back is turned or he's otherwise distracted.

A phone pings somewhere in the room. A jarring, intrusive sound that cuts through the casual chatter and laughter. As I glance up from my chopping, Ralph's hand dives into his pocket. He slides out his mobile, holds it at his side, and subtly turns his head to check the message.

'No!' Marcus yells so loudly, I jump. He smacks his hands down on the counter. 'No phones tonight!'

The room is stunned into silence. Everyone turns and gawps at him, shocked by the sudden outburst.

'Henry needs to concentrate without distraction,' Marcus rants. For a fraction of a second, a dark cloud of irritation shadows his face as his true colours bubble to the surface. And then it's gone, dissolving into another charming smile. Did they even notice?

'We want this to be a fabulous evening, don't we? I need your focus on the food, the amazing tastes and the great company. Tonight, consider your phones the enemy of everything we're trying to achieve. I don't want anyone distracted by texts or calls or checking their Insta accounts, okay? There'll be plenty of time for that later. In fact, let's remove the temptation, shall we? I want you all to hand over your devices, and we'll put them out of the way until the end of the evening.'

The look on their faces, it's as if he's suggested cutting off their arms.

'Hang on a minute,' Johnny says, as Marcus picks up a glass bowl on the side and approaches them. 'I need my phone in case the babysitter —'

'No distractions. You'll thank me for it later.' He's so disarming when he says it, they all fall for it.

Ralph shrugs but doesn't protest as I thought he would. One by one, they surrender their phones, dropping them in the bowl until it's almost full.

Marcus approaches me last.

'And you, Henry.'

My phone is my lifeline out of this hell. If I give it up, I have no way of calling for help. But I guess Marcus knows that. Taking our phones has nothing to do with keeping everyone focused on the food and everything to do with cutting us off from rescue.

I can't give that up.

'I wanted to take some pictures,' I say in desperation. 'You know, as a reminder of the evening.'

Marcus rattles the bowl in front of my face. 'No exceptions,' he says, his cold eyes cutting through me. 'I'll take some photos and I'll share them with everyone later.'

Up close, he's more athletic than I remember, with muscular, broad shoulders and a thick neck. The sleeves of his jacket strain around his biceps and he has at least a three-inch height advantage over me. It rules out any thought I have of being able to physically overpower him, at least not without a weapon.

With a sigh of resignation, I drop my phone into the bowl.

'Good,' Marcus says. 'I'll leave them by the door and you can pick them up on your way out later.'

He marches out of the room, into the hall. It's my chance to grab a knife. Some insurance should I need it later. But the block by the sink is empty. He's moved them all. The carving knives. The paring knife. Even the bloody bread knife. I scan the worktops, but I can't see them anywhere. Only the utility knife I have in my hand, and I need that to finish the shallots. He's already several steps ahead of me.

Then I hear the chilling sound of keys turning in the locks on the front door and the bolts being slotted into place.

He's locking us in!

Bizarrely, nobody else seems to notice. Probably just as well. I don't want anyone to panic. Everyone needs to keep calm.

'How's it going?' Abi sidles up to the counter and leans across it, fondling the stem of her champagne glass.

'Yeah, good.' I hope she doesn't pick up the tremor in my voice. What am I supposed to say?

Actually, not so good, darling. It's not your fault, but you've been duped by the dangerous and deranged lunatic who's been terrorising us for the last two weeks and now he's locked us in the house, taken away our phones so we can't call for help and is probably planning to murder us all.

A thud from upstairs reminds me the girls are in danger, too. My gaze automatically shoots to the ceiling.

'Don't worry about them,' Abi says. 'They're happy playing. Tim said he was going to make them some child-friendly nibbles for later when we eat.'

I don't want Marcus going anywhere near them, and so I need to make sure that whatever they do, they don't come downstairs. The only way I can ensure that is to speak to them. Make them understand how serious this is. I rush for the door, aiming for the stairs, but Marcus intercepts me, blocking my way.

'Going somewhere?'

'I was going to see if Norah and Katie are okay. I've not seen them all day.'

'They're fine,' he says through gritted teeth. 'You don't have the time to disappear upstairs. There's a lot of work to get done if we're going to eat on time.'

He doesn't give me much choice, so I turn and drag myself back to the shallots. As I pick up the knife, he comes up behind me and puts his mouth to my ear. I catch the stench of alcohol on his breath.

'Don't think about trying anything heroic tonight, Henry,' he hisses, 'if you want everyone to get out of this alive. This is my kitchen now and my rules. Do exactly what I tell you and nobody needs to get hurt. Understood?'

I swallow a lump in my throat as I nod.

He takes a step back and I release the breath I was holding.

'So,' he says, raising his voice above the chatter, 'it's just gone five now. The plan is that we'll have you seated and eating at seven-thirty on the dot. And trust me, you won't be disappointed.'

There's a ripple of appreciation around the room, but I shudder.

He's started the clock, the countdown to whatever it is he's planning.

It's the moment he's going to reveal himself, I'm sure of it. It's when he finally plans to avenge the death of Sally-Anne.

Unless I can stop him.

But I don't have long.

Two and a half hours.

Two and a half hours to figure out how the hell I'm going to get us all out of this mess alive.

Chapter 39

With shaking hands, I toss the chopped shallots into the pan of smoking, buttery oil and use a wooden spoon to stir them as they sizzle and spit.

'As soon as they've softened, we need to start on the gnocchi,' Marcus says.

Abi's in deep conversation with Colette and Felicity while Ralph and Johnny have taken themselves into a corner where they're huddled conspiratorially. Nobody's paying any attention to us.

I take the opportunity to quiz Marcus.

'What are you doing here?' I ask under my breath, trying to sound menacing. I don't want him to know how frightened I am. That would only feed his ego.

'I'm helping you cook the best meal any of your loud-mouthed friends have ever eaten,' he says.

'You know what I mean. What do you want from us?'

'Want? Nothing, Henry.' The smile that creeps across his lips is pure evil, especially the way he narrows his eyes like a snake. 'Now come on, you need concentrate. There's a lot of work to get through and we have little time.'

'I'm sorry about Sally-Anne, but her death wasn't my fault and I can't bring her back.'

I'm surprised by how quickly he moves across the kitchen, pressing his body against mine, his lips at my ear again. He prods something into my kidneys. A knife?

'Don't you dare mention her name,' he hisses with a flare of anger. 'You keep your mouth shut and you work. My kitchen, my rules.'

'Alright, alright, I'm sorry,' I gasp. I've crossed a line. I can't afford to make him angry. If we're going to come out of this alive, I need to keep him on side. At least for the moment.

'And when you're in my kitchen, you'll call me "Chef". Understand?'

It's a title that needs to be earned through respect, not fear, but I have no choice. 'Yes, Chef,' I say, the word clawing in my throat.

The menu turns out to be one of the most complicated, demanding and technical I've ever attempted and I'm actually glad Marcus is here to guide me through it and help with timings. I'd have never managed it on my own. And at least as I throw myself into a frenzy of chopping, peeling, frying, simmering, beating and blending, with sweat dripping from my brow, it helps take my mind off the seriousness of the situation.

Abi's taken the two couples through into the lounge, leaving us to work in peace, but there's no let-up for me as Marcus continues to bark out instructions, pushing me beyond what I thought I was capable of, determined to make this meal the best it can be. Who knows, it could be our last.

But I'm trying to juggle too many things, keep too many plates spinning, and my nerves are shot. Without thinking, I grab a pan with my bare hand, forgetting it's been sitting on a hot flame. A searing bolt of pain pierces my palm like I've been stabbed.

'Shit!' I scream, clutching my wrist and staring dumbly at the angry red welt that's appeared.

Marcus is immediately at my side, inspecting the injury and guiding me to the sink, where he holds my hand under a stream of cold water.

'You need to take more care,' he says. It almost sounds like he means it.

'Yes, Chef.'

'Do you have a first aid kit?'

I nod to a drawer on the other side of the room. He finds a dressing and bandages my hand. I flex my fingers. It's not too bad and although the burn stings, I'm good to carry on. There's no more time to lose.

Eventually, with the mushroom consommé finished and most of the prep completed for the octopus salad, I spot a narrow window of opportunity.

'I need to use the bathroom,' I say, wiping my hands on the tea towel I have tucked into my belt. 'Too much coffee earlier,' I add with a grimace.

Marcus squints at me and then nods. 'Be quick.'

I toss the tea towel on the side and hurry out of the kitchen without waiting to be told twice. In my haste, I almost bump into Abi in the hall.

'Everything going okay?' she asks.

'Fine.' I don't have time to stop and chat, and I don't want Marcus getting suspicious.

'What have you done to your hand?' she asks, noticing the dressing on my palm. 'Are you hurt?'

She tries to take my hand, but I pull it away. 'It's nothing.'

Colette's in the doorway to the lounge. 'It smells so good,' she says with a slight slur. They need to slow down on the champagne or they're all going to be under the table before we've eaten.

'Go back in the lounge,' I tell Abi, guiding them both back inside. 'It won't be long now.'

I check over my shoulder, half expecting to find Marcus watching me. But the coast is clear. I tiptoe to the front door and, sure enough, it's locked and bolted. What's more worrying is that there's no sign of our keys. They're usually in the papier mâché bowl, but both sets, mine and Abi's, have vanished. Nor is there any sign of the bowl of mobile phones Marcus was going to leave for people to collect on their way out.

My worst suspicions are confirmed. Marcus has locked us all in the house and removed any way of us calling for help. We don't even have a landline these days. Since we always use our mobiles, there seemed little point in keeping it. And of course, we can't even climb out of a window. The bars I'd had installed to keep Marcus out, now cage us inside the house with him.

The irony of the situation isn't lost on me. We're entirely at his mercy and I don't know what we're going to do.

If nothing else, I have to find a way of getting Norah and Katie out. They're too young to suffer at Marcus's hands. I don't know how, but I have to save them. It's a primaeval instinct, stronger even than the desire to save myself. They're my priority.

I creep up the stairs, wincing at each tread that creaks under my weight. Marcus will look for me soon. I don't have much time.

They're both in Katie's room. All their dolls spread out across the floor and a duvet strung over the back of a chair to make a den.

'Daddy!' Katie squeals, jumping up and launching herself at me when she sees me at the door.

I shush her quiet, worried Marcus might hear, and hug her tightly with unexpected tears pooling in my eyes.

There's no way I'm going to let him hurt them. I'd rather die first.

'I'm hungry. Mummy said she was going to bring us a snack.'

Norah pokes her head out from under the duvet den. 'I'm hungry too,' she says.

I lean over and kiss the top of her head, savouring her smell, apple shampoo and the lingering staleness of school.

'I'll bring something up in a minute, but you have to stay in your room. Promise not to come downstairs, unless I tell you it's okay. No matter what happens. Do you understand?'

'But why?' Norah whinges.

'Because it's grown-up time. Do you promise?'

'Okay, Daddy, we promise,' Katie says. 'Now, are you going to get us some snacks?'

'Yes, I'll be back soon. I love you both very much.'

Norah dives back under the duvet with a squawk of delight as I step out onto the landing and pull the door closed silently.

What have I done? My poor girls don't deserve to be caught up in Marcus Arquette's twisted nightmare. I'd lay my life down for them both. In a heartbeat. But that might not be enough. Marcus is still obviously grieving the loss of his own child. If he's looking for vengeance, to make me suffer the same way he's suffering, I have to accept he won't spare the girls just because they're children. But as a parent, my number one duty is to protect them, no matter what it takes.

But what if I can't?

No, I will. I can't think like that. Those girls make my heart swell with so much love and pride that sometimes I think it's going to burst. I won't let Marcus take that away. He is not going to destroy my family. My daughters are innocent. It's not fair they're caught up in this through no fault of their own.

Just as it wasn't fair that Sally-Anne lost her job at the worst possible time in her life, pregnant with her first child and soon to be married. I can't imagine the depths of despair into which she'd fallen to think the better option was to take her own life. It's a horrible tragedy, but Matunde said himself the restaurant didn't close because of the review on my blog, even if the staff thought so. Sally-Anne didn't lose her job because of me. I regret she was named in the piece and humiliated in public, but it doesn't warrant what Marcus is doing.

I'd try to reason with him if I thought he'd listen. I suppose I should at least try. He needs to know the truth, even if he doesn't want to hear it.

Before that, I need to get the girls out of the house.

But how? The doors are locked, Marcus has hidden the keys, and all the windows are barred. There must be another way. There has to be.

I glance up at the ceiling and back down to the floor. Abi's cleaned off the mud marks and vacuumed up the dirty clumps of spider yarn. Evidence that Marcus had been in the house, I'm sure. Felicity was adamant she hadn't left that mug of warm tea in the kitchen, so it has to be him. But how did he get in?

It's suddenly so obvious, I can't believe I haven't worked it out before.

He crawled through from Paul and Linda's attic. There's only a thin skin of plasterboard separating the two roof spaces. Mice have already chewed holes in it. It would have been easy to break through, even with his bare hands. That's why his footprints were directly below the loft hatch and it explains where the dirty spider yarn came from. The rafters are thick with it.

Excitement bubbles in my stomach as a new plan forms in my mind. If Marcus got into our house by crawling through the roof space, it's how I can get the girls out safely.

Then my heart sinks as I remember the closed curtains at Paul and Linda's. The lights out. The look of desolation about the place. What's he done to them? I close my eyes and say a silent prayer. Please don't let him have hurt them. They really don't deserve that.

'Henry?' Marcus's voice echoes angrily up the stairs. 'Where the hell are you? We need to get the octopus on.'

I nip into the bathroom and pull the flush.

'Just coming,' I holler back.

Chapter 40

I paint a fake smile on my face, but I'm worried about my neighbours. If Marcus has hurt Paul and Linda to get to me and my family, I won't be able to live with myself. At least I now know there's a way to save the girls. I just have to find an opportunity to put my plan into action.

'Where have you been?' Marcus grumbles.

'To the bathroom. I told you.'

'What took you so long?'

I raise an eyebrow.

Marcus points a carving knife at me. I still haven't worked out where he's hidden the rest of the knives.

'I warned you, don't try to be a hero,' he says.

I hold up my hands. 'Alright, I'm sorry. I popped in to see the girls. I've not seen them all day.'

He lowers the knife but keeps his eyes fixed on me like he's trying to work out whether he can trust me. I plaster what I hope is an expression of innocence on my face. I need him to believe I'm not being difficult, that I'm going along with his demands. I fear it's the only way any of us are going to get out alive.

'We need to finish the octopus,' he says. 'Ever cooked it before?' He's laid out six tentacles on a chopping board.

'Never.'

'It needs tenderising, and that's going to take some time, so you'd better get a move on.'

He instructs me to wash the tentacles in cold water and place them in the pressure cooker with onion, coriander seeds, white peppercorns and coriander stalks. But my mind's no longer on the cooking. I'm going through the motions. All I can think about is how I can distract Marcus while I help the girls escape. As I work, a plan forms in my head.

It will be asking a lot of them, especially as they're so young, but they're our only hope. I wish there was another way, and that I didn't have to ask them to do this. It's such an enormous responsibility, but time is running out.

I need to find another opportunity to give them the instructions and impress on them the importance of what I'm asking. I'll have to tell them what's going on. Or at least some of it. I have no choice. As parents, we sometimes keep the truth from our kids to protect them, but I don't have that luxury. If they're going to do this, they need to understand the seriousness of why I'm asking.

The problem is, I doubt Marcus is going to let me out of his sight again.

'Put this in the fridge,' he says, handing me a bottle of mango and apple vinegar.

'Sure,' I smile. I want him to believe I'm playing along. I don't want him to think I'm being in any way difficult.

I slot the bottle onto the shelf in the door next to a carton of milk and notice a tray of handmade sausage rolls, mini pizzas and chicken goujons covered in cling film.

'Are these for Norah and Katie?' I ask, spotting my opportunity.

'It's for them to snack on while we eat,' he says.

I blow out the air from my cheeks. 'It's probably going to be a bit late for them to eat by then. Why don't I quickly run them up now?' I slide the tray from the fridge and grab a couple of plates from the cupboard.

'They can wait,' Marcus snaps. 'You need to get on with this octopus.' His mood has been swaying dangerously all evening. One moment he's charm personified, and the next he's ready to chew my head off.

I'm going to have to take my chances.

'I'll be right back,' I say, hustling out of the kitchen before he can stop me. 'They get really grumpy when they're hungry, and I don't want them to keep popping downstairs for food. Then I'll sort the octopus.'

I leave the room expecting Marcus to snatch my arm and drag me back. I hear him grumbling, but he makes no physical effort to stop me.

There's laughter and chatter coming from the lounge. None of them knows the danger we're all in, but for now, it's best it stays that way. I don't want them panicking, or Johnny or Ralph trying something stupid and getting us all killed. They can stay in ignorance for a little while longer, at least until the girls are safely out of the house. I need to keep the situation as normal as possible for as long as I can, even though it's anything but a normal situation.

I trot up the stairs and get rid of the trays of snacks in our bedroom. The girls need to focus on getting out, not on their stomachs.

They're pretending to hide from me in their makeshift den, but their suppressed giggles give them away. I snake my hand under the duvet until I find their knees and squeeze until they're both writhing and breathless with laughter, begging me to stop.

They crawl out with sweaty, rosy faces and damp hair. I push the door closed so we can't be heard.

'How do you fancy going on an adventure?' I whisper.

'What kind of adventure?' Norah asks, suspiciously.

'A really quiet one, so quiet no one hears you.'

Norah frowns. 'Why?'

'Come on, it'll be fun.'

I stand and grab their hands. They're warm and sticky. I squeeze them tight, trying not to think of all the things that could go wrong with what I'm about to ask of them.

Then I explain exactly what the game entails, how they need to silently crawl through the attic into the neighbouring house, and drop through the loft hatch. That's going to be the most dangerous part because unless Marcus has left a ladder out, they're going to have to jump. Then they need to raise the alarm, hopefully with Paul and Linda, but if anything's happened to them, they're going to have to go knocking on doors on the street.

Oh my God, what am I doing?

I'm sending my kids through the loft into the house next door where, for all I know, Paul and Linda might be dead, and then asking them to go knocking on strangers' doors. It's insane. If there was any other way, I'd grab it with both hands. But there isn't. There is no other choice.

Norah looks up at me with her big, brown eyes, her brow knotted. 'But why do we have to find someone? Won't Paul and Linda be there?'

'They might be hurt, sweetie,' I say. 'And we can't get out of the house because the chef who's come to cook for Daddy's birthday has locked us all in and hidden the keys. That's why it's really important you find someone and tell them we need help, okay?'

Norah nods solemnly. 'Okay, Daddy.'

'Are there big spiders in the loft?' Katie asks.

'No,' I lie. 'There are no spiders. It might be a little scary, but you're big, brave girls. I know you can do it.'

Katie is looking apprehensive. Neither of them has ever been in the loft before. I guess the fear of the unknown is worrying them and they don't really understand the gravity of the situation. They need another motivation.

'And if you both complete the adventure, why don't we all go to Legoland as a treat?' I say, grasping at the first thing that comes to mind.

Katie cheers and I have to shush her quiet.

'Remember, it's a quiet game. Nobody's allowed to hear you. Are you ready?'

The girls nod.

I open the door and peer out onto the landing. A crackle of laughter from below echoes up the stairs.

'Okay, come on,' I say, coaxing them out of the room.

I can't believe I'm asking them to do this. Abi would never agree to it if she knew what I was doing. She'd think it was too dangerous. Accuse me of putting the girls' lives at risk. But what else can I do? If they don't do this, the chances are we could all die. If I don't do something, Marcus is going to kill us all.

Chapter 41

I straighten my chef's jacket, take a deep breath, and hurry back down the stairs. Our fate is now in the hands of my daughters and whether they can raise the alarm. I helped them up the loft ladder, gave them a torch, pointed them in the right direction and silently closed the hatch behind them. There's nothing more I can do but wait and pray.

Abi is in the kitchen talking to Marcus, whose face seems to darken with every passing minute.

'Go easy on him. It's his birthday. I guess he just wanted to spend some time with his daughters,' she's saying.

'Sorry about that,' I say breezily. 'The girls didn't want me to go.'

Abi turns and grins at me. I can see from the glaze in her eyes that the champagne has continued to flow freely.

Marcus glowers. Does he suspect something?

'Check the octopus and start on the panna cotta,' he orders.

I guide Abi out of the kitchen with a hand on her lower back. I don't want her anywhere near Marcus

Arquette.

'I just came to see how you're getting on,' she says, slurring her words.

'Great. I'm learning a lot. But there's lots to do. We shouldn't be too much longer.'

'I was going to pop up to see if the girls are okay,' she says.

'No! They're fine. I've just been up there. They're having something to eat,' I say, remembering I was supposed to have taken them their snacks. 'Leave them.'

'Abs, darling, is there any more champagne?' Colette appears wobbling on her high heels.

I snatch another bottle from the fridge, pop the cork and hand it to Abi. 'Make sure everyone's glass is full,' I say.

'Okay, love you.' Abi pecks me on the cheek.

'Love you too.' I mean it. I really, really mean it, but I can't tell her that without worrying her. There's something about facing down your own death that focuses your mind on the things that are most important in life.

I check the clock on the wall as the women totter off.

Fifteen minutes before we're due to serve the first course.

Fifteen minutes for the girls to make it out of the house and find help.

'How's the gnocchi coming on?' Marcus barks. 'Is it nearly ready?'

'I just need to sauté them.'

'Then what are you waiting for? Hurry.'

I step up to the hob with Marcus watching my every move. I have to stay calm. He needs to believe everything is going as he planned.

But what if Norah and Katie have lost their nerve? What if they're up there in the loft cowering in a dark corner, alone and afraid, unable to do what I've asked? They're only children, for pity's sake. I hate myself for forcing them to do this, but I hate Marcus more for putting me in this position.

I toss some butter in a pan and when it's melted and bubbling, I throw in the gnocchi.

'I'll get everyone to the table,' Marcus says, walking away. He steps into the lounge and I hear him clap his hands to get everyone's attention. 'Ladies and Gentlemen, if you'd like to go through to the dining room, we're about to serve the first course.'

I listen to the murmur of excitement. Usually, at this stage I'm buzzing. I love presenting new dishes to an appreciative audience, but this evening my only focus is on how to keep my family alive.

'I think they're done,' I say as Marcus returns.

He peers into the pan and nods.

'Get plating up. You have five minutes.'

I switch off the gas and wipe my hands clean on a tea towel. I still don't know what's going through Marcus' head and what he's planning. He's locked us in the house and hidden our phones, so he's clearly up to something.

'What are you up to?' I ask, fixing him with a hard stare. 'I mean, what's tonight all about? I don't understand.'

'Shut up and start plating.'

'I know you've locked the doors and hidden the keys, but how can you possibly expect to overpower us all?

There are six of us and only one of you. There are too many of us. And what have you done with our phones?'

'You don't need them.'

'It's not too late,' I say. I need to stall him to give the girls more time. 'Give us back our phones, unlock the doors, and we'll say no more about it. You've made your point.'

Marcus frowns. 'But Henry, it's your birthday. I've planned a special night for you.'

'It doesn't feel special.'

'I'm doing it for Sally-Anne and the baby,' he says, taking a step closer. He towers over me like a playground bully picking on the puny kid in the corner. 'You and your vacuous friends have a lot to answer for. Tonight it's time for a reckoning.'

His lips curl into a snarl and there's venom in his eyes. He's totally deranged. If I ever had any doubts, they're instantly dismissed. He intends to kill us all.

I glance around the kitchen, hoping he's left a knife lying around, but he's not that careless. I can't see anything I could realistically use as a weapon against him.

'Henry, switch on!' he yells, making me jump. 'I'm not having you late with the first course. Now get plating up!'

Marcus passes me six bowls. I reluctantly lay them out on the counter. I pray that at any minute we'll hear the wail of sirens and an officious knock at the door as the police swoop on the house. But for now, I have no choice but to follow Marcus's instructions.

'Four minutes!' he bellows like a drill sergeant. It's worse than being in a professional kitchen.

Steadying my hand, I carefully place three gnocchi in the centre of each bowl and dot the confit tomatoes between them. Marcus hands me a jar of pickled mushrooms and I add three to each plate, then garnish them with a sprig of chervil before adding the hot consommé .

Marcus inspects each bowl and nods his satisfaction before wiping away a few drips with a clean cloth.

'Not bad', he says.

Even though I despise Marcus with every cell in my body, I still feel a swell of pride. He might be a deranged madman, but he knows how to cook and winning his grudging approval feels like a minor victory.

'Get them to the table', he orders. 'You're a minute over already.'

I balance five of the bowls on my arms and creep into the dining room. Everyone's sitting at the table. Abi is at one end with Colette and Ralph on her left and Johnny and Felicity to her right. They clap and cheer as I walk in, making me wince with embarrassment. It doesn't feel right. Not tonight. But, of course, they don't know they have anything to fear. Not yet.

'Bravo, Henry!' Ralph raises a glass in my direction. I can't look him in the eye.

I feel bad for keeping them in the dark. If it was me, I'd want to know what was going on and that my life was in danger. But I can't trust Johnny or Ralph not to try something heroic, which I know would end in disaster and bloodshed. No, I'm right to keep them in ignorance. At least for now.

Abi wafts a hand over her bowl, drinking in the aroma from the consommé . 'Oh my God, smells so good', she says.

Marcus stands by the door with his arms crossed, observing silently.

I clear my throat. 'To start, you have a mushroom consommé with gnocchi, confit tomatoes and pickled mushrooms,' I say, trying to keep the tremor from my voice while sounding enthusiastic, even though I don't feel it. 'Enjoy.'

'What about you?' Colette asks, noticing I've only brought five bowls. 'Aren't you eating with us?'

'You'll have to excuse him,' Marcus says before I can reply. 'He still has some work to do on your main. He'll eat later.'

'Seems a bit mean,' Johnny says. 'It's his birthday after all.'

But I don't mind. I've lost my appetite anyway and I'm grateful to be excused from the charade of pretending to enjoy the food.

'Please, start,' I say. 'No need to stand on ceremony.'

Johnny and Ralph don't need to be told twice. They dive in with relish, making appreciative murmurs of pleasure.

'Top-notch grub, mate,' Johnny says, raising a thumb.

But Felicity is poking around her bowl with her spoon, fishing out the mushrooms and putting them to one side. She glances up and sees I've caught her.

'Sorry, I probably should have mentioned it earlier,' she says, 'but I'm not a great fan of mushrooms. You won't be offended if I leave them and only eat the gnocchi, will you?'

'It's fine —' I say.

But Marcus springs forwards in a fiery rage, slamming his hands on the table, making the glasses rattle.

'Do you have any idea of the effort that's gone into making that dish?' he screams at Felicity. 'Well, do you? Henry's worked his bloody socks off, so just eat it, will you, you ungrateful, skinny-ribbed cow.'

The room is stunned into silence. Ralph's spoon freezes halfway to his mouth as all eyes fix on Marcus. Felicity lowers her gaze and for a moment, I think she's going to burst into tears.

'Hey,' Johnny says, his expression tightening, 'don't speak to my wife like that.'

I want to tell him to shut up, that he needs to let it go. I don't want anyone provoking Marcus. He's unpredictable and dangerous. But I can't say anything, so I watch in muted horror.

Marcus doesn't pay any attention to Johnny. He's entirely focused on Felicity. He leans over the table so she has no choice but to look at him.

'I said just fucking eat it.' He lowers his voice to a low grumble, which perversely sounds more threatening than when he was shouting.

'Give me your mushrooms, I'll eat them.' Johnny holds his bowl out to his wife.

It feels like everyone's standing on a cliff edge, waiting to see how Marcus reacts.

'No!' he shouts, pushing Johnny's bowl away.

Felicity shrinks in her chair, her eyes wide with fear.

'You'll eat your mushrooms and you'll fucking well enjoy them!' Marcus is right in Felicity's face. Spittle flies from the corners of his mouth.

'That's enough!' Abi jumps up from her chair. 'How dare you speak to my friends like that.'

'It's okay,' Felicity whimpers. 'I'll eat them.' She scoops up a mushroom and tentatively puts it in her mouth with a grimace while Marcus watches.

I will Abi to sit down and shut up. There's no telling how Marcus is going to react.

'You don't have to do anything you don't want to,' Abi says.

'I don't mind. I don't want to spoil the evening for Henry.' Felicity puts another mushroom in her mouth and closes her eyes as she swallows. I can't watch.

'That's enough, Felicity. You don't have to eat them if you don't want to.'

Marcus smirks as he steps back from the table.

'I'm sorry,' he says, holding up his hands. 'I shouldn't have shouted.'

'No, you shouldn't,' Abi says, with fury in her eyes. 'What were you thinking?'

'My apologies, Abi. I was out of line.' The charming Marcus is back, deferential and smiling. 'I just wanted everyone to taste what Henry had cooked.'

'Right,' Abi says, retaking her seat and smoothing her napkin across her lap. She's still smouldering, but Marcus has apologised and she's hoping that's an end to it. If only she knew who we were dealing with. 'My friends are my guests. They didn't come here to be shouted at.'

'No, of course.' Marcus retreats with his head bowed, a totally different character. 'Come on, Henry. We need to get on with the main course.'

He nods to the door and I slip out of the room, glad to leave.

Chapter 42

Marcus is cutting brown shrimp jelly into cubes and I'm wiping the plates ready to serve when I hear a crash of furniture coming from the dining room, followed by a cry of pain.

It's Abi. It sounds like she's hurt.

'What was that?'

Marcus doesn't look up from what he's doing. It's as if he's not heard anything. Or doesn't care.

Abi stumbles into the kitchen, hanging off the door and clutching her stomach. Her face is deathly pale and contorted in agony. Sooty lines of mascara are running down her cheeks and her bright red lipstick is smeared across her chin. Her sparkly top is stained with vomit and spittle bubbles from her mouth.

'Abi?' I gasp. I race to her side as she collapses. 'What is it? What's wrong?'

The stench of vomit makes me recoil. She doubles over and dry-retches, her eyes bulging. I choke back the bile that rises from my stomach and glance at Marcus. He's leaning against the worktop with his arms folded and a stupid grin on his face like he's enjoying the show.

'Everyone's sick,' Abi says.

'Everyone?'

What the hell is she talking about? My mind races. What's going on? It's not that I don't believe her, but I need to see for myself. I leave her slumped on the floor and step into the dining room.

The scene that greets me is utter carnage. There's a stomach-churning stench of vomit in the air. Glasses have been knocked over and the tablecloth rucked up. Felicity is curled up on the floor in a foetal ball. Johnny is sitting with his back against the wall at Felicity's feet, gripping his stomach and groaning in pain.

On the other side of the room, Colette and Ralph are still in their chairs, but Ralph is doubled over as Colette, with a hand clamped over her mouth, stares at him in horror.

They were all fine when I left them a short time ago and now...

Have they all suffered some kind of allergic reaction to the food? Were the mushrooms off? I don't understand.

I rush back to Abi. Her head is flopping dangerously from side to side. Panic tightens my chest.

I've poisoned them. There's no other explanation for such a sudden outbreak of illness.

'Get me some water,' I yell at Marcus.

But he doesn't move. He's still leaning against the counter, watching with a look of amusement on his face.

I run to the cupboard, grab a glass, and fill it from the tap. Abi's hand trembles as she takes it from me. Her brow is burning hot.

'Sip it slowly,' I say, stroking the hair out of her eyes.

She retches again, a deep guttural groan straining from her belly.

'What have you done?' I glance up at Marcus. He's enjoying this. 'You bastard.' I stand up, my panic turning to raw anger.

He shrugs.

I knew he was planning something. I'd been waiting for it, but I was confident we had the advantage in numbers to overpower him if he tried anything. But he hadn't needed a knife or a gun to attack us. All he'd needed was poison. I should have seen it coming, but I've been blindsided.

'What is it?' I yell at him. 'Was it something in the consommé ?'

He laughs. 'It was your food. You cooked it. You served it to them. That makes you responsible.'

What had I missed? My head spins as I try to work out how he did it. Had he slipped something into a pan while I was distracted? While I was upstairs with the girls?

'If it's any consolation, I'm told death caps are delicious,' Marcus says. 'Fatal, but delicious.'

Death caps? It's like a punch in the face. He'd brought a jar of pickled mushrooms with him and I'd happily added them to the dish without a second thought. I'd served them to my wife. To Colette and Ralph. To Johnny and Felicity. And now they're all desperately sick. I need to get them to a hospital, fast. If I don't, they'll all die. It's as simple as that. But we're trapped in the house with no way of calling for help.

I could kill Marcus with my bare hands. Rip his head from his shoulders. I edge towards him, my fists balling, but he must read my mind or recognise the rage in my eyes. Suddenly, a carving knife is at my throat, the cold steel sharp against my skin.

'Back off,' he hisses.

Behind me, Abi groans. 'What have you done to us?' she gasps.

'It's okay, Abi,' I say. 'It's going to be alright.'

'You've poisoned us. Why?'

Marcus laughs cruelly. 'You still haven't worked it out, have you, Abi?'

I take a step back with my hands up in surrender.

'Marcus?' Abi's eyes narrow as she stares at him.

'That's right. I have to say I'm a little disappointed. I was sure a clever lawyer like you would have worked it out before now.' He grins like a maniac. 'It's hard to watch someone you love suffering, isn't it, Henry?'

'Please,' I beg. 'Let me call an ambulance. You've made your point. We can't sit here and watch them all die.'

'Why not?' Marcus looks genuinely baffled.

'Come on, where are the phones? Let me call for help. It's not too late to end this. We can say it was a mistake, but not if you let them all die.'

Abi retches again, the effort draining her energy. Her head slumps onto her chest.

'We don't have time to make phone calls, Henry,' Marcus says. 'You haven't finished the main.'

I stand there perplexed, totally at a loss to understand what's going on in his head.

'You're insane,' I say. 'You can't seriously expect me to carry on cooking after you've poisoned everyone.'

'After *you've* poisoned everyone,' he says. 'And anyway, it would be a shame to waste all that lovely octopus.'

'This is murder.' I let the word hang in the air, heavy and expectant. 'But not if we can get everyone to hospital. It's not too late to save them.'

A thought strikes me as I picture the girls clambering through the loft. Had he poisoned the snacks he made for them too? Of course, he had. He has no reason to let them live. Thank God I got rid of the tray in our bedroom and didn't let Norah and Katie eat them.

Marcus shakes his head. 'It's too late, Henry. Did you know death caps are one of the most poisonous mushrooms in the world? And that they kill more people every year than any other mushroom?' He reels off the facts like we're at a pub quiz. 'It's probably because they look so innocent, and they're not actually that difficult to find if you know what you're looking for.'

'You're sick.'

'Here's another fact for you. Cooking doesn't destroy their poison. Isn't that amazing?' Marcus says.

'Shut up.'

'It attacks the liver and kidneys, and when they're destroyed, death is guaranteed. I'm afraid you've killed them all, Henry. But don't worry, you still have plenty of time to say your goodbyes. They'll be in agony but alive for a few hours yet.'

There must be a way to counter the effects. Something I can do. Would milk reverse the reaction? Or water? Fuck. I wish I could google it.

'I'm going to kill you,' I say.

Abi tries to scrabble to her feet.

'Take it easy.' I ease her back down to the ground. If the poison acts like a snakebite, an increase in her heart rate could speed up the flow of the toxin around her body and quicken her death.

'Am I going to die?' she asks with terror in her eyes.

'No, I won't let you die.' It's an empty promise, but I need her to hang on to the hope I can save her.

There's no way out of this mess unless the girls have made it. Are they still in the loft? Have they been able to find Paul and Linda? Or are they knocking on doors in the street right now, asking for help?

Abi pushes me away weakly and gets back to her feet.

'I need the bathroom,' she says. 'Check on the others.'

'You need to rest.' But she won't listen to me. She staggers into the hall and climbs the stairs.

In the dining room, Ralph is now on his hands and knees. He's thrown up all over the floor and trails of saliva hang from his mouth. Johnny looks like a ghost, pallid and haunted, while Colette seems mesmerised, staring around the room, horrified at what she's watching. I guess it's only a matter of time before she succumbs to the mushrooms, too.

What am I going to do? Everything rests on Katie and Norah. We're totally reliant on an eight and a six-year-old for salvation. God help us.

And what about me? I've not eaten the mushrooms, but I can't believe Marcus plans to let me live. Or is that destined to be my punishment? To live with the deaths of my wife and the others always on my conscience.

I march back into the kitchen, where Marcus is calmly frying the octopus tentacles.

'Look,' I say, swallowing my pride. Maybe it's time to start begging. 'We should never have published the review or included Sally-Anne's name, but it wasn't the reason Matunde was forced to close the restaurant and lay everyone off.'

He stares at me with a wild look in his eye. 'You still don't get it, do you?' he says. 'You took everything from me. The love of my life. My unborn child. My future.'

'I'm sorry, I can't imagine —'

'You treated Sally-Anne no better than if she was mud on your shoe. You humiliated her in that stupid blog. How do you think that made her feel?' Marcus waves a wooden spatula at me while the octopus crackles and hisses in the pan. 'And to top it all, we both lost our jobs.'

'I don't know —'

'You should be ashamed of yourselves. Can you imagine how miserable you'd made her that she even considered taking her own life and killing our baby?'

'But this won't bring either of them back. Do you really think this is what she would have wanted?' I ask.

'Two lives gone in an instant, all because you had to wait for a table. Because your food was delayed for a few minutes. Because Sally-Anne was rushed off her feet and made a mistake with your order. Well, now you can see what it feels like to have nothing left to lose. They're the lucky ones,' Marcus says, waving the spatula in the direction of the dining room. 'Their suffering is going to be over soon. You're the one who's going to be left burdened with the grief and the guilt. You're going to lose everything, just like I lost everything when Sally-Anne died, and I can never forgive you for that.' He takes a deep breath, calming himself. 'Now, are you going to finish this octopus, or not?'

Chapter 43

How could I possibly rationalise with someone like Marcus Arquette? One moment he's casually poisoning our guests and the next all his energy is focused on finishing a plate of food, with no thought to the five people in the house suffering a slow and agonising death.

Marcus glances up as he continues to stir the octopus tentacles. 'Well?'

'You're not serious?'

'It would be a shame to see it go to waste after all the work you've put in,' he says.

His cold, flat expression suggests he's deadly serious. He actually wants me to finish the meal.

'What's the point?' I flamboyantly toss my arms in the air like a petulant child. 'They're all as sick as dogs, puking their guts up. Nobody's going to eat it!'

Marcus extinguishes the flame under the pan and puts the spatula down on the side. He licks his lips and wipes his hands on his jacket.

'If you finish the meal, I'll let you call an ambulance,' he says.

I don't know whether to laugh or cry. Does he mean it, or is it just more mind games? His face is blank. Unreadable.

'You'll let me call for help?'

He nods.

'And what are you going to make me put in it this time? Arsenic artichokes? Ricin cakes? Deadly nightshades tuiles?' I ask.

Marcus laughs, although there's nothing funny about any of this. 'I hate wasting good food,' he says, 'and I promised your wife I'd give you a lesson preparing a three-course meal. You can't quit after the starter.'

I study his face. Is he just trying to waste precious time, or will he really let me call for an ambulance if I finish the meal?

'How can I trust that you'll keep your word?'

'You can't, but you can either watch your wife and friends die a horrible, painful death, or you can finish the menu.'

Although I've never had much time for Johnny and Ralph, I've never wished them dead. Well, not seriously. But now their lives are in my hands, I feel the weight of it heavy on my shoulders.

'It's not a good feeling, is it?' Marcus asks. 'Watching the people you care for the most suffer and not being able to do anything about it.'

'That's all this is to you, isn't it? Everything in the last two weeks has been about making me suffer. To pay for the crimes you think I've committed.'

A sly grin plays across Marcus's lips.

'All the time you were just playing with me. The letter. The texts. The rock through the window. It was all about softening me up. But this was your big plan to make me pay all along, wasn't it? Do you really think this is going to make you feel any better? My suffering won't cancel out your pain. How can it? Sally-Anne's gone and I'm sorry for your loss, but killing five innocent people won't bring her back.'

Marcus's eyes narrow as his grin slips and fades.

'An eye for an eye, Henry.'

'And the fire at Joseph Farrow's house? Was that your work too?'

'Of course,' Marcus says. He looks pleased with himself. 'You were looking totally in the wrong direction. I needed to refocus your attention and make you understand that this is about what you did to Sally-Anne. Although it took you long enough to work it out.'

'Two people died.'

'They were leeches. Vermin. The world's better off without people like that. I wouldn't lose any sleep over it.'

I shake my head. 'You're a monster.'

'And what about you? You drove the woman I love to kill herself and my unborn child. That's pretty monstrous, wouldn't you say?'

Marcus grabs a handful of shallots from a basket. He peels and chops them with the carving knife he threatened me with, his hand a blur as he slices and dices.

'So, are you finishing this menu or not?' he asks.

How can I refuse? If the girls are still stuck in the loft, it might be the only way to save Abi and the others. With heavy legs, I drag myself back to the counter.

Marcus plugs in a food processor and pushes it towards me.

'Blend the garlic and ginger into a smooth paste,' he instructs, passing me the ingredients.

I drop them in the blender and give them a short blast until they're mushed up into a biscuit-coloured pulp. But my mind's not on the cooking. All I can think about is the poison that's slowly killing Abi, Colette, Felicity, Johnny and Ralph. Even if Marcus allows me to call an ambulance, what lasting damage might those mushrooms have already done?

'Now fry the shallots,' Marcus says.

I light the gas under a pan, add a drizzle of oil and grip the worktop to steady myself as I wait for it to heat. We bought the pan in France. It's made of cast iron. Heavy. Solid. Maybe I could use it as a weapon. I'd need to catch Marcus by surprise, but it might do the trick, especially with the hot oil in it.

But its heaviness makes it unwieldy and I'm not sure I have the strength. I'd only have one shot. If I didn't do it right, Marcus would probably kill me.

He prods something sharp into my side.

'And don't do anything silly, if you want your wife to survive,' he says, as if he knows what's going through my mind.

It's too risky. I'm going to have to trust that he'll keep his word and let me call for help if I finish the dish.

As the oil starts to smoke, Marcus nudges me.

'Now add the shallots. We don't have all night.'

I scrape them off the chopping board into the pan, and stir them half-heartedly as they slowly turn golden.

'Now add the ginger and garlic paste.'

The mixture releases a pungent aroma as it hits the smouldering oil. I can't believe I'm actually doing this while people are dying in the room next door. It's obscene.

'Good, and now some chilli to add some heat.'

Marcus picks up a bowl of red cayenne peppers he'd sliced earlier and holds it out for me to take. Like a thunderbolt, a flash of inspiration strikes me. The germ of a plan forms in my head. It's audacious, but it might work.

It has to.

If the girls don't succeed, I have nothing else. It has to be worth a try.

With half an eye on the pan I'm stirring, I reach for the bowl of chillies, but deliberately let it slip through my fingers, so it looks like an accident. The bowl falls and cracks into three pieces, shedding chillies across the kitchen floor.

'Shit, I'm sorry,' I say.

'Fucking idiot,' Marcus hisses at me. 'Pick them up.'

'We can't use those now they've been on the floor,' I say, although a mild dose of bacteria from my kitchen lino is hardly going to do anyone more harm than the poisonous mushrooms they've already eaten. 'I have some chillis we can use.'

I don't wait for him to argue. I dash across the kitchen to the window and pluck three wrinkled orange chillies from the naga plant Johnny gave me the last time he'd been for dinner. They're much more potent than the cayenne peppers I've spilt on the floor, too overpowering for the dish I'm preparing, but I have no intention of cooking with them. I have a much better idea.

As Marcus watches mutely, I drop them on the chopping board and squash them with the heel of my palm, popping open the flesh and releasing the potent oils inside. I'd never normally touch the fruit without gloves, but there's no time to worry about such niceties.

'Shall I chop them?' I ask innocently.

I glance up and catch his eye, surreptitiously prodding my fingers into the raw chilli flesh, coating them in its oils.

'No, I'll do it,' he says, stepping forwards to nudge me out of the way.

I back off and hold up my hands to show him I'm no threat. He grunts and, as he produces a knife from his pocket, I lunge at his eyes with my fingers, smearing his eyelids and crawling them down his cheeks.

It only takes a second, but the damage is done.

He shoves me away. But it's too late. He roars with anger and pain, stumbling backwards, screaming. His eyes streaming with tears. Blinded.

He drops the knife. I kick it away. It skitters across the floor and disappears under the oven.

He throws himself blindly at me in a rage. Arms wheeling. Anger seething. Grasping for me. Trying to kill me.

I sidestep out of his reach. Move behind him. And shove him in the back, hard.

He stumbles. Loses his balance. Yelps as he puts a hand down straight into the hot pan on the hob. His skin pops and sizzles like frying chicken. A sickening sound. His howl of frustration becomes a scream of agony.

The pan flips over as he knocks its handle and flames leap into the air, flickering around his sleeve. And then his entire arm is on fire. Orange flames engulfing one side of his body with a raging intensity that warms my face.

It all happens so fast, I hardly have time to think. I edge away, watching in horror.

I should put out the flames. Save him.

But I'm frozen, mesmerised by the horror of it all as the fire spreads rapidly, taking hold across Marcus's chest and licking his neck and face. His arms flail wildly. He spins around, screaming blindly.

Still he's hunting for me with arms outstretched, trying to grab me, a sickening version of blind man's buff. But as his jacket melts in a sticky, tarry mess, his legs buckle. He bounces off the fridge, puts a hand on the counter and sets a tea towel alight.

By now, thick, choking smoke is filling the kitchen, pouring off Marcus's clothes, rolling in waves off the white painted ceiling like a ferocious and deadly sea.

He finally stops screaming as he sinks to his knees and collapses on the floor, disappearing behind the counter in his own personal inferno.

I can't help him now.

And I can't watch anymore.

I have to get everyone out of the house before the entire building is razed to the ground and we all end up dead.

Chapter 44

I almost knock Colette off her feet as I race out of the kitchen and into the hall. She's stumbling out of the dining room with a hand clutched to her chest and a haunted zombie-like look of fear on her face. But strangely, no other apparent symptoms of illness. Not like the others. She's not doubled over in pain or throwing up.

'What's going on?' she yells at me over the piercing scream of the smoke alarm. 'What's wrong with everyone?'

There's no time to explain. I've already started choking on the thick smoke and if we don't act quickly, we'll all be dead, long before the flames reach us.

'Did you eat your mushrooms?' I ask, puzzled.

She shakes her head. 'I don't like them either, but after your chef yelled at Flick, I didn't like to say anything. I spat them out into my napkin.'

I could have hugged her.

'There's a fire. We need to get everyone out of the house. Hurry!'

She's in such a state of shock, she seems not to have noticed the acrid stench of smoke or the deafening

348

alarm. It's only when she glances over my shoulder into the kitchen that her eyes open wide in surprise.

'What the — '

'He's locked all the doors and hidden the keys', I tell her. 'We need to get everyone upstairs quickly. Help me.'

'Upstairs?'

'Yes! Come on! Hurry!'

She turns back into the dining room and rushes to Ralph's side, leaving me to worry about Felicity and Johnny. Felicity's still on the floor, balled up and moaning. Johnny's at her side, rubbing her back, but he looks like death. His skin has lost all its colour and his face is hollow.

'Get up, Johnny', I scream. 'There's a fire.'

He looks at me blankly.

'What the fuck did you give us?' he mumbles.

I grab his arm and try to pull him to his feet, but he's a dead weight.

'Johnny, if you don't get up now, we're all going to die! Move!'

Yelling at him is the only thing I can think to do. I can't physically lift him.

'I feel terrible.'

'I know. We need to get you to hospital. All of you. But we're locked in. And there's a fire in the kitchen. It's spreading fast. We need to get everyone upstairs.'

'That's a bad idea', he groans.

Normally, I would agree. Every idiot knows heat, smoke and flames rise. But there's no escape if we stay downstairs.

'I know a way out', I yell at Johnny, 'but I need your help to carry Felicity.'

He winces and clutches his sides. God knows what damage those mushrooms are doing, whether they've reached his liver and kidneys yet, slowly destroying them.

As a wave of pain subsides, he tries to get up. I offer him my hand and I lift him to his feet.

'When this is all over, I'm going to kill you, Henry,' he says, with a grimace that could be an attempt at a smile.

'Yeah, yeah, let's concentrate on getting out alive first, shall we?'

Together, we rouse Felicity. Like Johnny, she doesn't want to get up, but with some cajoling, she finally stands. I wrap her arm around my neck and with my arm coiled around her waist, we shuffle into the hall, following Johnny.

Colette is waiting with Ralph. His skin is grey and he can't stand up straight. He has spittle all over his chin and his eyes are bloodshot.

I glance into the kitchen. The fire has engulfed the cupboards and appliances and is crawling up the walls and rolling off the ceiling. Suffocating black smoke is billowing out into the hall, making everyone cough. And the heat is building. I already have a sheen of sweat across my brow and my T-shirt under my chef's jacket is soaked through. At least there's no sign of Marcus. It was a horrible way to die, but he brought it on himself. I never asked for any of this.

'Everyone up the stairs, now!' I scream, slamming the kitchen door shut. It might just buy us the time we need to escape.

'Where's Abi?' Colette asks, looking frantic with worry.

'In the bathroom upstairs.'

'And Tim? The chef?'

I shake my head. 'His name's Marcus, but he's dead.'

'Dead?' Colette says.

'I don't have time to explain. We need to get everyone upstairs! Now!'

Colette nods and goes first, half-carrying, half-dragging Ralph. Johnny goes next and I help Felicity. Progress with her is slow-going. She's only semi-conscious and is dragging her feet. Fortunately, Johnny helps and we regroup on the landing outside the girls' rooms. They all turn to me, looking for direction.

'What now?' Colette asks. She's normally so calm and collected, but I see panic bubbling under the surface.

Ralph has slumped to the floor with his chin on his chest, muttering something incomprehensible.

'I need to find Abi,' I say, stepping over Ralph's legs as I head for the bathroom.

The door's locked. I hammer on it with my fist.

'Abi? Are you in there? Open up! It's me!'

I wait for a second or two, but when there's no answer, I fear the worst. Is she unconscious? Dead? No, I can't think like that.

I take two steps back and kick the handle with the heel of my foot, like I've seen on the TV a million times.

The door shudders but doesn't move.

Shit. It always looks so easy in the movies.

I try again, but it jars my knee, a jagged pain shooting up my leg.

'Abi!' I scream.

What if I can't open the door? What if she is unconscious? The smoke's already snaked its way up the stairs and is swirling around the ceiling. It won't be long before it's too thick to breathe. Time is against us.

I try again, taking three steps back, ignoring the pain in my leg, kicking with a more explosive movement this time. The plaster around the frame cracks, but the door remains intact.

A figure appears at my side. It's Johnny, looking worried.

'Abi's trapped in the bathroom.'

'Let me try,' he says.

He copies the way I kicked the door, pivoting on one leg, but his kick is less effective than mine. He doesn't have the strength and nearly overbalances. At least the plaster has cracked a little more.

I push Johnny out of the way and kick again. And again. And again. Until finally, with a loud crack, the lock gives up and the door swings open.

Abi is crumpled on the floor next to the toilet, her breath shallow and her face a ghoulish white.

'You're alive. Thank God.' I scoop her up gently and put her on her feet.

She moans and cracks open an eye. She looks like she's been in a car crash, wobbly and dazed. I help her onto the landing and leave her with Colette, who holds her up by her elbows when her body goes dangerously limp.

A cough catches in my throat as sooty smoke swirls around my face. I feel it in my lungs, burning. My chest tight.

'What now?' Colette wails. She's the only one who seems to have grasped the seriousness of our predicament.

The others all seem out of it, lost in their own misery. But I can't have Colette losing her head now. I need her help.

'We're going up through the attic,' I tell her, pointing to the hatch above.

I pull open the airing cupboard door, snatch the long pole we use to release the hatch and drop it open. Then I snag the ladder and pull it down, making sure its feet are firmly positioned on the ground before testing it's stable. Just as I did earlier when I sent the girls to get help.

Where the hell are they? It's been ages since they left. I hope nothing's happened to them.

Felicity coughs, rolling onto her side, struggling to catch her breath. We need to get her out. We need to get everyone out.

I hurry into our bedroom to find the torch I keep by my bedside in case of emergencies, grateful to find that for once the batteries aren't dead. It shines a powerful beam of light across the room.

I hand it to Colette.

'You first,' I say. 'Take the torch and lead the way. There should be a gap in the plasterboard that takes you into next door's roof space.'

Colette stares at me like I've completely lost the plot, but she doesn't argue. She puts a hand to her mouth as she coughs, then nods and climbs the ladder up through the hatch, which is sucking up all the smoke from the ceiling.

I watch impatiently as she climbs slowly and hauls herself into the darkness above.

'Okay, I'm up,' she says, her face appearing in the gap above my head.

'Johnny, let's get Felicity up next.'

Felicity pushes us away when we try to pull her to her feet. She's delirious with pain and I'm worried the carbon monoxide fumes are taking their toll.

Johnny yells in her face. 'Felicity, listen to me! Get up that ladder now! Do it!' For an awful moment, I think he's going to slap her.

Her head rolls on her shoulders and her eyes flicker open. She glances up at Colette and nods, like she finally understands what she needs to do.

I climb the ladder with her, taking her weight on my shoulders as she slowly ascends. Colette grabs her hand and pulls her up.

Abi's next. It takes all my strength to push and shove her limp body up the ladder, as she seems barely capable of doing it herself. My arms and legs tremble and burn with the effort, but finally Colette and I somehow bundle her through the hatch.

Ralph's suffering too and is much heavier than Felicity or Abi, and it takes both me and Johnny to force him up the ladder.

The only one who makes it on his own apart from Colette, is Johnny. I stand behind him, ready to catch him if it looks as though he's going to fall, but he makes it all the way up by himself, coughing and spluttering.

I'm the last one. The flickering glow of flames reflects off the walls up the stairs and there's a roar below as the fire hungrily devours everything in its path. I doubt there's much left of the rooms downstairs and in a matter of minutes, the bedrooms and bathrooms on the first floor are going to be consumed, too. There's no time to lose.

I jump onto the ladder as a loud crash below echoes through the house. My legs feel weak as I climb, either from helping the others or simply from the relief of knowing we're going to be safe. But it feels like more of an effort than it should. I suck in another lungful of smoke and cough until I think I'm going to be sick.

The air is cleaner and cooler in the loft as I stick my head and shoulders through the hatch, but it's rapidly filling up with smoke. I can see it dancing in the light from Colette's torch as she guides everyone towards Paul and Linda's house.

With one last effort, I swing a leg over the lip of the hatch.

But my movement is halted by something tightening around my other ankle.

A hand, gripping tightly. Pulling me back down into the house.

Marcus's blackened face is like something from a horror movie. His eyes are sunken in his exposed sockets and he snarls with a set of bared teeth where his lips used to be. It's an image that's going to haunt me for the rest of my life.

He should be dead. But his grip on my leg is surprisingly strong and I can't shake him off.

He's pulling me down and I can't stop him. He's trying to kill me.

'Help!' I try to scream, but the word dries up in my throat, parched and burned by the smoke.

The others are disappearing through a hole at the far end of the attic, following my instructions to the letter. Running away to safety, following the path the girls took. They have no idea I'm in trouble.

I grasp for one of the roof trusses and howl in agony. It's the hand I burned on the pan earlier. A bolt of pain, like electricity, shoots up my arm. But I can't let go or he'll pull me off the ladder.

Instead, I grip more tightly, the wood rough and full of splinters, while I try to kick Marcus with my free leg.

I smash him in the face, twice. His head rocks back, but he doesn't let go.

He's like a man possessed.

But my grip is slipping, and he has the advantage of gravity on his side.

A second hand, charred and deformed, reaches up for my foot. If he gets two hands on me, I'll never be able to fight him off.

I'm holding on by my fingertips now. I'm slipping. I'm going to fall.

I push myself up through the hatch and aim another brutal kick downwards with every ounce of strength I have left.

My heel connects with his forehead with a sickening crunch and his grip loosens.

I kick again. And again. The final blow catches him where the bridge of his nose used to be. He howls, I think more out of frustration than pain, as he loses his grip and my ankle is freed.

I drag myself up into the loft and when I look back, he's lying twisted on the floor at the foot of the ladder, his lidless eyes staring at the ceiling. It's a horrific image I wish I'd never seen and my final, lasting memory of Marcus Arquette.

But I'm not taking any chances. I thought he was dead once before. I haul up the ladder and close the hatch, shutting out the nightmare below.

Chapter 45

I take a moment to catch my breath, enveloped by the cloak of darkness, my chest rattling and whistling. At the far end of the loft, I pick out the pinprick of Colette's torch. I can't stop. I need to keep moving. It's only a matter of time before the smoke becomes overwhelming and the flames take hold.

I crawl on my hands and knees across the rough chipboard floor, navigating around cardboard boxes, bin bags of old clothes and even an old metal cage that used to belong to Norah when she had a hamster. Eventually I reach a ragged hole that's been ripped through the plasterboard wall that separates our roof space from Paul and Linda's. It's just about wide enough to squeeze through.

I wriggle through and collapse on the other side, panting and wheezing. The others are circled around an open loft hatch, waiting for me.

'Henry, are you okay?' Colette asks, shining the torch in my face.

I hold up my hand to shade my eyes. 'I'm fine, but come on, let's hurry. Everyone out.'

'But there's no ladder.'

Everyone's looking at me again, waiting for me to tell them what to do. Even Johnny and Ralph. Only a few hours ago, they were laughing at how badly I hit a golf ball. Now they're relying on me for survival. How our fortunes have changed.

I take the torch from Colette and shine the light onto the Lambs' landing. It's only a drop of about eight or nine feet. It's not that far and the girls must have managed it, but Abi, Felicity, Ralph and Johnny are sick and weak. I'm not sure they'll willingly make the leap. They can barely stand up, let alone lower themselves out of the hatch safely.

'Stay here,' I tell them. 'I'm going to get you all down.'

With aching arms, I lower myself out of the hatch and dangle my legs above the carpet. Then let go and fall to the floor, my ankle twinging with a stab of pain as I land awkwardly.

I stand gingerly, testing it. It seems okay. A little tender, but thankfully it doesn't appear to be broken or sprained.

The house is silent and in total darkness. My fingers crawl along the wall, hunting for a light switch, and when I find it, the light that floods the landing is blinding.

'Hello?' I call out. 'Anyone home? Mr Lamb? Paul? Linda?'

There's no reply. The ceiling creaks as someone shifts their weight above me, but the rest of the house is quiet. Too quiet. There's something wrong. Where are the Lambs? And why are all the lights off?

The noxious stench of smoke pours off my clothes, my skin and my hair, but it doesn't mask the vile, sickly sweet tang of decay seeping through the house. It's the smell of death. I raise a hand to my nose as my stomach cramps.

I push open a door on my left where the smell seems to come from. I don't want to see it, but I have to know for sure. I flick on a light. The room is sparsely furnished with two single beds, side by side.

The smell makes me gag. I pull up my T-shirt over my nose and mouth. Even though I'm expecting it, the sight of the two figures lying on top of their beds, their faces staring at the ceiling, is a shock. My knees buckle and I grab the wall for support.

Paul and Linda's eyes are open and their hands have been folded on top of their chests. They look strangely serene, but the ugly, purple bruises around their necks suggest their deaths were anything but peaceful. They've been murdered. Two victims of Marcus Arquette's deadly determination for vengeance. Two innocents killed for the sole crime of being my neighbours.

What a senseless waste.

I'd had a pang of guilt when I'd left Marcus to his fate in our kitchen, blinded and his clothes alight. I hadn't tried to save him or put out the flames. I'd abandoned him. But now I see it's nothing more than he deserved. He's killed two of the nicest people I've ever met, purely because he wanted to get to me, my family and our friends.

Sally-Anne's death didn't warrant that. It didn't warrant any of this. He killed in cold blood, tossing Paul and Linda aside like they were worthless distractions. They had nothing to do with Sally-Anne's death, but died because they had the misfortune to live in the house next to ours. That bastard deserved to die.

I squeeze my eyes shut as a solitary tear runs down my cheek.

But we're still not out of the woods and I don't have the time to grieve just yet. I need to get everyone to safety and find Norah and Katie. I back out of the room and pull the door shut, preserving the scene for the police.

In a spare room at the back of the house, I find a rickety wooden stepladder splattered with paint. I place it under the loft hatch and help Felicity, Abi, Colette and the others down. They congregate on the landing, holding their hands to their mouths and noses. They can smell it too, but the way their stomachs are right now, I don't tell them what it is. They'd never be able to handle it.

Instead, I lead them down the stairs, clutching Abi's hand as she stumbles on weak legs. The front door is swinging open on its hinges. A sign, I hope, that Katie and Norah made it out safely. I only hope they didn't discover Paul and Linda's bodies. They've been through enough already without having that memory seared into their young minds.

Outside, the cool air hits me like a tonic. I take a huge gulp, filling my lungs. It makes me cough violently, but after all the smoke I've inhaled, it tastes so good. So pure. So clean. I fall to my knees on the drive with Abi at my side, spitting out sooty, black phlegm.

Colette drags Ralph out of the door and props him against a low brick wall. She runs her fingers tenderly up and down his neck as his body is racked by a bout of spluttering and retching.

Felicity and Johnny have collapsed on the drive in each other's arms. They're both trembling and coughing, but at least they're safe.

In our house, I can see the living room lit up with golden flames that lick and dance at the window like they're trying to escape through the bars.

'The girls...?' Abi moans, rolling onto her side, her hands pawing at her stomach.

'I don't know,' I say. 'I sent them to get help.'

An icy shiver runs down my spine. I don't know where they are.

I pull myself to my feet. We might be out of immediate danger, but I still need to call for help. Abi, Felicity, Johnny and Ralph all need urgent medical attention to treat the poison in their bodies.

I catch the urgent sound of sirens, growing louder, coming closer. And then I spot a fire engine racing up the street in a wash of blue pulsing lights. It pulls up at the end of our drive and a dozen firefighters spill out, pulling on breathing equipment and rolling out hoses.

Two police cars follow. And a couple of ambulances.

My legs give way with relief and I fall to my knees again.

'You're going to be okay,' I say to Abi, taking her hands and rubbing them between mine. They feel so cold. 'Abi?'

Her eyes flutter and close as her head rolls to one side.

Please, no!

'Help!' I scream, as two paramedics come running towards us. 'Please don't let her die.'

'Can you tell me what happened?' one paramedic asks. 'Did she breathe in the smoke?'

'Yes, but she's also eaten poisonous mushrooms. Death caps,' I gasp.

He glances at me briefly but shows no emotion.

'The others as well. They've all eaten them. I'm so sorry, it was all my fault.'

'Don't worry, they're in good hands now. We'll take it from here.'

More paramedics arrive until the drive feels crowded with people and equipment, busy and urgent.

'Daddy! Daddy!' My heart skips.

'Norah? Katie?'

The girls burst out of nowhere and throw their arms around me. Behind them, I spot the couple from across the road. I don't know their names, but I'm sure as hell going to find out.

'We did it,' Norah says. 'We climbed out of the loft and knocked on the doors until we found someone to help.'

'You did an amazing job,' I say, pulling them both close and hugging them tightly. I'm never going to let them out of my sight again.

I mouth a silent 'thank you' to the couple hovering in the background, emotion tightening my sore throat.

'What's wrong with Mummy?' Katie asks as she watches the paramedic fit an oxygen mask over her face. 'Is she going to be alright?'

I stand and lead them away, letting the paramedics get on with their work. The girls have been through enough tonight already. They don't need to see this.

'Yes, she's going to be fine,' I say. 'They're going to take her to hospital and make her better again.'

It might be a false promise, but what else am I supposed to tell them?

Chapter 46

THREE WEEKS LATER

Lawyer reveals she was deliberately poisoned on night she miraculously escaped house fire

Renowned criminal lawyer Abigail Pilkington-Hutton has spoken publicly for the first time about her miraculous escape from a fire that gutted her home – and of being deliberately poisoned in an attempt on her life just hours before the blaze.

Mrs Pilkington-Hutton, 38, spent nearly a week in hospital after her ordeal but says she's now made an almost complete recovery.

The lawyer, who earlier this year successfully prosecuted brothers Jimmy and Dean Farrow for the murder of pensioner Billy Bowden in his Canterbury home, is now planning to return to work and says she wants to put the entire episode behind her and move on.

She said: "I'm lucky to be alive. I could have died twice that night, but someone must have been watching over me."

Police believe that chef Marcus Arquette targeted Mrs Pilkington-Hutton and her husband, Henry, after blaming them for the death of his pregnant fiancée, Sally-Anne Pearson.

Sally-Anne took her own life after featuring in an unflattering review of *Meld*, the restaurant owned by celebrity TV chef, Matunde Yeboah, which was posted on a food blog hosted by Mr Hutton and subsequently widely shared on social media.

Mrs Pilkington-Hutton explained: "Marcus used a false identity to pose as a private chef and convinced me I'd won a competition to have him cook a meal for six of us at our home.

"As it was Henry's fortieth birthday, it seemed like an ideal present, especially as part of the prize was a cookery lesson and Henry's a bit of a frustrated chef."

But things turned sour when Arquette locked the hostess and her guests in the house and - unknown to everyone else - added death cap mushrooms to his menu.

"Four of us ate them and became sick very quickly," Mrs Pilkington-Hutton said. "I've never been in so much pain in all my life. It was like someone had stabbed me in the stomach with a dagger and was constantly twisting it. I thought I was going to die."

Amantia phalloides, or death cap mushrooms as they are more commonly known, can be fatal if ingested, rapidly affecting the liver and kidneys.

Mrs Pilkington-Hutton and three of her friends who attended the birthday celebration and who'd also been poisoned by Arquette were taken to a London hospital where they were treated with silibinin, an experimental drug derived from the milk thistle.

"It was like a miracle cure for us," Mrs Pilkington-Hutton said. "Doctors said we all suffered a small amount of liver damage, but it's nothing that can't be managed. We're just grateful to be alive. I can't thank the medical staff who treated us enough for their diligence and dedication."

The lawyer and her husband were not Arquette's only victims. Police believe he was also responsible for the deaths of

Mrs Pilkington-Hutton's neighbours, retired GP Paul Lamb and his wife, Linda.

Detective Superintendent Chris Abbott, of Kent Police, said: "It appears Arquette tricked his way into the Lambs' home with the sole intention of putting himself in proximity to Henry Hutton and his wife.

"Unfortunately, he seems to have treated the Lambs as a minor inconvenience to his plans. We're treating their deaths as murder and I can confirm we are not looking for anyone else in connection with the crime."

A post-mortem examination revealed the couple were killed by strangulation.

Curiously, Mrs Pilkington-Hutton believes Arquette was not only watching them from the Lambs' house next door but had entered their property through a shared loft space.

"We don't know how many times he gained entry to the house while we were out, but we know he did it on at least one occasion as he'd left a mug out on the side in the kitchen for us to find.

"He wanted us to know he could get to us at any time, even though we'd changed all the locks and Henry had even had bars installed on the windows.

"The only mystery is how he knew he could get into the house through next door's loft. We think that after he'd befriended Paul and Linda, they must have mentioned we were having problems with an infestation of mice which had chewed through a flimsy plasterboard wall that separated the two properties. But as Arquette and the Lambs are now dead, I guess we'll never find out for sure."

The remains of Arquette's body were later found in Mrs Pilkington-Hutton's house in the aftermath of the fire, which started after Arquette and Mr Hutton fought in the kitchen.

As the fire raged, the couple and their friends found themselves trapped with no way of escaping.

Not only had Arquette locked the doors and hidden their keys and phones, but the bars the Huttons had installed on all the windows prevented their escape.

"It was Henry's idea," Mrs Pilkington-Hutton said. "Arquette had previously made threats against our family and later smashed a window, so Henry didn't want to take any chances. Sadly, what was supposed to protect us almost cost us our lives."

In the end, it was the couple's brave young daughters, Norah, eight, and Katie, six, who escaped and raised the alarm.

"Henry finally worked out Marcus must have been coming in through the loft and realised it was the only way the girls could escape and call for help. I'm immensely proud of them, but also guilty that we had to ask them to do it. It was a tremendous responsibility on their young shoulders."

And what of the food blog that started the unfortunate chain of deadly events? Will that continue?

"I'm not sure yet," Mrs Pilkington-Hutton said with a wry smile. "Our only focus for the moment is rebuilding our lives and getting back to a kind of normality for the girls' sake."

Chapter 47

After Abi came out of hospital, we moved into a rented property on the outskirts of town, but reporters still found us and we had a constant string of journalists knocking at the door offering silly amounts of cash for an exclusive interview. I didn't want Abi to talk to them. Enough had already been written about the fire and the events of that night, but she thought it would get them off our backs and allow us to control the narrative. If we didn't tell our side of it, she said they'd fill the vacuum with half-truths and lies about us. She had far more experience with the press than me and I trusted she knew what she was doing.

She didn't ask for a fee on the condition the article would be syndicated and made available to any news outlet who wanted to run it. She didn't want to do a TV interview, but allowed the reporter who interviewed her to record the audio and release it to the radio stations. It was the best way, she felt, of being fair to everyone and getting our side accurately reported.

I run my eye over the article on my phone for a second time, trying to ignore the photo that appears alongside it. They made us sit on the couch with the girls on our laps. Abi looks amazing as usual, but I never take a good photo. I look gormless, like a grinning village idiot.

'Frustrated chef?' I glance up at Abi, who's sitting on the opposite side of the table sipping coffee.

'What? You are.'

'I think I might have phrased it differently,' I say. It's not a flattering description.

'If you'd have bothered to have been there for the interview, you could have corrected me.'

I shudder. 'No, thank you.' I'd taken the girls off to another part of the house while Abi sat for an hour with the reporter and only reappeared when they wanted to take our picture.

'Then don't complain.'

I go back to my phone and flick through various other news websites. Most of them have run the story, and apart from the picture, we seem to have come out of it in a good light. Abi's done an excellent job.

Norah and Katie come flying down the stairs sounding like a herd of elephants.

'Can we watch TV?' Norah asks, hanging off my chair and grinning.

'Go on, then. Just for half an hour.'

They scamper off into the other room. The TV comes on far too loud.

'Turn it down a bit!' I yell.

'They're coping okay, aren't they?' Abi says. 'You know, all things considered.'

I'd asked the unthinkable of them, to climb through a dark and draughty loft space to get help while we were being held hostage by a crazed psychopath. And yet they hadn't batted an eyelid. They'd found their way into Paul and Linda's house, run across the road and explained to Roger and Mel (I now know their names) that we were in trouble.

Fortunately, they hadn't discovered the Lambs' dead bodies. They said that when they discovered the house was silent and in darkness, they ran down the stairs and let themselves out, too frightened to investigate.

'They take after their mother. Resilient and brave.'

Abi's smile fades. 'Are you taking the piss?'

'Would I? Although it reminds me. I did promise we'd take them to Legoland if they got out and found help.'

'You'd better sort it out then.'

Later that evening, after we've eaten and the girls are in bed, Abi's phone buzzes. She snatches it off the arm of her chair and frowns.

'What is it?'

'A message from one of Sally-Anne's friends,' she says. 'One of the girls I reached out to when I was trying to find her address. She says the papers have got it all wrong about Sally-Anne. She wants to meet up. She wants us to know the truth.'

'What truth?'

Abi's fingers tap away at her phone. 'I don't know, but I've suggested meeting at a cafe in town to talk.'

The girl's name is Laurel. She's pretty, with sandy hair and furtive eyes, and slips into the café, where we've arranged to meet, with her gaze cast down to the floor as if she's afraid of being noticed. Abi must recognise her from her profile picture because as soon as she walks in, she waves to catch her attention. I've bought Norah and Katie milkshakes and ice cream to keep them quiet while we talk and true to their word, they sit silently as Laurel shuffles apologetically towards our table.

When she sits down, she looks up from under long black lashes that look too full to be natural. I buy her a latte and watch as she stirs in three sachets of sugar with a long spoon. Abi and I are both on the edge of our seats, but we don't want to rush her. So we talk about the weather, the state of the traffic and the roads. Anything but the reason she agreed to meet us.

'I'm sorry about what you went through,' she says, finally. 'I read all about it. It must have been horrible for you.'

Abi shrugs and smiles. What can she say? We've been through it a million times, playing out so many scenarios. How things could have ended up so differently. We were lucky not to have died that night.

'Were you and Sally-Anne close?' Abi asks.

'We went to school together,' she says. 'When we was kids, we was always together. Our mums used to joke we could have been twins. We never kept secrets. Once, we even made this promise that we'd never let a boy get between us. Shame she couldn't keep that one.'

Laurel toys with an empty sugar packet. 'Sally-Anne was clever, but she was shy. She should have gone to college but ended up waiting tables when she could have had any job she wanted, really.' She sighs and rolls her eyes to the ceiling. 'I wish I'd never said nothing to her now.'

'What do you mean? What did you say?' Abi asks.

'I told her she should apply for a job at that fancy new restaurant that was opening,' she says. 'I thought it would be better than working in a café.'

'*Meld*?'

'That's it.'

'Where she met Marcus?'

'When they first got together she was happy. Really happy,' Laurel says. 'She couldn't stop talking about him and what a perfect gentleman he was, always buying her presents and flowers and stuff. But I never liked him. I only met him a few times, but I thought he was...' She seems to struggle to find the right word. 'Possessive.'

I glance at Abi, but she's entirely focused on Laurel.

'What do you mean?' Abi asks.

'Like if we was out, he had to be constantly touching her, but not like in a caring way. More like he was claiming his property. D'you know what I mean? Me and Sally-Anne used to go out all the time, shopping, the cinema, the pub. Just hanging out, yeah? But when Marcus came along, she was either too tired or said Marcus was taking her out. It was weird the way she changed. She used to be a real laugh.'

I despised Marcus Arquette for the way he came after me and my family, but Laurel makes me view him in an entirely new light. I didn't think it was possible to hate him any more than I already did.

'Things got worse when Marcus moved in with her. She'd found this nice place near to the restaurant, but when Marcus got chucked out of his flat, he pressured her into letting him move in. She didn't want that, but she couldn't say no to him. I didn't see much of her after that. He stopped her from going out or seeing any of her friends. She wasn't even allowed on social media. I wouldn't be surprised if he hadn't started checking her phone, too.

'A few months later, I bumped into her in the supermarket. We used to be so close, but she looked terrified when she saw me. Actually, she tried to pretend she didn't see me. I went up to her. She was trying to cover up this bruise on her cheek. She said she'd tripped over, but they all say that, don't they? I don't think she knew how to leave him.

'But you know the worst part? While he made her stay at home, he was seeing other women. I saw for myself when I was out. But what was I supposed to do? Maybe I should have made more of an effort to see her and let her know what was going on, but you know, she'd cut me off and there was other stuff going on in my life.'

Her eyes are red and wet with tears.

Abi reaches across the table and takes her hand. 'It's not your fault. You're not to blame for Marcus's behaviour.'

'I was supposed to be her friend!'

Abi hands her a tissue from her bag and Laurel takes a moment to compose herself.

'Did you know they'd lost their jobs at the restaurant?' Abi asks.

Laurel dabs her eyes with the tissue and nods. 'When I heard it had closed down, I went to see her. I waited until Marcus was out and found her in the flat in a pretty bad way. She wasn't dressed, hadn't washed her hair, and she'd obviously been crying. She looked awful. That's when she told me about the blog.'

I stare into the bottom of my coffee cup, ashamed. I really wish Sally-Anne hadn't been named in the review. It was so cruel on top of everything else she was obviously going through.

'She was gutted her name had been used and that so many people had read it. She was sure that review was the reason she lost her job,' Laurel says. 'She was sure it was why the restaurant had to shut.'

'It's not true!' The words blurt out of my mouth. I can't help myself. 'The owner lied to her because he couldn't face telling them it was his fault, that he'd miscalculated the costs of running a restaurant.'

Laurel looks startled by my outburst, her fake eyelashes fluttering rapidly. 'It don't change the fact they both lost their jobs though, does it? She was worried about how they were going to pay the rent. I offered to help, but she wouldn't take my money.

'I knew there was more to it than just money worries.' She flicks a strand of hair out of her pretty blue eyes. 'She told me she was pregnant and how it had been a big mistake. The way she talked about the baby was weird, like it was a bit of Marcus growing inside her she didn't want. She said she wanted to end it.' Laurel's bottom lip quivers and she looks down at the tissue she's twisting between her fingers. 'I thought she was talking about an abortion, although I don't suppose Marcus would have agreed to that. I never thought for one minute she was seriously thinking about taking her own life. If I'd have known, I would have...' Her words dry up. I'm not sure she knows what she would have done.

'I found out from my mum, who'd heard it from one of the neighbours, a few days later. She'd waited until Marcus was out and strung a length of washing line over the door. Isn't that the most horrible thing you can imagine?'

'Yes', Abi says, squeezing Laurel's hand. 'It is. I'm so, so sorry.'

'It was horrible. And so was your review. It was a terrible thing to write about my poor Sally-Anne, but I wanted you to know, I don't think it had anything to do with why she killed herself like they've been saying in the news. There's only one person who drove her to that, and thankfully he's dead.'

Chapter 48

I check my watch and tap the envelope on the counter impatiently. I expected Abi to be home from work by now. She promised, in the light of everything we've been through, she'd spend less time in chambers and more time with me and the girls. She's only been back to work for a week, but I fear she's already slipping into old habits.

Keys rattle in the lock and I jump up, my pulse cantering.

How's she going to react? Surprise? Shock?

'I'm home,' Abi calls from the hall as I hear her kicking off her shoes. 'Sorry I'm late. The traffic was a nightmare.'

'I'm in the kitchen.'

Abi waltzes in and snatches a quick kiss on her way to the fridge, hunting for wine.

I hold up the envelope, keeping my face emotionless, waiting to see how she'll respond.

She freezes with a bottle of pinot grigio in one hand. 'What's that?'

'I think you'd better open it. See for yourself.'

She puts the wine on the side and swallows hard, glancing from me to the envelope and back again.

'Henry?' There's a tremor in her voice.

'Just open it.'

It's a plain white envelope. No address. No stamp.

She snatches it from me and peels it open. Her breathing is fast and shallow. She pulls out the contents and relief floods her face.

'You scared the life out of me,' she says, smiling. Then punches my arm.

I laugh, pleased with my little prank, as she studies the two plane tickets.

'Paris? Oh my God!'

'It's only a long weekend, but I thought it was time for a bit of spontaneity. I've booked a hotel on the banks of the Seine.'

'I'm impressed.' Abi throws her arms around my neck and gives me a long, lingering kiss. 'And I thought I was going to be the one with all the surprises tonight.'

Now I'm curious.

'I've booked a table at that new tapas restaurant you were talking about,' she says.

'Seriously? That's amazing. But are you sure?' It's been a long while since we've eaten out. It didn't seem appropriate after all we'd been through, especially as Abi's stomach is still delicate.

'Absolutely, I thought the six of us could...'

She tries to keep a straight face but bursts out laughing when she sees my expression.

'I'm kidding. It's a table for two, booked for eight o'clock. Johnny and Felicity are coming to babysit.'

Actually, I wouldn't have minded. My relationship with both Johnny and Ralph is much improved since the fire. Finally, they've started treating me with respect. I guess that's what happens when you save someone's life.

Like Abi, they'd been in a bad way after those mushrooms, but they'd all been treated in the same hospital by the same doctors who'd worked a miracle, given that I thought they were all going to die. I'm not sure any of them will ever touch a mushroom again, but at least Johnny and Ralph have both learned some humility. Neither of them are anything like the boorish, arrogant pricks they used to be. I quite enjoy their company these days.

❧

The tapas restaurant couldn't be any more different from *Meld*. It's a family-run place with flickering tealights on the tables and uplighters under a wooden bar at the back. We're seated at a table in the window and choose half a dozen dishes from a menu scribbled on a chalkboard on the wall. Boquerones and tortilla de patata, chorizo serrano and smoky albondigas, croquetas and olives and queso manchego, all served in miniature terracotta bowls by a waitress with the widest smile and most infectious laugh.

Obviously, we avoided anything with mushrooms. Abi turns green at the merest mention of them and I would certainly never cook with them again.

'So?' Abi asks. 'What do you think?'

'It's nice. It's got a friendly atmosphere.'

There are only eight tables in the whole restaurant, which means the waiting staff have the time to be attentive without being suffocating. It's the sort of place I'd always imagined I'd like to run. One day.

We've almost finished, replete with good food, when the owner sidles up to our table. He's probably my age, but with less hair and a bigger waistline. A man who enjoys the good things in life.

'How has everything been for you this evening?' he asks.

'Really good, but then I'd heard good things,' I say.

He dips his head, looking slightly abashed. 'Thank you, we do our best.'

We chat like old friends. He tells us about his plans to open a string of restaurants and how his son is training to become a chef.

'What made you want to open a tapas restaurant?' I ask. He's clearly not Spanish, so it seems a curious decision.

'I've always loved cooking and I've always enjoyed Spanish tapas,' he says. 'So when the bank made me redundant, I thought I'd take the plunge. It seemed like fate.'

'Any regrets?' Abi asks.

'Only one,' he says. 'I wish I'd done it earlier. Life's too short not to follow your dreams.'

He withdraws with a bow and moves onto the next table.

Abi finishes her wine and takes my hands. 'Can you imagine yourself running a place like this?' she asks.

I look around at all the smiling faces of people enjoying good, honest food. 'Yeah, maybe,' I say.

Or maybe not.

It had always been an ambition to own a restaurant, but the experience at Meld and talking to Matunde had opened my eyes. It's not an easy industry. Margins are tight and I'm no businessman. I love to cook and show off in the kitchen, but it's a big step to translate that into running a profitable restaurant.

I let the idea roll around my head in the taxi on the way home. It's a pipe dream, that's all. Never say never, but for the moment I'm happy cooking for family and friends. I don't need the additional stress. What I want is to spend more time with Abi and the girls, because if the last few months have taught me anything, that's what I care about most. Nearly losing them has brought my priorities into sharper relief than ever before.

The house is quiet when we let ourselves in. Johnny's fallen asleep on the sofa and Felicity is watching a film with the volume turned down so low I'm amazed she can hear it.

'Good night?' Johnny says, sitting up and rubbing his eyes when he hears us come in.

'Really nice,' I say. 'We should go back, all six of us. I think Ralph would really enjoy it.'

We crawl into bed with our stomachs full. I think about reading a few pages of my book, but I'm too tired. I switch off my light, kiss Abi goodnight and roll over.

Abi puffs up a pillow behind her back. 'Don't you think we should get the review written while it's still fresh in our minds?'

'Can't it wait until morning? I'm shattered.'

I'd given the blog a lot of thought in recent weeks. It was what had landed us in this hot mess. Part of me wanted to retire Nosher and the Nosher Bites Back blog. After Sally-Anne's death, it seemed the right thing to do. We posted a tribute to her on the home page, apologised for naming her in the Meld review, and removed all references to her in it, although there was nothing we could do about the content still flying around on social media.

It was the honourable thing to do, but I wasn't sure about closing down the blog altogether. After all, it wasn't the review that had led to Sally-Anne taking her own life. It was Marcus. Laurel had confirmed as much.

Abi wanted me to carry on with it, too. It had been her idea to start the blog in the first place as a way of channelling my interest in food, and now the publicity had increased its readership, she thought I'd be a fool to throw it all away. So, after much soul searching, I found myself in agreement with her. But in the future, I'd be much more careful about what I published. And I had a new rule - any reviews had to be about the food and the premises. Nothing about the chefs or the waiting staff.

'Better do it while it's fresh in your head,' Abi says. 'It won't take long.'

'Such a hard taskmaster,' I sigh.

I reach down by the side of the bed and grab the laptop from the floor where it's been on charge.

It feels like a big moment. The first *Nosher Bites Back* blog review since we'd eaten at *Meld* all those weeks ago. So much water has flowed under the bridge since then.

'So?' Abi says as the computer whirrs into life. 'What did you think of the food?'

'Top marks for the boquerones and the tortilla. They were both exceptional. But special mention has to go to the smoky albondigas. The way the chef blended in little bits of crispy baked chorizo to the meatballs was a sublime twist to a classic recipe.'

'That's great,' Abi says. 'And the queso manchego?'

'Delicious. A perfect accompaniment to that rioja,' I say. 'Not sure how I would describe it though. It's an unusual taste.'

I can summon up a tasty plate of food from pretty much any set of ingredients. It's my special talent. But I've never been much good at stringing a sentence together.

'Well, it was delightfully nutty, but not overly buttery and had delicate, slightly sweet overtones,' Abi says. She's so good at this sort of thing.

'Perfect,' I say.

I pass her the laptop and she positions it on top of her thighs and flexes her fingers. Then she begins to type.

'It shouldn't take too long,' she says. 'No need for you to stay up. You can sign it off in the morning and get it uploaded when you're ready.'

'Thanks, Abi.' My eyes flutter closed with the rhythmic tapping of the keys. 'Don't stay up too long.'

She's such an excellent writer and there's a real skill to writing engagingly about restaurant food.

There's no way I could do it by myself.

Acknowledgments

When I sat down to write **Nothing Left To Lose**, it was with the clear intention to write a conventional psychological thriller with an everyday hero who becomes embroiled in an escalating and terrifying situation through, what he thinks, is no fault of his own.

It's the sort of story that could happen to anyone.

All it takes is the wrong word said in anger while behind the wheel of your car. A misplaced comment on social media. Or, in Henry's case, a critical review he posted on his website.

I guess it's a reflection on the divided world we now live in, where people are increasingly polarised in their views and one misguided comment can quickly escalate into ill-feeling and hatred.

It was also written during a global pandemic, a strange time for us all when we came to fear an invisible threat in the shape of Covid 19 that hung around us in everything we did, from socialising with friends, going to work in our office or buying groceries in a supermarket.

We've had to think twice about doing all the things we used to take for granted, to save ourselves and protect the people we love.

I hope you liked Henry and Abi as much as I enjoyed creating them and putting them through the wringer. If you did, I'd be grateful if you could leave a brief rating and review on Amazon to help spread the word.

And if you use social media, why not give the book a shout out to your friends.

The book will always hold a special place in my heart as it was the first full-length novel I've written since becoming a full-time author.

But it would be unfair to suggest it was produced in splendid isolation. As with all my novels, it would never have seen the light of day without the unstinting support of my wife and fellow thriller author, Amanda, my plot doctor and number one proofreader!

Special thanks also to my wonderful editor, Rebecca Millar, who always pushes me to be better as well as being a hugely supportive friend and colleague, and Sarah Hawes for her keen eye for detail on rounds of proofreading.

Also to Stuart and Natasha Bache for their collective creative genius in producing jaw-dropping artwork for the covers.

And finally, to the dedicated family of bookbloggers and reviewers who see me through the dark days of doubt with their glowing words, and especially to Cathryn Northfield, Lyndsey Gallagher, Vikkie Wakeham, Elspeth Vines, Teresa Collins, Christi Truck, Gabi Rosetti, Alan 'Down Under' Smith and many, many others.

You know I couldn't do it without you and for your support, I'm forever grateful.

◈

Find out more about me on my website,
ajwillsauthor.com
Or on my social media channels:
Facebook
Instagram

Also by the author

His Wife's Sister
The Kindle Number 1 Bestseller

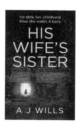

He stole her childhood. Now she wants it back.

Mara Sitwell was only a child when she went missing nineteen years ago. After being found alive and well, she tells investigators she was abducted and imprisoned - but her brother-in-law, Damian, doesn't think her story adds up.

To protect his young family from her, he'll have to prove what really happened to all those years ago. Even if Mara's not ready to give up her secrets just yet...

She Knows

Some secrets are worth dying for...

Esme and her husband, Frank, have lost everything and are taking refuge in a quiet island town where no one knows their secret.

On the same island, Sky is trying to rebuild her life after her mother's brutal death. But following a chance encounter between the two women, Sky becomes convinced Esme is in mortal danger.

But when Sky tries to help, she finds herself caught up in something far bigger than she could ever have imagined and accused of a murder she has no memory of committing...

Between The Lies

The perfect girlfriend – or a perfect stranger?

Jez thought he'd finally found happiness when he met Alice. But when Alice goes missing with her young daughter and the police accuse him of their murders, his life is shattered.

The only way to prove his innocence is to find them alive.

But that's not so easy when Alice is running from a grim family secret - and she doesn't want to be found...

Printed in Great Britain
by Amazon

75027273R00232